THE PALACE OF STRANGE GIRLS

THE PALACE OF STRANGE GIRLS

Sallie Day

Harper
Press

Harper*Press*
An imprint of HarperCollins*Publishers*
77–85 Fulham Palace Road
Hammersmith, London W6 8JB
www.harpercollins.co.uk

First published by Harper*Press* in 2008

1

Sallie Day asserts the moral right to
be identified as the author of this work

A catalogue record for this book
is available from the British Library

This novel is entirely a work of fiction. The names, characters and incidents portrayed in it are the work of the author's imagination. Any resemblance to actual persons, living or dead, events or localities is entirely coincidental.

Hardback ISBN 978-0-00-726939-6
Trade Paperback ISBN 978-0-00-728034-6

Typeset in Minion by Palimpsest Book Production Limited,
Grangemouth, Stirlingshire

Printed and bound in Great Britain by Clays Ltd, St Ives plc

For Julian

1

I-SPY AT THE SEASIDE

Hello, children! Welcome to your very own I-Spy book. In these pages you'll be able to look for all kinds of secret, exciting things that are found only by the sea. As you spot each of the things pictured here – and answer the simple questions – you earn an I-Spy score. It's fun!

Blackpool, Tuesday 12 July 1959

Beth has had it with Jesus. She's kicking the skirting boards to prove it and she hopes He's watching. Mrs Brunskill at Sunday School says He's watching all the time, even when you're asleep. It's amazing. You'd think He'd be too busy (what with all the cripples and foolish virgins) to be bothered with Beth. Thus assured of an audience, she pauses in her assault and eyes the heavily varnished wood. Beth is disappointed; the skirting boards are as yet undamaged, so she changes leg and carries on kicking. Flakes of dirty cream paint and grey plaster spiral down from the wall above her head and the picture of a little boy crying rattles in its frame. Beth carries on kicking.

'You big bugger,' she mouths on the off chance He's listening as well as watching. Beth has learned the word from the dustbin man, Mr Kerkley, who lives next door. Mr Kerkley shouted 'You little bugger' at Beth's best friend Robert when he dragged a club hammer into their coal shed and reduced all the big shiny lumps of coal into powdered shale. Beth had repeated the story to her mother. Word for word. She'd hoped to witness a satisfying gasp of shocked disbelief and disapproval from her mother, but her tale had the reverse effect. Her mother took her by the scruff of the neck and washed her mouth out with soap and water for using dirty words. Since then the offending word has been a constant resource for the child, who mouths it silently on a daily basis.

Beth woke early this morning. Wiping the sweat from her face, she sat up and dangled her feet out of the bed, waving them back and forth through air thick with the smell of bacon fat, unreliable plumbing and floral disinfectant. After a moment she slipped on her sandals (ignoring the shiny steel buckles that must always be fastened) and rummaged around under her pillow for the book. She has had the I-Spy book for four days now. Beth's initial reverence for the volume has been replaced with an obsessive fascination. Its white pages have softened to cream under Beth's sweaty-fingered perusal. It was purchased at the newsagent's on the first day of the holiday and Beth will not be parted from it. By day she carries it around in her pocket or, failing that, inside her knickers. By night she sleeps with the book under her pillow and her hand on top of it. Beth is at a loss to decide which is the best part – the book itself or the codebook that came with it. And then there's the membership card, the source of her present frustration.

The green card announces in heavy type 'Official Membership Card – Issued by Big Chief I-Spy, Wigwam-by-the-Water, London'. Underneath there are four dotted lines for the member's name and address. Although Beth can write her first name easily enough, her surname is long and fraught with difficulties. It has to be perfect. Bearing this in mind, Beth reached reluctantly for her glasses. The pink clinic glasses have a plaster stuck over the right lens. It is there to correct a lazy eye. The flexible wires hook ferociously round her ears and the frames dig in across the bridge of her nose. The discomfort always serves to concentrate Beth's mind. The 'B' for Beth went down wobbly but correct, the 'e' and 't' were easy and even the string on the 'h' was almost straight. She paused before attempting her surname, Singleton. The task demands a deep breath before she starts and, in the face of her inability to write the letter 'S', something approaching a miracle. Where should she start? Does the snake go this way or that? Within minutes the virgin card is smeared with rubber and gouged with the swan-necked traces of continued attempts. It makes no difference how hard she tries, the 'S' always comes out back to front. Beth cast around for a solution to her dilemma. An idea occurred. The verse she had to learn and recite at Sunday School last week was,

Ask and it shall be given. Seek and ye shall find.

The memory slipped back unbidden into Beth's head as she surveyed the wreckage of her once pristine membership card. It might be worth a try.

Beth placed her palms together and scrunched her eyes shut in an effort to attract the Almighty's attention and asked. She then set the point of her pencil to the card. When she finally opened her eyes, eager for the promised miracle, she found yet another backward 'S'. The letter lay fixed on the page. Eternally, immovably wrong. Beth stared at the card in disbelief. This is why she is now venting her fury on the nearest thing – the skirting boards.

The room that Beth shares with her sister is devoid of any luxury other than a dusty blue rug between the two single beds and a similar grey offering underneath the washstand in the corner. This is the Belvedere Hotel ('Families Welcome, Hot and Cold Water in Every Room, Residents' Bar'). Management do not supply eiderdowns in their fourth-floor bedrooms, nor do they supply dressing tables, trouser presses, suitcase stands or any facilities for hanging clothes other than two hooks behind the door. Not that either girl is discomforted in any way. Save for the washstand and the film of dust, room forty-eight is exactly the same as their attic bedroom at home. Except that Beth wouldn't dare kick the skirting boards like this at home. Beth lands another almighty kick on the woodwork.

The noise wakens her sister Helen who, aware of the damage that Beth, clad only in her vest, is visiting upon the toes of her new Startrite sandals, is quick to respond. 'For goodness' sake,

Beth! Stop that kicking. You'll ruin your sandals doing that. What's the matter?'

'I can't do it,' Beth shouts.

'What can't you do?'

Beth gets down on to her knees by way of reply and searches under her bed. Helen yawns, scrapes her fingers through her thick blonde fringe and flips the rest of her hair behind her shoulders. Helen has been trying to grow her hair to shoulder length for over a year now but her mother, who considers long hair to be an open invitation to nits, has constantly thwarted her. Normally Helen would have had her hair cut at the beginning of the Easter term but her mother was distracted by other things and Helen escaped. It is now July and her hair has grown long enough for a ponytail. Her mother has told her that she will have to have it cut before school starts again in September. But Helen isn't inclined to have her hair cut and she'd rather be dead than go back to school.

At last Beth retrieves the card and wipes it down the front of her vest to dislodge the dust, fluff and flakes of discarded skin.

Helen yawns again and says, 'Is that all? Flippin' 'eck, Beth. It's just a membership card. Oh, for goodness' sake! Don't start crying. Give it here and get me something to rest it on.'

Beth hands over the card and watches as her sister gets out her white clutch bag. There had been an upset when their mother had first caught sight of the bag. Helen had claimed that it was 'soiled goods' that couldn't be sold at the shop, so Blanche had given it to her for working late one Saturday. Ruth remarked that it didn't look soiled to her but Helen insisted that it had been and she'd managed to get the mark out of the plastic with soap and water. The truth was somewhat different. Helen had purchased the bag from the brand-new spring range at Freeman Hardy & Willis. She'd have preferred leather but plastic will do – just so as it's this season's colour: white. She'd got the money in the form of an unofficial cash bonus from Blanche. Blanche is keen to escape the attentions of the taxman and Helen is equally anxious to avoid her mother getting wind of the extra cash. Helen is expected to hand over her untouched wage packet to her mother every Saturday night. Ruth takes the little brown packet and, having counted out the ten-shilling notes, gives Helen the residue of change back as spending money. It's called 'bringing the old cat a mouse'. The sudden appearance of Helen carrying a brand-new bag rattled her mother, who would never dream of buying a white clutch. Ruth makes do with a more serviceable brown handbag with strap handles that she's had since the war. She was suspicious of Helen's explanation but limited herself to saying, 'I don't know why Blanche let you have a bag. You've nothing to put in it.'

'I've got my purse and a handkerchief,' Helen replied, waiting until her mother was out of hearing before adding, 'and the rest of my bonus.'

Helen, stung by her mother's dismissal, has made it her immediate ambition to fill the bag. Her first secret purchase with the hidden money was a miniature diary and notebook from

Mayhew's and she intends to buy a whole range of forbidden items in the future – a lipstick, mascara, powder, maybe even cigarettes. With one pound, two shillings and sixpence the possibilities are well-nigh endless.

Beth is impatient. She pushes the I-Spy book into Helen's lap and says, 'Can you write my name and everything? Can you do it now?'

The bag opens with a sophisticated click and Beth watches transfixed as Helen pulls out a tiny gilt case with matching gilt pencil topped with a rubber. The card is thin and creases easily under Beth's clumsy fingers, but after Helen rubs the paper it's so clean that there's barely a trace of Beth's abortive attempts. When she's satisfied Helen asks, 'Do you want it big?'

Beth nods enthusiastically.

Helen picks up the pencil and writes the word SPUTNIK in block capitals. Underneath, where it says address, she writes 'COAL-'OLE-BY-THE-TOILET, BACKYARD, BLACKBURN'.

Beth's face is a picture.

'What's wrong? That's your name, isn't it? It's what Dad calls you.'

Beth clenches her teeth and her hands bunch into fists. Helen laughs. 'Well, what do you want to be called then? What shall I write?'

'Elizabeth Singleton.'

'Oh, Elizabeth, is it?'

Helen goes into her bag again for her mottled blue Conway Stewart pen with the fat gold nib and begins to write. Helen is nine years older than Beth and her handwriting is beautiful; she puts little circles over her 'i's and even draws little flowers inside the letter 'B'. When she's finished Beth's name looks so pretty, so grown up.

Beth is elated. She reads the card avidly until she reaches the space for her Redskin name. She looks up at her sister and points at the blank space. 'I thought you weren't supposed to fill that in until later,' Helen remarks. This is true. Beth must fill in every page of *I-Spy at the Seaside* and send it to Big Chief I-Spy who will send her a certificate and a feather to prove she's a proper Redskin. Only then can she choose any name she likes. But Beth is impatient – she wants a name now.

'What about "Little Cloud" or "Laughing Waters"?' Helen suggests.

Beth looks unconvinced. She wants to be called something frightening. 'Wolf Teeth' would be good. Or 'Growling Bear'. Beth needs to find another club member so that she can join their tribe instead of being by herself all the time. She's been absent from school for a long time and all the friends she used to know are now friends with someone else. It would be better if Beth could join in at playtime but her mother has told the school that Beth is not allowed to swing, climb, skip or run. As a result Beth just sits and watches at playtime. Waiting for someone to play marbles with her.

Of all the myriad rules there is one above all others that must not be broken. Beth must never, ever, for any reason take off her wool vest. As a result the vest (Ladybird age 5) is Beth's closest companion. It is only removed once a week when Beth is bathed and is immediately replaced by another vest fresh from the airing cupboard and smelling of Lux soapflakes. In this manner Beth's shame is kept from the sight of all but her mother.

'For goodness' sake, Beth! What are we going to do about your sandals?' Beth looks down at the scuffed leather. She has had the sandals for six weeks but has only been wearing them since Saturday, the start of the holiday. It seems that only Beth is subject to this particular rule. All Beth's friends have been wearing their sandals since Easter and Susan Fletcher has been wearing hers even longer. All year round, in fact. But that's because Susan Fletcher's mum works and she 'doesn't care what state she sends her daughter to school in'. At least that's what Beth's mother says.

'I hate these,' Beth complains, kicking off her sandals. 'Only boys wear brown sandals. I didn't even get to stand on the thing that makes your feet go all green like a skellington.'

'You mean the X-ray machine. No one will notice they're brown. Anyway they match your hair,' says Helen, in a moment of inspiration.

They are interrupted by a sharp rapping at the door. Both girls jump.

'That's Mum! Quick, get your sandals on or we'll both catch it.'

Ruth Singleton, her arms full of clothes, waits in the hallway, her right foot tapping on the varnished floorboards. If her patience is short today it's due to her husband's ill-starred attempt at marital intimacy this morning. Surely he can see how she is after all these months of anxiety? But not Jack. No. Jack thinks a bit of early-morning sex is on the menu now they're on holiday. Ruth had tolerated his caresses until his increasing insistence had forced her to push his hand away and say, 'Don't, Jack. I have to get up to get the girls ready.'

He hadn't said anything, had limited himself to a drawn-out sigh. Ruth felt an answering rush of anger. Does it always have to come down to this?

Ruth is prised from the memory by the sound of the door finally opening. None of this palaver with locks would be necessary if it weren't for her younger daughter's recently acquired habit of sleepwalking. This is bad enough at home, but there's no telling what trouble the seven-year-old might get into in a hotel the size of the Belvedere. In a doomed attempt to allay Mrs Singleton's worst fears, the hotel manager has sworn on his mother's life (a lady much missed since her demise three years previously) that the room locks are made by the same firm who supplied the MOD during the war. Even the 'blasted Hun' couldn't breach the security of the Belvedere's rooms and thus Beth's habit of going AWOL at night has been curtailed. This desirable state being attained not by the hoped-for Yale lock and chain, but by the effect of damp salt air on turn-of-the-century iron locks. All of which means that Helen must use the combined strength of both hands and the leverage of her shoulder to release the door.

Though barely topping five foot six, Ruth appears much larger. Her face is scrubbed to a shine and her brown hair (already falling victim to the stealthy approach of grey) is brushed and fixed neatly into a Victory Roll that evokes memories of the war years and oppressive rationing. She is an energetic woman. A woman devoted to hard work. A woman reliant upon the writings of Elizabeth Craig to guide her through the minefield of domestic practice. Once in the room, Ruth dumps the clothes on the nearest bed and heads straight for the window to let in the sunshine. This involves coaxing, flicking, tugging and hauling the pea-green damask curtains to either end of a buckled and sagging wire. Halfway through this daily ordeal Ruth is distracted by the sight of the hotel yard, four floors below. It is lined with overflowing bins and a miscellaneous collection of mops, buckets and rusty chairs occupied by members of the hotel staff during their tea breaks. There, in full view, stands a line of sullen grey dustbins on an island of cracked concrete; the whole amply irrigated by the backwash of overflowing kitchen drains. Ruth's whitewashed backyard boasts two bins, double the capacity of her terraced neighbours'. One (supplied by the local council) for ashes, and the other (privately purchased) for household waste. Ruth always wraps potato peelings and the like before disposal. Only by wrapping everything in fresh newspaper can Ruth ensure that the inside of her bin remains as clean as the day she bought it.

The sight of the hotel bins is aggravated further by the appearance of two overturned buckets that roll back and forth as the wind shifts. Surely the hotel owns more by way of cleaning equipment than that? Ruth has a whole selection of buckets in her backyard. One for gathering up the hot ashes from the kitchen fire, one for scrubbing floors, another for washing windows and, finally, a monstrous aluminium bucket, twice the size of its iron counterparts, for 'best'. In line with its elevated status this bucket stands in glorious isolation in the scullery, immaculately clean and gleaming with potential, waiting for the next load of cottons that need starching.

Ruth's ruminations on household equipment are interrupted by a cry of protest from her older daughter: 'Isn't it time I changed my skirt, Mum?'

Ruth turns her gaze from the window. 'I don't know what you're fussing about. That skirt will do another day. You've got clean underwear. You wouldn't have that if I hadn't spent half an hour in the laundry room last night.'

This is not quite the irksome job it might appear. The hotel laundry room houses a brand-new Bendix Twin Tub. Under the pretext of hand-washing the family's underwear, Ruth has admired the top-loader lids and neat hoses on the twin tub, seen the spinner in action. As the adverts say: 'This is the future of household laundry.' Ruth has a Hotpoint Empress at home. With its built-in 'automatic' wringer and Bakelite agitator it used to be the last word in laundry. But the advent of the Bendix Twin Tub has changed all that. Who would want the backache of hauling double sheets through the wringer if they could drop them in a spinner and pull them out forty minutes later drip free? This is the modern world of post-war Britain. A world made familiar to Ruth through magazines. A world she is determined to enter.

Ruth turns her attention to her younger daughter. 'Have you washed your face, Elizabeth? Elizabeth!'

Beth has her head firmly in the I-Spy codebook. She is practising stroking her cheek in the manner prescribed at the beginning of chapter 3 'Greeting other Redskins'. Beth has been rehearsing this move for the past four days but no one has yet responded.

'Elizabeth!' Ruth says, taking her daughter firmly by the arm. 'Are you listening? Have you washed your face?'

'Yes.' It is a small lie. So small that it barely deserves the name. But it affords a morsel of revenge, a minor victory in the guerrilla war Beth has been waging since Easter, a war that Ruth is only dimly aware is being fought.

'Looks more like a lick and a promise to me,' Ruth says, scanning her daughter's face. 'You could do with using a bit of soap next time.'

'Can I have a summer dress today? Please. I hate wearing shorts. I look like a boy in them.'

Ruth holds up the brown shorts. The weave is a right-hand twill, perfect for rough wear because it will resist snags and tears. And it won't wear out. 'Well, if these shorts and those sandals aren't summery I don't know what is,' she says. 'I've only brought your jumper because we've got to keep you warm.'

'Can I wear this?' Beth asks as she pulls a smocked cotton dress from the bottom of the pile. Beth has inherited the dress from her sister but has yet to be allowed to wear it.

Ruth holds up the dress. 'It might do,' she concedes. There

follow a frantic ten minutes while Ruth tries and fails to fit the dress over Beth's wool vest and fleece-lined liberty bodice. 'It's no good, Elizabeth. It's not going to fit. Hold your arms up while I get it off.'

Beth raises her arms as the dress is pulled up over her head, bringing the vest and liberty bodice with it. By the time Beth emerges from the struggle her face is the colour of the rising sun – for a minute she looks healthy. In her haste to protect her daughter from any potential draughts Ruth yanks the vest back across Beth's skin so sharply that the child flinches with pain. In another moment she is dressed in the prescribed brown knee-length shorts, olive-green jumper and thick socks to take up the slack in her sandals.

'There. Now you're done.' Ruth heaves a sigh with the effort involved in arming her daughter against all the sharp winds and torrential rain that Blackpool can offer in the middle of July.

2

RED-EYED SANDHOPPER

These little animals live between the tidemarks, chiefly under stones and in the rotting seaweed at the top of the beach. They are white with bright-red eyes and five pairs of legs. Score 10 points for a bleary-eyed sandhopper.

Jack has escaped early to buy a newspaper. With this end in mind he has made his way to the promenade in holiday mood. The sun is still a bit fitful but the air is fresh. He is easily tempted by the sea and so wanders over the tram tracks and pink tarmac to the edge of the promenade, takes a deep breath and gazes over the railings. The run-up to the annual Wakes Week holiday has been hectic. The weaving shed where Jack is foreman has been buzzing with talk of closure. Jack has spent the last week sorting out one problem after another, reorganising shifts, dealing with strike threats and all the while continuing the daily struggle to keep output steady. Jack takes another deep breath and, determined to relax, gazes out to the horizon. The tide is coming in and the remaining strip of sand is empty save for a single figure, shoes in hand, making its way painfully over sand hard rippled by the tide. It's Dougie.

'Mornin', Dougie! Up an' at it already?' Jack shouts.

The figure looks up and glares. Dougie Fairbrother is knee high to a grasshopper and walks like he's fighting a gale. When he comes within hailing distance he yells, 'What time is it, Jack?'

'Just comin' up to twenty past.'

'What?' Receiving no immediate reply, he adds, 'Twenty past what?'

'Seven.'

'That means I've been on this friggin' beach for the best part of two bloody hours,' Dougie says as he makes his way slowly up the concrete steps that separate the beach from the prom. Jack shakes his head. He has known Dougie Fairbrother all his life. Jack was the first person Dougie went to when his wife walked out and it was Jack who got him sorted out with a solicitor. Dougie has developed a fair thirst since his divorce back in the spring. It's eight in the morning and he's still drunk from the night before. When Dougie finally reaches the top of the steps he stops to catch his breath. Dougie has worked in the weaving shed since he was fourteen, that's the best part of twenty years filling his lungs with lint and dust.

While he is puffing and blowing Jack remarks, 'Aye, well, they say there's no rest for the wicked. What happened to lying in bed, Dougie? I thought your lad had booked a double room.'

'He did. But it's otherwise occupied at the moment. The little bastard has got a lass from over yonder in with him.'

Jack follows the direction of Dougie's thumb and sees a strip joint on the corner opposite with all the hatches battened down. 'Who's he got in there?' he asks, hard pushed to hide his incredulity.

'One of the strippers. I didn't stop long enough to get her name and there were no bloody point asking Doug. Pound to a penny he wouldn't know.'

'So where did you sleep?'

'I kipped down in the Residents' Lounge. I was OK till the cleaners turned up at six and threw me out. I've been hanging around here on the off chance one of the lads turned up. I'm chilled to the bloody bone and gasping for a drink. They won't open the hotel doors before nine at the earliest.'

Jack puts his hand in his pocket and gives Dougie half a crown. 'That'll be enough to get you a pot of tea and some breakfast.'

Dougie brightens immediately and says, 'Thanks, Jack. E-e, but you should have come with us last night. We had a grand time. It was a good do.'

'Looks like it,' replies Jack.

Dougie blinks his bloodshot eyes and rubs a calloused hand over his sickly face. 'We started off at Yates's but, God help us, we ended up at the King o' Clubs.'

'I'm surprised you went back there. I thought you'd been thrown out last time,' Jack says as they cross the tramlines.

'We were. It was Tapper's fault. We sat through this load o' guff about how we were going to see amazing things. Some tart wi' her own version of ping-pong, half a dozen Egyptian dancers, that sort of thing. We'd gone in to see Sheba, the star of the show. She was billed as "six foot of exotic woman, naked as God intended, from the distant reaches of deepest Africa". Tapper jumped up halfway through the spiel and yelled, "Well, bloody bring her out! I've summat here from Blackburn waiting for her!" It took three of us, mind, but we managed to get Tapper to sit down again and button his flies. Nowt would have come of it if some lard-arse next to us hadn't said summat smart. Tapper only got to throw three or four punches before we were out on our ears. Never a dull moment wi' Tapper.'

That much is true. Eddie Tapworth is the best tackler in the cotton shed. A giant of a man, he is built for the heavy job of lifting beams. He can keep his looms running all day. He's not one of those tacklers who hang around making the weavers wait while they sort out a trapped or broken shuttle, or grumbling at Jack to chase up a shortage of spindles from the spinning rooms. Tapper sets to and does it himself. He could replace the used shuttles and put a fresh cop in faster than you could draw breath. He is one of the few tacklers who can reckon how much the shaft speed will increase when the leather drive belts from the looms shrink in the heat. If all the tacklers were as capable as Tapper, the foreman's job would be a damn sight easier. When he's sober, Jack has a good deal of time for Eddie Tapworth. But drunk it's another matter. A few pints and Tapper would fight his own shadow if it followed him.

'We're off to the Winter Gardens tomorrow night,' Dougie continues. 'You'd like. It's Kenny Ball and his Jazzmen. Why don't you come?'

Jack rubs the angle of his jaw and shakes his head. 'No, I'm not that bothered, Dougie.'

'Come on! You've not lost your taste for jazz! I've known a time when I couldn't get you to play a waltz straight without jazzing it up. We lost work for the band because of it. You were Blackburn's answer to Jack Teagarden.'

Jack's expression is transformed by the memory. Laughter rumbles from deep in his chest while his grey eyes all but disappear above the curve of his cheekbones. He and Dougie got up to all sorts in the band before the war. He played trombone to Dougie's trumpet. Jack had started off as bandleader – top hat, silk scarf, the lot. But it hadn't taken long to sort out that it was the players who were getting all the girls. The bloke with the trombone in particular. Eddie Cummings couldn't shift for skirt. When Jack promoted Eddie to bandleader and borrowed his trombone, things started looking up. Jack's broad shoulders and ability to charm make him popular even now with the women. He may be in his late thirties but he takes care of himself. His blond hair is cut by the best barber in town and combed back into a series of shiny Brylcreemed tramlines.

'No, I'll give it a miss, Dougie. Kenny Ball's a bit tame for me. I like the proper stuff – I saw Count Basie at the Tower a couple of years back. Cost an arm and a leg to get in, but it was worth every penny. Kenny Ball is just an amateur in comparison. I listened to a fair bit of jazz in Crete during the war.'

'We were damn lucky to get Vera Lynn where I was stationed. Wasn't it Crete where you met that bloke . . . the one that . . . ?'

'Yes. Nibs turned up one day with a gramophone and half a dozen jazz records. He'd brought them over from Greece. Got them from a black GI who was being posted back home. Only the Yanks would think to take a gramophone to war. I couldn't get enough of it. The first time I heard Meade Lux Lewis playing "Honky Tonk Train Blues" I cracked out laughing.'

'Aye, well, Kenny Ball's the best Blackpool can come up with. You sure you won't come?'

'No, I'll give it a miss. I promised to see Tom Bell tomorrow night.'

'What? The Union bloke? Now isn't that a surprise!'

'Oh, it's nothing serious. He just wants a chat.'

'Chat my arse. He'll have summat up his sleeve. I bet he's got wind of Fosters' offer.'

'You haven't said anything, have you, Dougie? Nobody is supposed to know. I haven't even told Ruth. I'm still thinking about it.'

'Why haven't you told Ruth? I'd have thought you'd have wanted to shout it from the rooftops. Bloody hell, Jack, they've offered you the top job. Manager of Prospect Mill. What's there to think about? It'll more than double your pay packet overnight. Get her told.'

'She's been distracted with Beth. And anyway I haven't said I'll take the job.'

'Then you want your bumps feeling, Jack. You should have bitten their hand off the minute it was offered. They should have made you up to manager years ago. You know more about cotton than all the Foster brothers put together.'

'It'll mean sitting behind a desk all day.'

'You won't catch Ruth complaining about that. I remember when we were kids on Bird Street. She had some fancy ideas even then. We used to tease the life out of her, but she'd never change her tune.

She was going to get married, live in a beautiful house and have two children – a boy and a girl.'

'That's Ruth. Always knows exactly what she wants. But I still think I'd rather be busy in the weaving shed than sitting by myself in an office pushing papers around. I'll get round to telling her. I've got other things on my mind at the moment.'

'Anything you want to talk about?'

Jack shakes his head. 'No, no. It's something and nothing. Not worth bothering with.'

'Well, think on. There'll be merry hell to pay if she finds out you've been keeping secrets.'

Jack looks at his feet and moves his hand unconsciously up to the inside pocket of his jacket where he has hidden the letter. There are enough secrets in there to keep him busy for a fair bit and then some.

'Anyway, how is she?'

Jack looks confused; his mind has been elsewhere. 'Who?'

'Your Ruth.'

Jack shakes his head. 'She's jiggered after all the upset with Beth. She didn't want to come away for fear that Beth wouldn't be up to it. We ended up having a barney about it. Ruth needs a holiday more than any of us. Still, you can lead a horse to water but you can't make it drink. The first thing she did when we got to the hotel was to set to and clean the washbasin.'

'But Beth's goin' to be OK?'

'Oh aye. Give her time, she'll pull round. She's a right little fighter.'

'And how's your Helen?'

Jack smiles. 'Still pushing to leave school this summer. It's the usual do – she's sixteen going on twenty-five.'

'They're all the same. Our Doug is only a year older and he thinks he knows it all. Never satisfied. "He wants jam on it" as my old dad used to say. Talking of which, just take a look at this.' Dougie reaches into his pocket and pulls out a square of fabric and hands it to Jack.

'Where did you get this?' Jack asks, turning the square over and back.

'One of the lads from Whittaker's. Says this is what they're turning out nowadays.'

'Are you sure Whittaker's are weaving this?'

'It's right what I tell you. Look at the state of it. Lowest possible thread count and sized to glory.'

Jack runs his thumbnail across the surface of the dry, brittle fabric and a small cloud of white powder rises. 'It must be hell to weave. There's no movement in it, no give.'

'There's more elastic in a tart's knickers.'

'I can't believe Whittaker's are using such poor-quality cotton staple that they've had to glue it together. They never used to use anything less than Egyptian or Sea Island cotton.'

'Times have changed, Jack. You know that as well as I do. There's no pride left in the business.'

Dougie and Jack reach the pavement where they part, Dougie for breakfast at the nearest café, and Jack for a *Daily Herald* and twenty Senior Service.

On the way back from the newsagent's Jack finds a bench on the prom, sits down and reaches for his cigarettes. The pack of untipped cigarettes is embossed in the centre with a picture of a brawny sailor. Jack runs his thumb over the familiar relief as he pushes open the pack and lights his first cigarette of the day. Smoking is barely tolerated at home. Jack may smoke in the backyard or, if it is raining, in the scullery. Tab ends to be disposed of directly into the ash bin. There isn't an ashtray in the house and Ruth refuses to buy one. Numberless though her household duties may be, emptying ashtrays is not one of them. Alcohol is subject to similar restrictions. The single bottle of sherry is brought out every Christmas and returned untouched to the darkest recesses of the sideboard every New Year. Ruth is running a house, not a public bar. She is teetotal, has been since the Temperance Society marched down Bird Street with their banners flying.

Jack sighs and opens the paper, but he's too distracted by memories of his friend to read. Nibs was barely five foot six, thin as a rake. He seemed to be in a permanent sweat. His skin shone like it was newly oiled and he couldn't speak without using his hands to illustrate his point. He looked like a windmill in a gale when he got upset. He had run a pet shop in London before the war. A typical Cockney – loads of patter and plenty of old buck when things weren't going his way. But he loved animals. It didn't matter where they were, there'd be some mangy mongrel or moth-eaten cat at his heels. In Heraklion Nibs had put his hand halfway down an Alsatian's throat to pull out a sliver of bone that was blocking the dog's windpipe. The dog had promptly vomited and then nipped Nibs on the ankle as he was walking away. He'd always taken in strays and the fact that he was in the middle of a war didn't make any difference. He argued that there wasn't much to choose between dogs and men. 'Sometimes, even with the best will in the world, you can't save them and there's no point in even trying. It's kinder to have done and put them out of their bloody misery.' The memory is a bitter one, considering how things turned out. Jack shakes himself and rubs his hand across his forehead as if to wipe away the memory. He lights another cigarette and stares out across the empty sands, a look of hopelessness on his face.

It is Gunner, the hotel dog, who finally rouses him. The dog wanders up out of nowhere and lodges his chin firmly on Jack's knee. Gunner is a Lakeland terrier, his coat a scrunch of grey and brown wire wool. One eye is dimmed with a cataract but the other is bright and what's left of his docked tail is permanently erect. Man and dog sit in companionable silence for a few minutes. The breeze freshens, shifting grains of sand across the pink flagstones and rippling the bunting tied to the promenade railings. Jack has spent Wakes Week at the Belvedere Hotel every year since the war and, as a result, is regarded as family by Gunner. Blackpool at the height of the holiday season might disturb and overexcite any ordinary dog, but Gunner is an old hand. It has been a long trip for Gunner from 'unofficial South Lancs Regimental mascot' to Mine Host at the Belvedere Hotel. The dog is subject to the unwelcome attention of passing children and his sleep is disturbed nightly by hotel guests in various states of inebriation gaining rowdy entry to the hotel lobby. Jack tickles the dog's left ear before taking a last drag and flicking his cigarette over the promenade railings. Standing up, he proceeds to fold the newspaper into three and, putting it under his arm, heads back to the hotel. Gunner meanwhile continues his route march along the prom in search of last night's chip papers.

'Looks as if it's going to be another hot one, Ruth,' Jack says when he sees his wife in the lobby. His glance strays to Beth, who is already wriggling with the itchiness of her vest, liberty bodice and wool jumper. 'Hasn't she got a summer dress to wear?'

'Not today,' Ruth replies firmly. 'It could turn cold again; the wind's got a nip to it.'

'Give over. I've been out there. It's not cold, it's fresh. It'll do her good to get some sunshine.'

Beth runs up to her father and wraps her arms round his legs.

'E-yo-yo, Sputnik!'

Jack bends down to pick Beth up. He puts his arm carefully round the back of her legs and lifts her gently. Beth might be fragile but the spell in hospital hasn't curbed any of her curiosity. She spots the letter in his inside jacket pocket in a flash. 'What's this?' she asks, her fingers closing round the corner of the letter.

'Never mind that. Are you ready for your breakfast? Plenty of porridge, that's what you need. It'll make your hair curl,' Jack says as he strokes back a fine brown strand that has escaped from her ribbon. 'I'll just nip upstairs and change my jacket – it's too hot for tweed,' he continues, turning to Ruth.

'I'll come with you,' she replies. 'I've left my scarf on the dressing table.'

'No, you're all right. I can pick it up at the same time.'

Once in the room, Jack reaches inside his jacket. The beige satin lining whispers conspiratorially against the thick envelope as he slides it out. He has had the letter for the best part of a week now and keeping it hidden is proving stressful. If he were at home there'd be no problem. Jack could have hidden it in his worksheets and textile patterns. As long as they're neatly stacked Ruth never bothers with them; she's no interest in loom specifications and the like. But here in Blackpool there's nowhere safe to keep the letter. Not in the suitcase. Dear God, not in there. She's in that case half a dozen times a day, pulling out fresh clothes for the girls and rearranging everything. She has a system. Everything in its place and a place for everything. At night she goes through all Jack's clothes looking for loose buttons and dirty handkerchiefs. She empties the contents of his pockets on to a brass tray on the dressing table and puts his wallet on top. Finally she brushes down his jacket and, resisting the lure of the hotel wardrobe, hangs it up behind the door. As a result of her efficiency Jack has been driven to distraction – forever moving the letter from jacket to trousers as the situation demands. He had been keeping it in his shirt pocket until he noticed her eyeing him suspiciously at breakfast yesterday. Discretion being the better part of valour, he had retired to the toilet and moved it to his jacket pocket where he'd reckoned it was safe enough for a while. Now he takes the letter, folds it in half, pushes it in the back pocket of his trousers and does up the button. Manoeuvre completed, Jack takes off his jacket, collects Ruth's scarf from the dressing table and locks the door behind him.

3

GANNETS

These are large seabirds with white feathers and black tips to their wings. They feed by plunging into the sea and catching fish with their long pointed bills. This habit of diving upon their food has led to their hungry reputation! Score 20 points for some greedy gannets.

Connie is run off her feet this morning. She has already seated an extra four families in the packed dining room when the Clegg family, six in total, turn up. 'There's a whole bloody tribe of them,' she complains to Andy, the chef, 'and I've only got a table for two left.'

Connie hasn't worked as a silver service waitress before, but the manager of the Belvedere knows a crowd pleaser when he sees one. Connie turned up on his doorstep a couple of weeks earlier and was offered the job on the spot. The Belvedere is very classy, a dream come true for Connie. Her last job was at Stan's Café, where she worked every weekend. She served behind the counter mostly, but she had to cook as well on Sundays if Stan wasn't feeling up to it. It was Stan who taught her how to carry seven plates at once. She'd got the knack eventually, but not before she'd turned up at school on a fair few Monday mornings with a giant plaster on the inside of her left wrist. Connie is a cracker, in more ways than one. She'd caused such a sensation at the café that the place was packed with lads every weekend waiting for her to lean over the counter or drop a fork. Connie is just that sort of girl. Her scarlet overall looked decent enough on the hanger when Stan gave it to her, but when she put it on there was something about her curves that resisted confinement. And what with the hotplates and ovens going full blast behind her, it was only natural that she should loosen the collar. Connie sees no problem in the degree of male attention she excites despite, or perhaps because of, the ladders in her stockings and the buttons missing from her bodice. Stan offered her full-time work when she left school, but Connie had bigger fish to fry. She'd heard that you could pick up seasonal work in Blackpool. What could be better than spending the whole summer in Blackpool and being paid for it to boot? Stan was sad to see her go. Still, Stan's loss is the Belvedere's gain.

The hotel supplies its waitresses with a black uniform and a white frilly apron with a delicate pin-tucked front fixed at nipple level with tiny gold safety pins. Black stilettos and seamed stockings complete the outfit, along with a wisp of lace that passes for a hat, which is secured to the back of the head with white kirby grips. Connie is friendly and easygoing by nature, and has already proved a big hit with the head chef, Andy. It is Andy who yells at the deputy manager to put up another table and find an extra couple of chairs sharpish, and Andy who advises Connie to put the Cleggs in the alcove. If Connie hesitates it's because her new friend Helen's family usually sit there. But Andy is adamant. He has her best interests at heart.

When she arrives in the palatial dining room Mrs Singleton is at first confused and then annoyed to see that the large table in its own private alcove (where the family has sat every day since their arrival last Saturday) is no longer available. Far from it. A family of six is occupying their table, leaving the Singletons no other option but to cram themselves round a tiny table inched in between the alcove and walkway. This new location not only affords them unwelcome glimpses into the kitchen with its blasts of steam and bad language, but, worse still, forces them into close proximity with the very people who stole their table in the first place. Jack sizes up the situation and, accepting that there is no alternative, indicates that they should all sit at the new table.

Ruth remains standing, staring furiously at the interlopers. The family appear not to have noticed but the moment Ruth finally relents and sits, the wife, a large florid woman with broad capable hands, pipes up, 'Have we got your table? It was the waitress what put us here. She said it were the only way what with there being so many of us and needing two high chairs for the twins. Do you want us to move?' All this said with the confidence of a woman who, once settled, even the H bomb wouldn't shift.

Ruth turns her head away and it is left to Jack to reply. 'No, no.

It doesn't matter. We'll sit here instead. There's room for everyone,' he says, raising his voice to cover the rustle of the letter in his trouser pocket when he sits down. 'It's Full English Breakfast wherever you sit!'

'You're right there,' replies the husband. He turns halfway round in his chair and offers Jack his hand. 'Fred Clegg,' he says and tilts his head in the direction of the florid woman. 'And that's the wife, Florrie.'

Jack nods at Florrie and shakes hands with Fred.

'We got here last night. We're still finding our feet,' continues Fred.

'Well, it looks as if you've brought the sunshine with you,' Jack says as he turns his attention to the breakfast menu.

'From over Blackburn way, are you?' Fred asks.

'Aye.'

'I thought I'd seen you around. I never forget a face. Where do you . . . ?'

But Jack, aware that the next question will be about work, interrupts: 'You're from the town then, are you?'

'Aye.'

During this exchange Ruth has had a good look at the Clegg family. The husband looks dishevelled, from the worn elbows of his brown cardigan to his nylon shirt that strains across a lovingly maintained beer belly. Ruth wouldn't dream of buying a nylon shirt. There's no need for nylon unless you're too lazy to iron. And as for all this craze for drip-dry – anybody with any sense knows that a good cotton twill will resist wrinkling and barely needs ironing. But Mrs Clegg doesn't look as if she'd care. She's wearing a faded blue dress with white polka dots. The dress is deliberately shapeless yet its generous gathers struggle to disguise her overwhelming bulk. The material stretches over unwanted curves and catches between rolls of excess. Only the eldest boy is decently dressed, the twins and the younger lad are in little better than rags. All her worst fears confirmed, Ruth turns and looks out of the window. High winds laden with salt spray have eaten away at the exterior paintwork. Ruth suspects it would only take a single swipe from a scrubbing brush to remove the lot but you'd risk removing the window at the same time. There isn't an ounce of decent putty left on the frame. No wonder it's draughty.

'We've not stayed here before,' Fred volunteers. 'We usually stay at Mrs Thornber's boarding house down at South Shore. Nearer for the Pleasure Beach. Three meals a day and less than half the price of this place. But what with one thing and another, we'd left it too late for Mrs Thornber's. So we thought we'd have a couple of days here instead. Makes a change.'

'Oh, you'll like it here. It's good plain food at the Belvedere and there's a bar every night,' replies Jack, who is momentarily distracted by the quality of the damask tablecloth. He turns the material over and back a few times remarking the precision of the surface pattern in reverse, speculating as to the thread count. He runs his nail across the grain of the fabric to assess how much of the stiffness of the cloth is due to the weave and how much to the application of starch. Jack learned long ago that once you start looking at weaves it's difficult to break the habit.

Fred sits back in his chair and looks around the dining room. The walls are covered in flock wallpaper: deep burgundy acanthus leaves against a pale plum background. The room itself is bisected by a series of white pillars that support a ceiling heavy with ornate plasterwork and oversized ceiling roses. It's what holidaymakers come to the Belvedere for – a bit of luxury. The hotel is fully booked and the room hums with the sound of mill workers and their families tucking into a three-course breakfast and making the best of an English summer.

Florrie Clegg beams at Ruth and says, 'It looks a nice place, this.'

Ruth looks unconvinced. She has noticed a slow but irreversible decline in standards over the years. Still, any hotel that can entertain that couple in room sixty-nine – the salesman and his 'wife' – is already well on its way to perdition without any further help from the Cleggs. And as for the 'good plain food' – that's a matter of opinion.

Shortly after they were married Ruth made Eggs Florentine. Jack stared at the eggs and spinach lavishly topped with a classic cheese sauce (made properly, mind you, with a flour and butter roux) and said, 'What sort of concoction is this? You shouldn't have gone to so much trouble, Ruth. What's wrong with broth on a Tuesday?'

Ruth may have crossed Eggs Florentine off the menu but she is still determined to use some of the fancy recipes she and her best friend Cora collected at night school. Cora always said that the French names alone were enough to make her mouth water (Poulet Bonne Femme, Moules Marinières, Boeuf Bourguignon). They'd both had a good laugh about the pronunciation. Cora had a talent for making French sound suggestive. She'd thought up a whole list of things that 'Moules Marinières' might possibly mean – including sailors' balls – until Ruth had blushed and covered her mouth with her hand. Despite her attachment to French cuisine Ruth is quite happy to leave out the garlic and downright glad to substitute water for wine. She has learned that it is no good putting Jack's tea in front of him and saying 'This is Quiche Lorraine' – he is a sight less suspicious if she says, 'I thought we'd have egg and bacon pie today.' Or 'I've picked up some fresh mussels from the market. I thought they'd make a change, boiled with a bit of onion.' He will set to and eat the lot until the bowl rattles with the scrape of empty shells and his fingers glisten with butter and flakes of fresh parsley. Ruth is running culinary circles around Jack. And as long as she only does it once or twice a week, Jack is prepared to let her.

Further conversation is abandoned as the two families order breakfast. Connie scribbles the orders down in her pad and disappears through the swing doors into the kitchen. Ruth has a set of rules garnered for the most part from *Good Housekeeping* and the writings of Elizabeth Craig. Rules are Ruth's sheet anchor in the troubled seas of marriage and child rearing. Over the years she has developed an encyclopedic knowledge of how to behave – table manners and etiquette being foremost in her present considerations. A glance down the table confirms that her daughters are behaving as she would expect in a public place. Their voices are suitably moderated, their spoons half filled from the far edge of the cereal bowls, their elbows well in and their movements slow. Ruth watches

Connie clearing the cereal plates from the Cleggs' table minutes after having served them.

'Just look at that family. Have you seen how they eat?' Ruth whispers to Jack. 'They're like a bunch of gannets. I'm surprised they bother with knives and forks. I've never seen anyone eat that fast.'

Beth taps her mother's hand. 'Can I have a drink, Mummy? I'm thirsty. Can I have orange juice like the other people?' Beth pokes a pale finger at the Cleggs.

Ruth shakes her head. There is nothing to drink other than a pot of tea. It is Ruth's first job, when she reaches the table every morning, to hand the jug of orange juice back to the waitress. Ruth does not hold with tinned juice, be it orange, grapefruit, or apple. Whole fresh fruit is to be preferred at all times. Water is not an acceptable alternative. Elizabeth is so clumsy she'd spill it.

'You'll have to wait until you get back to the room. I can't be having you making a mess,' Ruth replies.

The Cleggs appear to have no such qualms; their jug of juice disappears within minutes of their arrival and is refilled. This is promptly followed by demands for tea, toast and marmalade to keep the family going while they wait for the main course. The Full English arrives with another pot of tea and extra toast. Fred Clegg sighs and says to his sons, 'Wire in, lads.' As if they needed telling.

Fred and Jack go on to chat about the weather forecast and Florrie turns to Ruth. 'What a pretty daughter you have,' she says, casting her eye over Helen. 'And how old is your little boy?'

Ruth feigns deafness and Florrie has to raise her voice in order to be heard over the noise of the twins nudging and pushing each other, and stealing food from each other's plates.

Ruth gives her a frosty look. 'Are you referring to my daughters?'

'Oh, it's a little girl! I'm such a fool. I should have known. It was the brown shorts that threw me. What's your name, pet?'

Beth is not allowed to speak to strangers. She looks to her mother for permission. Ruth inclines her head – a nod imperceptible to outsiders – and Beth replies, 'Beth.'

'Elizabeth,' her mother interrupts. 'I don't hold with all this shortening of names. It's lazy.'

'Well, long or short, it's a pretty name. And how old are you?'

'Seven. And my sister is sixteen.'

'Well,' says Florrie, turning to Ruth, 'aren't they grand? You must be very proud of them. There's the same gap between my lads as there is between your girls. 'Rob' – she points to a sallow-skinned boy who is wearing an Indian headdress with three feathers – 'is nine.'

The boy pulls a packet of Barrett's Sweet Cigarettes from the pocket of his grey shorts and, extracting a cigarette, he taps the end on the front of the packet and lodges it in the side of his mouth. When he is assured that he has Beth's shocked attention he inhales deeply, glares at his mother and says, 'I'm called Red Hawk.'

Florrie ignores him and continues, 'There's the twins, of course. And my eldest, Alan. He's eighteen. Training as a clerk,' Florrie remarks with some pride.

Helen glances sideways at Alan. He is leaning back in his chair drinking his tea and flicking the ash from his tipped cigarette into the saucer. He is a remarkably sharp dresser, from his wide-checked blue gingham shirt to his white socks and shiny slip-on shoes. His hands are small but clean, the nails well manicured. He is shaved and scrubbed to such an extent that his neck glows red against his collar. His ginger hair is parted precisely on the left and combed into a solid quiff. Helen is impressed. Aware of her attention, Alan pulls out a large leather wallet and flicks it open to reveal serried ranks of fivers, pounds and ten-shilling notes. Helen immediately looks away, but this calculated display of wealth earns a wink from the passing Connie.

The Cleggs have finished their breakfast but seem unwilling to leave the dining room. Their table looks like a bombsite. The cloth is crumpled and smeared with butter, and there's dirty cutlery everywhere but on the plate, while only the folded napkins remain pristine. The Singletons' table is an oasis of order and calm in comparison.

Florrie relaxes and pours herself another cup of tea. After a few moments she arches her back against the wooden chair and addresses Ruth. 'How long are you here for, Ruth?'

'We leave on Saturday,' Ruth replies and busies herself with collecting the used napkins. She is relieved when Red Hawk's demand for some spending money interrupts the conversation. Florrie takes two sixpences out of her purse. She gives them both to the boy and whispers in his ear. Red Hawk nods and, before Ruth can put a stop to it, he has given Beth a sixpence.

'There's really no need, Mrs Clegg,' Ruth says. 'Elizabeth already has some spending money.'

'Oh, call me Florrie,' Mrs Clegg insists. 'Well, it's the least I could do after my silly mistake. It's only a sixpence. I'm sure you'll be able to find something to spend it on, won't you, pet?'

Beth looks at the sixpence in disbelief – this is twice as much as the spending money she gets every Saturday. Aware of the extravagance, she holds her breath, awaiting her mother's intervention, but there is silence. When Beth finally tears her eyes away from the sixpence and looks up, her mother glares at her and says, 'What do you say, Elizabeth?'

'Thank you,' she whispers and wraps the coin carefully in her best handkerchief. Sixpence will buy a Range Rider Lucky Bag, a tuppenny sherbet fountain and a liquorice Catherine wheel with a pink sweet in the middle. Besides the usual sweets and cards all Lucky Bags have a toy inside – with a bit of luck Beth might get a monkey on a stick instead of the usual whistle.

Outflanked by Florrie's generosity, Ruth is reduced to tightening her lips and watching, with mounting disapproval, as Red Hawk slides up and down the varnished walkway in his stocking feet. Beth is transfixed by his misbehaviour. He is wearing three feathers stuck in a rubber band round his head. His thick grey school shorts are ripped at the pocket and worn to a greasy shine on the bottom. Round his waist is a red and blue elastic belt that fastens at the front with a snake clasp, though it is not much use keeping his shorts up since the waistband is missing two of the belt holders. Beth is impressed. Red Hawk has several club badges pinned to his jumper. Beth has been trying to join clubs for the past year. All she's managed so far is the Golliwog Club, and she isn't really a member of that until her mother has finished sufficient jars of jam to send off for a badge. Beth has been campaigning for a golliwog pirate badge – much more exciting than the golly bus conductor or, worse still, the golly golfer. Red Hawk is wearing a Cub badge. Beth had harboured hopes of joining the Brownies but Brown Owl only wants Brownies who can join in the various activities like dancing in a circle round a papier-mâché owl on a toadstool and going away to Brownie camp. There's the Girl Adventurers' Club, but it's not very adventurous. Unless you count always being polite to adults and kind to sick animals exciting. There's Uncle Mac's Children's Favourites Club, but that's hardly exclusive; anyone can join just by switching on the wireless.

Red Hawk has already bumped into one table and got tomato ketchup down his front, and now he's shooting a bow and arrow at the ceiling. When he knocks over and smashes a couple of side plates his mother gives him a fond look and says, by way of explanation, 'You have to let them have their heads. It's only once a year. Holidays are holidays, aren't they?'

Breakfast is finished by the time the couple from room sixty-nine appear. Jack has spoken to him in the bar once or twice. He's a travelling salesman and Ruth reckons his 'wife' is out to get what she can – which will be a fair amount if you look at the way she's dressed. All she ever has for breakfast is dry toast and straight black coffee. Not, Ruth notes, that it stays straight for long. He's forever pulling out a hip flask of whisky to put a kick in it. 'Hair of the dog,' he says with a wide grin.

There's some winking and groping under the table before she

says, 'Behave yourself, Harry. What will people think?' It's obvious from his reply that he couldn't care less. He has a laugh like Sid James.

Breakfast complete, Jack and Fred Clegg wander into the Residents' Lounge for a cigarette, deep in conversation about whether or not Blackburn will make the cup final next season. The eldest boy, Alan, remains seated next to his mother but his attention is concentrated on the other side of the dining room where Connie and Helen are standing.

'Our Alan works for an accountant,' Florrie tells Ruth.

'Turf?'

'Oh no, a proper accountant. With a fancy office and everything. Our Alan has been there for the past couple of years since he left school. It's a responsible job. They rely on our Alan to do the local deliveries in the morning. It's very serious. Some of those letters have statements, bonds, or even cheques inside. The senior partner, Mr Tyson, calls our Alan his right-hand man. And he's a smasher at home. So good with the twins. They listen to every word he says.'

Florrie lifts the occupants of the two high chairs – a couple of heavy, flat-faced three-year-olds with matching sagging lower lips and dull grey eyes. Freed from restraint, the twins immediately fall into a fight, which progresses out of the dining room, through the lobby and looks set to continue into the street. It only stops when one twin cracks his skull against the sign that reads: 'Guests are requested to ensure that their footwear is free of sand before entering the hotel.' The infant bursts into tears and howls with such ferocity that his twin feels compelled to join in.

Deaf to the uproar, Beth watches entranced as Red Hawk continues to crawl around the dining room. When he disappears into the lobby Beth asks to be excused from the table and gets down from her chair. She moves to the doorway of the dining room and peeps into the lobby. Red Hawk is still shooting arrows. When one falls at her feet she picks it up. Close to she can see that he has a green and white I-Spy badge pinned to his collar. Beth solemnly strokes her cheek three times. Red Hawk signals back. A friendship is formed.

'Are you a proper Red Indian brave?' the boy asks. Beth nods eagerly. 'Where are your flippin' feathers then?' Beth looks blank. 'Look.' The boy points to his headband. 'I've got three feathers.' He points to each of them in turn and says, 'This one's for *I-Spy Birds*, the middle one's for *I-Spy in the Street*, and this one at the end is for *I-Spy Car Numbers*. I'm on my fourth now. And I'm head of the Wild Jaguars tribe. What tribe do you belong to?'

'I haven't got a tribe yet, but I've got this.' Beth extracts *I-Spy at the Seaside* from her pocket and pushes it under his nose.

He barely glances at it before he hands it back. 'That one looks too easy – I'm doing *I-Spy Buses and Coaches* now. They're more difficult but I bet I finish the whole book by Saturday.'

Beth is unable to give Red Hawk's achievements her full attention since she has spotted Gunner relieving himself against one of the impressive magnolia pillars at the hotel entrance. She has spent hours trying to make friends with Gunner. Beth is not allowed a dog of her own. She has asked her mother for one countless times, but the answer is always the same. Dogs are far too dirty to keep, they carry fleas and ticks, along with all sorts of diseases and they don't care where they make a mess. There being no hope of acquiring a dog of her own, Beth is therefore on permanent lookout for a dog she can adopt. She is fearless in her pursuit, despite having once been bitten by a poodle on Halifax Road. Beth is convinced that Gunner can be persuaded into allowing her to stroke him if she is persistent enough. But Gunner is not amenable to approach. His tolerance for children as a subspecies is substantially below zero and remains so despite having been severely tested by Beth's persistent kindness and relentless affection.

Beth, ignorant of the dog's pathological hatred of children, still believes that she can make friends with Gunner. 'Here, Gunner. You'd like a stroke, wouldn't you?' Gunner doesn't look convinced. Beth, hand outstretched, creeps forward. Unable to whistle like the boy in *Lassie*, Beth is reduced to making clicking noises with her tongue and purring, 'Here, Gunner. There's a good boy. Here, Gunner. Here, boy.'

Beth and Red Hawk watch as Gunner bolts past them in the direction of the hotel kitchens. 'I'll get him for you,' says Red Hawk, loading his bow with the remaining arrow and aiming at the dog's retreating backside.

'No,' shouts Beth, grabbing the arrow. 'I'll never make friends with him if you hurt him.'

'I wouldn't bother,' volunteers Red Hawk. 'That bugger bloody bit me when I pulled his tail. I wouldn't care but it were only a joke.'

Back in the dining room, Connie is clearing the tables. She and Helen have become good friends over the past few days. They can be found giggling together in a corner somewhere most mornings once the dining room empties. Connie sneaks a swift cigarette and a milky coffee, while Helen listens open-mouthed to the waitress's salacious account of the previous evening's activities. Connie is forever encouraging Helen to accompany her on these soirées but so far she has drawn a blank. She may be a couple of months younger but she has a wealth of experience hitherto denied Helen. Even Helen's Saturday job in a dress shop can't compete with Connie's obvious experience.

'I'll tell you what,' whispers Connie at her most confidential. 'Kitchen and dining-room staff get two hours off every afternoon. We all go out together. Why don't you come with us? We usually meet up at the pier for a drink and a laugh. It's a scream. Andy bought me four Babychams yesterday afternoon and I was seeing double by the time I got back.'

'I can't,' Helen says. 'I'm not allowed on the pier.'

'What? Even during the day? Hellfire! My dad's in Strangeways and even he gets let out every now and again.'

Helen is embarrassed. Not just because her parents treat her like a child but also for her friend having a dad in prison, but it doesn't seem to bother Connie.

'You're lucky to have a dad like yours. He's great, isn't he?' Connie sighs and casts a glance over at Jack.

'He's OK, I suppose. He's not as strict as my mother.'

'She's like bloody Hitler. However did she get her claws into your dad? I mean, he's good-looking enough to get anyone he wanted. He doesn't even look old, does he?' Connie changes the subject when she sees the look of disbelief on Helen's face. 'Anyway, what's the gossip about that new bloke?'

'Who?'

'Mr Wonderful in the check shirt on your old table. Go on, what's the gossip? Spill the beans, Helen.'

'I don't know a lot – he's called Alan and he works for an accountant.'

'Oh, very fancy! Did you see him flashing his wallet around?'

'Yes.' Helen is awestruck by such a display of wealth.

'I saw him. He couldn't take his eyes off you.'

Helen blushes. 'Well, I'm not interested in him. Well, I mean, he's all right.'

'Would you go out with him if he asked?'

'I might.'

'I thought you said you had a boyfriend at home?'

'I have,' Helen replies, trying to sound casual. She has been forced to invent a boyfriend with whom she is 'going steady' in order to deflect Connie's constant queries as to why she doesn't go out at night.

'Ah, well, a bit on the side won't do any harm. What the eye doesn't see the heart doesn't grieve over. That's what my mum always says when she's out with a new bloke. I'll bet Mr Wonderful over there would give his right arm to take you out. Oh, God! He's looking this way.'

Helen is forced to put her hand over her mouth to muffle the laughter. Far away, at the other end of the dining room, Alan looks on.

'I know what! If you can't come on the pier with me why don't we go to that new coffee bar?'

'Where?' Helen asks.

'Rico's. That one on Victoria Street, just behind the Tower. I went there with Andy last week – he'd fixed it so that we both had the same day off. There's a great jukebox and they serve that frothy coffee. Your mum can't object to you having a cup of coffee, can she? Let's go this afternoon.'

'Where shall I meet you?'

'You know where my room is, don't you? Through the Staff door in the lobby, down the stairs and it's on the right. I'll see you there at half past two.'

'I know Blackburn like the back of my hand,' Florrie says. 'Which part of the town do you come from?'

'Oh, we're on the outskirts,' Ruth replies as she hurries to finish her tea.

'Oh?' Florrie thinks she might have cottoned on to something. The silence that follows is deafening. When it's obvious that Ruth has no intention of supplying further details Florrie starts again: 'You're a long way out of the centre, are you? A terrace, is it?'

Ruth nods by way of reply. She neglects to mention that the house is an end terrace. It is not in Ruth's nature to be boastful, particularly with strangers. Both women know perfectly well that there's a class hierarchy in terraced life. The further out of town, the better the terrace. The Singletons own an end terrace. It might as well be a semi. Ruth has only one immediate neighbour – although with the noise the Kerkleys make it sometimes sounds as if she's got more. The Singletons' end terrace is situated at the tree-lined town boundary, overlooking the town below and the moors beyond. It is, to quote the estate agent Ruth has had round recently, 'a little gem'.

'I lived on Le-banon Street before I was wed,' Florrie volunteers. Ruth's face is a picture of restraint. 'They're a good crowd on Le-banon,' Florrie continues.

Ruth bites her lip. She is not only capable of pronouncing the name Lebanon correctly, she could point to the country on a map and quote freely from the Bible on the subject.

'So, whereabouts on the tops are you? Anywhere near the Black Bull?'

It is a common habit locally to tie the location of anything in the town to the nearest pub. Ruth is not prey to this habit. She allows herself a vague 'm-m-m' as she replaces her cup in the saucer.

'Oh, they're all pastry forks and bay windows up there, aren't they? Wouldn't suit me. No, I like to be in the thick of things. I like to know what's going on. Don't you find it a nuisance being so far out of town? It means a lot of travelling,' Florrie says as she's sweetening her Alan's second cup of tea for him.

'It's nice and quiet on the tops,' Ruth replies, biting back the urge to say that it's worth a three-bob bus journey to be away from dirty backstreets and the stink of mill chimneys.

'There,' Florrie says after she's taken an exploratory sip, 'that's just nice.' She passes the sweetened cup of tea over to Alan. Ruth can sense her nose turning up. She's seen her mother do it countless times for her father; indeed, Ruth might have sweetened and sipped Jack's tea herself had she not seen the light at night school. Quite apart from what constitutes good table manners, the practice is unhealthy and encourages the migration of germs. Elizabeth Craig is adamant about this.

'They're building some new houses up there, aren't they?' Florrie remarks casually.

'Where?'

'Up on the Boundary. Three-bedroom semis. I told Fred, I said, "They'll never sell them! Who'd pay a fortune to live that far out of town?" It's not even a local builder, is it?'

'No, I don't think it is.'

Florrie gives Ruth a shrewd look and says, 'Got your eye on one of them, have you?'

This is an understatement. Ruth has not only got an eye on one of the new semis, she's got a copy of the plans and the deposit as well. Not that she would ever admit to this. Talk of the semi involves two forbidden subjects: family and money. Ruth gets up from the table, anxious to make her escape.

'She's small for seven, your little girl. You did say she was seven, didn't you? She looks nearer five to me. Very quiet, isn't she?'

Ruth has heard the same from Beth's teacher at school. 'You know, Mrs Singleton,' the teacher had ventured, 'Beth, er, I mean Elizabeth is a bit too quiet, if you see what I mean. I've known children who appear quiet. But they're not really. They're hiding for some reason.

They imagine if they're quiet no one will notice them. Someone or something has frightened them. Have you noticed anything?'

'Nothing,' Ruth had replied with a firm shake of the head.

'Well, she may not be breaking her toys or screaming, but this doesn't mean she hasn't got problems. She's likely to tell you if you find the time to ask and listen to what she says.' Seeing the expression on Ruth's face, the teacher had added, 'Well, perhaps I'm wrong. Maybe all she needs is a good cuddle and some reassurance. All of us could do with that, couldn't we?'

The teacher had said all this in such a caring and reasonable tone that Ruth had been quite worried about it. Until, that is, she sat down and thought about it. Then she realised that it was all nonsense. Elizabeth is obedient because that's the way she's been brought up. Ruth expects her to be quiet and polite at all times. Who wants a cheeky daughter who's forever shouting and misbehaving? Ruth stopped calling in at school after that. But the accusation still makes her angry.

Faced with Florrie's comment, Ruth pushes her chair firmly back under the table. She gives Mrs Clegg a bleak, tight-lipped look but Florrie continues, 'The poor mite. She's so thin and pale. She looks as if she could do with plenty of good food and a nice bit of sunshine, wouldn't you say?'

Ruth ignores the remark. She heads out into the lobby where there is a brief exchange of views between mother and daughter before Beth drops the newly won sixpence into a collection box for the local disabled.

Blackburn, November 1958

The revelation of Beth's illness came as a direct result of Mrs Richmond having syringed her husband's ears and thus rendered audible to him the heart whisper, the rhythmic sigh of a leaking valve and phantom echo of escaping pressure, that had accompanied the Singletons' younger daughter throughout her six years. Beth stands before the old doctor as her mother peels off the layers of jumper and blouse, liberty bodice and vest. Dr Richmond places two pallid fingers above her shoulder blade and raps them sharply with the crooked fingers of his left hand. The exercise is repeated over the child's back, Beth alive to the uneasy vibration and flinching away from the discomfort when her chest is sounded. Dr Richmond reaches for his stethoscope, places the steel nodes in his ear and rubs the bright circle on the palm of his hand. There is complete silence. Ruth presses her lips together, too frightened to breathe, resisting the urge to join in while Beth inhales and exhales to order. Both mother and child pant briefly when the stethoscope examination is concluded, Ruth for oxygen and Beth with pain.

Dr Richmond removes the stethoscope from his neck with deliberation and folds it carefully until the ancient black rubber settles into its accustomed cracks. Ruth immediately stiffens in the hard-backed chair she has been occupying since she and her younger daughter were summoned from their sojourn in the doctor's waiting room – a two-hour wait during which Ruth had silently rehearsed all the reasons why she mistrusts the good doctor. If he'd been faster off the mark when she'd come to see him about her stomach pains back in 1950 she might have carried the child to full term.

Of course, she doesn't have any proof that it was a boy that she lost at thirteen weeks. But Ruth knows, as clearly as any real mother would know, that it was a boy. Sitting again in the same room waiting to see the same doctor, she had felt the old anger rising.

Dr Richmond sighs and says, 'You can get this bonny little girl dressed again now.'

Ruth has recognised a number of traits in Elizabeth since birth, but 'bonny' is not one of them. It makes no difference how well she feeds Elizabeth, the child remains weak and tires easily. Her shoulders are permanently hunched over her chest, she sweats too easily and she still asks to be carried up hills. It is a back-breaking task for a woman over forty. Ruth has resisted seeing the doctor before now. Her relationship with old Dr Richmond is not an easy one.

In order to cover her impatience Ruth now busies herself with dressing the child, stretching the wool vest over her head and struggling with the curling rubber buttons on the Ladybird liberty bodice.

When decency is restored Dr Richmond ventures his professional opinion. 'There might be a slight problem, Mrs Singleton,' he says. This example of kindly understatement is characteristic of Dr Richmond. He has had cause on many occasions, when delivering bad news to anxious mothers, to adopt a certain reassuring ignorance of fatal consequences. He has no cures for pneumoconiosis (a familiar complaint among the miners at Bank Hall Colliery) or pulmonary embolism, or parietal gliomas, or any one of the number of terminal conditions he is forced to witness within the space of a single day. The varnish of confident infallibility afforded to the newly qualified has worn away over the years to reveal his humanity in all its uncertainty and inadequacy. He spends his mornings on call. His white starched cuffs are stained brown with iodine and rasp against his wrists as he takes pulses, measures blood pressures, pinches swollen ankles and tests stubborn joints. He rubs the folds of his softening jowls as he considers prescriptions or waits for the arrival of the ambulance. By late evening he has listened to a litany of complaints and drunk his way through all manner of liquid that passes for tea in the houses of the poor.

Only then does he return home to the silent remembrances of former patients. His house bulges with mortuary gifts: gold watches, pipe stands, copies of the Bible and amateur paintings of local landmarks. Patients leave wills that afford him war medals from battles fought in the Mediterranean or North Africa while he was busy delivering the next generation in the cold austerity of Bank Hall Maternity Home. Financial bequests from wealthier patients are spent on repairs to the roof of his surgery, coal fires in his waiting room, lollipops for his infant patients, outstanding rent for miners laid up with lung disease and weavers laid off with mill closures.

Ruth is aware of Dr Richmond's reputation but, since she is not in need of charity or sympathy, she persists in her interrogation. 'What is wrong with her?'

'A slight chest irregularity. Probably minor, nothing to be anxious about. I have a colleague who might have a look at her. Mr Tomlinson at the hospital.'

'He's a heart man, isn't he? Is it her heart? What's wrong with it?'

'It might be a circulation problem. You yourself have noticed she's breathless sometimes. I thought I heard a slight whisper when I listened to her chest, but I could be mistaken. We doctors aren't infallible.'

'What do you mean, a whisper?'

'Let's wait until Mr Tomlinson has seen her, shall we? Then we'll be sure what we're talking about.'

'And when will that be?'

'I'll have a word with him first thing tomorrow. He's a good man. Can you take this little girl up tomorrow around two o'clock? Save all the bother of waiting for an appointment. Now I must get on, there are patients waiting to be seen.'

Ruth quits the surgery with some reluctance. She senses that there is something seriously wrong, but can get no further with old Richmond. She is too clever to be misled by his diagnostic hesitation, or the sudden availability of a hospital appointment. There is something wrong with her daughter and only Ruth's iron restraint in the company of strangers keeps her from crying in the queue for the bus home.

4

SHORE CRAB

This crab often hides under the sand with just his eyes and feelers showing and so he may be difficult to spot. He can also appear unexpectedly from under a stone but beware! The green and black shore crab has two very sharp pincer claws; once he latches on to something he won't let go! Score 20 for an unexpected appearance.

'Bloomin' 'eck, Ruth, how much longer?' Jack has been hauling three deckchairs around the sands for all of twenty minutes while his wife searches for a suitable location. The perfect spot has to be at the furthest possible point from the pier (roughnecks), sewage outlets (polio) and any patch of sand that has even a trace of tar. It's not an easy task. Jack's patience, along with the muscles in his right arm, is stretched to the limit. It is only when Ruth stops, turns and begins to retrace her steps along the beach that

Jack drops the three deckchairs, windbreak and bags in the sand and says, 'That's it! This'll do, Ruth.'

Ruth looks unconvinced. She stops and assures herself that they are still some distance from the sea. This is important if they are to get their money's worth out of the deckchairs. But it is only when she catches sight of the hordes of holidaymakers flooding down on to the beach behind her that she nods in agreement and Jack sighs with relief.

Jack puts up the deckchairs and windbreak, while Ruth unpacks the bags. Thus engaged, it is too late by the time they notice Mr and Mrs Sykes to take avoidance measures. Harry and Irene Sykes are, to quote their favourite expression, 'bang up to date' as only childless couples in their thirties can ever hope to be. Harry, sporting a pair of black winkle-picker shoes and green drainpipe trousers, sidles up. He has an extravagant quiff that teeters in the wind, and sideburns a good couple of inches longer than is decent for a man his age. Harry is foreman at Alexandria, a mill owned by Foster Brothers, the same company that employs Jack. He and Harry Sykes have known each other since Jack joined the firm but they have rarely, if ever, seen eye to eye. Despite this, Harry Sykes puts down his deckchairs next to Jack and says, 'Fancy seeing you here, Jack. Mind if we join you?'

'Of course not, Harry,' Jack replies, suppressing the urge to bolt. Ruth meanwhile gives the interlopers the briefest of nods, then turns her back and begins to empty her grey tartan shopping bag of towels, sun cream, knitting and this week's copy of *Woman's Own*.

Irene Sykes perches prettily on the edge of the deckchair that Harry has assembled for her with a single flick of his wrist. She puts the white stilettos she has been carrying since she reached the sands under her chair, opens her handbag and pulls out a pink enamelled compact decorated with the silhouette of a black poodle. She checks her lipstick in the mirror first, using a brightly varnished nail to wipe away the inevitable smudges of matching pink lipstick from the corners of her mouth. Snapping the compact smartly shut, she flashes Jack a brilliant smile. In present company Irene may have both youth and beauty on her side, but still she regards Ruth with a careful eye. 'Hello, Mrs Singleton,' she ventures. 'How are you?'

'Very well, thank you, Mrs Sykes.'

'And how's little Beth. Getting better now, is she?' Irene gives the child a look of heartfelt concern. Beth is wearing a blue mohair coat that ends just above her grey ankle socks and her head is wrapped in a yellow scarf.

'Elizabeth is very well, thank you,' Ruth replies in a tone designed to stifle any further questions.

'Poor little mite.' Mrs Sykes bends down and tickles Beth under her chin. 'I knew you when you were a tiny baby.'

Beth gives Mrs Sykes her whole attention.

'Your mum used to bring you to Baby Clinic every Tuesday. You were so good, you never cried. I had to weigh you every week to make sure that you were putting on enough weight and then write everything down in a special file. She was very late walking, wasn't she, Mrs Singleton?'

'I don't remember,' Ruth replies.

'Oh, but she was. I recall the doctor and I were very worried about her at one point because she was so far behind the other babies.' Ruth glares at Irene. 'But of course you were ill. That's why you were slow.'

Beth looks disappointed and returns to carving pictures of dogs in the sand.

Six years on and the memory of Irene Sykes writing 'slow walker' in the Baby Clinic file can still raise Ruth to fury. Irene Sykes may be a nurse, but she's no children of her own so what on earth would she know about anything?

'But you had the sweetest nature, Beth. Like a little angel.'

A lump rises in Irene's throat. 'How is she now, Mrs Singleton? I heard at work that she'd had the operation.'

'She's very well, thank you.'

'The physiotherapist told me that you'd cancelled any further visits. I know she was quite concerned.'

'She doesn't need any more physiotherapy. I'm sure Miss Franks has other patients who need her attentions more than Elizabeth.'

Irene is doubtful, but the look on Ruth's face persuades her to let the subject drop. In the ensuing silence Ruth picks up her knitting. 'And how's Helen?' Irene asks, turning to the teenager.

'Very well, thank you, Mrs Sykes.'

It is obvious that further attempts at conversation are a waste of time, so Irene leans back in her deckchair and lazily crosses one immaculately groomed leg over the other, showing off her evenly tanned legs, her white net petticoat and next week's washing in the process. She raises both arms, arching her slender back against the striped canvas. Her breasts rise against her scoop-necked bodice. Satisfied she has attracted the glance of every man in the vicinity, Irene closes her eyes against the glare of the sun and, smiling, relaxes.

Helen is overjoyed with her copy of the *New Musical Express*. There's a big poster of Bobby Darin in this week and a two-page spread. It's the only reason Helen bought the magazine. She flicks past the other articles ('Things Elvis Keeps Dark', 'Marty Wilde and Bert Weedon – So Much in Common' and 'Jerry Keller's "Here Comes Summer" Hits the Right Note') and turns to the poster. According to the article Bobby has 'a flashing personality, golden-brown skin, expressive eyebrows and dazzling white teeth'. The photo is only in black and white, but Helen can tell the description is all true. Bobby is wearing a tight shiny suit and he's dancing. His left arm is raised while the fingers of his right hand curl round the blunt bulk of the microphone. He must be dancing because Helen can see his legs are bent and one knee is twisted out to reveal his shiny winkle-picker shoes. It's enough to make Helen feel dizzy. She's looked in her *Collins School Atlas* more than once to see where Bobby lives. She knows it's a long way to America, but when she puts her thumb on Lancashire and her forefinger on New York it isn't far at all. In her dreams it's barely the distance of a breath and she's there in Hollywood, slow-dancing with Bobby. Even now, in broad daylight, she's irresistibly drawn to his photograph – the expression on his face when he looks directly into her eyes is enough to make her feel light-headed. Eventually she tears her eyes away from the poster and moves on to the columns of small print. Bobby, it says, was brought up in a rough neighbourhood where there were drunken fights and stabbings. Helen's mouth falls open as she reads that Bobby grew up surrounded by cheats, thieves, drunks, armed Mafia gangs and prostitution (whatever that is) on every corner. The family was very poor, but Bobby says, 'You could walk in our house and not see any furniture or anything, but love would hit you square in the mouth.'

Helen is deeply moved. It is terrible to think that her idol was brought up in a slum. Helen sometimes comes home from school with a bit of ink on her cuff and her mother always shouts, 'Take that blouse off this minute. Anybody would think you'd been brought up in a slum.'

Helen's grandma Catlow lives on Bird Street and her mother says the house is no better than a slum. This is why Helen only ever sees her grandma once a year at Christmas when Mum brings her up on the bus from Bird Street to visit. Still, it's nice that Bobby has such a close, loving family. The only thing that hits Helen square in the mouth when she walks in after school is the smell of polish and the sound of her mother scrubbing.

Bobby doesn't think school is up to much. He says, 'You don't know people or life through books. You learn by living and doing. You gotta go out in the world.'

Helen couldn't agree more. Bobby says that when he told his mother he wasn't going back to school she was disappointed, but she didn't try to stop him. He told her, 'Mom, it's time I got out to see what makes it tick.' Helen wishes she could leave school and get a job like Connie, but she doubts that her mother will let her. She looks again at the picture of Bobby. She caught sight of him yesterday on the television at the hotel. He was singing his hit song 'Splish Splash' followed by his new record, 'Dream Lover'. Bobby Darin has been Helen's dream lover ever since the moment she saw his photo on the front of *Boyfriend* magazine. He's half Italian and you can tell. He's got dark wavy hair and a brilliant smile. He's a great dancer too. Not like the boys at school.

The memory of her last school soirée is still fresh in Helen's mind. Not that it was any different from usual – the girls sitting on forms at one side of the gym and all the boys standing around at the other side. There was the usual mad rush when the music started, the thunder of pumps across the wooden floor as the boys raced across to grab the best girls. Helen had hoped that David Cooper, with his shock of strawberry-blond hair and black winkle-picker boots, might ask her to dance, but Hanson had got to her first. It happens every year – Hanson runs for East Lancs Schoolboys. Helen was refusing to dance even as Hanson was dragging her into the centre of the gym. As a result Helen spent the first part of the evening limping around the floor in the clutches of Hanson and the latter part watching in despair as her best friend Susan monopolised David Cooper. It would have been so different if Bobby had been there.

* * *

'I hear the bastards are looking for a new manager at your place.'

Jack is familiar with Harry's habit of referring to the mill owners as bastards and, under normal circumstances, barely bats an eyelid. But Ruth is easily offended and has a bee in her bonnet about bad language, especially in front of the girls. Jack looks pointedly at his daughters before giving Harry a warning glance and saying, 'Aye. Tom Brierley finished last Friday.'

'Irreplaceable, that one,' Harry mutters, 'they'll not find another crawler that fast.'

Jack sighs and shakes his head. It was Brierley who refused to have Harry back as foreman after the war, so the company shifted Sykes to Alexandria Mill. Harry took it badly. Alexandria still has the old looms and as a result weaves tea towels rather than the fancy work that's done in the weaving shed where Jack works. Even promotion to head foreman at Alexandria Mill failed to sweeten the pill where Harry was concerned – he was, as he was always at pains to point out, still being paid less than what he would have got if he'd stayed put. Worse, Jack replaced him as foreman at Prospect. All this has resulted in the relationship between Jack and Harry Sykes being strained, to say the least. If there's a smile on Harry's face at the moment it's because he's after something. 'Any idea who's taking over?' he asks.

'No idea,' Jack replies, squinting at the sea and opening his paper.

'I suppose we'll find out when the bosses are good and ready.'

'Aye.'

'It's a puzzle, though,' Harry persists. 'I've been keeping my eyes open ever since I heard Brierley was finishing, but there's been nothing in the paper. I asked that Union bloke . . . what's his name? Tom Bell. I asked him, but he's keeping his mouth shut. Claims he's no idea who'll get the job. I wouldn't mind a shot at it myself. A damn sight more money than Alexandria. Bastards must have it sewn up. I reckon one of the family will take over, what do you think? There must be a useless uncle or idiot cousin somewhere who's after a slice of the cake.' Harry throws the question casually, but he's watching for Jack's reaction.

'Aye, probably you're right.'

'They've always kept management in the family. Up until Brierley. And Brierley wouldn't have got the job if both Foster brothers hadn't jumped ship when war was declared. They viewed World War II from the comfort of their London club along with the rest of the fireside fusiliers. And Brierley wasn't slow to cash in. God knows how much he made in bribes from cowards keen to be designated "reserved occupation".'

Jack has heard all this before. Some people haven't moved on since the war – instead of looking ahead to the sixties they seem to be still stuck in the forties. Jack is usually optimistic, always looking to the future but things have changed. The letter in his back pocket has drawn him back into the past so effectively that he struggles even to remain in the present moment, let alone consider the future. Jack suppresses a sigh and says, 'Weather's not bad, is it?'

'Looks to me as if it's spoiling for rain later. I hear you had a rough do last week. Little bird told me that you very nearly had a walk-out.'

'It was nothing. Just a few troublemakers.'

'Well, you can't say you weren't warned. You were bound to get trouble the minute you brought those Pakis in.'

'The Pakistanis are doing the jobs that no one else wants, so they're not taking anyone's job. They're working the night shift because no one else will.'

'Well, I warned you. I said you'd regret the day you let foreigners in. They don't know the first thing about weaving. You've got your regular weavers coming in of a morning and not able to do a decent day's work. Those Pakis on night shift leave their looms in a right state. They're either broken or choked with muck. How are the day shift ever going to make a decent wage if half their looms are out of action? They're standing around waiting for a tackler to fix the mess. It's why I won't take on Pakis, I wouldn't even let them sweep the mill yard. They're all the same. More trouble than they're worth.'

'They're not all the same.'

'Well, they look it. Can you tell the difference between one Paki and another? It's beyond me.'

'They're not all Pakistanis. Some of them are Sikhs from the Punjab or Muslims from Bangladesh.'

'There's no difference. They were all swinging in trees before they came here and made a beeline for the National Assistance. Fuckin' Fosters – they draft in all these wogs and expect the British workers to lay out the welcoming mat. Buggers that were happy to work all hours for a bowl of rice back in India – no wonder they think they're well off when they get here. And once they are here, this bloody country will keep them for the rest of their lives, one way or another. No wonder the minute they get here they're filling in the forms to bring across their whole bloody tribe.'

Jack has heard this argument countless times and it never fails to annoy him. 'There's nothing wrong with the Pakistanis. I've not had any bother with them. They're quiet, they work hard and keep themselves to themselves. Our weavers aren't beyond sabotaging their looms before the night shift comes on and they don't complain. And I've yet to see a Pakistani turn up to work still drunk from the night before.'

'But that's just it. They don't kick up. Management can do anything it likes, and that bunch will roll over and ask for more. Seven quid nine and ten a week and they aren't complaining. It's a fortune to them.'

'Aye, and how long does it last when landlords are charging them the earth just for a roof over their heads? And any money they do manage to save is sent back abroad to feed their families. They're no different from you and me – they're trying to do their best for their families just like us.'

Jack has first-hand experience of the sort of squalor that immigrants have to cope with. There's so much prejudice locally that the only accommodation they can find is in houses that should have been pulled down years ago in the worst part of town. Last month there'd been a mix-up with the wages and Jack had ended up going round to drop off Ahmed Khan's overtime money. He'd found Ahmed along with a dozen fellow Pakistanis sharing the same house. No furniture – just mattresses on the floor of every room. No curtains, just blankets flapping with the draught. They'd had a bunch of local lads round a couple of nights before shouting abuse and smashing the windows. The landlord was charging them twenty-five bob each a week. Despite this he refused to get the windows repaired. Claimed it was a waste of time – they'd just get broken again. No heating whatsoever and the back gate had been kicked in. Jack has read about the West Indian riots in London a year ago and he reckons that Lancashire's Asian community won't be far behind.

'I blame the government,' Harry says. 'They're saying there'll be another election before the end of the year. The Tories have been a bloody waste of time. They behave as if we still had an empire. It's not two minutes since they were showing bloody Gandhi around the Lancashire mill towns. They should have kicked his chocolate arse and sent him home. No sooner have we given these darkies their independence than the buggers are getting on the nearest banana boat and coming here. And it's not just these wogs turning up on our doorstep; there are thousands of them brown bastards back in India flooding our markets with cheap, coarse staple cotton.'

Jack sighs with frustration. Lancashire cotton has been threatened by foreign competition before, but it has always risen to the challenge. The industry has invented new fabrics like Fabriflex – a combed cotton weave bonded to a plastic backing – and special luxury finishes on cotton shoe linings that make them feel like finest kid. There's even talk now of producing fake fur fabric, if the Cotton Board can sell the idea to the clothing industry. Once the car trade had been sold the idea of replacing leather seats with cotton-backed plastic Leathercloth they couldn't get enough of it. Leathercloth is wipe-clean, lasts a good deal longer and resists the stains that ruin leather. It's a nuisance that Leathercloth smells of plastic rather than rich leather, but appearancewise there's not a lot to choose between them. With the invention of all these new British fabrics foreign competition really shouldn't be the worry that it is. Jack turns to Harry and says, 'Give it a rest, Harry. I don't want to spend my holiday arguing the toss with you about work.'

Beth has been sitting cross-legged at her mother's feet during this exchange of views. She turns now and taps her mother's knee. 'What's a wog?' she asks in a stage whisper. Ruth appears not to hear. She is apparently immersed in her *Woman's Own*.

'Mummy! What's a wog?'

'What?'

'What's a wog? Is it like a golliwog? Like one of those golliwogs on the jam jar?'

'Shut up and play quietly.'

'But what is it? What does it mean?'

'It's what ignorant people call other people with different-coloured skin. It's very rude. Don't ever let me hear you using that word.'

'But Mr Sykes does. Mr Sykes says there are loads of wogs at the mill.'

'Do you want a slap?'

Beth shakes her head and moves out of range of her mother's hand.

Jack returns to the relative safety of his newspaper and Harry, keen to make amends, says, 'Aye, well. How are your lasses getting on, Jack?' Sykes's eye lingers overlong on the figure of Helen sitting in a deckchair at the other side of her father, her head still buried in the *NME*. 'Would they like an ice cream?'

'Well . . .' Jack hesitates; he is anxious not to reject this peace offering but aware of Ruth's silent fury.

'Come on, Jack. They're on holiday. Irene! Here's five bob. Go and get the kids some ice cream.'

'All by myself?' Irene objects.

Jack nudges Helen. 'Give Mrs Sykes a hand with the ices. Small ones, mind.'

5

ICE CREAM

Everyone loves ice cream, especially on a hot day. Where did you buy your ice cream? From a shop or from an ice-cream van parked on the sands? Score 5 points for a big ice cream!

'Haven't I seen you working at the dress shop on Penny Street?' Irene asks when they're out of earshot. 'Do you like?'

'Oh, yes. I love it. I just work Saturdays, but Blanche has offered me full time over the summer.'

'I thought you were still at school.'

'I am,' Helen admits, 'but I want to leave this summer.'

'I'll bet that hasn't gone down too well with your mother.'

'No,' agrees Helen. 'She goes mad every time I mention it.'

Helen looks closely at her confidante. Mrs Sykes has a look of Debbie Reynolds. Her hair is newly bleached and permed. A professional perm – nothing like the frizzy Toni Home Perm that her mother uses every few months. Mrs Sykes is the last word in style and not a hair out of place, despite the breeze.

'I got this dress from Kendal's in Manchester and I bought the hat at the same time. What do you think?' Mrs Sykes raises a hand to the white feathers that curl round the crown of her head.

'It's a lovely dress,' breathes Helen, 'and the hat looks nice against your hair.'

Helen knows that the dress alone will have cost the best part of ten guineas. It's pink with three-quarter-length sleeves and white turn-back cuffs.

'Thank you.' Mrs Sykes smiles. 'That's quite a compliment from someone who works for Blanche.'

It is Helen's turn to be flattered. 'Oh, I'm just the Saturday girl but you'd be surprised how many customers we get in to buy last-minute dresses for their holidays. And lots of them ask me what I think. We've barely a rail of summer dresses left. Blanche has had to order more from the suppliers. She'll have been busy with all the work pressing and pricing up . . .'

Helen's voice trails off in disappointment. It is not merely the money she could be earning; she misses the excitement of all the new dresses and the crush of customers all wanting her attention. Helen is treated like an adult from the moment she starts work until the shop shuts and she reluctantly returns home.

'You must be worth your weight in gold to Blanche.' Helen smiles and a blush of pleasure advances up her cheeks. 'Do you get paid a bonus for all the dresses you sell?' Irene asks.

It is common to discuss money and terribly impolite to ask

about anything as personal as wages. Helen would love to tell Mrs Sykes that she gets five per cent on every dress she sells but years of conditioning prevent her.

Helen has a natural aptitude for sales. It is to Helen that Blanche turns for an 'up-to-date opinion' when a customer can't make up her mind between a shot satin decolletage and a backless velvet cocktail dress. It is an unwritten rule that Helen recommends the more expensive gown, thereby maximising Blanche's profit margin and Helen's percentage. There has only ever been one exception to the rule. Mrs Taylor came in shortly after Helen started working in the shop. She was in search of an outfit for her daughter's wedding and was very taken with a bright-blue suit that drew attention to her varicose veins and drained her face of colour. Helen managed to persuade Mrs Taylor into a cheaper floral dress in peach with matching jacket. It was only when she was ringing up the sale that she noticed Blanche looking daggers from the entrance to the dressing rooms. A sharp exchange between owner and assistant followed Mrs Taylor's triumphant exit from the shop. Despite Helen's hopes that the customer, content with her purchase, might return to the shop on future occasions Blanche was adamant, 'That beggar won't come in again this side of Preston Guild. Eileen Taylor's a cheapskate. She buys mail order.'

This is the worst insult Blanche can ever bestow. Mail order sells mass-produced ill-fitting summer dresses for a fraction of the price. A thirty-five-shilling dress from Gammage's Mail Order Catalogue retails at nearer four guineas in the front window of Blanche Fashions. Customers at the shop are provided with a personal fitting service undertaken by a qualified member of staff (Eva during the week and Helen on Saturdays). Their purchases are lovingly folded in tissue paper to prevent undue creasing and placed reverentially in a candy-striped box with pink rope carrier handles. Certain clients, due to their long-standing custom or the professional nature of their husbands' work, are deemed worthy of the personal attention of Blanche herself. Such was Blanche's fury following Mrs Taylor's purchase that Helen was forced to stay late to sponge face-powder stains off necklines and press various garments before returning them to their hangers. Helen would have had to stay longer had she not pricked her finger while mending a hem ripped earlier by a careless stiletto. It wouldn't have mattered if the dress had been black, but Blanche, terrified of getting blood on the cream crêpe de Chine, snatched the dress out of Helen's weary grasp and dismissed her with a wave.

'What do you spend your wages on? Do you get cut-price dresses?' Mrs Sykes asks.

'No. I mean I could if I asked, but Mum thinks the sort of dresses Blanche sells are too old for me. Anyway, I'm saving up for a Dansette record player.'

'Oh, do you like Cliff?'

'He's OK, but I like Bobby Darin better. He's gorgeous. I wish I could see him.'

'It was rock and roll night at the Mechanics' Institute last Friday. You should have gone. They were playing all the hit parade. Tommy Steele, Cliff Richards, Billy Fury.'

'Oh, I wouldn't be allowed to go to the Mechanics' – there's a bar on Fridays, isn't there?'

'They wouldn't throw you out, you know. It's mostly teenagers that go there.'

'Oh, well, I normally go to the Methodist youth club on Fridays.'

Irene Sykes bursts out laughing. 'Oh, poor you! I don't suppose they allow any dancing there, do they?'

'Well, you couldn't anyway. There's no record player. But there's table tennis and the only reason they don't allow darts is in case someone gets hurt.'

'They're a po-faced lot, the Methodists. Don't crack a smile from one year's end to the next. I'll bet they have you hymn singing every five minutes, don't they?'

Helen shakes her head. 'We don't sing hymns but there's a prayer at the end. After we've said the Lord's Prayer, that is.'

'Oh, for goodness' sake! Anyway, I heard Bobby Darin is coming to do a concert in Manchester next year. It'll be expensive. You'll have to get your dad to buy tickets. You'll have loads of money if your dad is made manager at Prospect. I expect he's up for the job, isn't he?'

'I don't know. Dad never talks about work.'

Mrs Sykes looks into the wide innocence of Helen's face and changes tack. 'I'll bet you have a lot of fun working at the shop. You must hear all the gossip.'

Helen smiles. 'No. Not really.' It has been drummed into Helen that it is common to gossip. This is a source of frustration to her since there is nothing more intimately satisfying than information shared with another woman. Confusingly, Helen is invited to retell gossip at home to her mother, but only when her sister and father are absent. Even when she tells her mother what has been happening in the shop Ruth, having listened carefully, doesn't react as she should. Helen's stories fail to elicit a single gasp or squeal of amusement from her mother. Ruth will only shake her head and say 'It's a disgrace', and carry on washing up. Mrs Sykes, on the other hand, looks like a woman who would appreciate stories garnered from the shop. It's a temptation.

'I hear Mrs Booth is spending like it's going out of fashion. I saw her last Wednesday coming out of that fancy hairdresser's on Scotland Road and carrying four bags from Blanche's. She must have spent a fortune.' Mrs Sykes pauses in the hope of Helen volunteering further information.

'I don't know. I'm not there during the week.'

'Haven't you heard? She's only come up on the pools! Her husband was too drunk to do it on Tuesday, so she filled the coupon herself – and she won! When he'd sobered up he was furious. Demanded all the money because it was his name on the coupon. When she refused he tried to get her drunk and steal it.'

Mrs Booth, thin as a stick and a committed member of both the Methodist Mothers' Club and the Temperance Society, is known locally for her aversion to all the sins and vices that afflict her fellow man. When Mrs Booth is on youth club duty she won't even let them mess about on the piano in case they play the boogie woogie or, worse, rock and roll. The idea of Mrs Booth filling in a pools coupon of all things is too much for Helen who, despite her best efforts, starts to laugh.

'And that woman who lives on Reedley Road . . . what's her name? Irishwoman – smokes like a chimney. Donahue. Mrs Donahue. She got into a fight in the chip shop and laid out the assistant. Talk about "fryin' tonight".' Irene winks, nudges Helen in the ribs and both of them burst out laughing.

Helen watches as Mrs Sykes opens her white leather handbag and takes out a Stratton compact. She flips the lid open and powders her nose while Helen looks on, filled with admiration and envy in equal amounts. Mrs Sykes's handbag overflows with sophistication. Besides a well-filled floral make-up bag, there's a packet of tipped cigarettes, a special back combing brush, nail clippers and a bottle of Soir de Paris perfume. Mrs Sykes takes her appearance seriously.

When they reach the head of the queue Helen, mindful of her complexion, refuses the offer of an ice cream. Mrs Sykes orders and pays for the most expensive ice cream available for Beth before Helen can stop her. Purchase completed, Irene and Helen head back. It is 11.30 and the beach is packed. Helen has read in the paper that a quarter of a million visitors have arrived in the resort this week and, by the look of it, they've all headed for the beach. There isn't a clear patch of sand to be seen between the striped deckchairs, windbreaks, sunburnt bodies and discarded clothes. Irene and Helen thread their way through a cheerful, noisy crowd of mill workers and their families breathing in boisterous lungfuls of ozone instead of coal dust and cotton lint. Progress is slow.

Both women are forced to step over bags and towels, inch round windbreaks and skirt a confusion of deckchairs and sunbathers. Frustrated, Irene guides Helen to the water's edge where the only obstacles are paddlers and the odd sandcastle. Once they are free of the crowd Irene asks, 'Do you see anything of Cora Lloyd? She's a friend of your mother's, isn't she? Or is Cora too posh nowadays for Blanche's shop?'

'Oh no, she comes in a lot.' Helen is anxious to defend Cora, whom she has known and loved since she was a child.

'You're lucky to see her. I sometimes wonder where she's hiding herself; I see so little of her nowadays.'

This is not quite true. Such is Irene's fascination with Cora that she tries to bump into her as often as possible. If there were any justice, Irene would see her every Tuesday at the Baby Clinic. Cora Lloyd has flattened enough grass in her time for it to be suspicious that she never falls pregnant. Irene's special interest in Cora dates back to before the war. Harry and Irene hadn't been courting very long when Cora made a play for him one night at the Red Lion. Irene was forced to confront Cora in the ladies' lavatory. She had, Irene argued, no right to be flirting with Harry when everybody knew he was 'spoken for'. Cora didn't bat an eyelid. She carried on powdering her nose and fixing her lipstick until Irene felt a fool standing there waiting for a reply. When at last Cora did speak it was to tell Irene that she wouldn't touch Harry with a bargepole. Cora could 'do a damn sight better than Harry Sykes'.

True to her word, Cora had married Ronald Lloyd – deputy manager at Barclays Bank – before the war was over. She thereby gained entry into an exclusive social circle that Irene would kill to be a part of. However, all attempts to get on to genial terms with Cora following her marriage have been marked by failure. Cora is not forthcoming. Irene is painfully aware that Ruth Singleton is always invited to Cora's parties, but it's like getting blood out of a stone trying to get anything out of Ruth. Irene thinks she stands a better chance with Helen.

'I remember when Cora was Cotton Queen,' Irene begins. 'Oh, long before you were born.'

'I didn't know she was a Cotton Queen.'

'Oh, yes. She was the talk of the town. All the men thought she was a real catch. It's amazing she stayed single as long as she did. Do you know her husband?'

'Yes, he comes in the shop sometimes.' Helen is familiar with Ronald Lloyd and she dislikes him intensely. He always tries to fumble her while Cora is busy with Blanche in the dressing room. It is hard to tell which is worse, her embarrassment or her disgust. Mr Lloyd is quick on his feet despite his size. He creeps up behind Helen at every opportunity with his sweaty hands and his unctuous smile.

'I hear she's been poorly,' Irene continues.

'Has she?'

'Well, I've not seen her out and about for a bit. When was the last time you saw her?'

'Last Saturday. She was in to buy dresses for her holiday.'

'I bet she bought loads.'

'I don't remember.'

'What were they like? I bet they were gorgeous. Strapped sundresses?'

'No, she didn't look at the sundresses. She was trying on dresses with matching jackets.'

Mrs Sykes looks shocked. 'Where is she going on her holidays? Somewhere nice, I bet. Certainly not Blackpool.'

'Blanche said she was going to the Costa Brava.'

'That's Spain, isn't it? That'll have cost a pretty penny. Well, she'll not be needing a jacket, it's supposed to be boiling hot there, isn't it? Blanche must have misheard.'

'No.'

'Then why would she cover herself up like that? With her figure it doesn't make sense.'

Helen thinks back. Cora had been in the dressing rooms when Helen had poked her head round the curtain to tell Blanche that the rep was asking for her. It was little more than a brief glimpse but Helen saw that Cora's right shoulder and arm looked bruised. Helen hadn't thought any more about it until Blanche had given her Cora's purchases to wrap. Four summer dresses with matching jackets or long-sleeved boleros. Cora has an account at the shop and Helen had watched her struggle to sign her name in the book. 'Have you hurt yourself?' she had asked.

'Just a fall. I shouldn't be so clumsy,' Cora had replied and that was the end of the conversation. Cora had arranged for the bags to be delivered and she'd left.

'She said she'd had a fall,' Helen says.

'A fall? Poor Cora. Was she badly bruised?'

‘I don’t know.’

‘But she is bruised. I knew it. That husband of hers is knocking her about.’

There’s a note of triumph in Mrs Sykes’s voice that makes Helen uncomfortable.

‘It was nothing. Just her right arm.’

‘You mean that’s all she’ll admit to.’

Helen purses her lips and resolves to say nothing more. The rest of the walk is conducted in silence.

Beth hates everything about the beach, from the concrete ripples of sand that hurt her feet to the sting of salt water. No trip to the sands is complete without her bucket and spade. The red-painted bucket used to belong to Helen and is rusted at the bottom with the residue of many summers’ salt water. The handle is a thick ridge of flaking tin that cuts into Beth’s fingers when she carries a load of water back from the waves at the edge of the beach. Although the top rim of the bucket is rolled over, the bottom edge is as sharp as a knife. The bucket bangs against the front of her thighs when she hauls it back from the water’s edge. The long spade is worse. When Beth grasps it halfway up the wooden haft the tin spade still takes the skin off the back of her heel as she drags it across the sand or cuts into her instep when she tries to dig. Playing on the beach is an activity that other children enjoy. Beth watches them building sandcastles, playing with beach balls and screaming as they run into the waves. This morning’s misery is interrupted by the return of her sister and Mrs Sykes.

'Here, young lady. I've got you a proper ice cream. There! I'll bet you've not seen one of those before,' Mrs Sykes says with some satisfaction.

Beth nods dumbly. She hasn't. Two scoops in a double cornet – chocolate one side and strawberry on the other. Beth's wrist strains with the effort of holding it upright.

Ruth is momentarily thrown by the sheer extravagance and then annoyed. 'That's far too much. You shouldn't have bought such a big one,' she says, pointing to the offending ice cream. 'I'd have thought you'd know how bad ice cream is for children's teeth. Not to mention the danger of a chill.'

'A chill? In this weather? What are you thinking of? Come on, pet, get it eaten before it melts.'

Both women stare at the child. Beth is anxious to please. She opens her mouth to take a big bite.

'You'll be sick,' Ruth says. And, as if by magic, Beth feels her throat rise. She is sitting cross-legged at her father's feet, in full view. There is nowhere to hide. Trickles of pink ice cream run from the soggy cornet and gather round her wrist and still she is watched.

'Hurry up and eat it before it melts. I shall be in bother with your mother if you get it all over your clothes.'

Beth takes a lick. Mrs Sykes smiles.

'Have you said thank you, Elizabeth?'

'Thank you very much, Mrs Sykes.'

'Pleasure, I'm sure.'

Another drool of melted ice slithers down her thumb. Unable

to win the argument, Ruth takes up her knitting with increased ferocity. Although Beth has her back to her mother she can still feel the backwash of maternal fury. Beth's wrist is beginning to ache from the strain. The twin scoops will topple from their temporary mooring on the cornet unless Beth keeps the whole monstrous confection upright. Above her head Mr and Mrs Sykes make preparations to leave and she is forgotten. With infinite care Beth moves forward on to her knees and crawls round the back of her father's deckchair. She scoops a big hole in the sand with one hand and, with the other, she buries the ice cream. When she crawls back round she catches her mother's eye. Experience has taught Beth that, under these circumstances, it's best to keep her head down and her mouth shut until the storm passes.

6

COLLECTION BOX

If you look carefully you'll often see collection boxes on the promenade. Some of them are quite unusual – perhaps it's an old mine from the war, or a big model lifeboat, or even a disarmed depth charge and thrower! Where is your favourite charity box? Score a generous 15 points.

The Singleton family are returning to their hotel room after lunch when Helen pulls her dad to one side. She waits until her mother and Beth disappear round the corner before saying, 'Can I go out this afternoon?'

'Where do you want to go?' Jack asks.

'Just for a coffee.'

'Have you told your mother?'

'It's only a coffee, Dad. I'll be back before teatime.'

Jack reaches into his pocket for a coin. 'Here you are.'

Helen takes the coin and is gone in a flash. Jack shakes his head and continues to make his way up the stairs.

The Belvedere prides itself on being a superior hotel, and so it appears from a casual glance, from its mock-Georgian portico to its oak-panelled main staircase. No expense has been spared. The plush crimson and gold pile carpet that graces the exclusive Residents' Lounge extends throughout the immaculate ground floor. Sadly this reputation for luxury and cleanliness falters and finally fails when Helen passes through the STAFF ONLY door. Once her eyes have adjusted to the darkness, she makes out a flight of steps that leads to a warren of dimly lit dog-legged corridors. The air reeks of overcooked vegetables and rising damp. She peers at each well-worn and heavily scratched door as she moves through the darkness. Connie, when Helen finds her, is in room three. She is leaning over the washbasin in the corner and squinting into a tiny mirror as she applies another layer of Mediterranean-blue eyeshadow.

'Hiya!' Connie shouts in answer to Helen's polite knock. 'Come in. Won't be a sec.'

Helen steps over the threshold and looks around. Connie appears caught in the eye of a storm of personal possessions. Along with the piles of indiscriminate refuse there are copies of *Boyfriend* magazine (a weekly that Helen would kill to read) and various piles of clothes. Helen is faced with a chaotic mêlée of items from hairclips to powder puffs and discarded food and drink. Various articles of clothing are scattered across the cracked brown lino. A greying bra with circular stitching round the cone-shaped cups is hanging off the back of a chair piled high with discarded skirts and tops. The ledge above the washbasin is crammed with cosmetics, perfume and an overturned can of talc, and the towel rail below is home to several odd stockings, a pair of knickers and a single hand towel. Under the sink Helen spots a curled pink corset with suspenders attached.

'You've got one of those new corsets. It's a roll-on, like in the adverts. Is it comfy?'

'Yeah. It's great. A lot better than the old-fashioned girdles. Those things dig in all over the place. It's a Playtex elastic. Dead easy. Just roll it on and roll it off.'

'I wish I had one. Mum won't get me one; she says I've no figure to keep in so I just have a cotton suspender belt. The waist has gone and it's always slipping down. You're so lucky, you've got so much stuff. I mean I can't believe you have so many clothes!'

'Oh, well, you're welcome to borrow anything. If you fancy any of my skirts or anything. Hey! I'll bet we're the same shoe size. Why don't you try on my new stilettos?' Connie flaps her free hand in the direction of the bed. 'They're under there, I think.'

Helen struggles to ignore the sound of her mother's voice in her ear: 'Never try on shoes that someone else has had on. You'll end up with verrucas . . . or worse, some kind of transmitted disease.' But the prospect of seeing herself in a pair of white stilettos is too exciting to refuse. Helen bends and pulls out a Freeman Hardy & Willis box from under the bed. It is disappointingly empty save for a couple of sanitary towels, an emery board and tenpence ha'penny in copper. Helen resumes the search. At last she spots one shoe in the bottom of the gaping wardrobe and the other under the washbasin. Helen slips on the shoes and struggles to her feet. The heels are vertiginous – so much so that she is afraid to walk and as a result is reduced to standing still and swaying slightly.

'They look great,' Connie assures her. 'I'm wearing them myself this afternoon otherwise you could borrow them.'

'It's OK,' Helen replies. 'I don't think I'd be able to walk in them anyway.'

'You have to practise, but you get the knack after a bit.'

Helen opens her handbag and pulls out a piece of newspaper. 'Here, look what I found in the paper.' Helen passes Connie a clipping that reads:

PLANS ASSISTANT

The Land Registry has a vacancy for a Junior Plans Assistant.
Applicants must be aged between 16 and 18 and have
a good general education (minimum 3 GCEs).
Salary £282 per year rising to £789.

'What do you think?' Helen asks.

'Not a lot, that's only about a fiver a week.'

'Five pounds eight shillings and fivepence a week,' Helen corrects.

'Bloody hell, Helen. I get a fiver a week when you include tips, and I get free meals and a room on top.'

'Do you? That's a fortune! But this job is permanent and the salary goes up the older you get.'

Connie yawns theatrically and says, 'Boring! Boring! Anyway, I'm ready now. Let's go and check out the talent at Rico's.'

Connie and Helen have been in the café the best part of an hour during which time they have purchased and drunk two cappuccinos each while admiring the exotic surroundings. Rico's is stocked with a series of Formica-covered pedestal tables with chrome ladder-back chairs with matching seats. There's a line of high stools next to the pine bar where a complex arrangement of chrome urns, connected with thin metal pipes, spout high-pressure steam to heat up and froth stainless-steel jugs of milk. Both girls watch amazed as Rico, a young man with skin the colour of the coffee he serves, juggles with black-handled steel filters of freshly ground beans. The sight of so much chrome and steam, and the clink of steel against clear glass cups and saucers are impressive. For Helen, who has only ever drunk tea, the rich, exotic aroma of coffee is exciting. Looking around, she sees that a huge jukebox fills one corner of the café. When not in use, a soundtrack of lively foreign-sounding music accompanies Rico in his chrome and steam empire.

Helen and Connie are sitting together by the jukebox, taking in the sights and sounds, and keeping a covert eye on the rest of the customers. They both look up when a group of four men in their late teens jostle each other through the double doors and head towards the counter. Adrian spots Helen immediately. She looks beautiful. So beautiful that he freezes for a moment, transfixed by the sight of her glossy hair and clear skin. He takes his time, hitches the collection box round his neck and begins at the opposite end of the café from where she is sitting. This CND lark is the best chat-up opportunity he has ever had. It's foolproof. Every Tuesday, while his fellow students are engaged in sporting activities, Adrian crams himself into the Union bus and heads to any one of a string of local towns to spend the day shaking his collection box at a variety of teenage girls and young women. Of course, there's the odd bloke who turns nasty when he says he's collecting for nuclear disarmament – mostly along the lines of 'The bloody Nazis would be in charge now if we'd chucked away all our bombs. What do you think stopped the bastards? Our superior weapons, that's what. If it's a toss-up between dropping bombs or offering them a cup of tea and the chance to talk, I know which I'd choose. I didn't fight in the last war to let weak-kneed idiots like you piss around with this country's security. Why aren't you doing your National Service?'

Adrian has learned that it's pointless protesting that he's already completed his National Service. He has spent two long years 'working hard for the empire', which in most cases boiled down to polishing his kit and hoping the ceasefire in Korea held. It's a rarity to come across any other male peace campaigners – the whole country is still revelling in the euphoria of winning a second world war. You'd expect the Labour Party to support disarmament, but Gaitskell can't seem to make up his mind. He doesn't want to be seen to be playing into Khrushchev's hands. The Labour Party avoid any open discussion of disarmament like the plague.

As a result the level of general ignorance is shocking – half of the people Adrian speaks to don't understand the first thing about the H bomb, but Adrian finds that girls, for the most part, are at least prepared to listen. In fact, they seem to hang on his every word. It's a satisfying way to spend an afternoon – collecting both money and women. Another few minutes and he'll have worked his way round to Helen's table. Bingo!

Helen has been watching the group of students from under the cover of her fringe ever since they walked in. She has been sitting quietly hoping that the good-looking one will come to her table. She's no idea what he's collecting for but she's determined to contribute.

'Look at that bunch of students,' Connie says, stirring another spoonful of demerara sugar into her cappuccino.

'How do you know they're students?'

'You can spot them a mile off. Duffel coats, jeans, beards and striped scarves. Layabouts, the lot of them.'

'I think the one with the dark hair and the long scarf looks nice.'

Connie casts a professional eye over Adrian and tilts her head from side to side. 'He's OK, I suppose, but you can't see a lot under all that hair.'

'Sh-h-h. He'll hear you!'

But it is too late, he's heading straight towards them. He must have heard. 'Hi! I'm Adrian. Would either of you ladies like to contribute?' He pushes the wooden collection box on to the table between them.

'Depends what you're after,' replies Connie at her most coy. 'What are you collecting for anyway?'

'CND. The Campaign for Nuclear Disarmament. You know, get rid of the bomb.'

'You've lost me, dreamboat. What flippin' bomb?'

'The H bomb. Haven't you heard? These bombs are enough to blow up the whole world and it could happen at any time.'

Connie shrugs and looks bored. Adrian turns his attention to Helen and struggles to prevent his smile from deteriorating into a leer.

Helen rummages for her purse and counts out two sixpences. 'Is that enough?'

'Another sixpence and you can have a badge.' He holds up a black badge with white lines representing a bomb.

Helen fishes in her purse a second time and finds a thrupenny bit and three pennies.

'Didn't I see you at Aldermaston last Easter?' Adrian asks.

'Where?'

'The protest march to the Atomic Weapons Research in Berkshire.'

'No, I don't think so.'

'Oh, well, there'll be another march next Easter. I think we made a real difference. People have started to take notice. Half of them think we're raging Communists – in league with Khrushchev. But that's what middle England usually calls anyone who's interested in people's rights. There was one old boy, a real dyed-in-the-wool right-winger, carrying a banner that said "Khrushchev's Bunion

Derby". He insisted on walking at the head of the march. You'd have laughed if you'd seen it.'

'Is that where you got your scarf? On the march?'

Adrian laughs and says, 'No. It's a college scarf. I'm in my second year at Manchester University.'

'What are you studying?'

'Politics, though I wonder whether there's any point doing a degree.'

'Why?'

'Because if we don't get rid of these nuclear weapons then there might not even be a tomorrow. Having a degree won't stop me being vaporised if someone drops the bomb, will it? I mean I might not even get the chance to find out your name.'

Helen can feel her heart racing. She takes a deep breath and says, 'I'm Helen and this is Connie.'

But Connie has already left and is perched on a stool at the pine bar chatting to Rico, who is making a big show of working the espresso machine.

'Looks as if your friend is busy elsewhere. Mind if I sit down?'

Helen whisks her cardigan off the spare seat and says, 'No, I mean yes. I mean sit there if you like.'

Adrian turns the pine seat round and sits with one long leg either side, folding his arms across the top of the chair back. He tosses his head and his fringe falls forward. This well-practised silent seduction seems to work. Helen blushes and traces a circular route round a knot in the wooden table top. Adrian leans further forward, rests his chin on his hands, smiles and says in a slow,

low voice, 'So, put me out of my misery. What do I have to do to bump into you again?'

'What? Sorry, I can't hear you.'

Adrian must raise his voice in order to be heard over the sound of the jukebox and the chrome Gaggia coffee machine. 'I said, are you from Blackpool, or just visiting?'

'Oh. I'm just here on holiday. I live in Blackburn.'

'So not too far away. I'm from Manchester. We've got a CND student branch meeting at the university a week this Saturday. Do you fancy going?' Helen hesitates. 'I mean, it's really important,' Adrian continues, anxious to dispel any suspicion that his intentions are anything less than honourable.

'But I'm not a student.'

'Aren't you?' Adrian senses from the look on Helen's face that he has overdone the incredulity so he adds, 'Well, it doesn't matter. I can get you on the Union bus.'

'If it's a Saturday I won't be able to go. I work Saturdays.' Helen slides the back of her hand under her hair and flicks it back over her shoulder.

Adrian watches, mesmerised. At last he pulls a leaflet out of his duffel-coat pocket. 'Here, write your address on this and then I'll let you know what's going on. I can get over to Blackburn any time.'

Helen takes the proffered biro, writes on the back of the leaflet and hands it back. She feels very daring – giving her address to a complete stranger. Adrian reads it out and Helen nods. 'But you'd better not come to the house,' she adds. Adrian looks at her and raises his eyebrows. 'I mean, I live on the edge of town. It's a long way from the centre. I could always meet you at the station if you come over.' She's blushing even as the words are coming out of her mouth.

'Great!' he replies. 'I'll write you when I'm coming over.'

'Great!'

They are interrupted by the sound of one of the students shouting over, 'Ade! Are you finished? Put her down, Ade, we're going. Coach leaves at half past.'

The café seems very quiet when the students leave until one of the lads in the far corner swaggers up to the jukebox and feeds in a handful of change. Seconds later, after a deal of mechanical shifting, sliding and switching, Billy Fury comes on. Helen looks around. Connie is still deep in conversation with the man behind the bar. Helen gets up from the table and takes her empty glass cup and saucer over to the bar.

Connie turns and says, 'Hiya. Are you going?'

'Yes, I'd better get back.'

'Hang on a minute and I'll come with you.'

The two girls are temporarily blinded by the sunshine when they step outside. The street is almost empty – the hot weather has drawn everyone to the beach.

Connie links arms and pulls Helen close. 'Did you see that bloke that was serving behind the bar?'

'The one you were talking to?'

'Yes, that one. He's called Rico. He's only a flippin' Eyetie!' Seeing the blank look on Helen's face, she adds, 'You know, Italian.

Mamma mia, you're slow! He wants me to meet him after closing tonight.'

'Are you going?'

'For God's sake – no! My mum would bloody kill me if I brought home a darkie.'

Thursby Road Congregational Church, Blackburn, June 1942

'Friends, we are here to celebrate the joining of two people, Jack Singleton and Ruth Catlow, in holy wedlock. With this marriage comes a further joyful union – that of two families into the wider family of the Church. With this in mind there will be a collection at the end of the service in support of world peace.'

Michael Ryecroft, minister officiating at the wedding, has a face from which the slightest hint of humour has been assiduously wiped clean. Weddings are a serious business, not an opportunity for general indulgence and off-colour jokes. His church attendance is shrinking week by week and it is only the odd wedding that raises the average monthly attendance figure above fourteen. A lesser soul might be depressed by the falling numbers of followers but Michael Ryecroft, mindful of what Jesus achieved with a mere twelve, remains hopeful.

It's ironic, Jack thinks. All this talk of joyous unions. A bit of a joke, really. The only joyous union he ever wanted was with Eleni. She's only been dead a year, but she seems like a dream now, a different lifetime. The initial disapproval on his mother's face when he announced his intention to marry Ruth Catlow has transmuted over the course of the last six weeks into one of extreme distaste. Jack's mother has witnessed this morning the massed ranks of Ruth's relatives making their way, somewhat tardily and with noticeable reluctance, from the back bar of the Old Red Lion to the front porch of the Thursby Road Congregational Church for the start of the wedding ceremony.

The Singletons, despite wartime restrictions, have dressed for the event, unlike the bride's family whose clothes display ample evidence of at least a decade of uninterrupted wear. Mr Catlow, five foot five in his stocking feet, has, in the absence of a clean collar (or indeed any collar at all), borrowed a raincoat from an equally down-at-heel acquaintance 'at the dogs'. Furthermore, he has laboriously buttoned said raincoat from a point just below his Adam's apple to a point just above his ankles. Old Catlow is not a stickler for the finer points of dress in general and buttons in particular. As a result this buttoning marathon has taken the time and the assistance of several further sporting acquaintances to advise, undertake and complete. The bride may have opted for a fashionably 'short' pink crêpe wedding dress but the father who accompanies her is forced to haul the front of his raincoat clear of the dusty steps as he passes along the way of penitents, leaning heavily on his daughter.

Despite the minister's conviction that all present are members of the same family under God, Mrs Singleton has her doubts. And since the voicing of these doubts to her husband coincides eerily with moments in the service given over to silent reflection, the rest of the congregation is all too aware of her reservations.

Anxious to restore a harmony, which in truth has never existed between the two families, the minister launches himself into a soaring panegyric on the virtues of Ruth Catlow: her constant help in the Sunday School, her cheerful shouldering of the arduous tasks of church warden and church secretary, her eager help at Jacob's Joins, her support of sick and elderly members of the church, her flower-arranging and tea-making skills, her work for charity and her enthusiasm for Beetle Drives, Bring and Buy, Sales of Work and other activities designed to raise funds for the church. Bearing in mind all her years of service to the church, Michael Ryecroft has taken as the theme of his wedding sermon the merchant and the pearl of great price (Matthew 13: 45–6).

'When I think of Jack Singleton I'm reminded of the wealthy merchant in the Bible who, having earnestly sought and joyfully discovered a single pearl of such immaculate perfection, is inspired to sacrifice all he has in order to buy it. He is seized by its beauty and worth, carried away by its singular superiority to all others. No price is too high, no sacrifice too great in order to own this immaculate pearl. In this manner does the spiritual seeker sacrifice all to enter the kingdom of heaven. In the same way Jack Singleton has found his own pearl of great price in Ruth. She is truly unique, of immeasurable value. A pearl among women.'

If members of the congregation fancy they hear a break in the voice of the minister it is only to be expected under the circumstances. Michael Ryecroft, retired plumber and bachelor of this parish, had at one time hopes of a closer relationship with Ruth. But as the Bible itself informed him when he opened it at random in an ecstasy of prayer, the likelihood of his winning the hand of Ruth was similar to that of a camel passing through the eye of a needle. It has taken every bone in his corporeal body for Michael to remain impassive while the woman he loves marries another.

This laudatory assessment of Ruth is not universally shared by the assembled company – far from it. When the minister identifies Ruth as the pearl of great price, Jack's mother is heard to remark, 'Well, we'll see about that!' This comment so antagonises the Catlows that they forthwith refuse to acknowledge the groom's family's existence. The wedding breakfast is conducted in silence with only the faint rattle of silver cutlery on china plates from one side of the table and the chink of brown bottle on pint glass from the other. The man with the camera, a quiet person chosen for his wide experience of wedding photography, recognises the fatal signs early on and does not even attempt a group photograph, devoting his time instead to assembling the bride and family for one shot and the groom and family for another. The single photograph of bride and groom is undertaken with extreme care. Opportunities for action photography at the reception are resisted. As a result there is no actual photographic evidence of the scuffle which takes place, no tell-tale flash when the bride's father raises his fists.

Despite this, the day is reckoned a success. Jack Singleton has secured his pearl and Ruth her rich merchant. The collection box, when it is opened by the minister in the privacy of his room, is virtually empty. The minister sighs. The cause of world peace appears to be even more remote than before. But there is no denying the fact that Jack has found himself a wife who openly worships the ground he walks upon. Nobody could doubt the sincerity of Ruth's intense attachment. There is nothing she would not do for him. Ruth's relationship with Jack over the past year, though conducted for the most part from a distance of several thousand miles, has been intense – or as intense as it is possible to be when everything she writes must pass the censor's gaze. For Ruth the line between passion and carnal sin has, over the months of their separation, faded to a near invisibility. Only Jack's insistence on marrying a virgin keeps her from mortal sin and drives her desire for him to even greater heights.

Jack too has felt an overwhelming passion, but it ended when Eleni died and he does not want to feel it again. Ruth Catlow is not the most beautiful nor the most talented woman Jack has known, but he fondly imagines that she can give him something that he longs for, something more permanent, more realistic – the stability, the day-to-day predictability and basic safety of a normal life. Jack has had enough excitement since Hitler invaded Poland to last him a lifetime. Ruth, in contrast, looks forward from her wedding day to all the excitement to come.

7

THRIFT

This delicate flower grows quite easily at the seaside. It has a thin stem and a filigree head with lots of fine pale-pink or white petals. Score 10 points for a sparing little flower.

Prospect, Fosters' first cotton mill, was built in 1756 on the principle of thrift. Economy was employed at every stage – from the initial utilitarian design in local stone to the purchase of second-hand Lancashire looms. Although late to the game, Elias Foster was nevertheless destined for success. He was intent on following in the footsteps of the first northern entrepreneurs. Those men with enough capital to borrow more and a taste for risk. It was these northerners who had seen in Lancashire – with its mists and fogs, its drizzle and rain – the perfect climate for keeping cotton damp enough to weave. Elias Foster was a modest but determined individual. He declined to join his fellow mill owners as they travelled together to the Manchester cotton market in a coach and four. Elias, guided as always by the principle of thrift, rose before dawn and walked. For the most part Elias was regarded with the natural suspicion that accompanies any newcomer to the trade. John Thompson of Lees Bank Mill had it on good authority that the diminutive owner of Prospect Mill was still hand-spinning in his front room the previous week. Some of the merchants and buyers were provoked to laughter by this and the sight of Elias Foster's spare frame hidden under a heavily patched and darned coat. Nevertheless it is this very attachment to thrift that will see Elias Foster through the long years of cotton famine between 1861 and 1865, when his fellow mill owners will struggle and finally sink. He lives modestly, cheek by jowl with his spinners and constantly close at hand to the mills he owns. When, in 1761, the new Mrs Foster presents Elias with twin sons the future of Prospect Mill is assured.

The mill, a four-storey edifice, occupies a triangular site between the road, railway and canal. It is tailor made to convert the maximum amount of raw fibre into fine cotton thread in the minimum amount of time. Bales of raw cotton are winched from canal boats up to the top floor of the mill, where they are weighed, cotton merchants being somewhat lax in supplying the full weight if they think they can get away with it. When the inspectors are happy with the weight and quality, the bales are opened and sent down to the cleaning room below. Here the cotton is thoroughly broken down, mixed, blended and beaten. Only then is it deemed fit to be passed to the next stage. Down in the carding room the cotton is stripped of all its impurities and combed into a single loose strand, then it is drawn so that all the straightened fibres overlap to strengthen the strand before it is spun. Here Mr Crompton's magnificent invention comes into its own, drawing and spinning the cotton into finer and finer thread, then twisting the yarn on to cones and spindles ready for weaving. Prospect Mill can produce 4,000 yards of yarn from every single mule of 1,200 spindles. Only when the cotton yarn has passed through all these processes does it reach the ground floor. From here it is shipped out to the waiting weaving sheds.

Within two years of opening, Prospect Mill has earned enough money to finance the construction of a weaving shed adjacent to the main building. The weaving shed is supplied with the latest 'fire-proofing' measures, the ceiling is supported by iron pillars and arched brickwork instead of wooden beams. The concertina-shaped roof is divided into a dozen triangles, each complete with north-facing glass roof lights to let in the maximum amount of daylight needed to weave the best cotton.

By the time Jack Singleton takes over as foreman, Prospect Mill weaving shed houses over 200 looms producing 1,000 yards an hour. And still it's not enough for Fosters to show a decent profit, even with added night shifts. The only way out of the crisis is to re-equip the weaving shed with automatic looms: twice the product at half the price. Elias would approve.

Blackpool, Wednesday 13 July 1959

Ruth is walking at a furious pace, her Gannex raincoat flapping and her shopping bag banging against her leg. It is Wednesday and Ruth is programmed to shop. Having put some distance between herself and the beach, she slows her pace and debates which road to take first. That's the beauty of an unfamiliar town – all the shops are scattered at random. It gives Ruth an extra thrill. In the year since she last sampled the Blackpool shops various businesses have moved into the town. It has been non-stop expansion since the war. Bigger, brighter stores that stock a range of luxury goods that Ruth can't get in Blackburn have replaced some of the old corner shops.

She calls at Timothy White's first to buy some calamine lotion and another bottle of Dettol for the hotel toilet. It rattles her to think that other hotel guests on the corridor will also have the benefit of her disinfectant, but it can't be helped. The task accomplished, she is free to move to the kitchenware part of the store and indulge her obsession. Ruth Singleton is a fool to herself. She is unable to resist the siren song of kitchen gadgets. Timothy White's have the ultimate domestic machine – a Kenwood Chef – on display. This is far beyond Ruth's price range, so she turns her attention to the more modest end of labour-saving utensils. She purchases these utensils in expectation, one day, of having the modern kitchen that she deserves. The day when she exchanges her pot sink and wooden draining board, complete with curtain to hide the pipes, for a stainless-steel model with a mixer tap; the day when she has a sparkling fifteen-guinea Frigidaire fridge, with special ice compartment, instead of a green-painted meat safe covered in wire mesh. The day when she is the proud owner of a Creda Carefree Electric Cooker, with hob settings for every occasion; that happy morn when she exchanges the old wooden kitchen table for wipe-clean Formica, and her brush and shovel for a brand-new Hoover vac.

To this end Ruth has learned to be thrifty. Every Friday teatime Jack comes in with his wage packet and opens it at the sideboard, while Ruth lays the table. She doesn't know precisely what Jack earns. It varies from week to week with overtime and now, after seventeen years of marriage, she has given up asking. He pulls out his wage slip first and glares at the tax and deductions, before turning his attention to money. He tips the wage packet upside down and catches the loose change, flicking the coins back and forth in his palm before depositing them in his trouser pocket. He then turns his attention to the bundle of notes. Green pounds, blue fivers and the odd brown tenner, his lips moving with the calculation. He extracts a few notes for his wallet and hands the rest to Ruth.

She, meanwhile, has a red Sovereign notebook where she keeps track of her housekeeping money. She scrimps and saves at every opportunity, making sandwich lunches, sewing all her daughters' dresses, knitting jumpers for Jack, buying scrag end for broths and cutting back on coal. She resists the lure of Camay ('You'll be a little lovelier each day, with wonderful pink Camay!'). She buys rough yellow blocks of carbolic soap instead, saving the residual slimy remnants to cram into a plastic swish basket for suds when she washes up. This thrifty approach informs everything she does. The Kleeneaze man would kill to get his selection of dusters and cloths past the Singletons' doorstep, but Ruth sticks resolutely to her own system of using up old clothes as cleaning rags. White rags are used initially for pressing collars, until they wear into holes, at which point they are used to clean windows until, in the end, they are boil-washed and used to staunch the nosebleeds that Ruth has suffered from since she was a child. Coloured rags serve as dusters and hand mops. Woollen jumpers are unravelled and reknitted. Anything left over is given to the rag-and-bone man in exchange for a donkey stone to whiten the front step. It is by thrift that Ruth has cut her weekly shopping bill to less than thirty shillings, allowing her quietly to put away a pound a week into her account at the post office. Ruth is determined to move to a bigger house where there will be space for all the gadgets, furniture and labour-saving electrical equipment she desires. Until that day arrives she must content herself with window shopping. And what better occupation could there be on a sunny afternoon in July?

Sheltered for the most part from the sea breeze, the shopping centre is a suntrap this afternoon. Ruth loosens the scarf round her neck and unbuttons her coat. When she catches sight of a sale banner in the front window of Kennet Quality Drapers her pace quickens, despite the heat. There's a tea chest outside the shop that's filled with neatly folded remnants. Ruth is sorting through the various fabrics with an eye to making a summer dress when the shop owner, a slim, elderly man, approaches her. 'Can I help you, madam?'

'No, thank you, I'm just looking.' This well-worn sentence is delivered in a firm tone that usually scares off pushy shopkeepers.

But this is Blackpool and Mr Kennet is not intimidated. He smiles thinly and says, 'Ah, I see you've found the blue seersucker. A quality Sea Island cotton, that. Long staple. Very hard-wearing.'

'Yes,' Ruth agrees.

'I have over a hundred different fabrics if you'd care to look inside.'

Ruth hesitates. She knows she is being soft-soaped, but she could do with making herself another dress. After some token hesitation she picks up her shopping bag and enters the shop. The shelves behind the long wooden counter are a riot of different colours and textures, from bolts of crimson velvet to magenta satin and black net. There isn't a single price tag to be seen, making Ruth immediately wary.

'I take it you're looking for dress material?'

'Yes, but I'm only interested in your sale fabric.'

'Oh,' Mr Kennet says with a wide smile, 'I think you'll find even our full-price materials are cheaper than elsewhere. Here on holiday, are you?' Ruth nods reluctantly. 'Well, I'm sure I can send you home with a bargain. What sort of fabric are you looking for?'

'Cotton.'

'Let me show you what we have.' Within the space of a minute the air is lavish with bright cotton fluttering from various bolts. The material is gathered and cast across the counter with casual artistry. Ruth is left breathless by the sight of so many colours splashed across the polished wood. She lines the tips of her fingers against the edge of the counter, her eyes filled with excitement.

'I have plain cotton, of course, but I'm sure you'd prefer this.' Mr Kennet unrolls a bolt of white cotton decorated with sprigs of primrose. Ruth knows at a glance that the style would be more suited to a woman half her age. She shakes her head. The next fabric is a lavender design and again Ruth shakes her head. There is too much wastage with a repeated pattern and it's a job getting all the seams to match. More bolts of cotton are taken down from the shelves. Ruth is not proving to be an easy customer. She examines each fabric closely, dismissing any printed cottons, aware that they will fade.

She is losing interest when Mr Kennet unrolls a bolt of fabric covered in giant pink roses and verdant foliage. 'This one is called "Romance". It's new in,' he says. 'Very sophisticated, isn't it? See,' he says, gathering the cloth into a ripple of soft folds. 'Look at the detail on the flowers. It's top quality.' Mr Kennet heaves an audible sigh of pleasure. 'Just look at the colour. The design is woven in. Won't fade.'

Ruth visualises how the material would look made up into a simple round-necked dress with a gathered skirt. It would look wonderful. Mr Kennet sees her expression. He swiftly gathers up the other discarded cottons and replaces them on the shelves, leaving only a lavish spread of the rose fabric across the counter.

Ruth is silent, drinking in the crimson and pink petals. At last she is roused to speak. 'It's British, is it?'

Mr Kennet hesitates. 'Let me see,' he replies, pretending to consult a book under the counter. He waits a moment before saying, 'Well, blow me! I could have sworn it was Lancashire cotton.'

'It's not foreign, is it?'

'It would seem so,' replies Mr Kennet, closing the petty cash book. 'But, of course, the price reflects that. It's substantially cheaper, only nineteen and six a yard.'

'I always buy British.'

'I quite understand,' Mr Kennet replies gravely. 'But it's difficult getting a modern design like this. It's rare to find anything with so much colour and style.'

'Have you nothing by Standfast?'

'I'm afraid not. I sell very little Standfast fabric nowadays. It's too expensive. My customers want something new at a competitive price. British designs aren't a patch on these German weaves.'

'German? No, thank you, I've changed my mind.'

Ruth turns and starts to leave the shop when Mr Kennet says, 'If you were to take a few yards, say a dress length, I could do it cheap for you.'

Ruth pauses. The material is extravagant. It knocks the other fabrics into a cocked hat. Jack would be furious if he knew she'd even been looking at imported cloth, let alone considered buying some. Every yard of foreign cloth that's sold is one more nail in the coffin of Lancashire's cotton industry. And this material is even worse. It's made in Germany. 'I'm sorry,' she says, picking up her shopping bag. She opens the door a fraction and a blast of salty air rushes into the shop, lifting the edge of the fatal fabric that is strewn across the counter.

'Just a moment.' The shopkeeper measures out a few lengths of the rose material against the yard-long brass rule screwed into the edge of the counter. Ruth watches as the fabric tumbles from the bolt. Within moments the counter is invisible under a profusion of roses complete with buds and crisp leaves. Mr Kennet cuts the cloth with a single stroke of the scissors. 'Here you are. There's a good dress length there. Retails at a fiver and you'd pay a good bit more in some places. You can have it for three guineas.'

Ruth looks him straight in the eye. 'It's a lot to pay for foreign cotton.'

'Three quid, then. Top-quality cotton. And I'm cutting my own throat at that.'

It is mid-afternoon when Ruth finally emerges from the draper's. She is carrying a square parcel neatly tied with string. She looks at her watch. There's time for a quick look on Queen Street before she must return.

Queen Street is home to the most exclusive of the town's shops. Jewellers, milliners, furriers and high-class chemists are housed along a graceful colonnade of shops. Ruth pauses at Roberto's to admire the display of Italian couture day and evening dresses. At the front of the window there's a range of handbags, diamante for evening and leather for day. Her attention is caught by a caramel-coloured calfskin shoulder bag and matching hand-stitched gloves. Roberto's is not the sort of shop that displays price tags. The shop's clients are not the type who count the cost. Ruth knows from experience that shoppers like herself who reckon in shillings and pence rather than guineas aren't the sort of clientele the shop wishes to attract. But the bag is beautiful. She is still gazing at the soft leather when a shop assistant opens the door for a customer about to leave. As Ruth swiftly steps aside she recognises a face. 'Cora! Heavens, you made me jump. What are you doing here?' Ruth asks.

'I might ask you the same thing.'

Even in her high heels Cora Lloyd is only just five foot tall. She is dressed in a plain cream shift with a matching long-sleeved bolero in a fancy brocade. Her legs shimmer under seven-denier fine silk stockings and her chestnut-brown hair gleams in the sunshine. Cora is immaculate. Nevertheless there is an air of fragility about her that has become apparent in recent months. A tremulous quality to her gestures, a brittle thinness in her laughter.

'Why aren't you in Spain? What happened to the holiday on the Costa Brava?'

'Oh, we couldn't go. Ronnie had a string of last-minute meetings and we couldn't have got down to London in time for the flight.'

'So you came to Blackpool?' Ruth is incredulous.

'Well, yes. Don't look shocked, Ruth. It's not the end of the world and it's a lot less travelling for a start.'

'Where are you staying?'

'At the Links over in St Anne's. It's convenient for the golf course. Ronnie was determined to fit in a few rounds while we were away.'

'Very nice for Ronald, I'm sure. Anyway, how are you? I barely recognised you with those big sunglasses on.'

'Oh, fine. I'm fine really.'

Ruth hears the slight tremble in her friend's voice and puts it down to disappointment. Ruth would be fed up if she were promised the Costa Brava and ended up in bloomin' Blackpool. 'Look, let's go for a cup of tea. I haven't seen you for a proper chat for ages.'

'Ruth! I only saw you last week at the party.'

Cora's Tupperware party the previous week had been a great success. Cora had served sherry to a select group of women while she outlined the advantages of the airtight plastic boxes and introduced the new additions to the range. Ruth was particularly impressed with the circular top that keeps an opened bottle of milk fresh (even without a fridge!). She had bought one on the spot and several other women had followed suit. Cora had gone on to demonstrate that only with Tupperware can you make food the day before and store it hygienically until it is needed. There was a full display of Tupperware on the walnut dining table. Transparent cornflake boxes that show how much cereal is left, containers to prevent highly flavoured foods like chopped onions from tainting other milder foods, sandwich boxes for packed lunches, tightly capped tumblers for carrying fluids and rectangular fridge jugs that save space and eliminate spills. The evening had been a triumph.

'We barely got a moment to ourselves at the party. For goodness' sake, Cora. You've time for a cup of tea, haven't you?' Ruth sees the hesitation in her friend's face. 'Unless you're expected elsewhere,' she adds.

'I shouldn't really. Ronnie always likes me to be there waiting when he comes in and I've already been out an hour longer than I intended.'

'Oh, blow Ronnie. You're on holiday! Come on – I'll pay. We'll go to the Emporium. The scones are on me.'

'The Emporium? That sounds very posh.'

'It's not. It's still the Co-op. They gave it a fancy name when they opened the new store.'

The women link arms and head down the street. At a casual glance they could be mother and daughter. Cora is thirty-seven – a full seven years younger than Ruth. Her long chestnut-brown hair is coaxed back into a neat French pleat. Ruth, shrouded in an over-large raincoat and shod in sensible shoes, looks much older. The two women have been friends for a long time. Cora was the first person Ruth told when she got engaged to Jack. The engagement caused a sensation at church. Half the girls thought it was a hoax. Jack Singleton marrying his old Sunday School teacher. Word had got round that it was one of Jack's jokes and the engagement would be called off next time he came home on leave.

But Cora didn't sneer or poke fun. 'Why, Ruth,' she'd said. 'You're a dark horse and no mistake.'

'He's six years younger than me,' Ruth had confessed with some pride.

'Fancy you landing Blackburn's very own heartbreaker. Why, I can hardly believe it! I'm so happy for you, Ruth.'

Jack had sent Ruth the money to get a ring. A modest sapphire, or maybe an amethyst. Ruth, aware of the gossip, decided that, whatever the cost, she would buy the best ring in the shop. In the finish she'd added £30 of her own money and bought the triple diamond.

'Now let them laugh,' Cora had said when she saw the ring.

The two women had been firm friends ever since.

The Co-op restaurant is up several flights of marble steps, on the top floor of the store, but the climb is worth it. There are views right across the promenade and out to sea. The restaurant itself is frugally lit by circular white glass globes suspended from the high ceiling. The waitresses scurry round the tables in semi-darkness.

'Which hotel are you staying at? I tried and tried to remember it this morning but I couldn't.'

'The Belvedere. We go there every year. Jack wouldn't dream of going anywhere else. He'll book and put the deposit down on next year's holiday before we leave on Saturday.'

Cora smiles and looks sympathetic. She knows that Ruth would give her right arm to go elsewhere. Ruth had suggested last year that it might be nice to try Llandudno for a change but Jack had shaken his head. He has holidayed in Blackpool since he was a child. The tea and a cake stand of scones arrive, and Ruth lifts the lid of the silver teapot and gives it a good stir before pouring.

It's only when Cora stretches out her hand to take the cup of tea she is offered that Ruth thinks she sees a shadow across her friend's wrist. She opens her mouth to ask but she's interrupted by Cora's laughter as she pokes into one of Ruth's shopping bags. 'Now, let me guess. No, Ruth, don't tell me what's in the bag.

M-m-m. Now what could you have been buying at Timothy White's? It's not another gadget, is it?'

'A kitchen timer – it'll come in useful.'

'Along with the rest.'

'What do you mean, I only have a few.'

'A few? Your scullery drawers are crammed with them – icing nozzles, whisks, biscuit cutters, two different sorts of peelers, apple corers, plastic spoons, bottle toppers and tongs, to say nothing of the measuring spoons, tenderising hammer, measuring cone . . . The last time I looked in your pantry you were busy screwing cup hooks on the underside of the shelf to accommodate all your graters, slicers and cutters. You're like a woman possessed, Ruth.'

'I'll have you know, Cora Lloyd, I use every single one of them.'

'Even the garlic press?'

'Perhaps not as much as the others.'

'Never.'

'Cheeky beggar. You'll see. One day I'll have a modern kitchen to put all these gadgets in.'

'Still yearning for one of those new semis? I don't know why. Your terrace is lovely and cosy, it's like a little palace.'

'Palaces are normally a bit bigger than two up two down. Anyway, I've got the deposit for a semi. It's just a case of persuading Jack that we can afford the mortgage. We really need a bigger house – a two-bedroomed terrace is too small. Oh, I know Mrs Kerkley next door has brought up four boys – but she's a right sloppy faggot. I've seen her sweeping down her backyard in her carpet slippers.'

'Well, at least she's doing some housework.'

'Give over. She's that mucky she's a breeder for Louis Pasteur. You can laugh, Cora. You don't have to live next door. When her oldest lad got Emma Bradshaw pregnant she just shrugged her shoulders and the girl moved in as well. If it had been my lad I'd have killed him. He wouldn't know what had hit him.' Ruth takes a bite of her scone and pulls a face. 'I wouldn't bother with the scones, Cora. They're rock hard – must have got the recipe from Jack's mother.'

'And what's this?' Cora asks, seizing the brown-paper parcel.

'I've bought some material.'

'What's it like?'

'It's pink roses. It'll look gorgeous made up into a dress.'

'Oh, let me see!'

Ruth unwraps a corner of the parcel enough to give Cora a glimpse of the fabric.

'Oh, Ruth. It's lovely. I'd love a dress made out of that.'

'It's called "Romance".'

The women exchange glances and laugh.

'I should be so lucky,' Cora says.

'What do you mean?'

'Well, look at me, Ruth. Married for all these years and still no sign of a baby. Oh, I long for a baby of my own to hold. I'm fed up of being "auntie" wherever I go. No one else has any problem getting pregnant. It's just me.'

'Don't be daft, Cora. Loads of couples have difficulties. And anyway, why do you think it's your fault? What about Ronald?'

'Well, I don't know. Ronnie has a difficult job and he's quite often tired. And, of course, he's out every night with one thing and another . . .' Cora's voice trails off.

'Well, there you are then. You'd better make the best of getting him on holiday.'

'It's not that simple.'

'Oh, it is. You'll see. You don't need to be clever to get pregnant.' Despite the dim light Ruth sees the beginnings of tears in Cora's eyes. 'There,' she says. 'Don't cry, Cora. It'll all come right.'

'How's Helen?' Cora asks, changing the subject.

'Driving me round the bend. She's forever telling me what Blanche does, or what Blanche thinks, or what Blanche says. I'm up to here with it . . .'

'Well, Blanche must seem very sophisticated to a girl Helen's age.'

'She's a bad influence. She was plain old Peggy Watson until she got her hooks into the mayor. You can laugh, Cora, but it's true. It was her horizontal charms that got her where she is today. And him married with five children. Of course, they'd been knocking around together for years. They were doing all their courting in the back of the mayor's car until he finally set her up in a flat on Scotland Road. It was above what used to be Redman's grocers. Anyway, the shop closed down during the war and the mayor bought it. The paper quoted him as saying that he was "setting an example by investing in local business". It was enough to make a cat laugh. Next thing she's changed her name and set up as "Blanche Fashions".'

'She's a woman and a half, isn't she?'

'She's a bad example. She treats Helen like a fellow adult and that's asking for trouble. She's still at school, for goodness' sake. Helen's so keen to work at the shop she didn't want to come away on holiday.'

'Well, she isn't the only one who had second thoughts about coming away, is she?'

Cora watches as Ruth shakes her head. 'I still think it's a risk bringing Elizabeth away so soon after her operation. She's not right in herself.'

'What do you mean?'

'She'll barely speak and she's still sleepwalking. She wakes up crying and she won't tell me what's wrong. She's not right, not right at all.'

'What do you mean, Ruth? They wouldn't have let her out of hospital if she wasn't right.'

'They let me bring her home because she wasn't getting any better after the operation. Not like she should. They thought she might improve if she was at home with her family.'

'And she has, hasn't she?'

'Not so as you'd notice. I don't think she's going to get better. If she catches a cold, with the state of her chest that'll be it. She won't pull through. Not a second time.' Ruth pulls out her handkerchief. 'I don't know what's worse – her dying in hospital or at home. And nothing I can do about it.'

'She's not going to die! You're worrying about something that's not going to happen. Buck up, Ruth.'

Ruth wipes her eyes. 'You don't understand. It's all my fault. When she was born I . . .'

Cora interrupts before Ruth can continue. 'It's not your fault. That's ridiculous. Come on. Oh, I know something that'll cheer you up. Guess who I bumped into last week? Miss Wren.'

'Our old teacher?'

'The very same. Now sit up straight and recite after me . . . "The efficient running of a house, the effective nurturing and bringing up of children in an ordered and hygienic environment is a science in the truest sense of the word. It requires intelligence, aptitude and full-time commitment. Never forget that, ladies."'

The memory of Marion Wren holding forth on subjects domestic at the college on Ink Street is enough to make both Ruth and Cora smile. The Diploma in Household Management course ran every Tuesday night. Over the four years Ruth and Cora learned everything from when to clean velvet drapes to how to cook for a family of four from the weekly rations. By the end of the first year Ruth and Cora were firm friends – if for no other reason than they were the only women who had a genuine interest in the lectures and assignments. Although she wasn't even courting at the time Ruth dreamed of getting married and having children, and Cora, already engaged to Ronnie, was determined to be the perfect wife. A diploma was awarded at the end of each year successfully completed. Ruth and Cora came out with a total of four diplomas for cookery, dressmaking, laundry and child-care.

'Do you remember prizegiving day? What a palaver we had

with your mother! I thought I'd die laughing when she put that hat on.'

'Don't remind me.'

Ruth's mother had lost all her hair when she was a child and, as a result, refused to go out. Collecting enough clothing coupons to get her a decent dress was the least of Ruth's worries – what was she going to do about her mother's hair? In the end Cora managed, by a mixture of charm and barefaced bribery, to get hold of a hank of real hair. Ruth sewed a little hat for her mother and they attached the roll of hair under the brim, only to find that the old woman had put it on back to front. Cora's mother died before the war and her father was too busy in the shop to attend the prizegiving, so Ruth and Cora clubbed together for a taxi and the three of them arrived at the college in style.

'You know, Ruth, I was thinking of going back.'

'To the college? Are they still running the course? I thought Miss Wren had retired now.'

'She has. But I saw they're starting an International Cookery course in September. Ronnie enjoys foreign food, you know. I thought I might give it a try.'

'What a good idea, Cora. You'll love it and it'll take your mind off things.'

'M-m-m.'

'You don't sound convinced.'

'Well, I thought it was a good idea, but when I asked Ronnie he wasn't keen. He's talked me out of it. He's right, I don't need to learn to cook fancy food – we have Mrs Maguire to do that.

And if we want something a bit special we can always go out to a restaurant. Ronnie always says, "You don't need to know how to cook me a moussaka, Cora. Just make sure you're looking beautiful when I get home. That's what you do best."'

'You can do a lot more than just look pretty, Cora. You won Best Student at the college three years running.'

'I don't think that cuts much ice with Ronnie. He'd laugh out loud if I told him that.'

Ruth tries not to look as angry as she feels. Ronald Lloyd was full of himself when he was still at school and he hasn't improved in the intervening period. Ruth would see a lot more of Cora if it were not for Ronald. Cora's husband has a clear idea about 'suitable friends' and Ruth suspects she isn't on the list. Ruth can count the number of times she's spoken to Ronald on one hand.

The waitress comes to the table with the bill and Ruth roots around in her purse. Eventually she pulls out a ten-shilling note and hands it over to the waitress, who clicks her tongue and says, 'Haven't you anything less?'

Ruth returns to the inner pockets of her purse and counts out one shilling and ninepence. 'I'm a thrupenny bit short – have you got the rest, Cora?'

'Er . . . No, I don't think I have,' Cora says, opening and promptly closing her bag. There is nothing for it but to send the waitress away with the ten-shilling note and wait for the change.

'You've not lost it, have you?'

'What?'

'Your purse.'

'Oh, no. I just forgot to bring it out with me. The truth is I don't bother carrying a purse. Not generally. Not nowadays.'

'Why ever not?'

'Well, I don't need to, do I? Ronnie does all the money. He's opened accounts for me at various shops. He says it's so much easier that way. It's the way his father dealt with things and his mother was certainly never short of anything. And anyway, Ronnie takes care of all the bills and the housekeeper does all the household shopping. I have an account with Blanche and at the hairdresser. I mean, there isn't a lot left to spend money on.'

'And what if you want to shop somewhere different?'

'What do you mean?'

'What if you fancy a different hairdresser? What do you do then?'

'Well, I don't. I mean I wouldn't, would I?'

'Why not?'

'Because Ronnie likes the way Sylvia does my hair. Don't be silly, Ronnie does this in order to make life easier for me.'

'Does he?'

'Well, of course.'

'And what are you expected to do with your time?'

'Anything I like. Although there isn't a lot for me to do in the house. Ronnie has been on to me to join the Townswomen's Guild.'

'Cora, even I'm too young for the Townswomen's Guild.'

Both women are still laughing when the waitress finally returns with Ruth's change. Basic thrift prevents Ruth from leaving a tip, but she does smile at the waitress as they leave.

8

PIDDOCK

A piddock is a boring mollusc about half an inch long and it makes its home inside rocks. Its pale-brown sharp shell helps it to bore into sandstone or any soft rock. Pick up a pebble to give it a shake! If you can hear a faint rattle then you've found a piddock! Score 75 points for a boring mollusc.

In the absence of her mother Beth is effectively marooned in the deckchair Ruth stuck her in before leaving. The shiny striped canvas resists all the child's efforts to escape and it is only after she has been wriggling for a full ten minutes that Jack finally looks up from his paper and says, 'Do you want to get down now, Sputnik?'

Beth nods and stretches her arms up to be lifted. Jack picks her up and swings her back and forth a few times, pretending to toss her into the sea before finally lowering her gently on to the sands. Once she's found her feet, Jack checks his jacket pocket. The letter is still there. Waiting for him.

'Can I go on the donkeys?'

'We'll ask your mum when she gets back from shopping.'

'But, look! That's Red Hawk. The boy from the hotel. He's having a ride. And he had a ride before. It's not fair. He's riding that donkey all the time.'

'Cheer up, Sputnik, he'll not be taking it home with him. He'd not get it on the coach, for a start.'

'How do you know?'

'Because your Uncle Dougie tried it once. For a bet. The daft beggar.'

Beth would have liked to see it, but the Singletons always come to Blackpool by steam train. Jack would rather pay the extra five bob and travel in relative comfort.

Old George Pomfret of 'Pomfret's Pleasure Trips' is notoriously selective about what he will allow on his coaches – particularly where non-essentials such as luggage, bicycles, boxes, musical instruments, etc. are concerned. In short, anything that can't easily be charged for is vigorously resisted. In the winter evenings of 1958 Pomfret has calculated precisely how much it costs to convey a standard-sized passenger with a single suitcase from Blackburn cattle market to Blackpool central. The differential between unit cost and the actual price of a return ticket warms the heart. But holidaymakers refuse to behave in any ordered, 'unit cost' manner. They pay for their ticket in advance and then turn up on the day with any number of suitcases, carrier bags, bats, balls, bags of food and bottles of lemonade. They expect to get the lot on the coach. Buckshee. There's the further problem of the odd passenger (usually of the feminine persuasion) who needs a whole seat to herself – this puts Pomfret's calculations into such disarray that he is forced to loosen his over-stretched braces and mop his ample brow. And, to top it all, there's the annual problem of Dougie Fairbrother. This particular customer is guilty of sneaking crates of beer in through the back emergency escape window. Every year there's havoc. The central aisle is heaving with bodies struggling to secure a few bottles for themselves before the coach has even set off. The suspicion remains fixed in the coach owner's mind that Dougie Fairbrother makes more of a profit on the trip than Pomfret himself. Running Wakes Week coaches to Blackpool is a right palaver and it's only a sense of civic duty that keeps old Pomfret going. That and the money.

Beth is bored. She runs the heels of her new sandals through the sand, raking up damp ramparts, then kicking them up in the air. Jack sweeps the airborne sand from his newspaper three times before he reaches into his pocket and says, 'Take your sister up on to the prom, will you, Helen? Here's some money for the slot machines.'

Helen, who is squinting at the small ads in the *NME*, groans as her dad empties a pile of pennies into her hand. 'I'm supposed to be on holiday, not babysitting.'

'A bit of exercise will do you good.'

'Can we go to the pier?' Beth asks the moment they are out of earshot.

'No! You know we're not allowed.'

'Well, I don't want to go ON it. I want to go UNDER it. The bit where the rock pools are. Over there. See?'

'The answer is still no.'

'But why? Mummy is shopping and Daddy is reading his newspaper. There's no one to see. Why can't we go?'

'Because you'll blab and I'll catch it.'

'I won't. I promise.'

'You will.' Helen sighs. 'You can't help it.'

'But I need to fill in my I-Spy.'

'Here, let me look.' Helen leafs through the book for a minute and says, 'It's no good, Beth. There's only a couple of days left, you'll never finish filling in the book. You'll have to cheat.'

The book is looking the worse for wear, the covers are creased and the once bright staples are covered in a dull patina that is a prelude to rust. Inside, the pages, though well thumbed, are empty of scores. Beth is not allowed to go exploring by herself so three pages of shellfish and jellyfish remain resolutely unmarked by her pencil, not to mention a further two pages about rock pools. Granted, she has found two different types of seaweed (bladderwrack and serrated wrack) and the odd shell (periwinkle, chipped cockle and half a razor shell), but overall she has scored no more than sixty-five points. She needs a minimum of 1,250 before Big Chief I-Spy can award her second-class honours and the rank of 'Beachcomber'. Nevertheless, when Helen suggests cheating Beth is horrified. 'I can't cheat! What if Big Chief I-Spy sees me?'

Over the past week Big Chief I-Spy has figured so large in Beth's mind that she has elevated him to a standing equal to that of Baby Jesus. He, like the Holy Infant, must be watching everything all the time. How else could he fill a whole book with things to see? Things Beth didn't even know existed.

Helen is not convinced. 'Don't be daft. Big Chief "I-Spy with my little eye" will never know if you cheat a bit. He's probably too busy boiling his socks at the Wigwam-by-the-Water in London to be bothered with you.'

'How far away is London?'

'As far as you can sneeze and then a lot further.'

Beth looks worried.

'Put it this way, you're not going to bump into him on the prom. London is a couple of hundred miles away, you nit.'

Beth considers her options. It's difficult to cheat with the book because you always have to write in where you saw the thing you've spied. Like the name of the lightship you've spotted, or the shape of the funnel on a tanker, or what colour legs the herring gull has.

'Look, what do you want to spot?' Helen continues.

'Shellfish.'

'OK, then. This way.' Helen veers away from the steps up to the prom and heads instead towards a little green stall in the distance, barely visible on the crowded sands.

'What d'you want?' The stallholder is a middle-aged man with muscular white fingers that are shiny with salt water and fish innards.

'What have you got?' Helen asks with her sweetest smile.

'Oysters, cockles, mussels, jellied eels, potted prawns, boiled lobster and crab. All fresh today. What do you want?'

Helen turns to her little sister who is frantically scribbling in her I-Spy book. 'Have you got that?'

'Nearly,' Beth says, pencil scrawling across the page.

The stallholder and Helen wait. A minute passes during which there is some shuffling and muttering in the queue.

'Have you remembered prawns?' Helen asks. There is a renewed flurry of activity while Beth finds the right page and ticks the box.

'Oi, young lady. I've got a bloody queue waiting here. Make up your mind. What do you want?'

'Oh,' says Helen, 'nothing, thanks. We've changed our minds.' Beth and Helen turn and walk away under the furious stares of waiting customers.

Beth is elated. That's two hundred and twenty points. 'Where are we going now?'

'Up there on the prom. Don't you want to spend your pennies?'

'No, I want to carry on spying things. There are pages of boats and ships and flags and things to spot.'

'You'll need a telescope to spot all those. Come on. I think we can risk spending a penny.'

Both girls laugh at the joke. They start to climb the wooden steps that lead up to the prom. Halfway up Helen stops in order to give Beth a rest. Looking down, she sees the grain in the wood planking has opened up under the onslaught of the salt water tide. The surface of the wood is pale, cracked and grooved with a scouring of sand. The step sags with the weight of summer visitors hurrying down with deckchairs, then returning with the tide, trailing tired children and dripping swimming costumes. Beth starts to move again and the sisters climb the rest of the steps. Once again Helen stops, leaning against the railings and looking out to sea while Beth gets her breath back. There are one or two dark spots on the horizon, but it's not clear whether they're ships or buoys.

The telescope is a penny for a look. Beth climbs the steps, pushes a penny in the slot and waits. 'I can't see nothing but black.'

'Well, take your glasses off, then.'

Beth pulls the pink wire clinic glasses off her face and drops them on the ground.

'You're supposed to close one eye,' says Helen.

'I still can't see nothing.'

Helen, who has been leafing through the I-Spy book, sighs audibly and says, 'Here, let me have a go.'

It's a miracle. Like in the Bible. A real miracle. Helen can see every kind of boat in the book. In less than a minute she's spotted a lightship (score 40), a pleasure steamer (10), a coaster (20) and a tanker (25).

But however hard Beth squints at the sea she can't see any boats at all. 'Are you sure? I can't see a trawler with an admiral's flag.'

'That's why they have telescopes, nit. That way you can see everything there is to see.'

Another minute and Helen reports sighting a lighthouse, lifeboat and an air-sea rescue helicopter until the penny runs out and the telescope shuts down. Helen has to rattle off the rest of her sightings from memory until Beth's pencil breaks and the I-Spying has to stop for the day.

The shops and stalls on the prom are ablaze with colour. Country and Western music whines from various stalls and the air is thick with the smell of fish and chips. There's a man standing at the 'Guess Your Weight' stall. After some discussion with the stallholder, a woman with a face as grey as her hair, the man booms, 'Well, what do you think I weigh, then?' The man puffs out his chest and proudly pats his stomach with a protective hand.

The woman eyes him from top to toe. 'Twenty-two stone three pounds . . . and sixpence lighter.' The woman holds out her hand for payment. The crowd cheer.

They pass a rock stall and Beth has a fleeting glimpse of the woman stallholder standing behind a bulwark of boiled sweets. Her mouth is missing several teeth and, even in repose, she looks as if she's ready for a fight. A white cap pulled low over her eyes frames her bright-red face and when she reaches forward to serve customers her hands are swollen and covered in burns and cuts. When Beth looks round the corner of the stall she can see into the back where a man in white is working the hot rock with giant tweezers and a hatchet that glints in the shadows. Beth eyes the pyramids of pink Blackpool rock wrapped in clear cellophane with a black-and-white photo of the Tower and the words 'A present from Blackpool'. Up on the sides of the stall hang walking sticks fashioned out of multi-coloured skeins of twisted rock. In pride of place there's a bunch of red rock dummies. Only babies have dummies. Beth has never had a dummy, not even when she was small. When she was in hospital there were poorly toddlers and children in the same ward, and they all had dummies. It's not fair. Beth gets into trouble if she sucks her thumb or even the buttons on her cardigan. It will spoil her teeth.

Helen pauses at a stall where sunhats are clipped to the low awning and Beth watches as the assistant twirls a thin stick round the perimeter of a huge metal rotating drum to catch the glistening threads of pink candyfloss.

Further along the prom there's bingo. A man dressed in a tight white cowboy suit with gold studs and fringes shouts the numbers over a speaker above their heads. He's wearing a black cowboy hat pulled over one eye and he's smoking a thin cigar just like a proper cowboy. 'Winner takes their pick of the stall – clocks, glassware, kitchenware, cutlery, bedding and toys.' The stall is filled with women sitting on high wooden stools at either side of a counter and marking off the numbers as they are called. When Helen walks past the cowboy whistles and invites her in but she pretends she hasn't heard and carries on walking.

When they get to a bank of slot machines the girls stop and Helen hands over half the pennies. The first machine will stamp out your name on a thin silver strip but this is boring and it involves spelling. You have to push a stiff metal arrow round a circle of letters and press a big red button to punch the letter in. Beth can think of better things to do with her pennies. Close by is a penny slide machine, which devours four of Beth's five pennies before Helen takes over and, with perfect timing, slips the penny in the slot and scoops up tenpence in the process. The winnings are duly shared out and the sisters wander further along the packed prom, weaving this way and that to make their way through the crowds.

They have come to a full stop outside a booth that Beth hasn't seen before. There's an illustration of a woman on the boards outside the entrance. Her brown skin gleams – it's the same colour as the thrupenny McCowan's Caramel Bar that Beth buys every Saturday with her spending money. Under a sign that says 'The Show They Tried To Stop' and 'No Cameras' there is another sign that says:

TIGER WOMAN

SEEN FOR THE FIRST TIME IN CAPTIVITY

SEE HER SCARS! HEAR HER SNARL!!

Tiger Woman is shown down on all fours, in the centre of a circle of men, her right hand raised as if to strike out. The men don't look too bothered. They're all staring wide-eyed at Tiger Woman with big smiles on their faces. She is wearing a ripped orange bikini and long strands of dark hair stream out behind her. Beth gets as near as possible to the picture and takes off her clinic glasses for a closer look. She can see that the woman's arms and legs are slashed with the same crimson scars that Beth imagines cover her own back. Tiger Woman stares out of the picture with an amber gaze, her red lips pulled back in a snarl. Beth is inspired. She has seen pictures of tigers before, but never one with a proper face.

Below the picture are some words Beth can't understand. She points to them and asks Helen what it says.

'It says "nothing for noseys".'

'Go on, tell me. What does it say?'

'It says "The Palace of Strange Girls" – satisfied?'

Beth looks up. The entrance to the Palace is guarded by a single bare-chested black giant wearing a scarlet bolero and baggy blue satin trousers. Beth stares at him. His skin is the colour of a penny liquorice. On his head is a large gold turban. Beth's mouth falls open. She has never seen anything like him before. Next to the giant stands a white midget on a high platform and he's in full flow.

'See Hairy Mary the ape woman – her mother was the missionary unable to resist the call of the wild! Toto the African Piccaninny – a child in all ways but one! Marvel at the world's best contortionist who can bend herself into positions that women will envy and men can only dream of! And Joanna Joe – the medical marvel of the age – she has fathered and suckled five children! See the Mermaid Twins from the Horn of Africa. Two girls presented as nature intended. Together they play the harp, joined for ever by a single mermaid tail. These girls have lured men to madness. Brought here at enormous expense. And top of the bill – Tanya the Tiger Woman. Carried off by a tiger, she still bears the scars. She has never spoken since she was rescued from a den of wild tigers. What is she? A woman? Or a tiger?'

'It looks really exciting,' Beth whispers. 'Oh, let's go! Please, please.'

Beth pushes her way to the front of the crowd to hear more, but Helen hangs back.

The man on the platform pauses for a moment and fumbles

behind the curtained entrance for a pint of beer which, holding it in both hands, he downs before turning back to the crowd. His eye finally alights on Beth. ''Op it, kid,' he says, jerking his thumb. 'See that sign? Adults only.' Beth looks miserable.

'Why don't you buy yourself a gobstopper?' Helen says, shepherding her sister away from the crowd.

'Can't I have a kali?' Beth has a particular trick with kali. With a good dose of the powder and sufficient saliva Beth can shoot the yellow powder back and forth through the gap between her two front teeth. The resultant froth will expand to twice the volume and leak from the corners of her mouth. This trick has caused several hitherto sensible adults (pre-programmed to expect medical emergencies from the child) to assume that Beth is having a seizure. Kali is now a banned substance and, seeing the look on her sister's face, Beth accepts the offer of a gobstopper. But she would have liked to see the Tiger Woman better.

There are rules concerning shop purchases. It is 'common' to start enjoying your purchases before you've even left the shop. The handing over of money is a solemn business. Only rough children open their comics immediately and read them in the street, or worse still, shove gobstoppers straight in their mouths instead of having them properly wrapped. Sadly, this particular shopkeeper isn't familiar with the practice. When Beth makes her request he slams the penny gobstopper down on the counter and says, 'Clear off, you cheeky bugger!' with such menace that Beth grabs the gobstopper, only for it to slip from her fingers a moment later and bounce down the step outside. Helen, who has been waiting for her sister, turns a blind eye while Beth retrieves it from the pavement and dusts it off. Next door the gift shop window is full of handwritten cards advertising flats to rent. Helen scans the adverts while Beth wanders over to a carousel of postcards where two women wearing 'kiss-me-quick, squeeze-me-slow' hats are standing giggling. They're looking at a picture of a grinning salesman with a bald head and shiny face showing a young blonde in a tight red dress a pair of nylon stockings. One of the women reads the caption out loud and Beth listens closely.

'The salesman's saying "They're on special offer. This pair comes with free fitting today."'

The other woman laughs so much that her hat falls off, which makes her laugh even harder. She staggers around scraping her stilettos on the pavement in an increasingly desperate attempt to retrieve the straw hat. Beth is at a loss to see what's so funny. The Kleeneaze salesman is always coming to the front door at home with special offers and her mother hasn't laughed once. Disappointed, Beth inches one of the postcards out of the wire holder. It is a picture of a man in a corner shop asking, 'Excuse me, Miss, do you keep stationery?' The shop assistant has very red cheeks and is saying, 'Well, sometimes I wriggle a bit.' Beth has more success with the next one. A lady hanging over a rail at the racetrack unaware that her knickers have fallen down. A man with a wide rubbery face, a pink shiny tongue hanging out of his mouth, eyes bulging with delight, points to the knickers on the ground and says, 'They're off!' Beth begins to laugh.

Helen, meanwhile, has spotted an advert for a flat: two girls in

Bispham looking for a third to share. This is much cheaper than the flat rents she has seen before. Cheaper than those in the local paper she saw this morning. There's a telephone number that Helen is in the process of copying down when she hears someone bellowing her name. Looking up, she sees Connie waving her hands over her head outside the entrance to the pier. Of course she's not alone. She's surrounded by a coterie of admiring males and the ever attentive Andy has his arm round her waist.

'Come over here!' Connie yells.

Helen shakes her head. 'I can't. I've got my sister with me,' she replies, pointing at Beth who has lost interest in the postcards and is now shadowing her elder sister, cheek bulging with the gobstopper and ears flapping.

'Hang on. I'll come over to you,' Connie yells.

Helen and Beth watch as Connie turns and says something to Andy. After some discussion he releases his proprietorial grasp of her waist. His narrow eyes follow her as she bounces cheerfully across the road. She is wearing a scarlet circular skirt with a full underskirt, and a skimpy black top and matching black stilettos. Helen sighs with admiration. If she weren't stuck at school, she'd be earning enough money to dress like Connie.

'Hiya!' Helen says when her friend gets within speaking distance.

'Hiya, Helen. Me and the lads are off for a couple of pints at the Laughing Donkey.'

'Where's that?'

'Over there! Isn't the sign big enough?'

Helen looks across the road and sees a huge hoarding. A cartoon donkey with crossed eyes and an oversized set of teeth is grinning from ear to ear while playing an upright piano. Overflowing pints of frothy beer are lined up on top of the piano. It looks good fun.

'Let's go!' Beth urges and pulls Helen's hand.

'Yeah, come with us,' Connie says. 'I'm with Andy and the kitchen porters. You'll like them. They're a right laugh.'

'I can't,' replies Helen. 'I've got to look after Beth and she won't be allowed in a bar.'

'They won't mind. They'll turn a blind eye, like they always do. And anyway we often have to stand outside when the bar is crowded.'

'I'd better not. If Beth lets it slip where she's been I'll be in bother. Anyway, is that a new top? It looks great!' Helen says, anxious to change the subject.

'This? Oh, it keeps on riding up. It's supposed to be off the shoulder but as soon as I move an inch it slips back up on to my shoulders and falls so low at the front you can see my bra. It's a good job I've got my black lace on today, isn't it?'

Connie gives a good approximation of embarrassed frustration as she adjusts the tight black top until it reveals her shoulders rather than her cleavage.

'I think it looks great. Where did you get it?'

'Co-op. This one was the last fourteen – but they've still got a couple of smaller sizes, if you're interested.'

Helen brings her head close to Connie's and whispers, 'I will be when I find a job. I've already seen an advert for a flat I could rent. I'll bet I could afford it if I got an office job.'

'So, you're too fancy to be a waitress like me.'

'No, I'm not. It's just that your job will finish at the end of the season, won't it? Where would I go then? I'd rather be dead than go home again.'

'She's a right cow, your mother. She barely lets you breathe without interfering. Fancy bringing you to Blackpool and not letting you have any fun. She wants you to be as bloody miserable as her. Will you fix the flat before you scarper?'

'Well, no. I'll need a job first.'

'You could stay with me while you're looking for a job. The room isn't big but we could manage.' Connie smiles at Helen and puts her arm round her and, aware that Beth is looking left out, she stops whispering and says, 'We need to cheer your sister up, don't we, Beth? Anyway – guess what?' Helen can't guess. 'That new bloke yesterday morning. What's his name? Clegg. That's it. He's only asked me out!'

Helen joins in the ensuing laughter, but her heart isn't in it. She'd cherished a hope that Alan would ask her out. It would be wonderful to tell Blanche that she'd met a boy on holiday. Helen is the only one of her friends who hasn't got a boyfriend. It's embarrassing and it's all her mother's fault.

'What did you say?' Helen asks.

'What do you think? I said no.'

'Why?'

'Have you seen him? He's a right creep, that one. I wouldn't trust him as far as I could throw him.'

'Why not?' Helen is amazed. Alan Clegg is nicely dressed and he works for an accountant.

'He's a bit too handy, if you ask me. Too fast for his own good. Won't take no for an answer. Got a touch of desert disease.'

'What's desert disease?' Beth asks and both sisters give Connie their full attention.

'You know.' Connie nudges Helen. 'The old wandering palms.'

Neither sister is any the wiser, but at least Helen manages to hide her ignorance. 'You're too young to understand,' she tells Beth.

'I'll bet that knocked the smile off his face when you turned him down,' Helen tells Connie. There's still a chance Alan might ask her out if Connie has given him the elbow.

'Oh, I'm not too sure about that. I've heard that he's wangled an invitation to join the porters for a drink tonight. I'll probably end up seeing him whether I like it or not. The pillock.'

Beth, whose attention has wandered back to the postcards, is suddenly alert, eyes open wide in surprise. 'Piddock? Did she say piddock?' she asks Helen.

'Be quiet, Beth. And don't swear.'

Beth riffles through her I-Spy book until she finds the right page. 'It's not swearing. A piddock is a boring . . .' Beth hesitates over the strange word. 'A boring molly something. Anyway it's worth seventy-five points!'

Both the older girls burst into laughter. Connie takes the book and glances at the page. 'I said he was a pillock,' Connie replies. 'Not a flippin' piddock.'

'Oh, I don't know. A boring mollusc,' says Helen, looking over her friend's shoulder. 'Sounds like a fair description to me,' she adds.

'Either way he's a nuisance. I've a good mind to complain to Andy about him. Andy would sort him out fast enough.'

'Who's Andy?' Beth asks.

'The chef at the hotel. Now shut up,' Helen tells her sister. 'So why don't you go out with Andy?' she asks, turning to Connie.

'I've told you before,' Connie replies. 'He's already breathing down my neck every hour God sends. It would be even worse if I went out with him. He's so possessive. I wouldn't get a minute to myself. Why can't I ever get a bloke like that one over there?' Connie points to a figure approaching them through the crowd. 'God! He's gorgeous.'

'Who?' asks Helen, turning round to follow Connie's glance.

'The one with the leather jacket. Looks like James Dean. He's bloody gorgeous. I'd kill to get a date with him.'

Helen spots a tall muscular figure dressed in tight jeans, a white T-shirt and black winkle-pickers. His brown hair is brushed into a DA at the back and coaxed into a shiny quiff at the front. 'Him with the studded jacket? Oh, I know him. That's Doug Fairbrother. His dad knows my dad.'

'Well, be quick and introduce me,' Connie whispers but there's no need.

Doug has spotted them and is making his way over. It's obvious he's going to speak. 'It's Helen, isn't it? I've seen you at Prospect, haven't I? I took you to your dad when you came to the mill one day.'

Doug gives Helen an admiring glance and watches with some satisfaction as she blushes.

Prospect Mill Yard, Blackburn, 16 April 1959

It is raining when Helen reaches the mill yard. Her mother is down in Liverpool visiting Beth in hospital and, as a result, there is a change in routine. Helen has to meet her dad at the mill rather than going straight home after school to an empty house. She does have an umbrella, but not one that she's prepared to take to school and risk losing. There's a hood on her school raincoat but there's no way she's going to use that. Not when she can see a really nice-looking bloke watching her from the high hatch in the gable end of the mill. There's two of them up there guiding in the bales of raw cotton from the winch. Helen can see they're laughing and waving at her, but she's too shy to acknowledge their shouted greetings and enthusiastic arm waving. 'I'll be down in a minute, luv,' one of them shouts. Helen bites her lip and looks at her feet, scanning the cobbles as if the cure for her embarrassment lies there.

'Hi! So what brings you here?'

'I'm supposed to be meeting my dad.'

'Who's he, then?'

'Jack Singleton. He works in . . .'

'I know where he works. I should do. You must be Helen.' Helen looks blank. 'I'm Doug – Dougie Fairbrother's son.'

'Oh! Your dad comes over to our house every now and again.'

'Yeah.'

There is a brief silence.

'Anyway, I'll take you to your dad, shall I?'

'He said to wait for him in the yard.'

'Not when it's pouring down! C'mon. At least let's get out of the rain.'

Doug guides Helen across the yard to a vast sliding wooden door painted green and padlocked top and bottom. There appears to be no way forward until Doug opens a small hatchway set in the woodwork. He bows his head and steps through the door into semi-darkness. Doug holds the door back, signalling her forward and Helen follows.

It is the sound that hits her first, before she has even taken a second step across the threshold. A demonic hum and crash that makes her want to scream in terror, fall to her knees and curl up, press her hands against the throbbing in her ears. It is the loudest sound she has ever heard, the wild whistling roar of a thousand steel-tipped shuttles as they shoot back and forth, and the titanic clash of iron-trimmed weaving beams as they shift and change the warp threads. And below all these sounds is the steady rumble of hundreds of giant leather drive belts that revolve from floor to ceiling, powering looms that glisten with oil and grime. And the heat. The imprisoned air burns the back of Helen's throat as her nose fills with the damp, rich smell of cotton and oil. Above her daylight filters through the north windows and illuminates a scene of frenetic industry and chaotic haste. And everywhere, everywhere, the air is alive with floating lint.

Helen turns back to the hatchway in search of a way out of the chaos and noise, but the exit is lost in the shadows. Doug turns and beckons her forward, so she follows. Her feet slip on the mixture of black machine oil and settled lint that covers the floor, and sweat pours down the back of her shirt beneath her school uniform. As she passes, weavers appear from the tangle of machinery and nod or stand with their backs to their loom and openly stare. Others talk to each other in a pantomime of silent speech in order to be understood through the constant thwack of picking sticks that drive the shuttles back and forth. And still the narrow corridor continues through section after section of looms that stretch as far as the eye can see. At last Doug turns back to Helen and indicates a doorway at the top of some steps set into a small glass half-partitioned wall. There's a peeling wood sign on the door that says 'Foreman'. Helen rushes forward, eager to escape the shed.

Once inside, Doug closes the door behind them and shouts in her ear with a laugh, 'First time in a weaving shed?'

Helen nods in reply, light-headed with the heat and not trusting her voice to be heard over the uproar.

'This is your dad's office – he'll be out on the floor somewhere now, but he'll be back in a minute. I can't stop. I'll have to leave you . . .'

'Don't!' Helen shouts and grabs his arm.

Doug laughs again. 'I've got t'get back. You'll be OK here. Stop 'ere an' wait for your dad or we'll all get hell.'

Blackpool, Wednesday 13 July 1959

Doug has cause to remember the day Helen turned up at the mill for more than one reason. He'd paid a high price for the pleasure of parading through the shed with a pretty girl at his heels. Once Jack Singleton had learned about it he'd dragged Doug across the tiles. Doug Fairbrother was employed in delivery and dispatch – he shouldn't have been in the shed in the first place. Still, looking at Helen now, Doug is convinced that the upset was worth it. If her face is anything to go by she won't forget him in a while.

He is still basking in the notoriety when the redhead breaks in: 'Hi, I'm Connie. Helen's friend from the hotel.'

'Which one?'

'The Belvedere.'

'Oh, I'd heard that you were staying there,' Doug says, looking at Helen. 'Dougie says you stay there every year.' Doug's habit of referring to his father by his first name makes Helen want to laugh.

'I work there. Just for the summer, like,' Connie says, redirecting Doug's attention to herself. 'I'm surprised I haven't seen you before. I get off most nights by eight and then we're straight down to Yates's for a drink and a bit of fun.' Connie's smile is an open invitation.

'Yates's, is it? I might see you and Helen down there some time,' Doug says.

'Make sure you do,' Connie adds.

The left side of Beth's face is aching, forcing her to shift the gobstopper to her other cheek. It tumbles out of her mouth in the process and all three girls watch fascinated as it rolls to a sticky halt between Doug's winkle-pickers.

Helen aches with embarrassment. 'Don't you dare!' she hisses when Beth bends to retrieve the sweet. 'Anyway, we'd better be going.'

'See you around, Helen. Nice meeting you, Connie.' And with that Doug is gone, leaving Connie staring dreamily after him.

9

STRANDED OBJECTS

If you look carefully you'll find lots of things on the beach that have been stranded by the tide. You might even find a message in a bottle that has come across the sea from far away! Score 30.

With his daughters gone and Ruth still in town shopping, Jack is left to his own devices. He folds up his newspaper, wedges it in the wooden frame of his deckchair and stares out to sea. Out on the horizon a packed pleasure boat inches across the bay. Jack takes several deep breaths, but still he can't settle. The moment he tries to relax, his thoughts return to the same old subject. Jack sighs and, casting a surreptitious glance around him, reaches into his pocket and pulls out the letter.

He has had it since last Thursday when he'd called round to see the old man. Jack was there alone – Ruth hasn't accompanied him on these visits since they were newly married. Jack had spotted the letter as soon as he'd walked in. It was propped up behind the one-eyed pot dog on the kitchen mantelpiece where his mother had always put important paperwork. Everything went there, from her current Co-operative Society Stamp Book to her Last Will and Testament and the latest crumpled receipt from the coal man, a known rogue who waits until there's no one at home and then charges for a couple of bags more than he delivers. Jack's mother died last year but the pot dog remains, still guarding vital communications. Jack saw what he reckoned were foreign stamps on the letter but he'd smothered his curiosity, knowing that the old man would get round to telling him in his own good time.

Father and son had sat at the green baize card table in front of the fire and shared a plate of cream crackers with a wedge of Tasty Lancashire. Conversation was punctuated by next door's dog howling its head off in the backyard. The meal finished, Jack had gone into the scullery with the dirty plates and, while waiting for the kettle to boil, he'd seen the dog stick its head over the high backyard wall. Jack had nipped out and given the poor bugger a scratch behind the ears. When he came back in his father was shaking his head.

'Dickie picked up that beggar for a couple of quid last spring in the Cat and Sardine on Mill Street. He'd been after a lapdog for Winnie, now she's stuck in a wheelchair with the arthritis. The bloke in the Sardine swore through a nine-inch wall that the dog was a fully grown pedigree and it was only for sale because it was too soft to go ratting. Dickie carried it back home under one arm. He'd be hard pushed to even lift it nowadays, let alone carry it.'

Jack has heard the story many times but recognises it would be churlish to deny his father the pleasure of telling it. 'I'll bet Winnie was pleased,' he volunteers. 'She's a soft spot for dogs, hasn't she?'

'She was suited to death. The minute that dog set eyes on her it knew she was soft in the head. It crawled straight up on her knee and curled up as good as gold. She called it Totty. They hadn't had it a month before they cottoned on. Not only was it a keen forager with a rare talent for thievery, it could eat like a mad horse. It'll chew anything – from backyard weeds and clothes on the washing line to pantry leftovers and bicycle tyres. Listen on it whining – they've put it out just so they can eat their tea in peace.'

'Well, it's a fair size for a dog.'

'Last time I saw Dickie I told him straight. I said, "You want to get a saddle on that bugger."'

'It's a shame.'

'Well, it's six of one and half a dozen of the other. He was daft buying a dog in a pub and she was dafter still nursing it. It doesn't matter how big that dog gets it's still after being nursed. If it's not trying to climb on her knee it's sat beside her wheelchair with its chin on her shoulder and a daft grin on its face. The big galoot. Winnie can't get on with her knitting without him snuffling around the back of her ears and dribbling on her wool. For two pins Dickie would have taken it back, but Winnie won't hear of it. She says that dog is the nearest thing they've had to family since the day they were married.' The old man heaved a sigh and said, 'You couldn't make it up, could you?'

It was only after they'd finished off the Lincoln biscuits and were drinking their mugs of tea that the old man tilted his head at the mantelpiece and said, 'That turned up a couple of days ago.'

'Oh, aye?' Jack replied, wandering over to the mantelpiece and retrieving the letter.

'Aren't you going to open it? Might be important. From the looks of it it's come a fair distance.'

'Has it?' Jack had said, but seeing the expression on his dad's face he'd added, 'I'll open it later. I'm about ready for another mug of tea, aren't you? I'll put the kettle on.'

The rest of the visit passed off quietly until it was time for Jack to make tracks.

'Well, enjoy yourself in Blackpool, lad. Here's a bit of something for the girls.'

'You don't have to, Dad. I'd rather you kept the money.'

'No. Take it. I've nowt to spend it on here.'

'You'll be going to the Pot Fair next week though, won't you?'

'Oh aye, I'll have a look around. But I've more sense than to buy owt from that bunch of rogues. You see these poor beggars walking away with cardboard boxes packed up with tea sets and the like. It's only when they get home and open the blessed thing that they find out it's full of chipped plates and cracked cups. And no way to get their money back. Bloomin' fair has already moved on. Still, it's a sight to see, the fair, and I could listen to the salesmen's patter all day. There were one bloke there last year sellin' glassware and he had folks rolling with laughter. You'll tell me if it's something serious?'

The abrupt change of subject had floored Jack for a moment. It was only when the old man pointed at the trouser pocket where he'd hastily stuffed the letter that Jack had cottoned on. 'It'll be something and nothing, Dad. I made a few pals in Crete, that's all. I'd not have got out in one piece if I hadn't.'

That was last Thursday and Jack hasn't had a moment's peace since. At first he'd been shocked that the letter had found him at all. But that's the Red Cross for you – or maybe it was the army that had handed out Jack's pre-war address. Either way, the letter had found him. On the way home he'd taken a detour through Victoria Park, the letter burning a hole in his pocket and his head full of memories of Crete. He stopped when he got to his favourite spot. Hidden behind a laurel hedge and sheltered from sight by the curve of a rhododendron, he sat down on a bench. This was where he'd done most of his courting before the war. He hadn't been back there for the best part of twenty years. It was there that he'd ripped open the letter. He found the photograph first and the shock had nearly killed him. He didn't know whether to laugh or cry. There she was, leaning against the back of the taverna, a lacy jumper tight across her breasts and the curve of her hips dark against the whitewashed stone; a broad sash belt round her waist and her hair spread in a black halo. Eleni; Eleni with her wide eyes and full lips; Eleni whom he'd believed dead these last eighteen years. He jerked his eyes away in an attempt to pull himself together.

The park's ornamental flower beds blurred out of focus. He wiped his eyes and looked again at the photograph. At the time he barely registered the pale figure who stood beside her. All his attention was focused on Eleni and still, after all these years, the familiar sensation, the way his breath stops short when he sees her face. In his memories she was always dancing – the embroidered hem of her skirt in one hand and a cup of wine in the other. Or she was sitting with her back against the trunk of the judas tree, laughing out loud and kissing his face as he tried to eat the picnic she had brought.

The news of her death had come the day after he'd been evacuated from Crete. He'd been sitting around with a bunch of soldiers who'd come through the village on their way to the coast. They said that the taverna had taken a direct hit. One of them had seen Eleni's body laid out by the roadside. Jack had cried openly. Later he had lain on the deck while the ship took them through to Egypt and willed himself to die of the pneumonia that was already sweeping through his lungs. To know that she was alive now was almost beyond belief.

That was a week ago and since then the letter has exercised his mind every waking moment. Now, in the absence of his wife and the relative anonymity of Blackpool beach, Jack runs his finger over the stamps and indecipherable postmarks and, setting aside the photograph, pulls out a single sheet of paper from the thin faded envelope.

Kalivis

Hello to you my old friend Jack,

I send greetings to you and hopes for good health. It is a long time since you and Nibs were here. Taverna bombed the night you left but walls and roof made good after war ended. My father died a few years back and now I run the taverna alone. Same customers but all a little older than we were. We often remember good times we had when the British were here. I heard what had happened to you from a soldier the monks were hiding at Preveli. Here is a photograph of me and my only child, Ioanis, seventeen. If you ever come back to Crete we would be very happy to see you.

Yours with love and remembrance,

Eleni Korakis.

Jack runs his finger over her signature – as if it would bring her closer. Of course, the truth had only dawned on him in stages. When he looks at the photograph now, however, it is glaringly obvious. The figure standing next to Eleni is her son . . . their son. True, he'd barely believed it at first. It made no sense. If Eleni had found his address now, why hadn't she found it seventeen years ago when the child was born? The boy is looking away from the camera, one hand in his pocket and the other holding a newly lit cigarette. An air of angry reluctance informs every muscle in his body. As if he would wish to be anywhere other than caught in such close proximity to his mother. The closer Jack looks, the more the photo hides as much as it reveals. The boy has pale hair that looks paler still against his obvious tan. His eyes, partially hidden under a heavy fringe, are fixed on the ground at his feet. If Jack doubted the colour of the boy's hair on the black-and-white photo, the appearance of his right hand is irrefutable evidence. Ioanis has the same broad hands and square fingers, the same shrug to his shoulders that characterised Jack's teenage years.

Even after examining the photo countless times, Jack is still in shock. He rereads the letter. His heart aches for Eleni. As the last line of her letter reminds him, he had promised to return. A bitter smile passes across his face when he reads this. He'd been on the last ship leaving the island. He was ferried on board by stretcher along with the other wounded. If things had been different he might have stayed in Crete. Plenty had. Hundreds of Allied troops hadn't made it to the beach fast enough and the rescue ships were long gone by the time they'd arrived. Things could have been so different.

It is apparent from the photograph that Eleni hasn't changed at all. She was little more than a girl back then and even now she barely looks thirty. Jack tries to concentrate on Eleni's smile, but his eyes are constantly drawn to the boy: Ioanis, his son. Times when his thoughts should be with Ruth and the girls the image of the boy will rise in his mind and bring a lump to his throat. Whether the emotion is one of pride or grief or even anger is unclear. Even now he cannot tell whether what he feels is joy or regret. It is odd to ache for the loss of Eleni after all these years. The sadness he felt at the time has now multiplied a hundred-fold. He feels torn to shreds. When he is not elated that Eleni is still alive, still beautiful, still remembers him, he yearns to see the son he has never known or even supported. Jack longs to tell someone. Anyone. He longs to hear another person confirm the truth that he suspects – that the boy is indeed his son. He has tried in the long hours of sleepless nights to reconstruct the last conversation he had with Eleni, the last words they exchanged before he kissed her and left. But it is hopeless.

Hania, North-west Crete, 20 May 1941

It is early morning when the Stukas come in. Jack and Nibs are queuing up for breakfast when they hear a restless, uneasy buzz in the air which, within minutes, increases to a roar: wave after wave of enemy aircraft heading for the airport at Maleme, five miles away. By the time Jack and Nibs have scrambled to their gun emplacements above Souda Bay, the sky has grown dark with the concentration of enemy aircraft. There have been rumours for weeks about a German invasion, but still the sight of that many bombers is overwhelming. In the distance Jack can hear the thump and boom of Allied heavy anti-aircraft guns firing greedily into the crowded skies above the airport. And so it continues, day after day without respite. Jack, still manning one of the heavy anti-aircraft guns on the escarpment above the beach, can only watch in amazement as hundreds of low-level gliders come in like a plague of dragonflies. Each glider lands on the beach in a storm of sand and disgorges a dozen fully armed troops, bent double and running for the shelter of the cliffs. And still the escarpment guns fire and reload and fire again, striving to beat off the aerial invasion. Another four days of fighting follow in a desperate bid to hold Maleme, but once the Germans have control of the airfield the battle for Crete is effectively lost.

After a week fighting, and now overwhelmed by the numbers

of invading troops, the order comes through to withdraw beyond the smouldering remains of Hania and Souda Bay into the cover of the daisy-strewn olive groves further inland. Jack, Nibs and three other lads find shelter in an empty bomb crater. Here they wait out another day, firing their Bren guns intermittently but mostly keeping their heads down as the Germans set up a series of creeping barrages on the slopes below them. Late on that day a message comes through from headquarters. A fighting retreat is ordered to Sfakion on the south coast where ships are stationed to take them off the island. Chaos sweeps through the ranks with some troops moving east to the apparent safety of the garrison at Heraklion while others make directly for Sfakion via the White Mountains.

When Jack sets out on the road to Kalivis with the intention of seeing Eleni one last time, Nibs tags along. At the end of the first day they are joined by Jonno and Tommy, two New Zealanders who have been cut off from their regiment. Together they make their way slowly up the only road that runs south. They hear the strafing attack and catch the smell of burning flesh on the wind long before they see the line of wrecked jeeps. The road is littered with the detritus of retreat: scattered documents, steel helmets, ripped canvas, empty shells, brass buttons, odd boots and torn webbing. And still the bombing and strafing continue, forcing them to desert the road and take the safer mountain tracks. A mile from Kalivis Jack skirts off from the group, promising to catch them up later.

She has seen him coming. Eleni, her dark hair blowing in all directions and her face pale with concern, meets him at the edge of the village carrying a rough sack filled with food and a flask of water. For the first time in over a week Jack relaxes. They embrace, giddy with relief at each other's survival. On this, their final picnic, they lie hidden in the shelter of an outcrop of rock. Their conversation is conducted against a backdrop of strafing attacks along the line of retreating troops on the road below. They part at sunset. Jack looks back at the last turn in the path, searches for her figure in the gathering darkness. A glimpse of her, nothing more, her pale arm raised against the darkness, her face hidden in the shadows, and yet still as close to him as his next step, his next breath.

They are waiting for him further up the valley. Jonno has built a meagre fire and Tommy is doling out rations. Nibs has his feet up, catching forty winks. They greet his return with relief. Jack, with his keen sense of direction and his constant chivvying, is the best chance any of them has of reaching the rescue ships. They spend an uneasy night making their way up the lower slopes of the White Mountains. Coming over a rise, they look down into a smoke-filled valley crowded with fires and spend the rest of the night in the shelter of a cave watching for the yellow flares from enemy aircraft. Dawn comes up to reveal the valley floor punctured with a smouldering orchard. The breeze lifts brief sparks that glitter crimson against the devastation. The flare of blackened branches against the pall of smoke stays in Jack's mind long after the details of their retreat to Sfakion are lost.

They keep moving during the heat of the day and into the chill of the night until, an hour before dawn on the second day, they stop and spend a fruitless hour trying to sleep. When the sun rises they slide down the side of a nearby creek in search of water, only to come across a group of fellow soldiers. These lads had overtaken them earlier, intent upon sticking to the road in the hope of finding a lift. Now they lie, their bodies crammed together like sardines, glistening in the thin dawn light, uniforms and flesh ripped apart by machine-gun fire. The sight is greeted with numb acceptance rather than surprise. Groups of retreating British troops are being hunted down all over the island. Invariably they try to evade capture by hiding in caves, concealed gullies and isolated shepherds' huts. Now that any form of organised resistance is in ruins, the German battle for Crete has resolved itself into a race to prevent the Allied forces from escaping. There is no food, little water and still the White Mountains surround them. Another day's walking takes them up to the Askifou Plain – a wild, inhospitable area covered by cypress forest. Purely by chance they come across an army dressing station at the head of the track. Jonno throws in the towel and takes up the offer of shelter by a local shepherd. Tommy is finished, his ankle broken after a fall during the previous night's march. He sits down outside the dressing station and refuses to move. Only Jack and Nibs take the track that leads down to the Imbros Gorge.

Blackpool, Wednesday 13 July 1959

Back on Blackpool beach Jack tries to shake himself free from the nightmare of the Imbros Gorge. He attempts instead to reconstruct in his mind's eye a photo he used to have of Eleni. It was taken in happier times with a Box Brownie borrowed from Nibs. She is sitting under the flowering judas tree, a flask of wine, bread and goat's cheese in front of her. Her head tilted back laughing and her arms raised towards him as he fiddles with the shutter of the unfamiliar camera. The photo was destroyed, along with the better part of his pack, during the bombing of Tripoli. He had lain at number 4 Dressing Station, covered in bandages, his eyes blurred with the loss. Jack shakes his head, as if to dislodge the memory, and returns the letter to its hiding place in his back pocket. Why hadn't Eleni told him she was pregnant before he left? But what does it matter now? He is married to Ruth. He is father to two daughters who between them claim the greater part of his affection. He could, he recognises, lose a number of things in his life. But to lose his daughters? Jack is filled with panic by the thought.

And then there's Ruth. What has his wife done to warrant his desertion? Jack's view of Ruth has changed over the course of their marriage. At first he was flattered by her faith in him, drawn by the reassurance of normality that she seemed to offer. He used to smile and shake his head when she said that he was tied on for success. 'After all,' she would argue, 'why be a weaver when you could be an overlooker? Why be an overlooker when you could be a foreman? The sky's the limit, Jack.'

As always, Ruth draws her inspiration from the Bible. The parable of the talents. After the war she persuaded Jack to attend night school classes to learn more about textiles. When he brought home his diploma she framed it and displayed it prominently in their front room. And it's been non-stop push since then. Ruth's constant striving for more success is wearing him out. She is never satisfied. It's all a long way from the life Jack had visualised back in Egypt when he wrote proposing marriage. He'd believed then that together they would create a stable life, an antidote to the terrifying flux of his years of fighting abroad. But seventeen years have passed and with them any notion of partnership.

In the headlong rush that is Ruth's ambition there are casualties. Intimate conversation being one and physical affection another. He is at first frustrated, disappointed by the lack of physical union, then troubled by guilt. He suspects that he is being unreasonable to expect Ruth (a woman permanently distracted by what she views as the fatal illness of her younger child) to find time for sex. In her silent rejection of his advances Ruth gathers a certain martyrdom to herself. And it would have continued that way had her demands for a new house not suddenly increased in intensity. Thus reduced to only two topics of marital conversation, imminent infant death and financing the purchase of a semi, Jack has taken avoidance measures. He seeks distraction in work, completing eighteen-hour days only to discover, when he finally collapses into the marital bed, that he has the energy to be angry. Nevertheless he continues, working all the overtime he can get. On Saturday mornings he brings home parts of faulty loom drives to mend over the weekend. He already earns more than all his friends, but a weaving shed wage will never buy his wife all the things she wants. Living with Ruth is hard work and Jack's life had looked set to continue that way until a week ago when the letter arrived and everything changed.

Every night since, Jack has dreamed of Crete. Sleep has allowed him entry to the happy illusion that he is back in the inn, drinking and dancing, that Eleni is once more so close that he can feel her pulse. Despite the bitter knowledge when he wakes that it is not reality but imagination, he can't stop thinking about her. He wakes immersed in a past that he had hoped to forget and now can only partially remember. He bears the daylight despair of a man fully alive only in his dreams. A man impatient for the privacy of sleep that brings with it the prospect of seeing her again. And still he feels cheated, as if he had reached out for the dancing figure of Eleni and, when the music stopped, found Ruth in his arms. As if his life is stranded here, on Blackpool beach, when he should be in Kalivis running a taverna, looking after Eleni and bringing up his son.

Ruth finds him staring into space when she returns and she is forced to nudge him with her foot in order to get his attention. 'Here, Jack. Give me a hand with this tea before I drop the lot.'

Jack gets up and, taking the battered tin tray from her hands, places it on the sand while she disentangles her shopping bag and the brown-paper parcel from her wrist. 'There was a right crowd at the tea van. I must have queued for at least twenty minutes. I'm gasping.'

Ruth unbuttons her raincoat and pours a stream of milky tea from the chipped white pottery jug into the two similarly battered mugs. Sugar is added separately with an outsize teaspoon from a green egg cup. Taking tea on Blackpool sands is a bit rough and ready. The proprietors of the tea van ensure the return of their crockery and trays by sticking a shilling on the price, refundable with the return of the tray. This has proved to be something of a money spinner since the majority of carefree holidaymakers are not prepared to queue again with the loaded tray for the sake of a bob. Thus the sands are dotted with abandoned trays harvested at the end of the day by local lads at sixpence a time. This is business Blackpool style.

'Where are the girls?'

'Oh, they're on the prom. I gave Helen a couple of bob for the slot machines.'

'How long have they been gone? You know that Elizabeth shouldn't walk too far.'

'Around ten minutes,' Jack replies, keen to avoid an argument. 'I've barely had a chance to look at the local paper.'

Ruth passes him a mug of tea. 'Well, you should see the prices of semis they're advertising in there. They're sky high. Best part of £2,000. Anyone would be hard pushed to afford a pre-war semi let alone a new one.'

'There's plenty of money in Blackpool. Still, you wouldn't have all the shops if there wasn't,' Jack remarks, eyeing his wife's shopping bag.

But Ruth persists: 'You could buy a semi at home for the cost of a terraced house here.' Jack presses his lips closed and turns to the cricket scores. Ruth tries another tack: 'You'll never guess who I saw in town. Cora!'

'Hmm.'

'You know, Cora Lloyd.'

'Ah.'

'She was supposed to be having a fortnight in Spain, but they've had to cancel. They're staying in St Anne's for the week. Anyway we went for a cup of tea and she was telling me that Ronald has been up to his ears at work arranging mortgages for couples wanting to buy one of those new semis they're building at the Boundary. You know, the ones we're interested in.'

This is wishful thinking. Jack is resolutely not interested in either taking on a mortgage or buying a semi. Their terraced house was bought outright for cash. Jack fires Ruth a warning glance. He has made his feelings known in the past and will do so again if she doesn't let the subject drop.

Ruth meets his gaze with studied indifference. 'Cora says at this rate there'll be none left by the time we get round to looking.' Jack refuses to rise to the bait. He takes another mouthful of tea and returns to his perusal of the cricket scores. 'I mean, it's not as if we don't have the deposit, is it? . . . Jack? Are you listening?'

'What?'

'I said we have enough to put down for a deposit.'

'It's got nothing to do with the deposit. It's the fact we'd be taking on a loan and interest that it would take twenty-five years to repay. I've told you what I think and I'm not going to get into another argument now.' From the look on his face it is obvious that he is in no mood for further discussion.

* * *

Ruth is unaware that Beth has stolen one of the comics from the Residents' Lounge. Beth has hidden the comic up her dress and only the elastic in the ruched bodice lies between her and immediate discovery. Mother and daughter have climbed the stairs to the second floor before the comic begins to slip. Beth is forced to fold one arm against her chest in order to prevent the paper from continuing its downward slide past her knickers and on to the floor.

'What's the matter with you, Elizabeth?' her mother asks. 'What's the matter with your arm? Are you hurting?' Beth nods. 'Is it your chest?' Ruth tries to keep her voice calm but when Beth nods her head again she is filled with anxiety. 'Do you want to stop and rest, or shall I carry you?'

Beth shakes her head and carries on climbing. This secrecy is vital. Ruth disapproves of children's comics. She will be angry if she discovers the contraband inching its way towards Beth's knickers.

Progress up to the girls' room is slow as many of their fellow guests are on their way down for afternoon tea. Mother and daughter regularly pause and stand aside to let people pass. Hotel guests invariably say hello and smile at Beth, but she refuses to speak or even meet their eyes. Mrs Clegg's pity for the child has translated itself into the urge to share her concerns with other guests. Adults now watch Beth with either a lurid fascination or outright pity. The salesman's 'wife' has bought her a little Welsh doll to play with. Beth dislikes dolls in general, but she reserves a special hatred for this particular doll, for its red lips and rosy cheeks that mock her. Beth's privacy is daily invaded by bending adults who stroke her hair, or big men who boom and push sixpences into her hand. Sadly, her mother, who invariably witnesses these monetary exchanges, collects the sixpences. Every time they pass the statue of the crippled boy outside the post office they stop and press the latest sixpence into the slot at the top of the boy's head. Beth is drawn to the statue. The boy has leg irons, but this is of little interest. The real excitement is the big brown dog sitting at his side. The dog has friendly eyes, his mouth is open and she can see a big pink tongue that might lick her hand if he were real.

Eventually they reach the room. Ruth walks over to the window and closes the curtains. Beth pulls out the comic from its hiding place and pushes it under her pillow. When Ruth turns back from wrestling with the curtains she sees that Elizabeth is already out of her dress and lying in bed, still as a corpse, with the covers pulled up to her chin. Ruth is gratified by the sight. This proves that she is right about Elizabeth needing rest. Ruth checks her daughter's forehead for signs of fever (the first sign of polio and thus of constant concern to Ruth). Satisfied that Elizabeth's temperature is normal, she kisses her daughter, tucks her in as tightly as possible between the thin white sheets and lavishly darned grey Utility blankets, and switches off the light before leaving the room.

Beth waits for some minutes before moving, listening to her mother's retreating footsteps. Once the sound has died away she begins the struggle to free herself from the binding of bedclothes.

This involves a degree of wriggling before she can worm her shoulders free, followed by some sharp twisting and turning. Once her arms are released it's relatively easy to pull aside the sheet and blankets. Despite this Beth is gasping for breath when she finally sits up and puts her feet on the floor. Triumphant, she reaches for the comic.

Her favourite story is about an orphan who is adopted by a cruel family who ignore her and are unkind. The orphan doesn't realise it, but really she's a princess who has been hidden away to keep her safe. One day a prince comes to the door and claims her, and she leaves the nasty house and moves to the palace where she belongs. Beth is entranced by the story. She reads it again and again, and traces the pictures with her finger. She is interested in becoming an orphan. More exciting still is the prospect of living in a palace like the Tiger Woman. But the Tiger Woman is pretty. Beth sits and mulls the problem over. She is already growing her nails into claws, but Beth's lips aren't as red as they ought to be. In fact, they're not red at all. Mrs Clegg said she thought they looked a bit blue at breakfast. Beth sighs and bites her lips hard, the way she has seen Helen do before she walks into the hotel dining room. But there may be a better solution. Beth opens the drawer in her bedside table and takes out a circular box. The label says,

Dr C. R. Coffin's American Dentifrice

prepared by Darling of Manchester.

An excellent preparation for the preservation of Teeth

Beth opens the cardboard box and sees it is still half full of pink powder. First of all she tries patting the powder on to her cheeks. Anxious to see the effect, she drags the chair over to the washbasin. Climbing up, she can just about see her face in the mirror. But Dr Coffin's powder hasn't worked. It is nowhere near dark enough and it falls off her cheeks the minute she pats it on. Beth stops and considers the problem. A solution occurs to her. She empties some of the powder into her hand and kneels down on the chair to reach the taps. With the addition of a trickle of cold water the powder not only turns dark pink but also stays put when she applies it to her lips. Beth stands on tiptoe to see her reflection. Her lips look a little lumpy but this is a small price to pay. All that remains now is to practise tiger leaps.

10

GYPSY

Have you ever had your fortune told by a gypsy at the seaside? Did you cross her palm with silver? Did she have a crystal ball? Score 20 points.

The Singletons are late for the evening meal. The corridors and stairs are deserted as they make their way downstairs. There's a queue for the dining room and when the family finally get there it's like a cattle market. The room is hot and noisy, the tables crowded, the air vibrating with the clatter of Sheffield steel against hotel china and the rumble of conversation. Florrie waves across the room at them and yells, 'Coo-ee, Ruth. Over here! I've saved your table for you.'

Ruth is torn between relief and annoyance. The last thing she wants is to be beholden to the Cleggs, but with the dining room as crowded as it is it's a relief to sit down. The meal starts with brown Windsor soup thick enough to stand a spoon up in. What it lacks in meat, Ruth observes, is more than made up for with pepper. The main course consists of a couple of lamb chops reared up against a mountain of mash, peas the colour and texture of spent shells and gravy that solidifies on contact. It's an approximation of lemon meringue for afters. Ruth bakes the pudding according to Elizabeth Craig. The lemon base should be clear and sharp to the taste in contrast with the sweet crispness of the meringue. Ruth bakes the pastry blind and allows the lemon to cool fully before she fills the case. Haste at any point in the baking of a lemon meringue is asking for trouble. Sadly, the chef at the Belvedere has made the basic mistake of over-sweetening the lemon. It runs from the pastry case like jam. And the rest? The meringue is chewy, the topping hasn't been sealed properly and the pastry is waterlogged. Despite this Ruth's daughters eat enthusiastically – as if they'd never tasted better. Probably it's the sea air, Ruth reasons, that has made them so hungry. The meal is consumed in record time and the families disperse, leaving Ruth alone with Florrie.

'Do you work?' Florrie asks, moving over to sit with Ruth and motioning to Connie for a fresh pot of tea.

'No. I don't have time to work. I'm too busy running the house,' Ruth replies.

'But what is there to do that would take you all day?' Florrie notes the look of disapproval on Ruth's face and corrects herself: 'I mean, what do you do when you've finished the housework?' In Florrie's world running a house doesn't qualify as work. If it qualifies as a job at all, it's what you rush through in a morning before going out to work and finish off last thing at night if it won't wait until tomorrow.

'I look for some more to do,' Ruth replies. 'I clean my windows every week, inside and out.'

'It would be a right waste of time cleaning windows down where we live. Scotley's mill chimney puts paid to clean windows and it doesn't do much for your washing either. Have you never worked?'

'I used to work as a clerk at the town hall, but that finished when I got married.'

'That's a shame – it's just the time when you need a bit of extra money when you're setting up home, like.'

'When Jack came back from service overseas all he wanted was to settle down and have a family. He likes a well-run house. It's what a man needs when he's busy at work.'

'I don't know about that. I've been a spinner at Lane End Mill since I left school.'

'Doesn't your husband object if there's no meal waiting for him when he gets home?'

'Does he heck. I'd like to see him object. I can't be in two places at once. It's money in his pocket if I'm earning. Anyway, I don't know that it makes that much difference, in the long run.'

'What?'

'Staying at home and looking after the house. I mean, are kids any better for it? My lads stay with Fred's mother and they don't seem any the worse for it, I must say.'

Ruth casts a sour glance at the state of the twins' socks. That alone is argument enough for staying at home and being a proper mother. Ruth wouldn't mop her step with those socks. The lad, Red Hawk, is sliding across the varnished floorboards at the edge of the room. His socks will be in holes as well before the week is out, let alone the dangers of splinters in his feet. Ruth can't bear to watch.

'It's odd, isn't it,' Florrie continues, 'how different folk are. I mean, my old dad did everything at home. My mother had eleven kids, nine surviving, and she hadn't a single varicose vein in her legs up to the day she died. I swear she had hands like a lady.' Florrie surveys her own worn and calloused hands. 'She was a one, my mother. I've seen her sit in a rocking chair all day long while my dad set to with the washing and stripping the beds. He'd even black-lead the stove. She was the boss of him and no mistake. I never heard her give him a kind word. I wouldn't reckon my chances of getting away with that with my Fred. You'll not catch him picking up a duster. Still, I don't do a lot of dusting myself. It only goes up in the air and lands somewhere else, doesn't it?'

Ruth knows full well that if you dust properly – using a damp cloth after vacuuming and moving methodically from top to bottom – you can shift the dust completely.

'Anyway,' Florrie continues, 'Fred's mother is a real gem. She looks after the lads Monday to Friday and I've never had a wrong word with her in all the years me and Fred have been married. I take it you've not been so fortunate with your in-laws, Ruth?'

'No.'

'Some of them are buggers, aren't they?'

'I've stopped out of the way.'

'How do you mean?' Florrie's face is full of sympathetic concern.

'I used to get out of the way when Jack's parents came over,' Ruth confesses. 'I'd make sure I'd left the house immaculate – I'd dust everywhere, polish the cooker. I'd clean the windows even though they never came until after dark when the curtains were shut. I knew well enough that his mother would be having a good poke around. I wouldn't give her the satisfaction of finding anything wrong.'

'But it doesn't upset you now, does it?'

'I suppose not. They don't come any more. His mother died last year.'

'I'm sorry to hear that.'

Florrie has such a way with her. A way of making whoever she's speaking to feel as if she's on their side. Her whole manner encourages confidences. Her expression is soft, her look uncritical, her smile engaging. Her broad face glows with feminine understanding. Despite her natural reserve Ruth finds herself drawn to the woman.

The two women lift their cups and take a sip of tea.

'My, but he's a grand-looking chap, your Jack. Don't you think he has a look of Charlton Heston? We took the lads to see *Ben Hur* last night and the minute he came on screen I said to Fred, "Now, who does he remind you of?"'

Ruth is not unaware of the attention Jack provokes, but she's learned to live with it. She even joins in when Florrie laughs.

'How did you and Jack meet?'

'We went to the same Sunday School. He didn't attend regularly, but I could tell the minute I walked in the church when he was there. Wherever Jack was there was always plenty of noise, the sound of people having a good time. It was a nightmare trying to calm the children down before the start of church. It didn't matter whether I was teaching about the commandments or the feeding of the five thousand, Jack would be pulling faces, or horsing around at the back of the class. The only time I ever got his attention was when I told the story of Daniel in the lion's den. He listened then.'

'Lads! They're a nightmare, aren't they?'

'I couldn't believe it when Reverend Ryecroft asked him to take one or two of the Sunday classes when I was busy with the Church Committee. I remember sitting in church listening for the uproar. But it was silent as the grave. Not a muff. When I went to the schoolroom at the end of church, the children filed out like little angels. It was a bit before I cottoned on. His Sunday School classes were packed to the gills because he'd abandoned the Bible in favour of cowboy stories. When I complained he switched to the slaughter of the innocents. With embellishments. There was nothing I could do about it. And it wasn't just church. I'd see him on Trafalgar Road while I was hurrying off to a church wardens' meeting. He'd have some girl on his arm, or he'd be sat on a bench in Victoria Park holding forth, legs at full stretch, showing off the socks his mother used to knit. He was working at Bank Mill then.'

'Is he still there?'

'No. Foster Brothers took him on before the war.'

'My Fred used to work for Edmondson's until they shut down last month. Out on his ear with nothing after twenty years. They promised him the earth if he'd go back to his old job after the war and he went. Despite the fact he could have earned more elsewhere. When I kick up about it Fred shrugs his shoulders and says, "Florrie, they don't pay you for loyalty." He finished last month and there hasn't been a whiff of a job since. He's tried all over but there's nothing. Nobody is even sure nowadays if they'll still be in work at the end of the week. It's a bloomin' good job I'm working – otherwise we'd be in a right mess trying to make ends meet on the dole. I'm sick to death of making do. There's never enough money for everything, is there?'

Ruth nods in agreement despite her own firmly held opinion on the value of thrift. She could give Florrie a whole series of money-saving tips and ways to stretch a limited budget, but she doubts that the attempt would meet with much success. Ruth has identified Florrie as one of those people who lead their lives with no thought for tomorrow, they spend as fast as they get, the sort of people who are out enjoying themselves at the weekend and penniless by the following Friday. In short, the sort of people, like her parents, who end up in a rented house on Bird Street.

'Well,' Ruth says, 'maybe there'll be something for your husband when you get back. There are always a few workers who retire at Wakes Week.'

'Yes, isn't that funny? A gypsy told me today that I was going to come into some money. Maybe she was right! Me and Fred were walking up to the Tower when he spotted her tent and paid for me to go in and see her. We spent the rest of the day laughing – she said I was going to have another baby. Fred said, "Well, we'll give it a good try!" You should go and see her, Ruth. She's a right laugh.'

'I don't think there's anything funny about cheating decent working people out of their money with a load of rubbish. Thieves and liars the lot of them.'

Ruth's face is so red and her tone so sharp that Florrie is shocked into silence. If she didn't know better, she'd think that Ruth was on the verge of tears.

Blackburn, 1 May 1952

It is Wednesday morning and Ruth, seven and a half months pregnant, is on her hands and knees scrubbing the flags in the scullery. The day's work has barely started and she is already exhausted. The scullery floor is covered in soap suds that swirl the breadth of the stones and fill up the nicks between the flags. It doesn't matter how hot Ruth gets the water it still turns cold the minute it hits the flags. The Vim powder she is using scours her palms and the clefts between her fingers, leaving her cuticles red and swollen. Scrubbing completed she is about to swill down with clean water when there is a knock at the front door. Ruth sits back on her heels and rubs her knees before she even tries to get up. She rises at last and takes off her heavy, sodden pinny and replaces it with her light floral waist apron. As Ruth makes her way through the kitchen Helen stops playing with her doll and follows her mother to the front door. The family only sets foot in the front room at Christmas. If at any point in the intervening 363 days anyone should knock on the front door, Ruth is at pains to direct them to the backyard gate. In this way the square of green and gold carpet in the centre of the room remains unmarked by the passage of dirty footprints. Blinding sunlight floods the porch when Ruth opens the door. As a result it's a moment or two before she realises that her visitor is a gypsy. Ruth automatically backs away and says, 'No, thank you. Not today.'

'Bless you, missus,' the gypsy replies. 'That baby you're carrying is going to be a beautiful boy. A baby brother for your little girl.' When Ruth hesitates the gypsy smiles, aware that the tide has finally turned her way after a morning of slammed doors and casual abuse. 'And a right bonny boy he'll be.' The gypsy takes a step forward and adopts a pious look. 'And as God is my witness, your little boy comes with a Romany blessing.'

Ruth lets go of the door and unconsciously slides her hand over her bulging stomach. She waxes with pleasure at the prediction.

Meanwhile the gypsy drops the ribbons she had hoped to sell back in her basket and draws out a black-and-cream purse instead. 'Can I show you a purse, missus? It's finest snakeskin, handmade. Look, it has space for your loose change, a pocket for stamps and a wallet section for notes. Look at the quality of the fastenings.' The gypsy opens the purse and demonstrates the press stud and bright metal compartment clips. 'It'll last you a lifetime, missus, quality like this. You won't get anything like as good elsewhere. It's a one off. Handmade.'

But Ruth isn't listening. She is filled with a sense of triumph. All the weight, discomfort and nauseous agony of this pregnancy will be worth it in the end. She is carrying a son. Unwittingly she smiles, her hand open, ready to accept the purse the gypsy proffers.

The snakeskin shines and ripples softly under her thumb. It is a fold-over purse that opens with three press studs to reveal a concertina of pockets and flaps. The first pocket is for coins, a metal clip closes the second. There's a separate pocket at the front of the purse for bus tickets and receipts, and a clear plastic pocket with a card for the owner's name and address. There's even a zip at the back of the purse, which will easily hold her child allowance book. Ruth is impressed. The purse is exuberant, eye-catching and wildly extravagant. Ruth is sorely tempted. She draws her eyes away from the snakeskin and asks, 'How much?'

'Four and six,' risks the gypsy.

'Four and six! There'll be no money left to put in it!' Ruth tries unsuccessfully to hand the purse back to the gypsy.

'You can take it for four shillings with a gypsy blessing for you. Take my word for it. That purse will never be empty. You'll look at this purse in a few months' time when your baby is born and thank heavens you bought it. You're a lucky woman. Take it! Take it for four shillings.'

Ruth hands over the four shillings. When the gypsy has gone Ruth empties the contents of her old purse into the new. She props the shiny snakeskin purse on top of the sideboard and sighs with satisfaction. The rest of the day passes in a haze of pleasure. She wants to shout the news from the rooftop but, taking her example from the Virgin Mary, she determines to keep the secret in her heart and tells no one. Every time she runs her fingers over the purse in the coming weeks she smiles. She ceases to worry about the forthcoming labour. She is confident that, when the baby is born, she will have a son. To this end she desists from any heavy housework – the scullery floor will not see a scrubbing brush for the best part of two months, curtains will go unwashed, windows unpolished. The burden she is carrying is too precious to risk.

Like her namesake in the Bible she is carrying a son. In the Bible Ruth names her son Obed, and Obed himself has a son called Jesse. Neither of these names strikes Ruth Singleton as suitable – particularly Jesse, a word her father reserves for idiots and fools. Further reading of the Book of Ruth is required before the mother to be discovers that the unfortunate Jesse begat David – King David. The name resonates with her, sends a tingle up her spine. Her own David who will slay giants for her, who will love her as fiercely as Jack loves his mother. Everything falls into place.

Bank Hall Maternity Home takes a dim view of older mothers. They are less easy to deal with, they have opinions about labour and how it should progress, they have complications, their babies are more likely to be ill, they recover from labour slowly and they are more demanding. Ruth is no exception. When the day arrives she resists the midwife's suggestion that she take some gentle exercise when the labour is slow. Ruth will not move from the bed for fear of harming the baby. She rejects both food and drink. She refuses an enema and complains bitterly when one is administered against her will. As the labour passes from minutes into hours she is assaulted by the fear that her son will be born dead. Fear for his safety impels her to push away the gas and air the midwife offers when the contractions increase. Ruth lies back on the thin mattress, grits her teeth and waits for the arrival of her son.

The baby is born at dawn.

'Another little girl for you, Mrs Singleton. Worth all the effort, isn't she?' The midwife lays the baby in Ruth's arms.

For a moment mother and child are frozen in a shocked silence. The news is incomprehensible, beyond belief, impossible to understand. Ruth has knitted blue bootees, a blue bonnet, hand-stitched blue smocking on the front of the tiny nightdress and stuck a blue teddy transfer on the top of the toy box. She has even replaced the pink duck on the corner of Helen's old cot blanket with a big blue rabbit.

'A girl? Are you sure? I was told it would be a boy. That's what I was expecting. A boy. It's a boy, isn't it? It has to be. That's what I was promised.'

The midwife pulls the cot blanket aside and shows Ruth the baby's sex. A wave of darkness sweeps over Ruth as she struggles to lay claim to a daughter she does not want. She searches the tiny face for some feature that might identify the baby as hers, something that might stem the breach that has arisen between them. The baby drags stiff fingers over pale cheeks and closes her eyes, resolutely shutting out the sight of her weeping mother.

'We'll get the baby checked over by the doctor,' says the midwife, assuming Ruth is distressed by the blueness of the baby's skin. 'Let me take her for a moment.'

The baby is hastily removed to a table under the window where she is held upside down and slapped on the back. The manoeuvre is repeated until there is a weak cry. The midwife loosens her grip on the baby's ankles and weighs her before passing the bundle to the doctor. Another cry, louder this time. The new mother barely hears the disturbance. She is numb with shock. Later she watches in despair as the baby struggles to suckle at her breast. At the earliest opportunity Ruth hands the baby back to the midwife and, pleading exhaustion, turns away.

Jack is unable to come at visiting time. He is on late shift and can't see the new baby until the following afternoon. Ruth is furious. She demands to know why he hasn't phoned the hospital to enquire about the baby. In a doomed attempt to lighten her mood with a little humour, he counters that there wasn't much point. He knew it would be another girl. He shakes his head and smiles at his new daughter. Ruth spends the rest of Jack's visit in stony silence, her arms folded across her aching breasts.

Ruth is moved to a side room on the ward when it is obvious that she will not stop crying. The ward sister speaks to her firmly. 'Now, Mrs Singleton, you must stop all this weeping and wailing. You're disturbing the other mothers and I won't have it. You've got a perfectly healthy baby and you're behaving as if the world has come to an end. Pull yourself together or you'll be sent home.'

Ruth is unrepentant. She is sent home the following day.

The baby, Beth, rarely cries. She requires so little, is barely owned by life. She is silent, deeply enclosed between the high sides of the kitchen drawer that now serves as a cot.

11

THE SEASIDE AT NIGHT

You might not think there's a lot to spy at night, but you're wrong! All kinds of things happen at the seaside at night. If you look you might see flashing lights. The light may be a revolving beam from a lightship anchored out at sea, or a flashing light from a lighthouse, or it may even be one of the pretty coloured lights on the promenade. What did you spot? Score 40 points for an exciting night out.

Jack and Ruth head back to their room after the evening meal, leaving their daughters in the television lounge glued to *The Six Five Special.* Pete Murray has grabbed the microphone. 'Here's something to get you cats jumping. It's Cliff with a cool new number. Take it away, Cliff, and let's get with the gas!'

Ruth would normally stay and keep her eye on the girls, but she is aware that she very nearly made a fool of herself in the dining room. Mention of gypsies always has the same effect. If she'd sat with Florrie any longer the whole miserable story would have come out. There is, though, a second reason for her accompanying Jack upstairs. She has been married to Jack long enough to know that he's up to something. She has caught sight of the letter a couple of times – the one that Jack has been keeping hidden. It's pointless asking him what it is because she knows he'll deny all knowledge and hide it so effectively that it'll never surface again. Ruth believed initially that it was a redundancy notice, but that idea has been dismissed since they came to Blackpool. Unlike the Cleggs, Jack wouldn't dream of forking out for a holiday if he'd no job to go back to. And anyway Jack is always positive about the prospects at Fosters. Surely the company must be doing even better since rival firms started shutting.

Ruth has caught a glimpse of the heavily creased envelope – it is an odd yellowy white. Business letters are invariably brown, like wage packets. A white envelope means it's likely to be a personal letter. It didn't come in the post to the house – Ruth picks up the post every day without fail – so it must have been handed to Jack. Who would be handing him letters at work? It is a puzzle that has been exercising Ruth since the start of the holiday and the opportunity to go through Jack's pockets is too good to miss. Jack takes off his jacket and heads off down the corridor to the bathroom. The minute the door closes behind him Ruth darts over to his discarded jacket and starts going through all the pockets. Nothing. She'd have bet a pound to a penny the letter was in his inside pocket at tea. She was sure of it. He must have switched it to his trousers when he was following her up the stairs to their room. Frustrated, Ruth bangs herself down on the bed and glares at the door, waiting for Jack to return.

When he knocks to be let in she opens the door and walks to the other side of the bed, her arms folded across her chest. 'I don't know why you're rushing out tonight,' she offers as an opening salvo. 'Where are you going, anyway?'

'I said I'd meet Tom Bell at Yates's.'

'Why?'

'Because he arranged it last Friday, before I left work. I didn't see any harm. I'll only be a couple of hours.'

Ruth tolerates Jack having the odd pint for one reason only. Jack doesn't drink like her father drinks. Jack doesn't come home after a night in the pub swearing his head off and throwing punches right, left and centre. Ruth's father, like Noah, has been 'drunken and uncovered in his tent' more than once. Ruth's dad has a familiarity with the contents of the Prayer Book, which only emerges when he's had one over the eight. He will quote freely from the Bible. 'Thou shalt drink of thy sister's cup which is deep and large' – this delivered in terms of an order while negotiating the back step. And 'I have digged and drunk strange waters' (Isaiah 36: 25) – this when he tripped and fell head first into the stone sink. There's no point in Ruth campaigning to go out with Jack, even supposing he ever asked her. Ruth can't stomach alcohol. Jack says he goes for the company as much as the beer. But Ruth is inevitably left wondering what's wrong with her company.

When Jack picks up his jacket from the bed Ruth says, 'Just a minute, I want to have a word with you. Are you sure there isn't something you need to tell me about?'

'Not now, Ruth. I haven't time for games. I'm going to be late.'

'Tom Bell is fully capable of keeping himself amused for a couple of minutes. You've had a letter, haven't you?'

Jack notes the look on Ruth's face. She's obviously spotted Eleni's letter and she's spoiling for a fight. Jack's head whirls with the effort of forming an acceptable reply. 'Yes, you're right. I've heard that it's likely the Union is going to offer me something. I didn't want to tell you until I was sure.'

This neat diversion has the desired effect. Ruth flushes with excitement and helps him on with his jacket. 'How much?'

'How much what?'

'Money, of course. It'll mean an increase, won't it?' Ruth gasps with pleasure. 'You'll be on a *salary*!'

'I'd bloomin' well hope so. Anyway, I don't want you to be disappointed – my information may be wrong. Let's see what they have to offer first.'

Jack can hear his heart thumping in his ears as he makes his way out of the hotel. He is aware that he's only escaped by the skin of his teeth. For some reason this makes the letter even more precious. His fingers run over the envelope where Eleni has stuck the stamps. The burden of his other family is made sweeter by the secrecy.

Out in the fresh air of the prom and safe from Ruth's questions, Jack slows his walk and admires the view. It is coming up to high tide and the sea defences cup a full, smooth curve of rising water. It's a clear night. A slight breeze sways the line of coloured lights strung between the lamp-posts. Beyond the promenade the sea is calm, beneath a serene sky. It's a fair walk down to Yates's. Plenty of time for Jack to think over the coming meeting. The Union offered him the job of area rep last month, a couple of days after Fosters offered him the post of manager of Prospect Mill. Only a fool would imagine it was a coincidence. Tom Bell will be expecting an answer from him this evening. Ten years ago he'd have stuck with the Union, come hell or high water. But things have changed. Cotton is under threat from all sides – if it's not the government trying to shut the mills, it's the market flooded with cheap foreign imports. As usual it's all down to the mill owners. If they can't be persuaded to invest in Lancashire cotton, they'll invest somewhere else and then where will the industry be?

Jack is a fervent believer in cotton. There are no qualities displayed by satin, silk, velvet or any one of the half-dozen other materials available that are a patch on cotton. Get the correct weave and weight (knowledge Jack acquired at evening classes at the Institute of Cotton Manufacturers in Manchester) and you can produce anything from the finest wedding lace to weather-proof canvas sails that will resist the worst Atlantic storms. Cotton is the only material known to man that will absorb twenty-four times its own weight in fluid and withstand 280 degrees of heat. The Lancashire cotton industry has supplied the world with everything from nappies to shrouds and all points in between. From cotton towels, blankets, tea towels, tablecloths, curtains and twill sheets to shoe linings, stockings, socks, skirts, trousers, overalls, pyjamas, underwear, blouses, shirts and hats. In the hands of Lancashire manufacturers cotton has been transformed into a giddy selection of brocades, crêpes, muslins and georgettes, woven into everything from coarse monk's cloth to delicate cloqué. There is no wastage with cotton as even the most inferior fibre can be used for shoddy and crash. The fabric is a source of endless fascination to Jack. He carries the memory of the different weaves imprinted on his fingertips. There are fabric samples in his pockets and blueprints for new designs in his head. There isn't a weave he can't recognise on sight.

Ruth watches Jack walk out of the hotel and turn left along the prom from the bedroom window. The sense of relief that floods through her makes her dizzy. The letter is nothing more than a note – it'll be to do with this Union job. The prospect of a semi has drawn immeasurably closer with the news. Jack will finally be earning enough to cover the increase in running a bigger house. Why, within a couple of hours she may finally have got Jack to agree to buying a new semi on Boundary Drive! The prospect is so exciting that it makes her restless. Ruth opens her magazine with a new enthusiasm. Before her lies the prospect of actually owning goods that previously she has only been able to dream about. She studies the adverts closely. Addis has brought out a new range of coloured plastic brushes, pails, flip-top bins and kitchen tidies, which divert her attention for a couple of minutes. She wouldn't buy red of course, but yellow would be a refreshing change.

Sandwiched between the problem page and this month's horoscopes, Ruth comes across an article by a Mrs D. D. Heatherington-Taylor. It's a piece about stay-at-home mothers. Ruth's interest is sparked. It's not two minutes since the government was bending over backwards to keep wives at home. That way the returning soldiers could pick up where they left off at their old jobs. Everywhere you looked there were posters saying thanks very much for your war work, but now it's time to return to the kitchen sink and bring up the first post-war generation. Ruth didn't need telling – that's precisely what she wanted to do. Now she reads an article, in *Good Housekeeping* of all places (they should be ashamed of themselves), recommending that wives desert domesticity in pursuit of personal achievement outside the home. It's outrageous. It's nonsensical. Ruth doesn't see herself as an individual. How could she be when she's bringing up two daughters? If she's doing it properly there isn't time to be an individual – when she's not the children's mum, she's Jack's wife. What decent mother has time to be an individual? But Mrs D. D. Heatherington-Taylor is adamant. She writes, 'Modern mothers who make no plan outside the family for their future will not only play havoc with their own lives, but will make nervous wrecks of their over-protected children and husbands.'

Ruth violently disagrees and is about to throw the magazine aside in disgust when there's a frantic knocking on the door. It's Helen. The girl is flushed with excitement and the effort of racing up six flights of stairs.

'What's the matter?'

'There's a phone call for you! The manager's wife told me to tell you. You can take it in the booth in the lobby.'

Mother and daughter hurry downstairs. Ruth picks up the phone with one hand and waves an inquisitive Helen away with the other. 'Hello?'

'Hello, Ruth. It's Cora.'

'Cora!'

'Can you come over, Ruth?'

'What? Now? Are you all right?'

'Well, yes, I suppose so. But I need to see you.'

'Why? What's happened? You were right enough this afternoon. What's gone wrong?'

'I can't really say. It's difficult over the phone.'

'Well, why don't you come over here? Jack's out with his Union pal. You could get a taxi.'

'Oh, I couldn't do that.'

'Why not?'

'He doesn't like me going out. Certainly not at night. If I want to go out I have to agree it with him in advance.'

'But you're not doing anything dangerous – you'd be nipping out to see me. We were friends long before you even knew Ronald.'

'It's no good. I can't ask him. He's downstairs in the bar with his golfing friends. He'll be furious if I interrupt.' Cora hears Ruth's impatient sigh over the phone and adds, 'It's not just golf they talk about, you know. It's business as well. Oh, can't you come over here instead? Helen won't mind babysitting, will she?'

Ruth hesitates but at last she says, 'No, Cora. I can't leave the girls. Not with Jack being out as well. I'm not keen to leave Elizabeth – she's barely out of hospital.'

'Of course. I didn't think. Well, why don't you and Jack come over to the Links on Friday?'

'If you want to talk I'd be better coming by myself.'

'No, don't do that. Ronnie will think I'm talking about him behind his back.'

'He's a big lad. He'll cope, I'm sure.'

'Promise you'll come over on Friday, Ruth. I really want to see you, and Jack of course. Both of you.'

Ruth considers all the good news she might have to tell Cora if Jack is offered the Union job. It could be a real celebration. 'All right then,' she replies. 'We'll see you at three on Friday.'

'Thanks, Ruth. I'm really . . . Oh, God, he's coming back. I have to go. 'Bye.'

And she is gone. Ruth can't settle after the phone call. Cora sounded upset, almost frightened, when she said Ronnie had come back. Ruth suspects that Cora's husband, for all his apparent generosity, is really a bully. Ruth is uneasy, worried about Cora. She wanders around the hotel room looking for things to do. At last she sits down and starts writing the postcards she's been carrying around in her bag for the past three days. At this rate she's going to be on her way back before they're posted.

Yates's wine lodge is a popular venue for Blackpool fun seekers. A wide Victorian portico welcomes customers into luxurious surroundings where they can sample the delights of its cellar. It's only eight o'clock but the place is already packed with evening drinkers jockeying for position at the highly polished brass and mahogany bar. The fine stucco ceiling complete with cherubs toasting each other's health is rendered virtually invisible by a pall of tobacco smoke. The floor is awash with spilled drinks. Drinkers in their 'kiss-me-quick' hats, drape jackets and winkle-picker shoes are engaged in a nightly attempt to drink Blackpool dry. There's a noticeable spreading of masculine chests and an exchange of friendly blows among the single men as the women look on, bright in their polka-dot dresses, their gathered skirts rising to reveal layer after layer of nylon net and the occasional stocking top. Yates's isn't licensed for dancing but this matters little to the revellers. Chairs are pulled back in a surge of excitement when the jukebox is switched on and couples rock to and fro in sweaty congress on the makeshift dance floor. Bra straps fail and suspenders snap under eager male embraces, but the dance continues regardless. There's some muttering from the older drinkers, but some bright spark has located the volume switch on the jukebox and Lonnie Donegan's 'Rock Island Line' effectively drowns out all opposition. All in all it promises to be a lively night.

Jack spots Tom at a table in the corner, a half-finished pint in front of him, and signals across to see if he wants another. Tom nods in agreement and Jack makes his way to the bar. He's not been there for more than a couple of minutes when a woman taps him on the shoulder and says, 'Here, let me. I'll get served faster.' He turns and sees that it's the waitress from the hotel – Helen's friend. He is still struggling to remember her name when she pulls the pound note from his fingers and whistles to the barman.

'It's all right,' Jack says. 'There's no hurry. I'm only after a couple of pints.'

But Connie has her back to him and is already pushing her way to the head of the queue. The barman, who hitherto has studiedly ignored Jack in the general crush, fetches up in front of Connie's cleavage the minute she leans over the bar. It's like watching one of Leonora's Dancing Dogs at the Tower Circus. Jack, embarrassed at the idea of a woman getting his drinks, looks around, anxious not to be spotted. Connie is wearing a black top and scarlet skirt that accentuates her curves, and her auburn hair spreads loosely over creamy white shoulders that sparkle with gold freckles. Jack has no idea how old she is, but she looks at least twenty.

'You'd better take one for yourself out of it,' Jack says as an afterthought.

'Thanks,' she says, flashing him a brilliant smile.

They both retreat from the bar with their drinks and stand at the edge of the crush. Jack, deliberately ignoring Connie's cleavage, is at a loss to know what to say. Happily Connie knows exactly what she wants. 'Have you seen Doug tonight?'

'Doug?'

'About my age. Brown hair, leather jacket. Beth says you work with him.'

'Oh, you mean Doug Fairbrother.'

'That's him.'

'No, I haven't,' Jack says. 'Who did you come with?'

'No one. The lads from the hotel are all over at the Laughing Donkey.'

'I should get over there if I were you. It's a bit of a rough shop, this. For a girl on her own, I mean.'

'Oh, I'll give it a bit longer I think.'

'Well, I hope Doug turns up. Anyway I'll keep an eye open for you. I'll be over there.' Jack points to the table in the corner where Tom Bell is looking increasingly impatient for his pint.

Unknown to both of them the youth in question has already poked his head round the bar door and, seeing Jack Singleton in conversation with Connie, has given up hope of bumping into Helen and beaten a hasty retreat.

Jack threads his way through the crowd to Tom's table and puts down both pints with a sigh.

'Reckoned I'd lost you there for a moment,' Tom says.

'What?'

'I reckoned you'd be happier spending the evening with the redhead.'

'Give over, she's a friend of Helen's.'

'Aye, well, you'll find they're the worst,' Tom remarks with a wink.

'Are we drinking or just gassing?'

'A bit of both. Cheers, Jack.'

Tom has been fitted with a new pair of dentures. He still had his own gnashers before the war, but the Italian campaign put the kibosh on his teeth along with his chest. False teeth were the only option after he was demobbed. The bottom set of National Health teeth are so loose they require some clever tongue and lip manoeuvring to keep them in place. Tom's conversation is interrupted on a regular basis by discreet attempts to wedge the bottom plate more securely into his jaw. Pronunciation of the letter 'l' is fraught with danger and his 's's whistle like the wind in the fireback on a winter's night. It would be easier to give up the fight and manage without dentures, but Tom still retains a shred of vanity. Despite being well over fifty he can nevertheless make women blush with pleasure. He makes out it's a terrible burden, this ability to charm the women. Blames it on the Union – having to talk to all those women weavers late at night. It never fails to make Jack laugh.

They sup the best part of their pints talking of this and that. Tom asks after Ruth, wants to know how Beth is after the operation and whether Helen is going to stay on at school. Jack admires Tom; even when they disagree over tactics the old man still manages to retain Jack's respect. Tom has been area rep for the Union since before the war. He is absolutely committed to the Union and members' rights. Jack has seen him speak for upwards of an hour, take questions from the floor, deal with the barracking from the hotheads and then pack up and move on to the next mill – and the next set of angry workers and obstinate management. They met when Jack heard him speak at the WEA on the future of the Socialist movement. Tom gave him a book by Marx, told him to read it and then tell him the Labour Party was Socialist in the true sense of the word. 'They're a bunch of phoneys, Jack,' Tom had said at the time. 'They wouldn't know Socialism if it got up and bit them on the arse.'

Since that time Jack has read every book that Tom has suggested. Today is no exception. He's not been sat down two minutes when Tom says, 'Here, Jack, take a look at this.'

Jack turns the book over and reads the title: *The Uses of Literacy* by Richard Hoggart. 'Never heard of him.'

'Me neither, but he's a good read. Better than Orwell at any rate. It knocked me sick to read him ranting on about "working-class decency". You'll not see a lot of that when there's no wage coming in. Hoggart is a sight less sentimental.'

'So what does this bloke think is wrong with society?'

'Consumerism, that's what. You've only to look in any shop window to see that there's a spending boom going on. Hoggart has a profound contempt for all this constant greed for material goods. He thinks we need to get back to real values instead of forever pushing for the latest fad. Everyone wants to fill their houses with white goods nowadays. And that bugger Macmillan' – Tom points to the picture of the Prime Minister on the front of his copy of the *Daily Herald* – 'is cheering them on. He's just shooting his mouth off again. He says we've never had it so good – it says here that two out of every three families own a television. Just because these politicians can point to some parts of British industry that are doing well, they think they can forget about cotton. I mean, what's the point of announcing all this expansion in the building industry? They're only building fancy new houses for people who've got the wage to buy them. There's thousands of weavers in Lancashire with no hope of paying the next week's rent, let alone collecting the money to put down on a house of their own.'

Jack stares at his pint, Ruth's demands still ringing in his ears. 'This new Cotton Act is going to shake things up a bit,' he says, keen to change the subject.

'Aye. Government has finally come up with an idea how to solve the cotton problem. It's easy. Just get rid of it, shut the mills. We've lost just short of 20,000 looms in the last twelve months – at this rate there'll be no industry left in seven years. And in case there are any buggers left who actually want to carry on weaving they'll be finished off anyway with all the foreign competition. They're calling it "modernisation of the industry" when it's nothing better than "Scrap and Shut".'

'But how can it be "Scrap and Shut" when there's going to be grants for modernisation?'

'Modernisation? What good is that when they're planning to lose 100,000 looms? These new Northrop looms mean that one weaver can run twenty-four looms instead of six on the old system. And there's none of the stoppage problems. Same amount of material, less than half the workforce. Where's the point in losing all that skilled labour? They've been going on about paying mill owners compensation for the loss of the old machines. Doesn't occur to them to pay weavers any compensation for losing their jobs, does it? If the government can afford to pay the owners compensation, why the hell can't they fork out for the weavers who've been running the looms all their working lives? They're still arguing that redundancy is the owners' problem, not theirs. Parliament won't touch any move to make redundancy payments compulsory. There's too many big hitters in the House who've made their money from paying workers a pittance.'

'I heard that the Union signed an agreement with the industry last week to pay some of the workers compensation.'

'They had to – the government has stipulated that none of the payouts to the employers can be used towards redundancy,' Tom replies. 'It sounds a decent deal, but if you look at the small print and get-out clauses you can reckon that less than half the workers are going to get anything. No, all the real money is to go on new Northrop Automatic machines. Anyway, I've not come here to argue the toss over modernisation. I've come to see if you've made up your mind yet whether or not to take over my job when I move down to Head Office in London.'

'There's no easy answer, Tom. It's not as simple as it looks.'

'Why not? This is a real opportunity, Jack. A chance to make a difference – not just at Fosters but in Union policy in general. More money than you're getting at the moment, travel expenses that'll cover the cost of a car. It'll suit you down to the ground – lots of travelling and not having to see the same old faces every day. You know how long we've been pushing for improvements? Bloody years. And nothing's happened – and nothing will until we get a few more like you working at higher Union level, making their voices heard.'

'I don't know about that, Tom. I spent last Wednesday night at the local meeting listening to the usual backbiting, arguing and time wasting. These meetings go on for hours and finish with meaningless resolutions that pander to every view and satisfy no one.'

'But you're talking about local level. You get a totally different perspective at area level. It's a different ball game altogether – there's none of this shop floor tussling.'

'Aye, you're right. They're well away from the shop floor. They're busy making decisions for a workforce they no longer recognise and barely understand.'

'I can't believe I'm hearing this from you, Jack. What's happened to workers' rights? You need national policy to secure them – national policy steered by area input. We'll survive this dip. We need to resist the closures. Strike if need be.'

'Striking is no good! How strong is the Union with half its members on the dole? No, Tom. The Union will do what it has always done. It'll bleat a bit and then it'll announce that it's going to protect all the jobs that are left. Management closed Portsmouth Mill with twenty-four hours' notice. The Union hadn't even got out of bed.'

'So you're selling out, are you, Jack? You're going to take up Fosters' offer. Manager of Prospect Mill and bugger the rest.'

Jack glares at Tom, resisting the urge to get up and walk out. 'No. I'm not saying bugger the rest. I haven't made my mind up yet. I just sometimes wonder if management have a better chance of turning the industry round than the Union.'

'God help us! Going to be the first mill manager with a social conscience, are you?'

Jack ignores the crack. 'I didn't say that. The truth is that without new markets there's no industry. And without modernisation there's no future for the industry. It's as simple as that. We need to get the owners to start investing in the search for new fabrics. We can import cotton cheaper than we can make it. We need to look to the future. That's what the Union should be doing, instead of harping on about the past. Anybody can see that if the market takes off following this modernisation the workforce will be able to call the shots, return on their terms, redundancy payments and minimum wage included.'

'You can invent new fabrics till kingdom come. You won't better Lancashire cotton.'

'Fosters are going to take a leaf out of ICI's book. They're going to start experimenting with new types of material.'

'How can you say that when it's bloody nylon that's caused half the problem in the first place? Fosters offering you a bonus for every weaver you get shut of? I suppose they think workers will take the sack better from you.'

There's an angry silence broken at last by Tom, who gets to his feet and says, 'It's getting crowded in here. I think I'll have a walk over to the Albion. It's bound to be a bit quieter there. Are you comin'?'

'No, Tom. I'll leave it. I should be getting back. Ruth's waiting.'

Looking up, he sees the ill-disguised contempt on Tom's face and struggles to defuse it. 'Anybody would think she's got me on a string,' Jack says with a self-deprecating smile.

'A bloody ball and chain more like,' Tom snaps as he's walking away.

The idea that he is tied hand and foot to Ruth offends Jack's dignity. He reaches forward and snatches up his pint, leans back in his seat and glares at Tom's retreating back.

Jack finishes the rest of his pint in a single swallow and is reaching for his jacket when Connie appears. 'You're not going, are you? I've just got a couple of drinks. I can't drink both, can I? Come on, I owe you one.'

Jack looks doubtful. But it's still early and won't do any harm to stay a bit longer. At least that way there's no chance he'll bump into Tom on the way back. Connie sees Jack hesitate and promptly sits down. 'I'm surprised you've nothing better to do. What happened to your date?'

'Stood me up, didn't he?'

'Well, there's plenty more fish.'

'I know and I think I just might have spotted one.' Connie relaxes back in her chair and gives him a calculated smile. 'Anyway, who was that you were talking to?'

'Oh, he's a bloke I know from work.'

'He left in quite a temper, didn't he? I'd better watch my step with you. I'm a bit on the timid side, you know.'

She gives Jack a look that makes a nonsense of her words and Jack laughs despite himself. 'You're all right, I won't bite. It's Connie, isn't it? How long have you been working at the Belvedere?'

Connie adopts an expression of world weariness and says, 'Too long. I'll stop here for the season, then I'll be moving on again. It's like something out of the Cartoon Capers in that kitchen.'

'What do you mean?'

'Everyone is terrified of the chef. You should see the waiters jump when he shouts. He puts the fear of God into the kitchen porters when he doesn't think they're moving fast enough. You should hear him curse! They say he's handy with his fists, but I've never seen it. I've never had any trouble with him.'

Jack listens while Connie gives him a full account of life behind the scenes at the Belvedere. She is an entertaining talker with a sharp sense of humour. Jack starts to relax. It's not as if he's doing anything wrong. He picks up their empty glasses and buys another round. The evening passes quickly until they call last orders. 'This'll have to be your last,' Jack says. 'You should be getting back, Connie. You've got work in the morning.'

It has turned rowdy outside when they leave. Jack puts out a guiding hand, barely touching the small of her back, and directs her across the road. They stop when Connie decides to demonstrate that she can still walk a straight line. The fat metal tramlines shine silver in the moonlight as she places one foot in front of the other with painstaking precision. An oncoming tram disrupts the demonstration and the couple retreat to the promenade where knots of stragglers make their beery way back to their hotels and tipsy couples share fish and chips in the darkness of the shelters. The wind has an edge to it. Jack removes his jacket and places it over Connie's bare shoulders. She catches hold of his hand and hangs on to it as they walk. It is only reasonable that he should see her safely back to the hotel. But Connie is in no hurry to return. She slows her walk until she comes to a full stop, pulls Jack's jacket closer and stares at the strings of fairy lights that trace the curve of the promenade down to Central Pier. In the far distance they can see the flashing white lights of the Big Wheel that turn and turn in the pitch-black sky, and below them they can hear the slow slap of the tide against the sea wall.

Connie is not allowed to use the hotel's main entrance. Staff quarters are round the back and cloaked in darkness ever since the floodlight gave up. Connie takes Jack's hand and navigates her way around the collection of dustbins and broken chairs that litter the backyard. It will, Jack reasons, only take a minute to see her safely to her room. Once there, Jack watches as she trawls through her handbag. She hands him the key and he opens the door on to a modest room lit by a forty-watt bulb. The room is bare of furniture save for a wardrobe and a single chest of drawers. Over the washbasin there's a cracked mirror screwed to the wall. Connie moves over the threshold and, turning, puts both arms round Jack's neck. Sensing his reluctance, she moves closer, running her hand under his jacket and over the small of his back.

Despite the surprise Jack is flattered, amused even. He takes her by the shoulders, intending to push her gently away. But the luminescent softness of her arms and the scent that rises from her skin fills his senses. He breathes an audible sigh when she kisses him. He bends and kisses her back with a fierce intensity that leaves them both breathless. He bends still further, strokes away the ringlets of hair that cover her right shoulder, buries his face in the warm curve of her neck. She responds immediately, her body tense, tight with excitement. Arching backwards, she draws him into the room, smiles as she locks the door.

A radio is playing next door, an old Dean Martin song that Jack half recognises from before the war. The effortless sway of the melody curls around the room, lazy with the sound of saxophones and rich with an underpinning of muted drumming. The curtains are open to the distant neon light of a backstreet peep show ('Makes Old Men Young!'). Jack is beyond thought. In the presence of this woman he is lost to himself. It is so easy to slip the dress from her shoulders. The zip slides away down to the curve of her back with a sound like a skate over thin ice. The music has changed. Bobby Darin is singing 'Beyond the Sea' and Jack is kissing her now as if his life depended upon it; as if he is twenty again and back in Crete; as if it is Eleni lying in his arms in the green shelter of grass and, above their heads, a tracery of boughs hang heavy with the sharp perfume of orange blossom.

Jack explores the body beneath him. She is all curves, moist to the touch of his fingers, open to the movement of his hand. When she rolls on top of him he is conscious of the glorious weight of her breasts against his skin, the hard press of her nipples. The sheets rumple beneath them as their hands move, pulling aside satin and cotton, careless of the temporary restraint of buttons. The pillow lies discarded on the floor along with remnants of clothing and shoes. The narrow room is filled to the brim, bursting with pleasure. Jack's hands are broad and warm across her stomach. His fingers measure the length of her inner thigh, elicit a shudder of pleasure that registers in her backbone so sharply that she pulls away. But in the next moment she presses herself against him again, greedy for the rough tangle of hairs that cover his chest and belly, the urgent rasp of his chin against her cheek, the rub of his fingers, the salt taste of his skin. He pushes her hand down the length of his belly, urging her on until she takes him within the circle of her hand and, rolling over, guides him inside her. For a moment he appears paralysed with the rush of sensation, afraid that he will come too soon. And then he is moving. Connie arching towards him when he enters her, her mouth wide with the shock of pleasure. When he moves against her she tilts, her legs wrapped smoothly round his hips. He rises above her, his hands covering her breasts. Connie draws him in closer and closer still until, in the final union, they occupy a single space, a single exultant moment. The sound rises from the bed and echoes joyfully around the walls before dissolving into the surrounding darkness. 'Eleni,' he whispers into the perfumed mass of her hair.

'Connie,' she says. 'I'm Connie.'

12

BRITTLE-STAR

Brittle-stars look like starfish. They have five thin arms which readily break off if they are grabbed by a predator. The miracle is that the brittle-star doesn't die when it is badly injured – it forms a scar and will grow another arm to replace the one it has lost. So the brittle-star isn't brittle at all! Score 30 points for a miraculous recovery.

Ward 4, Liverpool Children's Hospital, 16 April 1959

Ruth is encouraged to accompany her daughter into the operating theatre. The surgeon explains that there are certain procedures (the insertion of a tube, nothing more) that have to be undertaken while her daughter is still awake. Prior to anaesthesia, that is. It is likely the child will be a little uncomfortable. The presence of her mother in these circumstances will reassure the child. The prospect provokes panic in Ruth. Providing reassurance to the child is a task best left to others. Ruth is keenly aware that the surgeon hasn't stopped for a moment to consider how distressing it might be for her to witness her daughter on an operating table. The surgeon listens carefully as Ruth outlines the difficulties that the bus timetable imposes, the overwhelming demands of family and, finally, the imminence of an unexpected but vital dental appointment. The subject is dropped. The surgeon is a man of few words. He steeples his fingers when he speaks of heart surgery techniques perfected on the battlefield. Three or four hours at most. A fifty/fifty chance of success. They must hope for the best.

It is dark when the nurse wakes Beth. The child smiles, thinking that she is at home in the attic bedroom, believing that the figure leaning over her is Helen, come to say 'night-night'. But it's not Helen. It is a nurse she hasn't seen before.

A man lifts Beth on to a steel trolley and buckles the leather restraining straps over her chest and knees with practised ease. 'Don't struggle,' he says. 'We're going to take you on a ride. It'll be fun!'

Beth turns her head and watches as the nurse riffles through the bedside locker belonging to the boy in the next bed. 'There's no need to be afraid. Nobody is going to hurt you,' the nurse says. 'Have you got a book?'

'Yes,' replies Beth. 'I've got *Sleeping Beauty*.' She tries to point to her locker but the leather straps are too tight to allow her to move her arms.

The nurse darts over to the ward toy box and grabs the nearest book: *The Big Book of Adventure Stories*. 'This will have to do,' she says.

Beth is now fully awake and wide-eyed with anxiety.

'You're not afraid, are you? You're a brave girl.'

'I don't want the straps. I can't breathe.'

'They're there to keep you safe. If you keep still and quiet I'll take them off the minute we get to theatre,' the nurse says.

They enter the lift. The steel doors close and the nurse and porter wait in silence while Beth struggles to stay quiet, swallowing back her fear, gasping for her next breath. The lift goes down, the steel doors open.

'Now,' the man says, 'we're going through the tunnel. It's exciting, isn't it?'

The nurse agrees enthusiastically.

'Heart, is it?' the man asks in an undertone. Beth watches as the nurse nods her head and puts her finger over her lips. 'Oh, well, you'll fall asleep and it'll all be over in a jiffy. You won't feel a thing. Do you want to go fast? My trolley is the fastest in the whole hospital. I can make it race. Hang on!'

There is a blast of cold night air and then they're in a tunnel. There are lights in metal cages set into the ceiling. Beth is forced to close her eyes against the glare. But the lights still register behind her eyelids, flashing by faster and faster. At the end of the tunnel they emerge into a rat-run of dark corridors swinging this way and that until they reach another set of double doors. Once through the doors, Beth is immediately blinded by light and surrounded by figures swathed in green. If these are people they are devoid of any recognisable features. They have no hair or mouths or noses, only eyes – unfamiliar eyes that peer out from the narrow slit between green hat and white mask. Eyes that frown and wrinkle while disembodied hands strip away her nightie and retighten the straps.

Above her, huge white lights angle and turn. Beth can feel their heat across her skin. Silent eyes that watch, eyes that flick towards her and then away. Other figures flit in and out of sight in a blur of movement. Beth clenches her teeth against the rattle of instrument trolleys and the clash of metal bowls. Her ears are assaulted by a cacophony of strange, unfamiliar noises: the thud of black rubber tubes, the urgent hiss of taps, the tapping of dials, the tearing of packages, gas tanks shaped like bombs on wheels that squeak, squeak, squeak. The background murmuring stills to a whisper. Everything stops, as if awaiting a signal.

A face bends close to her. 'Hello, Elizabeth. There's no need to be frightened. We just have to do one or two little things before we put you to sleep. Just a couple of little nicks. The nurse is going to read to you. Oh good, it's an adventure book. We're all going to be very quiet and listen.'

The nurse begins to read as the surgeon engineers the first cut in his patient's ankle and moves on, heedless of the answering scream. Within seconds the nurse's voice begins to rise and rise until she is shouting in order to be heard over the patient's sobs. The child is hysterical with fear and pain. She is wild, fighting against the hold of the leather straps, tears coursing down her cheeks, stinging against the corners of her open mouth. The surgeon is a compassionate man. He is familiar with the sound and appearance of pain. Still, the child's screams are piteous and the straps are not wide enough to ensure she is perfectly still. Words are exchanged. The straps are unbuckled and three sets of hands continue the job of restraint. Beth's legs are held rigid, soothing words are uttered but still the child fights and screams. The nurse at her head raises her voice, bringing the book up to Beth's face. 'See,' she offers. 'Look at the picture!'

A man dressed in a beige shirt and shorts, long grey socks and a pith helmet is walking through the jungle. A tiger, half emerged from undergrowth, springs on the explorer's back. The animal has already clawed open the explorer's shoulder blade and the force of its attack has caused the man to drop his shotgun. The tiger's eyes burn bright red, his jaws open to reveal a set of vicious fangs. In the background three native bearers in bracelets and feathers throw down their loads and, arms waving, run for their lives. It is an action-packed picture that promises the sort of thrilling distraction sadly absent from the lives of most six-year-olds. But Beth cannot be distracted. She has no interest in the man's survival. At a sign from the surgeon, the nurse abandons the adventure book. She places her arm across Beth's chest to prevent the child from rearing up while her other hand strokes a cotton towel across the patient's face. Beth's nose streams; her cheeks run with sweat and tears, her mouth open like a wound.

Thursday 14 July 1959

It is past midnight when Beth wakes from her nightmare. She wriggles beneath the weight of the eiderdown and turns over. It is slightly less painful if she lies on her right side, the scar is on the other side of her chest. In the next bed Beth can just make out the comforting shape of her sister. Responsibility for Beth's present sleepless state lies firmly at the door of the Palace of Strange Girls, in particular with the Tiger Woman ('See her Scars! Hear her Snarl!!'). Beth has been able to think of little else since yesterday afternoon. Inspired by the Tiger Woman, she has spent hours playing shadow tigers on the bedroom wall with the help of the pink bedside lamp. Beth is not allowed to touch the lamp itself in case she breaks it or electrocutes herself, but nothing has been said about the on/off switch. After an hour spent practising the crouch and low crawl, Beth is convinced that she would make a good Tiger Woman. But she will need to grow her nails.

Beth has come out of hospital with several things she didn't take in. A propensity for nightmares, a knack of sleepwalking and a habit of biting her nails. This last trait is obviously the most serious since it impinges upon outward appearance. Ruth has attempted to dissuade Beth from this nasty, unhygienic habit by painting her nails with green aloes. Beth continues to bite her nails but, as a result of the bitter aloes, she has now taken to pulling a face while she's doing it, thus increasing her mother's despair. Tiger Woman has long scarlet nails filed to vicious points. Beth is determined to have the same. Beth already has the required scars. The raw gleam of cuts in her ankle, her knee and her hip. They aren't as large as Tiger Woman's but they might increase in size as Beth grows. As to the big wound across her back, Beth hasn't seen it, but other people have. In Beth's experience once people have seen her scar they don't want to look at it again. Dr

Richmond visited before they came away on holiday and said, 'The little one is healing up nicely, isn't she?'

And her mother had replied, 'It looks no better to me. It's such a mess . . . disfiguring. I don't know how she's going to cope when she's older. Because it'll always be there, won't it? There'll be no hiding a scar that size, will there? Who is going to want her looking like that?'

Dr Richmond shook his head and shot Beth's mother a sharp look. 'What the eye doesn't see the heart doesn't grieve, Mrs Singleton.'

Since that day Beth has tried to twist herself into a position where she can see the scar. But it is hopeless. There are only two mirrors in the house. One inside her parents' bedroom, where she is strictly forbidden, and one in the bathroom above the wash-basin, which she is too short to reach. In the end, of course, it doesn't matter that Beth can't see the scar that stretches across her back and curls under her left armpit – she can see the disgust in her mother's eyes and feel the revulsion in her touch. That alone is enough to persuade her that the scar looks as bad as it feels. If only she were pretty like the Tiger Woman at the Palace of Strange Girls. Beth has experienced only limited success with Dr Coffin's tooth powder. She needs something more permanent to redden her cheeks. She wouldn't be odd at all if she was a Tiger Woman at the Palace of Strange Girls. She'd fit in perfectly. She wouldn't mind having to scratch and snarl. She wouldn't mind it at all.

Beth hears the sound of muffled sobs from the other side of the room. 'Helen? You're crying! What's the matter?'

'Nothing. Shut up, Beth. You're supposed to be asleep.'

'But I'm not,' Beth replies, twisting from side to side in an attempt to struggle free of her tucked-in sheets and blankets. Eventually she tears her way free and, Houdini-like, stretches her arms up into the air before jumping the short distance to Helen's bed.

'Get off! Go away!'

'Why are you crying?'

'I'm not.'

'You are. I heard you. Is it because Mum won't let you go out with Connie tonight?'

'If Connie doesn't see Doug she'll meet someone else. She's really popular, she's had loads of boyfriends. I'm older than her and I haven't had a single one. And she's got a room full of clothes. She buys something new every week when she's paid.'

'But you're a lot prettier.'

'I don't care. I don't care about anything any more. I wish I were dead.'

'Don't say that! I don't want you to die, it's horrible. Horrible.' Beth sobs.

Helen sits up in bed, shocked by Beth's distress. She pulls her sister close and wraps her arms round Beth's skinny frame. 'I didn't mean it. I didn't mean it,' she says. 'Nobody is going to die.'

'Promise me.'

'I promise, now get back into bed. You should be asleep.'

'I'm not tired,' Beth replies. 'I know. Let's look out of the window like we do at home. We might spy some tipsy.'

Tipsy is the word given to men and women who stagger out of the Four Lane Ends pub every Friday and Saturday night. Tipsies do a lot of laughing, even when they're sick over the Singletons' front garden wall, which is surprising. Beth has been sick more than once over the previous few months and she hasn't laughed once. Beth pulls back the curtain and peers down through the open window into the yard below. There isn't a lot to see. Minutes pass and Beth's feet begin to get cold. She is about to give up when there are signs of movement in the yard. 'Helen! Look! Come quick! I think I can see Connie. Just look! She's got a boyfriend. She's holding his hand!'

'Liar.'

'She is. I'll prove it. Come and look.'

Helen gets up and pulls the curtain wider. There's very little light down in the yard, but she can see the outline of two figures and hear the sound of Connie's unmistakable throaty laughter. Helen strains to try and make out who Connie is with. It certainly isn't Doug, he's got the wrong-coloured hair. Has she ended up with Alan Clegg after all? The man looks faintly familiar, he's wearing a jacket like her dad's, but in a moment both figures have disappeared. The sisters stay by the window for a while. There is a fish and chip shop round the corner and the aroma of hot batter and sharp vinegar makes their mouths water.

'I'm hungry,' Beth complains.

'You'll have to wait for breakfast.'

'But I can't!'

'If you promise to get straight into bed you can have a spoonful of rosehip syrup. Mum left it on the washbasin this morning by mistake.'

Beth scrambles back into bed, her mouth open wide like a fledgling.

Ruth has spent the whole evening sitting in a faded pink wicker chair by the window in their hotel room worrying about her daughters. Helen is a pain in the neck with her constant demands. She wants everything too soon. And then there's Elizabeth – a constant source of worry. Ruth believes that her daughter's illness is a judgement from God. Divine retribution for what she calls her 'disappointment' when the child was born. Ruth's God is an Old Testament God. A vengeful God. A judgemental God. Ruth barely expects her to last out the week. God, she suspects, has only allowed her daughter to live this long in order to make her final demise all the more bitter. Not that Ruth is going to give up without a fight. Elizabeth suffered a collapsed lung after the operation, forcing her mother, in the hope of outwitting the Almighty, to institute a regime of comprehensive care. No child alive is subject to the same pack drill of health-giving home remedies. Although she recognises that she can't mend Elizabeth's heart, Ruth has left no stone unturned in her search for a cure for her daughter's weak chest. To this end Beth faces a bowl of porridge every morning ('sticks to your chest and keeps you warm') prior to spending the morning either traipsing around after any passing tar wagon ('Big breaths, Elizabeth!') or suffocating over a bowl of steaming water intended to 'clear her tubes'. After her weekly bath Beth's chest is rubbed vigorously with Vick ('fights respiratory infection') before she is squeezed into her wool vest, her fleece liberty bodice and her winceyette nightie.

Under the onslaught of Ruth's capacity to worry the evening has flown by. It is past midnight and contemplation of the perils of infant mortality raises Ruth into such a frenzy that she begins to pace the room. There is nothing for it but to distract herself with housework – but the cleaning options available at the Belvedere are limited. Not that the grime is not present – anyone with half an eye could spot it – but she is handicapped by the absence of a bucket and anything approaching a scrubbing brush or mop.

This attachment to cleaning began some seventeen years previously with the shifting of her few spinster belongings from her parents' house on Bird Street and into her first (and so far only) marital home – a terrace on St Cuthbert's Street that Jack had bought prior to their wedding. With the move Ruth set her foot on the road to her own personal Damascus with her blinding revelation occurring in the form of a desire to clean. As a result Ruth has the tiny two up two down in a state of constant chaos. Items are shifted, cleaned and replaced on a daily basis. Everything she touches is transformed – polished brighter, ironed smoother, washed cleaner. Polish is applied, sheets are stripped, windows are washed. The house is a hive of activity from dawn to dusk. It is an uphill struggle. Even while the family sleep dust is settling, pyjamas are being creased, pillows stained with spittle and flakes of skin shed. The house demands the whole of Ruth's attention and energy to complete the innumerable tasks. Ruth has read the statistics. A full eighty-five per cent of the dirt in a house is lodged in the carpets. There are five different kinds of ground-in dirt, all of which really require the use of a proper Hoover vacuum cleaner to remove.

And still the house is not perfect. It seems to Ruth that the sofa is in the wrong place, the kitchen chairs stand at an awkward angle, the vase needs replacing, the photos dusting. There isn't time enough in the day to do all she must accomplish. As a result Jack must drink his cup of tea immediately his fist closes round the handle. Ruth has no time to waste. The sweet liquid burns his throat while Ruth stands beside him to snatch the empty mug from his grasp. Anxious to run it under the tap, polish it dry and hang it back on the hook. There is no peace of mind for Ruth until her household chores are completed. Instead of the stay in a hotel being a welcome rest, Ruth finds that her anxiety levels rise by the day. Her only recourse is to clean. She is leaning over the washbasin, handkerchief in hand, scrubbing at the tidemark of soap scum and whiskers when Jack returns.

He is strangely subdued. 'You're not cleaning again, are you? For goodness' sake, Ruth, it's gone midnight. Why don't you leave it for the chambermaid?'

'They don't do it properly.'

Jack sighs and takes off his jacket.

'Anyway,' she continues, 'I've been waiting for you to come back. I thought you weren't going to stay out late.'

When her husband fails to reply she stops scrubbing the washbasin and turns to look at him. He looks dishevelled. When she crosses the room he steers round her, snatches the towel from the rail under the sink and says, 'I think I'll go and have a shower, Ruth. Don't you wait up. I'll try not to wake you when I get back.'

'What? Are you daft? Having a shower at this time of night? The water was only lukewarm when I put Elizabeth to bed at seven – it'll be stone cold by now.'

'Well, it'll clear my head if nothing else, won't it?' Jack is out of the door before she can reply.

The Belvedere Hotel boasts some superior fixtures. Each of its six bathrooms is fitted with an independent shower as well as a full-sized iron bath with giant taps and claw feet. At the apex of some complicated and rusty pipe work is a single shower head. It is the size of an imperial dinner plate. Hotel guests unfamiliar with its workings force open its central tap and experience an ejaculation of water sufficiently fierce to floor them. Jack, however, is aware of the unique quality of the Belvedere's ablutions and is fully prepared. He stands rigid under the blast of icy water that robs him of breath, as if the force of water alone is sufficient to wash away more than just the smell of Connie's perfume. He grabs a rectangle of green soap stamped with the hotel crest and rubs his hands together vigorously. It might as well be a piece of stone for all the lather it produces. Frustrated, Jack spots an ancient loofah hanging dustily from a hook – a long tubular network of grey fibres that initially resists the lure of water. Jack attacks his skin with the loofah, intent upon scrubbing away every trace of her lipstick from his neck, every particle of her from under his fingertips, every memory of her from his skin. It is a long exercise. He cannot face Ruth until the job is done properly, until he is scrubbed clean.

She is hanging up his discarded jacket when he returns. 'This jacket will need a good airing. It stinks of beer and cigarettes. Have you been celebrating?' she asks, her voice full of hope.

Jack shakes his head, refusing to meet her smile.

'Well, don't keep me in suspense. What happened? Did he offer you the job?'

'I've decided against it, Ruth. It's not the right move.'

'You've turned it down?'

Jack nods, pulling on his pyjamas with an uncharacteristic modesty and getting into bed. 'It's for the best.'

'You've turned it down? Without even asking me?'

'Don't start, Ruth. It's too late to get into an argument. We're both tired. We'll discuss it tomorrow.'

Ruth could weep with disappointment. She gets into bed and, to Jack's relief, turns her back on him. She has been sitting by herself all night waiting for him to come back and when he finally turns up he won't even look her in the eye, let alone tell her what has happened. Jack shuts his eyes and falls into a deep sleep of exhaustion. But Ruth is left awake, staring into the darkness.

13

QUEEN SCALLOP

This pretty shell is easy to find. It's two to three inches wide and it has striped ribs that are coloured from the palest pink to almost red. These shells are sometimes called 'Queenies'. Score 5 points for some pretty pink stripes.

Belvedere Hotel, Thursday 14 July 1959

'I've been wearing this skirt for ages now. Can't I have a change?'

Ruth is becoming weary of the constant struggle with Helen about clothes. Not a day passes without some argument or other.

'I look awful in it,' Helen continues. 'It's all pink and stripy. I look like a stick of flippin' rock.'

'Less of the "flippin'". Speak properly,' Ruth replies.

'But just look!' Helen holds out her arms, the better to demonstrate the effect of the candy-striped material that hangs in depressed gathers from her waist. Ruth has recently spent an evening letting down the hem of the skirt in the hope of camouflaging her daughter's knees. Needless to say this 'improvement' was greeted by a howl of despair when Helen woke up the next morning and saw the end result.

'Don't be ridiculous,' Ruth replies, undoing the buttons on Beth's nightie. 'I don't know what you're complaining about,' she adds as she tugs the nightie up over the child's head. 'That's a new skirt. Give over mithering. It'll do.'

'It'll do for a flippin' deckchair,' Helen mutters.

Despite her mother's intransigence Helen knows that there is still hope for the candy-striped skirt, if only she can persuade her to stretch to a proper underskirt. To this end she begins again. 'But this skirt is creased all over the place. I can't go out looking like this.'

'It wouldn't be creased in the first place if you weren't forever fiddling with it.'

'It's supposed to stick out. That's the way they wear it.' Helen fluffs out the sides of her skirt to demonstrate.

'I don't know what all the fuss is about. There's the best part of six yards in that skirt. It couldn't do anything *other* than stick out.'

'But not like it's supposed to. The skirts that Blanche sells are right. They're stiff with lots of layers of white net so that when you twirl round people can see them. If I had a proper underskirt like that, this skirt wouldn't droop around my ankles.'

'I've told you before, a cotton underskirt does just as well and it's better for you. It lets your skin breathe. It's called an underskirt because that's what it is. It's for under your skirt. Nobody is supposed to see it. I'm not having you walking around with your underskirt showing. And I won't buy nylon.'

'But that's the fashion. It's the way people wear them. Blanche says . . .'

But Ruth interrupts: 'I'm sick to death of hearing what Blanche thinks, or Blanche does, or Blanche sells. I'll decide what's best for you and I don't need some miserable trollop, who's no better than she ought to be, telling me any different. Now be quiet and finish getting dressed.'

'I can't. I can't wear this skirt – it's missing a button.'

'Let me see.' Ruth takes the skirt by the waistband and squints at the site of the missing button. 'Where is it?'

'How should I know?' Helen replies, anger overcoming her attempt at innocence. This is not quite the truth. The button is in the backyard four floors below where Helen threw it earlier this morning after she'd managed to pull it off with her teeth.

Ruth sighs and reaches into her pocket. 'We're going to be late for breakfast at this rate. Here, you'll have to use this safety pin. You can look for the button later. Watch out! If you pull the waistband too tight that safety pin will rip the material and then there'll be some darning to do as well as sewing the button back on. Are you listening?'

Frustration and anger get the better of Helen. She glares at her mother for a moment and says, 'Mrs Sykes says that Cora's husband is knocking her around.'

'Don't be ridiculous. You don't know what you're talking about. And don't go repeating gossip – especially gossip from Irene Sykes. She's forever sticking her shovel in where there's no muck.'

'Cora told Blanche that she'd fallen downstairs at home.'

'That sounds nearer the truth.'

'But Blanche thinks . . .'

'How many more times? I don't want to know what Blanche thinks. It's all nonsense and anyway she shouldn't be saying things like that in front of a schoolgirl. I'm glad now I didn't agree to you working there over the holidays. She's got the morals of an alley cat and a mouth to match.'

'Well, it doesn't matter anyway.'

'What?'

'I told Blanche I'm not going back to school in September and she offered me a full-time job. She says she'll train me to manage the shop.'

'She'll do no such thing. I've never agreed to you finishing school. A-Levels start in September.'

'If you don't let me leave school I'll leave home anyway.'

Ruth raises her right hand and slaps Helen across the back of the head. 'You'll do as you're told.' Helen glares at her mother, her eyes filling with tears. 'Now finish getting dressed and remember to lock the door behind you.' Ruth takes Beth by the hand and makes her way downstairs.

Victor, the hotel manager, spots Jack while the latter is idling in the hotel lobby. Jack looks as if he could do with a sympathetic ear. He'd barely woken up this morning before Ruth had demanded to be told all the details of the Union job. The discussion had degenerated into a full-scale argument. It had finished only when Ruth stormed out of the room. Jack is keen to escape further questioning from his wife concerning last night and equally desperate to avoid seeing Connie. The hangover that woke him this morning continues to make his head throb. There's an unwelcome whistling in his ears and the edges of his vision flicker like Blackpool lights. He must have slept heavily because he's woken up with a dry throat and a tongue that feels too big for his mouth.

'Mornin', Jack,' Victor proffers.

'Mornin',' Jack replies.

'You look a bit worse for wear. You should do your supping in my bar – there's less distance to stagger to your bed. Want me to get you a hair of the dog?' Jack groans by way of reply and shakes his head. 'Still, if you can't get pie-eyed on holiday when can you?'

Jack raises his chin and, with some visible effort, focuses on Victor's face and says, 'Well, at least you look in fine fettle.'

'I don't know why. It's nothing but bad news at the moment. I took a day off last week and went over to see my cousin. I went by train from North station. They were advertising it as the last steam engine journey on the Blackpool–Leeds line. They're switching over to diesel this weekend, you know. Anyway, we chugged along through Preston and then on straight through Blackburn, Accrington, Burnley, Brierfield and Nelson before going up the valley to Colne. What a mess!'

'What do you mean?'

'I mean the bloody mills. It was a sight to see. Every other one was closed down. Mile after mile of weaving sheds all shut up and deserted. Half-demolished mills silent as the bloody grave and not a single sound window between them. Half the mill chimneys were gone. Smith Brothers was still standing, but not for long if what I hear is right.'

Jack nods in agreement. He too has remarked on the devastation apparent from the train window during the trip through the cotton towns. The rising feeling of despair was curtailed by Beth climbing into his lap to escape the burgundy mockette pile on the seats that was irritating the backs of her legs. Together father and daughter stared out at the passing scenery, the railway sidings littered with discarded rubbish, the banks of dirty pink willow herb, chickweed and nettles. Wright's Spinning Mill had already been demolished, though cynics might argue that it was next to derelict anyway and had been for the past decade. All that was left was an open empty space, punctuated by a single pile of rotten plaster, broken bricks and shattered north lights. The weaving-shed door alone had survived the carnage and lay discarded among the rubble. It was a sad, hopeless sight and one that made Jack hold his daughter tighter. In an effort to lift his mood Jack had looked away and focused on the faded sepia prints of holiday resorts that flanked the mirror screwed to the carriage wall opposite, but his eyes were continually drawn back to the window. In the finish he was driven to pulling down the leather blind to prevent any further sight of the devastation.

Jack slides back out of memory and listens again to Victor's lament.

'I mean, what future do people like me have in the hotel trade when half our customers are thrown out of work? I haven't met a man yet who could afford to take a holiday on what he gets from the dole. I've had one booking after another cancelled. And it's not just the weavers and spinners, it's every other business that relies on the mills – from loom makers to corner shops. Everyone is suffering.'

Victor is a slim, angular man with soft grey eyes, a mobile face and a love of hard work. The Belvedere is his sole focus and he takes any threat of failure personally.

Jack inwardly groans; fond as he is of Victor, he's sick to death of hearing from the prophets of doom.

'You mark my words, Jack. It's the beginning of the end for Blackpool. The town won't stand it.'

'Never! You look full enough to me, Victor.'

'Full? Don't make me laugh. This isn't full. Not full like the place used to be when my old dad ran it. He was cramming them up to the rafters every year. They were lined up there like ruddy bats. One year he even filled the staff quarters with guests.'

'And where did you sleep?'

'Residents' Lounge and, failing that, kitchen floor. Now *that*'s being full.'

Jack has known Victor the best part of twenty years. They are as close as two men can be who see each other for one week out of fifty-two. Victor took over the management of the Belvedere when his dad died just before the war. If his mother had hoped to cash in on billeting troops, thereby persuading the powers that be that Victor, her only son, was essential to the war effort at home, she was disappointed. Hostilities had barely started when Victor announced that he'd joined the RAF and was due to start his pilot training the following week. He met his wife, Elsie, a WAAF with legs like Rita Hayworth, a ready laugh and a sex drive that matched his own, while he was on leave in London. He survived the Battle of Britain by the skin of his teeth, only for Elsie to be killed during the Blitz while she was cycling back to her flat near the docks. She'd swapped duties with a fellow WAAF whose boyfriend had managed to get theatre tickets. Jack had caught up with Victor briefly in 1942 when he'd brought Ruth to the Belvedere for their honeymoon. It was 1946 before they met again and Victor was running the hotel full time.

It is a lonely job, ensuring that the shifting population of the Belvedere's one hundred guests are well fed, comfortably accommodated and constantly entertained every day from March to November. Marginally less miserable is Victor's job of running the Residents' Bar every night. It is here that he has cemented his friendship with Jack and a few dozen other hotel regulars. The atmosphere is relaxed, the notice advising guests that ties are necessary has long since become obsolete. So too is the notice informing drinkers that management reserves the right to refuse to serve certain customers. Victor Titherington has never once found the need to refuse alcohol to any of the Belvedere's guests, although he has, on occasion, had to enlist the help of the night porter to ensure the safe passage of certain guests to their rooms.

'I mean, is your job safe, Jack?'

'Aye, safe enough for the time being. Things aren't as bad as they look.'

'How can you say that when the papers are full of mill closures? If it goes on like this there'll be nothing left.'

'But it won't. Closures will slow down and stop altogether in another six months or so.'

'What makes you so sure?'

'The government is handing out grants to cotton manufacturers to shut down. But the owners have to apply before next March. If they shut before this August they can claim an extra five per cent premium. That's why so many mills are toppling over themselves to shut before the end of the summer. Once the trade has been modernised and updated the mills that are left will be looking for workers. Things will improve.'

'I don't think I'll ever get the Belvedere back to full capacity. I reckon if cotton finishes then Blackpool will finish soon after. We'll have to rely on the Scots and bloody southerners for business. It's not just the mills closing, you know. It's these new travel companies offering a week in Majorca for thirty-nine guineas each, all included. I reckon the real future in the hotel trade is there or in Spain. They're planning to build new hotels all along the coast in the south and they're looking to British hoteliers to move out there so that our holidaymakers can have a bit of home from home. They reckon these new resorts could be as popular as Blackpool but without the rain. I'll look at my takings this season, but if they're down I'm minded to start over again in Spain.'

'Do you speak the lingo?'

'Do I hell! A pint is a pint wherever you are, isn't it?'

'Well, in the meantime your dining room looks to be filling up nicely.'

'That's due to casuals. That's what I'm down to. Accepting any passing trade in order to keep the hotel looking full. It's a case of keep up or go under. Stop by the bar tonight and we'll have a drink.'

'I take it it'll be on the house.'

'Go on, then. Seeing as it's you.'

Jack makes his way to the dining room. He sits down at the usual table and hides behind a copy of the *Daily Herald*. Every time a waitress passes he slides lower in his chair, anxious at all costs to avoid Connie. When she does appear she comes up on him from behind and places her hands over his eyes. 'Guess who, lover,' she whispers as she kisses the back of his neck.

Jack pulls her hands away from his eyes and turns in his seat. 'Stop it, Connie! Are you mad?'

'I was only teasing,' she protests. 'Anyway, what can I get for you this morning, lover.'

'Nothing. I don't want anything. I'm waiting for Ruth and the girls.'

'OK, keep your hair on! We can always talk later.'

Connie pulls her order pad and pencil out of her pocket and

moves on to the next table. As the dining room fills Jack sinks further into his paper, keen to escape the attentions of his fellow guests. When she finally appears, his wife is accompanied by Beth and she's in no mood to exchange pleasantries. Jack looks at Ruth and reflects that he may have had sex for the first time in over a year but last night with Connie is neither adequate comfort nor suitable revenge for the present state of his marriage. They might as well be on different planets for the difficulty he has trying to reason with his wife. 'Where's your sister, Sputnik?' he asks. He is unsure whether or not Ruth is prepared to speak to him following their argument.

'She's coming in a minute,' Beth replies. 'Can I have cornflakes today instead of porridge?'

'If you like, Sputnik,' Jack replies.

Beth, keen to make the most of her mother's refusal to speak, adds, 'And orange juice?'

Jack pours her a glass and returns to the shelter of his paper.

With the arrival of a tearful Helen some minutes later the family is ready to order. Connie is all smiles, anxious to know how Jack wants his scrambled eggs (runny or set?), how many pieces of fried bread (one or two?), tomato (fried or grilled?). And so the enquiries would have continued had Ruth not intervened. When Connie returns with the plated breakfasts she serves Jack first, placing the Full English Breakfast before him like a sacred offering. 'I've managed to sneak you an extra sausage, Mr Singleton,' she says, bending over him, her left nipple inches away from his lips.

Breakfast is consumed in complete silence. Only Helen looks

up from her plate, still hoping to have a word with Connie. She's keen to hear all about her friend's night out with the bloke she and Beth spotted from their window.

Jack eats his breakfast in record time and escapes to the Residents' Lounge, but Ruth waits for Beth to finish her scrambled eggs. Neither mother nor daughter will leave until the plate is empty.

Meanwhile Helen hangs on until the dining room is almost empty and the waitresses have started clearing the tables. She finds Connie sitting in the corner having a black coffee and a Pall Mall cigarette. 'Hiya, Connie!'

'Hi, Helen.'

'Did you have a good time last night?'

'Great.'

'Where did you go? Yates's?'

'Yeah.'

'Well, go on, what happened? Did Doug turn up like he said he would?'

'No.' Connie adopts a deliberate vagueness. 'I don't think so.'

'So did you meet up with the lads from the kitchen, then?'

'No.'

'So who were you with? Me and Beth were looking out of the window and we thought we saw you coming back with a bloke.'

Connie gives Helen a narrow look. She puts down her coffee cup and stands up and starts to move away.

Helen catches her shoulder as she passes and says, 'It must have been someone exciting. Who was it?'

Connie looks Helen in the eye, opens her mouth and then

appears to change her mind. At last she says, 'Now that would be telling, wouldn't it?'

Florrie meanwhile takes advantage of Jack's absence to occupy his seat at the Singletons' table. 'Mornin', Mrs Singleton,' she says and, receiving no reply other than a small tilt of the head, adds, 'My but your little girl is looking tired out this morning. Hasn't she slept? She's as pale as a sheet. She could do with a bit of colour in her cheeks, couldn't she?'

Beth silently snarls and, beneath the cover of the damask tablecloth, curls her fingers into claws.

A couple of miles south along the coast Cora Lloyd has awoken to an empty bedroom and an immediate sense of profound relief. She is alone. Granted this state of affairs is not one normally associated with pleasure in any previous occupants of the Excelsior Suite, especially when they are as young and attractive as Mrs Lloyd. But Cora is no ordinary woman, not by a long chalk. Cora Lloyd is a very fortunate woman, the envy of her friends and proof, if proof were ever needed, that there is no limit to what a pretty figure and an engaging smile can achieve. Mrs Lloyd is heralded to the daughters of ambitious mothers as a glowing example of what heights might be scaled by the simple expedient of a 'good marriage'. Cora Lloyd (Blake as was) used to run a set of six looms at Prospect Mill – not, it has to be said, the fastest weaver but by far the most attractive. She was out dancing most nights and was known to travel any distance with any man if there was the prospect of some fun.

Cora dresses carefully this morning. This is important. The slightest mistake in her appearance – a button left undone, a stocking seam not quite straight, the careless migration of powder from face to collar – could have serious consequences. Mr Lloyd, deputy manager of the local bank, requires his wife to attend to her appearance. He is easily raised to fury by mistakes. However, he is not an unreasonable man; that his wife should maintain her appearance is not a lot to ask. After all, as he would be the first to admit, this was the whole reason he married her. Appearance, the presentation of a public face, the maintenance of a certain standard is entirely right when one considers the style in which Cora is kept. Other lesser women may fill their lives with shopping, cleaning and cooking, but this is not the life Ronald Lloyd has chosen for Cora.

Ronald observed from early in life that love was a greatly overrated consideration when it came to marriage – it's a mistake to imagine there is any observable financial gain to be had from such emotional decisions. It is as great a mistake for a man to marry for money. Some of his acquaintances had done this and quickly discovered that there is nothing so uppity as a woman with her own income. Given these considerations, no one was more surprised than Ronald when the answer came to him through the letter box of The Hallows with the delivery of the local paper. Cora Blake's trim waist and pretty face smiled out from the front page under the banner headline THIS YEAR'S COTTON QUEEN. She had, he read, already attended the annual Cotton Ball in London, where she met several sour-faced minor royals, the Lord Mayor and Lloyd-George, who marvelled at her cotton dress and promptly invited her to Downing Street.

In that moment Cora's future is decided and Ronald Lloyd's courtship begins. It is not an easy task. The angular beauty of Ronald's early teens has long since disappeared under the daily onslaught of school puddings, a taste for which accompanies him throughout the rest of his days. He derives a similar pleasure from rough sex, with the added piquancy that only violence can afford. The passing days of the courtship are marked by increasingly large bouquets of flowers, culminating in a basket of sixty 'crimson fire' roses the day Ronald proposes marriage. The appearance of his wedding ring on Cora's finger signals the closing of the deal. Ronald has removed from Cora the necessity of carrying a key to The Hallows and the tiresome responsibility of handling her post office account. No longer tied to her six looms at Prospect, she is, to all outward appearances, as free as a bird. Free to be immaculately groomed, free to keep her mouth shut in company, free to stand beside her husband whenever and wherever required, free to await his return home every evening, to serve him with food and drink at whatever hour he pleases, and free at last to kneel at his feet and remove his shoes.

14

WEEVER FISH

Beware if you're paddling in shallow water at low tide looking for shrimps – you may find this little fish instead. It buries itself in the sand and you won't know it's there until it stings you! Score 20 points for a painful experience.

'Mrs Clegg asked me what I want to be when I grow up and I said I want to be a weaver and she said, "I don't think your mum will make much of that idea" and then laughed. Why did she think it was funny? What does a weaver do?'

Father and daughter are in the Residents' Lounge waiting for the arrival of the rest of the family. They have already been sitting here for ten minutes and Beth is getting bored. Since there's no immediate answer from her father she asks again, 'So what does a weaver do?'

Jack Singleton looks at his younger daughter and smiles. 'A weaver makes cloth.'

'What kind of cloth?'

'All sorts. Everything you're wearing has been woven. Those curtains have been woven too – and the chair covers, and carpets, and the tablecloths in the dining room and all the napkins.'

'But how do they do it?'

'Spinners spin a long piece of thread and then the people who run the looms weave it.' Beth looks blank. 'Like this,' Jack offers. He takes the ribbon from his daughter's hair, undoes the knot and stretches out his left hand, splaying his fingers wide. Then he threads the ribbon over one finger and under the next. 'See? My fingers are the warp threads and this ribbon is the weft.' Jack wraps the ribbon round his thumb and weaves it back towards his little finger. 'Can you see the pattern? This is a plain weave but you can make the weave as fancy as you like.'

Beth runs her fingers across the weave and says, 'What is a fancy weave, then?'

'Oh, I haven't enough fingers to show you a really fancy one. But I can show you a twill. Stretch out both hands like mine and I'll weave your fingers together.'

Beth holds out her hands and Jack takes the ribbon. 'With a twill the weft goes under two warp threads and then over one. Under two and over one. On and on like that until it makes a pattern.'

'Like my blouse?'

'No, your blouse is a seersucker.'

Beth laughs. 'A what?'

'A seersucker.'

Beth runs her fingers across the stripes in her blouse and says, 'What's a seersucker, then?'

'You change the weave so that one stripe on the cloth is a loose weave that lies flat like this.' Jack points to the smooth stripe in Beth's blouse. 'And the next stripe is woven very tight so that it crinkles. That's the way a weaver would make seersucker. But if it's a cheaper cloth it's all woven at the same tension first and then it's put through a machine that puts stripes of a special acid paste down the material that makes the alternate stripes wrinkle up. But the best seersucker is woven in – the other kind will lose its crinkle when it has been washed a few times. It's the same with patterned cloth – the best patterns are woven in, not painted on afterwards.'

'So what sort of weave are the curtains?'

Jack walks over to the window and takes the edge of the curtain. 'That's a brocade.'

'How do you know?'

'You can tell when you run your thumb over it. See, these twill flowers stand out from the flat satin-weave background.'

'How do they make the flowers do that?'

'They use a loose weave and a different kind of thread. The flowers are made in silk and the background is cotton. You need a special kind of loom to weave brocade – a Jacquard. But that kind of loom is very complicated and expensive.'

'And what kind of weave are the chairs?'

'They'll be chintz.'

'They're pretty, aren't they?'

'Yes, but those roses are printed, not woven.'

'And they're shiny too.'

'That's a special glaze they put on the material after it's woven and printed. It's a shiny coating that stops dust and dirt getting into the fabric. It'll wear off in time.'

'Do you need a special loom for chintz?'

'No, just an ordinary one will do.'

'Like the ones you bring home?'

Jack looks puzzled for a moment. 'Loom? Oh! You mean the loom drives I sometimes bring home to mend. I seem to remember I've caught you fiddling with the machines more than once.'

Beth blushes at the memory. The machines are irresistibly shiny and complicated. There are wheels that cry out to be pushed, screws that are made to be turned, handles that are meant to be pulled. Her father brings loom drives home on Friday night and puts them in the front room where they stay all weekend hidden under an oily rag. No one is allowed to go near the machines, let alone touch them. But the lure of the screwed knobs, the shiny brass bezels and turning wheels is too much for Beth to resist. As a result when her father turns his attention to the machines on Sunday he is faced with the sight of tiny fingerprints that race all over the brass balancing wheel and the odd neglected nut or refugee screw rolling around the base plate. Beth is still too young to hide the evidence of her mischief and too distracted to remember to dry her oily fingers anywhere other than down the front of her dress. When her father finds her meddling with the machine he sends her out to the backyard to play with her ball.

If her mother discovers the crime there is uproar – fiddling with the machines is a punishable offence equal only in wickedness to running across the road without looking, or sneaking food upstairs.

Jack Singleton tries to maintain his look of stern disapproval but it is difficult. 'If you can manage to keep your fingers off the loom drives then I might take you into the weaving shed. Then you'll not only see the looms, you'll be able to hear them running too.'

'Will you take me when we get back? I'll need to see the shed if I'm going to be a weaver, won't I? Helen has been in the shed – why can't I?'

'When you're a bit older. Children aren't allowed in the weaving shed. It's too noisy and too dangerous.'

'But it sounds like fun.'

'Oh, it can be fun all right. A right barrel of laughs some days.'

Beth picks up the change in her father's tone but the meaning is lost on her.

Upstairs, Ruth and Helen have just crossed swords again over what constitutes suitable wear for a day that promises rain. They have not managed to agree. Ruth has won the argument but the insolent look on Helen's face makes the victory seem hollow. Anxious to assert the fact that she is fully in charge she says as they are making their way down to the Residents' Lounge, 'Your dad and I are going out for the afternoon tomorrow, so I want you to keep an eye on Elizabeth. We'll be back for tea.'

'Where are you going?'

'St Anne's.'

'Why?'

'We're going over to see Mr and Mrs Lloyd. They're staying at the Links.'

'You're going to see Cora? Oh, can I go too? Cora's such good fun! Let me go. Please.'

'I need you to look after Elizabeth, and anyway, you barely know Mrs Lloyd.'

'I do. I've told you. She comes into the shop every week for one thing or another and she always talks to me. She bought a load of summer dresses last week.'

'I wonder what's wrong with the ones she bought last month? They looked nice enough to me. Anyway you can't go, you have to stay here and look after Elizabeth. The Links is just for adults. You're too young. I'll put Elizabeth down for her afternoon nap before we go and you can spend the afternoon reading. That way you can keep your eye on her at all times and I won't have to worry.'

Helen has a face like thunder when they get to the Residents' Lounge. 'What's the matter with you?' Jack asks.

'I'm fed up!'

'You're spoilt, more like,' Ruth chips in.

'I never get to do anything. Connie goes out every night and she's younger than me.'

'Give over!' Jack replies. 'Pull the other one! You're nowhere near as old as Connie. There's no call to exaggerate.'

'I'm not! I'm two months older than Connie. She may be working at the hotel but she's still only fifteen.'

Jack is speechless, struck dumb by the revelation. Helen looks at him. She is filled with a sense of injustice and is keen to hear his reply. But Jack is lost for words, desperate to keep his mounting sense of horror from showing all over his face. A minute passes. At last Jack pulls himself together and volunteers, 'Well, she doesn't look it. And she shouldn't be drinking at that age.' And that's not the only thing Connie shouldn't be doing, Jack thinks. He is gripped by panic when he thinks of the possible consequences of what he has done.

'I look younger than her, don't I?' Helen counters, aware that she's finally hit on a fact that her parents can't dismiss. When Jack fails to reply she continues, 'You see, that's proof! I look about twelve. I work in a dress shop and I'm not even allowed to buy my own clothes. I can't even choose what to wear when we're away on holiday.'

Ruth, who has been buttoning Beth's coat and pulling up her daughter's socks, comes over to where Helen and Jack are standing and says, 'Keep your voice down, there are other people in this hotel. Do you want everyone to know our business?'

Helen ignores her mother and continues to glare at Jack. She senses that her complaints are falling on deaf ears. It's obvious that he isn't listening. He is staring at the scarlet and gold carpet beneath their feet, his expression grim. She raises her voice. 'I'm not stupid, you know. I'm sixteen but I'm treated no different from Beth. I'm surprised Mum doesn't make me have a nap in the afternoon as well. Anyway, I won't stand for it. I'm not going back to school in September. I'm going to get a job here in Blackpool. Connie says I can stay with her.'

Helen notes with some satisfaction that these words have had the desired effect. Her dad seems to freeze for a moment before looking up horrified. 'You can't do that! You can't leave home. You'll end up like Connie!'

Jack hesitates, struck by this hypocrisy, but he recovers quickly. 'I haven't time to talk about this now. Get your coat on, we're going out.'

15

VENUS SHELL

The Romans named their most beautiful goddess Venus. She was not born but emerged from the sea in a shell. This triangular shell is named after the goddess and is decorated with multicoloured concentric rings. Score 10 points for an emerging Venus.

Rain or shine, there's always something to do in Blackpool. The amusement arcades, cinemas and Winter Gardens raise a cheer even when the resort is windswept and rainy. Rough weather is a godsend. It prevents holidaymakers from spending cheap, lazy days on the beach. When it rains everyone makes for shelter. Damp holidaymakers congregate in the Olympia to play the slot machines or queue for tickets at the Tower Circus. Money changes hands. It might be like Noah's flood outside but still Blackpool is booming and all is well with the world.

Ruth Singleton is in no mood to partake of the holiday

atmosphere today. She is so fed up after the argument with Helen and the disappointments of last night that she doesn't even remind the girls not to breathe when they pass the black-and-white striped lighthouse that disguises the town's sewer ventilator. When it is apparent that the rain has set in for the morning the Singleton family retreat to one of the promenade shelters; Jack to nurse his hangover and come to terms with this morning's shock revelation, Ruth to read her copy of *Woman and Home*, and the girls to kick their heels and watch the rain. By dinner time the whole family look dispirited. Jack folds up his newspaper and says, 'Come on! Buck up! I fancy fish and chips for dinner. My treat. Come on, Helen. You can help me carry them back.'

Helen doesn't look enthusiastic but Beth pipes up, 'Let me, Daddy! I want to go. Can I help carry them back?'

'No, you can't,' Ruth says. 'You stay here with me. You'll only get wet and catch a chill.'

'I don't want to walk all the way into the centre,' Helen moans.

'Come on, pet,' Jack continues. 'It's only just a bit further along the prom. We'll be back in less than an hour if the queue's not too bad.'

Helen sighs heavily and stands up. She buttons up her coat, adjusts her ponytail and combs her fingers through her fringe before picking up her handbag and venturing out of the shelter. Jack leans over the promenade railings and waits for his eldest daughter to catch up. Down below, the rainswept beach is deserted, even the donkeys are sheltering under the pier along with a smattering of disconsolate holidaymakers. For a moment Jack is reminded of the empty beach at Souda Bay where he and Eleni used to sunbathe and swim. In his memory she is turning her heart-shaped face towards him, chin tilted up, eyes closed against the glare. 'You'll come back? When it's all over, I mean. You'll come back and find me?' Jack's eyes sting. He shakes his head and wrenches himself from the memory as a reluctant Helen catches him up.

There are still quite a few people on the promenade, heads down and hurrying through the rain. Jack and Helen settle into an easy pace. Jack forces his mind back into the present. 'Come on, chick. Buck up! We're supposed to be having a good time.'

'Well, I'm not,' Helen replies. 'I could have earned a load of money at Blanche's this week. It's boring sitting on the beach every day. I'm not allowed to do anything here. And I just know that all my friends from school are away having a good time. I couldn't get a word out of Connie this morning.'

'Maybe she was busy.'

'She was at Yates's wine bar last night. I bet she had a really good time. She must have done because she's got a new boyfriend.'

'How do you know?' Jack asks, forcing himself to stay calm.

'Me and Beth saw her bringing somebody back to where she lives. In the staff quarters, I mean.'

'Ah,' Jack manages.

'I thought it might be Alan Clegg, but it didn't look like him. This bloke had a different jacket on.'

Jack forces himself to carry on moving his legs back and forth; walking slowly; keeping calm. But when Helen opens her mouth again he interrupts her, afraid of what she'll say next. 'I've been thinking about what you said earlier this morning. The exam results will be out next month. You might change your mind when you see how well you've done. It would be a shame to end up working for Blanche when you could earn a lot more with a couple of A-Levels. If you stay at school you could keep your Saturday job, keep all the money you earn, spend it how you want. I'll square it with your mother.' Seeing Helen hesitate, he adds, 'And I think you deserve a treat for finishing your exams, don't you? Here, go and buy yourself a new blouse or something. Whatever you like.'

Jack pulls out his wallet and gives Helen a couple of notes. She is speechless for a moment, fixed to the spot while the couples in plastic macs drift around her. 'What? Now? Can I get myself a blouse now? And a proper underskirt too?'

'I can't see any harm if there's enough change left.'

For a moment it looks as if Helen is going to burst with excitement. She points to the nearby Co-op. 'I'll go in there. That's where Connie got her top.'

Jack opens his mouth but manages to smother his objections. 'OK,' he says. 'I'll walk on up the road to the chip shop and wait for you there.'

Helen flies into the Co-op and, ignoring the lift, takes the marble stairs two at a time until she reaches ladies' wear on the third floor. The whole floor is filled with forbidden fruits. Drip-dry nylon blouses, pencil skirts in Tricel, rayon dresses and Terylene trousers. Helen is momentarily overwhelmed. Blanche doesn't carry anywhere near this much stock. Within moments Helen has been spotted and a smartly dressed shop assistant bears down on her. The woman's demeanour is enough to frighten off the casual shopper but Helen stands firm. She knows precisely what she wants. She wants a black top with scarlet piping just like Connie's. But they've sold out. There's only pink with white piping left. The assistant guides Helen to the changing rooms and stands sentry outside the curtained cubicle. Once Helen has got changed she realises that, although it may be pink instead of black, the top is satisfyingly tight when she pulls it on. The deep neckline clings to the very edge of her shoulders before curving round the top of her breasts. Helen has to slip her bra straps off her shoulders to avoid them showing.

'Is this the right size?' Helen asks the assistant when she emerges from the cubicle.

The older woman gives her a professional glance and says yes, any bigger and the top will drop off her shoulders. Helen knows that her mother will be outraged. Ruth has an aversion to tight clothes and this, allied to her habit of buying blouses and skirts with one, or preferably two, years' growing space has ensured that Helen has spent her childhood and adolescence turning back cuffs and hitching up waistlines that droop and settle on her hips.

Helen subtracts the cost of the top from the notes in her hand and reckons that there's still enough left for a full-blown layered net underskirt. The saleswoman measures Helen's waist and disappears. When she reappears it is with a net underskirt so generously gathered that it springs up over her face as she carries it into the changing rooms. The white net layers shine and sparkle under the light. They are edged with white ribbon and there is a pink rosebud and bow at the waist. Helen pulls the underskirt up under her skirt and settles it at her waist. She is transformed, turned from schoolgirl to prima ballerina. Helen shifts from foot to foot with excitement. Glancing out of the window it seems that the weather has changed to match her mood. The rain has stopped and the streets are bathed in sunshine. She refuses the saleswoman's offer to wrap her purchases and only asks for a carrier bag for her old blouse. It is a new Helen who steps out of the shop. Her cotton skirt billows out from her waist, the new net underskirt is just visible beneath the hem, the satin ribbon edging skimming her calves. Her face, neck and shoulders gleam white against the pink top as she hurries through the rainy streets to find her father.

Jack has bumped into Dougie outside the fish and chip shop. It's one o'clock and Dougie has already sunk a couple of whiskies to dry himself out. Dougie is keen to hear the news. 'How did you get on last night, Jack? What's Tom Bell after?'

'Someone to replace him as area rep when he goes up to headquarters in London.'

'Are you taking it?'

'I don't know. I'd set out with the idea that I'd accept whatever the Union could offer, but now I'm not sure. I don't reckon Fosters will last – not unless they modernise. Nylon wasn't supposed to last five minutes but look at the market now.'

'Whichever way you look at it you'll earn more money as a manager than you'll ever do with the Union. Stands to reason.'

'I don't know about that – it more or less evens itself out on a day-to-day basis. But there again there'll be a manager bonus if we have a good year.'

'Have you told Ruth?'

'I just said I hadn't made up my mind. She still kicked up merry hell this morning. Started trying to tell me about my responsibilities to her and the girls. As if I needed telling. She was all for me going with the Union, but only because she doesn't know about the manager's job at Prospect.'

'Have you still not told her? Why the hell not?'

'Because Ruth is only concerned with the short-term future. She wants a semi. She wants it now, no matter what the cost. She doesn't care about anything that doesn't directly involve the family. She doesn't understand that every time a mill goes under it weakens the overall strength of the whole industry, never mind that it puts hundreds of weavers out of work with no redundancy and precious little dole. That sort of thing doesn't even register on her radar.'

'Cheer up, man! You look as if you lost a shilling and found sixpence.'

'I wish it were that simple. Look, Dougie, why don't we have a couple of beers at the Albion tonight? Eight o'clock suit you?'

'What's the matter? Come on, Jack. Spit it out. You've had a face like a wet Monday all holiday.'

'It's nothing. We'll have a chat tonight.'

Jack is spared any further explanation by the arrival of Doug. 'What do you want?' Doug asks his father.

'Usual,' Dougie replies.

'Where's your money?'

Dougie checks his pockets. 'I'm all out. I don't know why. I only had a couple in Yates's.'

Doug knows that Jack has been offered the manager's job at

Prospect – his father let it slip one night when he was drunk. Doug wasn't surprised by the news. It's only what he has come to expect from Jack Singleton. Doug has heard all the stories about Jack's womanising when he was in the band and all the tricks he used to get up to when he was still a tackler. He's even heard how Jack was mentioned in dispatches during the retreat from Crete. If there were any justice in the world he'd have had Jack for a father instead of Dougie. Maybe then his mother wouldn't have walked out. 'Can I get you summat, Mr Singleton? I may as well get them all together. No point in us both queuing.'

'It's OK, Doug. I'm waiting for our Helen. She should be here in a minute or two. She's just nipped into one of the shops. Oh, there she is now.' Jack raises his hand and waves.

Doug follows his gaze down towards the beach. Making her way up the street with the sea at her back is a figure dressed in the height of fashion from her skimpy top to her fully flared skirt that swishes round her knees as she walks and kicks out to reveal a sparkling white net underskirt. Her blonde hair gleams against the blue of the sea and her face shines with happiness. Jack and Doug are struck dumb by the transformation. It is left to Dougie to pipe up: 'By the left, she's changed, hasn't she? I wouldn't have known her.' Doug stares, open-mouthed. No wonder she didn't turn up in Yates's last night. She must have had at least half a dozen better offers. Dougie sneaks a look at Jack. If anything, he looks even more shocked.

When Helen reaches them she smiles at Dougie and says, 'Hiya, Dad. Hello, Mr Fairbrother.' She turns to Doug and he stares back at her like a complete fool.

The chip shop is full. Doug and Helen are forced to queue out on the street and, since they are still within hearing distance of their fathers, Doug keeps his mouth shut. He's had more than a taste of his father's mockery in the past and isn't keen for another dose. The queue shuffles forward over the threshold of the shop. Once safely inside Doug clears his throat and says, 'Did you get to Yates's last night?'

'Oh, no. I didn't. I expect Connie did, though.'

'Did she have a good night?'

'I don't know, I haven't seen her today.'

'You planning to go anywhere tonight?'

Helen is at a loss to know what to say. She can't face the embarrassment of admitting that she's not allowed out at night, but there again she can't think of where she could claim to be going. She eventually settles for a bland 'Oh, I don't know.' As she turns away she feels the net underskirt rustle and crush against Doug's thigh and is pleased by the sensation.

'I hear you've a Saturday job,' Doug says, anxious to keep her talking.

'Yes. I work at Blanche's on Scotland Road.' Relieved to be on less dangerous ground, Helen rushes on. 'I should be working now but I decided to come on holiday instead. Blanche has offered me full time.'

'Will you take it? I heard your dad telling Dougie that you were going to stay on at school.'

Helen shrugs her shoulders and tries to look as if she doesn't care. She finds Doug's habit of referring to his father by his first name alternately amusing and unsettling. Doug is standing with his thumbs hooked into his jeans pockets. He is *so* cool and so good-looking. It feels dangerous just standing next to him. When he moves his leather jacket wrinkles and shines, and the heavy collar rubs against his sideboards.

'Have you ever been to the Winter Gardens?' Doug asks.

'Lots of times.' Helen is still easing into the part of an experienced social butterfly. And it is true in a manner of speaking. Helen has seen three Christmas pantomime matinées at the Winter Gardens. On each occasion she was accompanied by the full church Sunday School.

'Lonnie Donegan is on tonight. I've got a couple of tickets. Do you fancy going?'

They have reached the head of the queue and Helen feigns deafness as she puts in her order for fish and chips with salt and vinegar. She pays at the counter and waits for the change. Her mind is in overdrive trying to work out a way she can go out with Doug without her parents finding out. But it's impossible. There isn't any way that she can manage it. 'I can't,' she says, swallowing hard and looking away.

'Already got a date, have you?'

'Yes. No.' Helen is anxious not to lose Doug's interest. She is at a loss to know how to turn down the date without either admitting she isn't allowed out or putting him off completely. 'Well, I think I might have. I don't know,' she concludes.

Doug glares at her and says, 'Well, let me know if you ever make your mind up. I won't be holding my breath.' And with that he turns away and studies the view out of the steamed-up windows.

16

SEA GOOSEBERRY

This little jellyfish looks exactly like a gooseberry except that its body is transparent. It blends into its surroundings and trails two long tentacles through the water to pick up any passing prey. When it moves it shimmers and takes on all the colours of the rainbow. Score 20 points for an invisible gooseberry.

It's Connie's turn to serve afternoon tea in the Residents' Lounge. She rearranges her hair and admires her reflection in the stainless-steel tea urn while she waits for the water to boil. Nobody has ever made love to her like Jack Singleton. Not even Father O'Connell. She'd had to sink three gins and orange last night before she'd had the guts to walk up to Jack when the bloke he was talking to left. After that it had been easy. He didn't use anything but it doesn't matter. She had sex with her geography teacher at school loads of times and she never got pregnant by him. It's only older women who get pregnant, not teenagers like her. Jack is a proper man, not like that idiot Alan Clegg, or Andy who's been dogging her every step this afternoon. In the end she'd stopped in her tracks, turned round and said, 'Look, Andy, I really like you but it's no good. I've already got a bloke and it's serious.' And she means what she says. It is serious. Connie is convinced that Jack must care for her. How could he not love her after last night? True, he'd got her name mixed up with someone else's, but anyone could see that Connie and Jack were made for each other.

Connie refused to go out with Andy and the lads after lunch and spent the early afternoon readying herself for her next meeting with Jack. He was a bit short with her at breakfast but all that is forgotten in her preparations for the afternoon. She has dressed carefully, releasing her hair from its usual rubber band, and slipped her feet into her best stilettos, the ones that will cripple her before the day is out. There's barely been a break in the rain all day and, as a result, Connie is hoping and praying that Jack will turn up for afternoon tea. There are butterflies in her stomach when she walks into the Residents' Lounge but she is immediately disappointed. There's no sign of Jack. Over in the far corner the couple from room sixty-nine, the salesman and his 'wife', are already seated. They're regulars for the afternoon tea. They throw it down and retire to their room for the rest of the afternoon. The chambermaid is always moaning that she has to change their sheets every day. There's the old couple from room five. They have to have a room on the ground floor because of her wheelchair. They're regulars too. Mr Stansfield wheels his wife along the prom every day after lunch to allow her to take advantage of the health-giving properties of ozone. They're both ready for a cup of tea come 3.30 p.m. Connie catches sight of Mrs Clegg and Jack's wife. Her spirits rise; if Ma Singleton is here it's likely that Jack will appear. Connie won't be able to speak to him, not with his wife there, but at least she'll be able to see him. Connie hurries forward with her tray.

The hotel provides a pot of tea and slices of Victoria sandwich for guests every afternoon. Ruth used to bake this cake on a weekly basis, specifically to annoy Jack's mother, so she knows how it should taste. She used the finest flour from Canadian wheat – not the sweepings-up her mother-in-law used to call flour. Fresh-laid eggs, not dried. And home-made jam with real fruit, not the commercial stuff that's all sugar and cochineal. Jack's mother was horrified by Ruth's culinary extravagances. As likely as not she'd say, 'There are perfectly good results from plain ingredients at half the price, you know, Ruth.' Or, 'You'll not mind if I don't finish the crust, it's all a bit too rich for me.' There is, of course, no 'crust' on Ruth's Victoria sandwich – the ingredients have been beaten over a bowl of hot water, whisked to within an inch of their life. As Ruth is fond of telling Jack, 'Just because you were brought up on shop-bought doesn't mean you have to continue missing out.'

Jack, for his part, has been known to protest that his mother's cooking wasn't 'shop-bought'. In fact, Jack's mother had her own bakery on Gas Street. It was so successful that she supplied four Dainty Shops as well, but Ruth dismisses this with a wave of her hand.

Ruth had walked into the Residents' Lounge hoping for an hour's peace and quiet, but this isn't to be. Mrs Clegg clocked her the minute she walked in and now the two of them are settled in the corner. If Ruth could have ignored the frantic waving she would have done, but Mrs Clegg isn't easily ignored. When Connie comes over Mrs Clegg orders a pot of tea for two.

Still hopeful, Connie turns to Ruth and says, 'And what can I get for you? Will anyone else be joining you?'

Florrie interrupts: 'A pot of tea for two will do us nicely. And we'll have some of your cake as well.'

Connie and Ruth look equally depressed.

Florrie starts immediately Connie has moved on to the next table: 'Where's your eldest girl, Ruth?'

'She's gone to the pictures for the afternoon.'

'Pictures! They're a blessing on a day like this, aren't they? We were going to take the lads up the Tower – on a good day you can see for miles and miles. You'd be hard pushed to see across the street today so Fred has taken them to the Tower Circus. Your youngest would like it. How is she today?'

'Better, thank you. She's having her nap at the moment.'

'I don't know how you manage it. The twins are coming up to four and they'd scream blue murder if I ever tried putting them to bed in the afternoon. It's bad enough getting them settled at night. Still, it's easier here. I think all that sea air wears them out.'

Connie has returned with their order and conversation pauses while Ruth clears a space for the tray.

Florrie looks in the teapot, stirs the contents for a minute and looks again. 'We'll have to leave it a bit,' she says.

Ruth picks up a side plate and reaches for a piece of sponge.

'Your eldest is going to be a real beauty, isn't she? She's certainly caught our Alan's eye. Will you be having any more?'

Mention of Alan infuriates Ruth. She's seen him leering at Helen more than once.

Florrie, suddenly aware of the silence, asks again, 'So, will you be having any more?'

'No.'

'You're not tempted to try for a boy?'

'No. I much prefer girls. And anyway, I was told I wouldn't be able to have any more after Elizabeth was born.'

'Oh, you're so lucky.' Florrie's chin wobbles. 'What a blessing. Oh, I envy you. My Fred says he's fed up to the back teeth of "getting off at the roundabout instead of going into Morecambe", if you take my meaning.'

Ruth is embarrassed by Florrie's frankness and searches for something different to talk about. Contraception doesn't figure in Elizabeth Craig's list of topics suitable for polite conversation over afternoon tea. 'Are you enjoying your holiday?' she enquires.

'We're having a grand time. I'm only sorry that tomorrow will be our last day. We'll be off on Saturday. We've decided we're going to splash out and go to the Tower Ballroom tomorrow night. You're welcome to come with us, if you like.'

'It's kind of you to ask but we'll be busy all day. We're off to St Anne's tomorrow.'

'Very nice. They're a bit posh over there, aren't they? What do you plan to do when you get there? There isn't much of a pier, is there? Will you be going by taxi?'

'No, we'll get the tram. We're just seeing friends. I've known Cora for years and Jack was at school with her husband.'

'Are your girls looking forward to it?'

'They won't be coming with us. Helen will be staying here and looking after Elizabeth. We'll only be away a couple of hours.'

'Oh, don't you worry. I'll keep my eye on your lasses.'

'There's no need. Helen will stay in her room while Elizabeth is having her afternoon nap and we'll be back before four.'

'You'll feel better knowing they're being looked after. And it means you can stay as late as you like, can't you? I know how time flies when you're chatting.'

Ruth can't refuse this generous offer without appearing rude. She struggles with the effort of sounding grateful. 'Thank you. That's very kind of you, Florrie.'

Florrie smiles and says, 'Make sure you and Jack enjoy yourselves without the girls. Me and Fred take every opportunity there is to get some time alone. It was our anniversary yesterday.'

'How long?'

'Twelve years.' Florrie sees the look on Ruth's face and adds, 'I married Fred when my first husband, Alan's father, was killed in Italy. How long have you and Jack been married?'

'Seventeen. We were married during the war.'

'Bit of a whirlwind affair then, was it?'

'No, not really. I'd already known him some years.'

'I'll bet he was one of the first to join up, wasn't he? Oh, didn't they look smart in their uniforms? At the beginning it was quite the thing to have a boyfriend in uniform. You used to see them when they came home on leave – swanning around the dance halls and surrounded by girls.'

Ruth nods. Jack had turned up at church in his khaki uniform. He used to wear his cap at an angle that implied he'd been in uniform since the day he was born. Even the regulation short back and sides looked good on him.

'Had you been going out with Jack a long time, then?'

'No, not really.'

After Jack joined up a number of other members of the congregation followed suit. Eventually there were no young men left in the church. After a while it was suggested that the church ought to keep in contact with members of the congregation who were fighting abroad. Ruth was acting secretary, so the task fell to her. She went round to the families and got the rank and service numbers, and started writing letters of support. Most of them were ignored, but every now and again she'd get a letter back – especially from those lads who didn't hear a lot from their families.

'So how did you get together?' Florrie is full of curiosity.

'We started writing during the war. I'd give him news of what was going on in the town – church events, money-raising drives for armaments, that sort of thing – and he wrote back. It went on from there, really.'

'There wasn't a lot they were allowed to tell you, was there? I know when I heard that my first husband had died in Italy I was amazed. I'd no idea he was out there. I thought he was still in France. Half his letters were censored. It used to make me mad. All I wanted to know was where he was and that he was all right. I wasn't after battle plans – I just wanted to know he was OK.'

Ruth nods, although her experience was somewhat different. To read Jack's letters you'd think he was having a whale of a time. He didn't mention the war once, though Ruth could tell from bits and pieces that he was fighting in Africa and later all over the Mediterranean. He filled his letters with tales of what he'd done on his leave and his plans for the dance band when he got home. He sent a photo of himself on a camel when he was in Palestine, said the locals were friendly. Looking at him, Ruth didn't doubt it for a minute.

'It always surprised me how those letters even arrived. The paper we wrote on was little better than blue tissue.'

'Yes, I'd write one way and write again across the lines when I came to the end of the sheet. Jack's letters were the same, like a coded puzzle when I opened them. I suppose I got to know him better and better over the months. He was mentioned in dispatches.'

'What for? What did he do?'

'Jack won't talk about it. He won't even talk about his time on Crete. But his mother said he'd carried a soldier to safety. He must have been in a fair state himself because he went straight into hospital when he got back to Egypt. Anyway, later, when I heard he had lobar pneumonia, I started writing to him regularly. We got married the next time he was home on leave.'

'He's an attractive man. You must have to put up with other women chasing him. It must be a right headache.'

Ruth stiffens at the suggestion. 'Not at all. I worry about a number of things, but I never worry about him being involved with anyone else.'

'But how can you be sure?'

'He'd rather die than do anything that would hurt his family. He's that sort of man. Family comes first. Anyway he'd be lucky to find another woman who'd care for him the way I do. He sits down to a full cooked meal and home baking every day. There isn't a spot of dust in the house, I make sure of that. He'd be hard pushed to find another woman who'd look after him so well.'

Connie has merged into the surroundings so effectively that she's been pretending to wipe down the next table for at least five minutes and nobody has noticed. She has been eavesdropping ever since she heard Jack's name mentioned. For all the attention the women have paid to her she might as well be invisible. The envy she feels is outweighed by an overwhelming curiosity. Ma Singleton's account of their marriage has inspired the waitress. Connie can do a lot more for Jack than just look after the house. And she intends to show him tonight. The moment the idea enters her head she is overtaken by impatience to see him. It is with this in mind that she ventures even closer to where Ruth and Florrie are sitting and asks, 'Will your husbands be in later?'

'Well, mine would,' Florrie says, 'if it was beer you were serving, love. And I don't think Mr Singleton will be down either. Didn't you say he was putting Elizabeth down for her nap, Ruth?'

Ruth nods her head and empties the hot-water jug into the teapot in the hope of diluting Florrie's brew. This is exactly what Connie wanted to hear. She abandons the table she was clearing and disappears with her tray. Back in the still room she makes up another tea tray with a giant slice of cake and pushes it in the dumb waiter. She then sprints up to the lobby and, seeing the reception desk empty, dips behind the counter. It is a moment's work to find the Visitors' Book and ascertain the Singletons' room numbers. The lift is out of bounds to staff – maintenance men, chambermaids, waitresses and kitchen workers are ordered to use the gloomy back stairs. Bearing this in mind, Connie looks both ways before she steps smartly into the lift for the third floor. Once there, she retrieves the tea tray from the dumb waiter, no minor achievement since she has to haul the rope the distance of three floors. She walks smartly to number 351 and knocks on the door. There is no reply. Frustrated, Connie imagines that Jack must still be up on the next floor putting Beth to bed. She picks up the tray and re-enters the lift. She's visited Helen's room often enough to remember the number. Once there, she stops and listens at the keyhole. She can hear two voices.

'Do I have to put my nightie on?'

'Yes. You don't want to get sand from your socks and shorts all inside the bed, do you? You'll be a lot more comfy in your nightie.'

'Why is my nightie hairy?'

'It's made of flannelette.'

'Well, it feels fuzzy to me.'

'That's because it has been finished. It's been put through a machine with lots of sharp teeth that raises the surface of the material.'

'What does that mean?'

'It means that it scratches the cloth so that the little cotton fibres come up from the surface. They trap the heat. That's what makes your nightie cosy.'

Connie listens to the conversation for several minutes, hoping that Jack will finish putting Beth to bed and come out of the room. At last she loses her patience and knocks on the door. It is some moments before there is any answer. The door opens a crack and Connie is elated to catch a glimpse of Jack. 'Hello, lover,' she says.

'Sh-h-h. Be quiet! She's still awake. What are you doing here?'

'Room service. I thought I'd bring you a cup of tea up seeing as you won't come down. I've cut you an extra big slice of cake – you'll need plenty of energy for what I've got planned for tonight.'

'This isn't a good idea. It's too risky. You have to go.'

'Well, that's a fine way to talk. You didn't seem that bothered about the risk last night. Come on, Jack. At least take the tray after I've gone to the trouble to bring it up. I was hoping we could sort out about tonight.'

'What about tonight?'

'Where we're going to meet. What you'd like to do with me – although I'll bet I can guess.'

Connie giggles but Jack appears to have missed the joke. 'You shouldn't be up here, Connie. You'll be in bother if you're caught.'

'I don't care. They can sack me if they want. I can easily get a job somewhere else. Anyway, what's happening tonight? Where shall I meet you?'

'You'll have to go. You're not supposed to be up here. What if my wife comes up?'

'She won't. She's stuck in the lounge with Ma Clegg.'

A small high voice pipes up from within the room: 'Daddy? Who's at the door?'

Jack looks over his shoulder into the room. 'Nobody. Go to sleep now, Sputnik.' Jack steps out of the room and joins Connie in the corridor. 'I'm sorry, Connie. I mean about last night. It shouldn't have happened.'

'Don't say that! It was fun. We can have some more fun tonight.'

'No. It was a mistake. All my fault. I should never have walked you back, should never have started it, but it has to stop now.'

Connie pushes out her breasts, balances the tray in one hand and slips the other inside his jacket but Jack backs away. 'Don't say that, Jack. You know I love you. I'll be finished by eight. I'll see you at Yates's. You said yourself, it's no place for a girl to be drinking alone.'

Connie throws her weight on to her left leg, pushing out her right hip and gives Jack a coquettish smile. Jack lapses into silence. He eyes the top of the white waitress apron that fails to cover Connie's breasts.

'That's fixed, then. I'll see you at Yates's,' Connie says before he has a chance to reply.

'No! I can't meet you at Yates's. Half the lads at work will be there. We'll be seen.'

Connie looks surprised. 'It doesn't matter if we're seen. People are going to find out eventually anyway.'

'No! I can't. You have to go now. You'll be missed.'

'You can come to my room, then. I'll wait for you there, shall I? Be there at eight.'

There is the squeak of bedsprings, the swish of covers being pulled back and a light patter of footsteps.

'I have to go,' Jack says, dipping back into his daughters' room.

'Eight o'clock then,' Connie repeats as Jack is shutting the door.

17

WARNING NOTICE

There are always warning notices at the seaside. They are put there in order to ensure the safety of all visitors. Some notices warn of high tides or flooding. Some warn of danger from overhead wires, or unexpectedly deep pools, or quicksand, or heavy currents. The seaside can be a dangerous place. You must obey every sign you see. Score 20 points for staying safe!

Beth has discovered a new game. It's called 'Follow Gunner' and it's the best game she's ever played. It all started when she plucked up the courage to ask Mr Titherington, the hotel manager, if she could take Gunner for a walk.

'If it's all right with your mum and dad, it's OK with me.'

Beth assures him that her parents won't mind at all. She would go upstairs and ask but she's been sent off to play and not disturb them. A smile crosses the manager's face when he hears this. Sadly, he is mistaken. Beth's parents have sought the privacy of their hotel room in order to finish the heated argument held over from that morning. Ruth is determined to get Jack to agree to chuck in the foreman's job and take the Union's offer of area rep. She has detailed the reasons on several occasions. Ruth can't understand why Jack still won't make up his mind. What more does he want?

Meanwhile downstairs their younger daughter is listening carefully to Mr Titherington. 'Here you are, then,' he says, passing the lead to Beth. 'Don't take him along the backstreets. He's a bugger for getting into dustbins. And mind, don't let him off his lead.'

'Why not?'

'Because he'll either get into a fight or scarper. You'll not let him off, will you?'

Beth promises to keep Gunner on his lead but secretly she feels sorry for the dog. She believes it's sad to tie up animals, they should be free. The nurse tied her to a trolley in the hospital and it isn't nice. It's frightening. The thought stays with her as she walks the dog up to the prom. Gunner is dragging on the lead. He isn't keen to go. Beth stops again and strokes the dog in the hope of encouraging him forward. Gunner takes a couple of steps and sits down, giving Beth a reproachful look. Beth is convinced that Gunner would like it much better if he were allowed to run free.

She reaches down to unclip the lead and suddenly has a good idea. Why shouldn't Gunner decide where he wants to go? If she keeps the lead slack he could pretend that he's free and just go where he likes. It would be even better if Beth closes her eyes – that way Gunner could take her anywhere. But how to get the dog started? Beth tries several ideas (clicking her tongue and flicking the lead across Gunner's back as if he were a horse; pretending she has a sweet in her hand; standing behind him and pushing) until at last she makes a noise like a steam engine: ch-ch-ch, the sound universally understood to indicate the presence of a cat. And he's off like a shot, dragging Beth down the nearest alleyway in search of the imaginary cat. Beth is elated. She is forced to run at full pelt to keep the lead slack. 'Go, Gunner!' Beth pants, shutting her eyes as the dog careers down yet another alley.

This is the most exciting game ever. Beth is tugged blindly down foreign streets, brought to an abrupt stop at the edge of roads and then, equally abruptly, dragged across at breathtaking speed. Dog and girl are in complete harmony, Beth giggling with excitement and Gunner snorting at every lamp-post and growling at passing dogs. Beth's chest aches with laughter. She opens one eye every now and again, keen to see where Gunner is taking her. Once she almost trips over a loose cobble and nearly goes head first, but Gunner is still pulling so hard she is dragged back to her feet. She is whipped round corners, dragged down alleys, hauled across roads. This is the best fun that Beth has ever had. Saliva drips down her chin as she gasps for breath, her nose is assaulted by the smell of food – from hot dogs and boiled onions to vinegar, chips and hot sweet rock. Beth imagines that they must be some way from the hotel now. Gunner has slowed down to a bright trot and Beth opens her eyes. She is in the middle of a backstreet she has never seen before. She can hear the passing of traffic and fairground music in the far distance. The backstreet is lined with high wooden gates, some of them locked shut and others wide open. Beth bends to stroke Gunner. 'Where are we?' she whispers.

Gunner is too busy snuffling at a patch of dirty yellow groundsel to reply. Together they wander slowly down the street. Every now and again Beth gets a glimpse into one of the backyards. Some are neatly flagged and crossed with lines filled with swags of drying clothes, while others are an uproar of bicycle parts, gaping windows, broken slates and dumped ash. Gunner ploughs on and Beth follows, the back of her neck tingling with excitement. They walk in step now, as if they belonged together, and the pain in Beth's chest slowly subsides. Beth's eyes are wide open, drinking in the new experience of being totally lost. The world around her is unfamiliar, an entirely new sight greets her at every corner. She is like an explorer setting foot in a different world. At last Gunner comes to a full stop in front of a solid black gate marked

KEEP OUT
STRICTLY PRIVATE

Gunner pauses a moment, then pushes his nose against the bottom corner. Beth steps back, pulling lightly on the lead and whispers, 'No, Gunner. It says keep out.' But Gunner scratches at the gate and looks back at her. '*No*! It's not allowed. It says so.' Impatient now, Gunner presses hard with his nose. The gate opens just enough to allow the dog to wriggle through. Beth is horrified and promptly hauls the lead back, but it's too late – the gate swings open.

Tiger Woman is lounging in a ragged deckchair with her feet up on a broken raffia footstool. Above her head is a washing line full of the most peculiar clothes Beth has ever seen – tiny trousers with turn-ups and covered in gold braid, a brassiere that's packed full – not like the empty ones her mother has – and lastly a huge grey bag that is painted with scales and ends in a tail. Beth can't think who would want to wear clothes like this. Tiger Woman looks different from what she looks like on the poster. She's got a cigarette hanging out of the corner of her mouth and she's reading a copy of *Titbits*. She must have just come off stage because Beth can see she's still wearing her costume under a big blue dressing gown. But if Beth is surprised to come face to face with Tiger Woman, then Tiger Woman looks equally alarmed to see Beth.

It is Tiger Woman who takes the cigarette from her mouth and finally breaks the silence. 'Well, come in, then. Let's be seeing you.' Beth gasps and her eyes open even wider. 'Come on. I won't bite!'

Tiger Woman must think this is a joke because she laughs. Beth edges forward into the yard, but keeps herself ready to turn and flee. 'That dog is a right scallywag, isn't he? He's round here every day looking for food.' Tiger Woman sits up straight in her deckchair and pats her knee. 'Come on, then.'

Gunner jumps straight into Tiger Woman's lap and the resultant jerk on the lead pulls Beth even further into the yard. 'What's the matter, pet?'

'You can speak!' Beth says.

'Of course I can! What's so special about that?'

'But when I saw the picture of you the man said you didn't speak. Not since the tigers dragged you away.'

'Which man?'

'The little man who shouts a lot. The one who told me to hop it.'

'Malcolm? Malcolm the Midget? You don't want to listen to a word he says.' Tiger Woman has to lift her voice to be heard over the sound of Gunner snuffling through her pockets. 'He's looking for a titbit. He's a right soft bonnet, aren't you? Is he your dog, then?'

'Oh, no. But I wish he was. I'm just taking him for a walk for the man that owns him. He's called Gunner.'

'Oh, Gunner, is it? And I've been calling him Scruff! And what's your name?'

'Beth.'

Tiger Woman runs her scarlet fingernails through Gunner's fur and the dog arches in pleasure, lying back in her arms and lifting his throat to be tickled. Tiger Woman takes her feet off the raffia stool and says, 'Here, you park your bottom, pet, while I get him his usual.' Tiger Woman passes the dog over to Beth, who is overwhelmed to receive the pliant bundle. She would never dare pick up Gunner by herself. He's supposed to be fierce. Dog and child stare at each other for some moments.

'Good boy, Gunner,' Beth ventures.

The dog half closes his eyes and remains silent. Beth cuddles him very carefully. The sound of Tiger Woman's return enervates the apparently slumbering form of Gunner. He is immediately awake and leaps out of Beth's arms to greet her. Tiger Woman skips down the steps from the back door with a bundle in a paper serviette in each hand. She hands one to Beth. The girl hesitates. It's very wrong to take presents from strangers. Girls who don't pay attention to rules like this end up in danger. Beth has been warned.

'Come on, pet. It won't be a hot dog for long. It's going cold already.' Beth still hesitates. 'Well, if you don't want it . . .'

Beth is at a loss to know what to do. To turn her nose up at the gift would be rude, but eating it might prove dangerous. There are implied but unspecified dangers involved in consuming 'junk'. She looks down. Gunner has polished off the bun and is now savouring the onion and sausage. Inspired, Beth takes the bundle and unwraps the serviette to reveal a hot dog in a bun. Beth has never before come this close to a hot dog. She's smelled them and seen pictures of them but her mother has always refused to buy them. Hot dogs are forbidden food. Beth takes a small bite. Her teeth sink into the fluffy bun. Heaven. Another bite brings her first taste of the hot dog sausage. Salty juices escape from her mouth and run down her chin. The mixture of smoky meat and boiled onions melts in her mouth. She has never tasted anything so delicious. Another bite confirms the sensation.

Gunner has finished his treat and is holding down the serviette with one paw while licking off the residue of onion. He looks up at his walking companion, eager to catch her eye. Beth ignores the dog and continues eating. The dog sits at her feet, willing her to look at him, but still Beth feigns ignorance of his presence. Gunner is not a dog to beg. He waits in the hope of any falling debris and when it doesn't arrive he treads firmly on the front of her sandal. Beth moves her foot and continues chewing. Aware that the girl is coming to the end of her hot dog and frustrated by his apparent failure to coax a titbit from her, Gunner moves in still closer and rests his chin on her knee. A sound somewhere between a yelp and a growl vibrates in the dog's throat. It is a difficult appeal to ignore, delivered as it is with a turning of brown eyes and a tilting of the head. Gunner's nose brushes the back of Beth's hand. Defeated, she picks a single sliver of onion from the bun and watches as the dog lifts it neatly from her fingers.

Once the feast is finished Beth turns her attention back to her benefactor. 'Thank you,' she says with complete honesty. 'That was the best thing I've ever eaten.'

'Give over! I can't believe you've never had a hot dog before!' Tiger Woman sees a look of embarrassment cross Beth's face and adds, 'Still, you have now and that's all that matters.'

Filled with the warm reassurance that only forbidden food can supply, Beth looks hard at Tiger Woman and says, 'Did you have to go into hospital for your scars?'

Tiger Woman is taken aback. She looks carefully at the girl before saying, 'No, I didn't go.'

'You're lucky.'

'Why? Have you been in hospital?'

'Yes. I've got a scar all over my back and under my arm.'

'Have you? But you're better now, aren't you?'

'I don't know. It could happen again, couldn't it?'

'What could happen?'

'Blue lips. People don't like it when I have blue lips. They don't want to play with me because I'm ugly.'

'You don't look ugly to me. Your lips are a pretty shape and the only blue I can see is in your eyes. They're a lovely blue, just like the sea.'

'Well, Susan Fletcher came to see me when I was ill. And she asked and asked me to show her my scar and when I did she was so sick she had to go straight home. And I didn't even get the lolly she said she'd give me. And now I'm never allowed to do PE on Tuesdays at school. Or Music and Movement on Thursdays or Dancing on Fridays.'

'That's a shame. Why don't you join a club?'

'Not allowed.'

'Well, haven't you got friends to play with at the weekend?'

Beth shakes her head. 'My sister works on Saturdays. And Sundays I have to go to Sunday School. Mrs Brunskill told me off last time. She gave me a drawing of Jesus to crayon and I made it into a picture of my sister instead.'

Tiger Woman laughs. 'Why on earth did you do that?'

Beth wrinkles up her nose and purses her lips. 'Jesus is boring. There's nothing to colour in for Him except brown for His hair and pink for His hands and feet. The rest of Him is white. I gave Him yellow hair like Helen and I coloured in her best blue dress and red shoes. It looked just like Helen when I'd finished.'

'So have you no one to play with at weekends? Are there no children your age who live nearby?'

'There's Robert but he's always getting into trouble. Mr Kerkley swore at him. And there's Kathleen and Mary who live at the bottom of the street. I really like them, but Mummy always sends them away when they call for me.'

'Why?'

'Because they're Catholics.'

Tiger Woman listens carefully, feels in her pocket for a hanky and leans forward in her chair to wipe the mustard and sausage juice from Beth's chin. 'That's no reason to send them away. Catholics are just the same as you and me. Why were you in hospital?'

'The doctor said I had a hole in my heart. But I've never seen it so I don't know. But then they made a hole in my back and it didn't have a hole before but it does now. I didn't have no scars until then and now I've got lots of them. And they said it won't hurt and it did. And I get smacked if I tell lies, but they don't. Anyway, I hate them all. I hate all of them except my daddy and Helen.'

'Is Helen your sister?'

'Yes, and she does my writing for me but she won't be able to when I go back to school. I'll have to do it myself and sometimes I can't remember how to do all the letters. And if I go to the bottom of the class then they'll move me into the "B" class and I won't pass my Eleven Plus, and then I won't go to grammar school like Helen.'

'That's not such a disaster, is it?' Tiger Woman replies, although she can see from a glance at her visitor's face that it is. 'Well,' she continues, 'at least you're better now, aren't you?'

'Dr Richmond said I was getting better, but I heard my mummy saying I was too ill to go on holiday. And she's always saying she might lose me, and I think it's because she doesn't like me now I've got scars.'

'Well, I always think that scars aren't too bad. I mean, by the time you have a scar you're better, aren't you? It means the cut has healed. The scars on my back hurt a lot when I got them but they don't hurt at all now.'

'Where did you get them?'

Tiger Woman hesitates before answering. 'Somebody hurt me.'

'In the jungle? Was it a tiger?'

'Oh, it was a long time ago. All forgotten now. I'm more interested in you. I don't think you'll be bottom of your class. Were you bottom before?'

'No, Susan Fletcher was bottom.'

'Well, there you are! I'm sure you'll never be bottom of the class. You seem very clever to me.'

'I'm not. I'm stupid. I can't read the clock. Everyone learned it in Mrs Williams's class when I was in hospital. And I can't learn it because I've got a lazy eye and I'm so far behind I'll never catch up.'

'I don't think so. And anyway, school doesn't matter that much. What do you want to be when you grow up?'

Beth sniffs hard and swallows. 'I'd like to be pretty like you.'

'Well, you don't need to be top of the class to be pretty. What else would you like to be?'

Beth begins to cry and Tiger Woman lifts her from the raffia stool on to her knee and strokes her hair.

'I'd like to be a Tiger Woman.' Beth sobs. 'Then they wouldn't dare do things to me if I was a tiger. I'd tear them to pieces.'

'Well, you're halfway to being a tiger already, aren't you? Tigers are very, very brave. Just like you.'

Beth shakes her head, remembering the operation. 'I'm not brave, not like a tiger.'

'Oh, you are. You're the bravest little girl I've ever met. You can be anything you want to be. Even a Tiger Woman. You have my word for it. I can spot a tiger when I see one.' Tiger Woman flexes her scarlet claws, bares her teeth and roars until the sound fills the air. Beth jumps and then laughs, delighted by the scare. 'So where do you live?'

'At home with Mummy and Daddy.'

'Not in Blackpool, then? You're here on holiday?' Beth nods. 'Well, I'm due back on stage in five minutes so I'd better go in and get ready. And you'd better be getting back – your mum will be worrying about you. Which hotel are you staying at?'

'The Bell-dear.'

Tiger Woman looks flummoxed for a minute before she bends down and looks at the tag on the dog's collar. 'Oh, you mean the Belvedere.'

'Yes. Do you know the way? I was playing a game on the way here and I don't know the way back.'

'It's one of those big hotels at North Pier, I think. Just a minute. I'll see what I can do.'

When Tiger Woman returns she takes Beth by the hand and leads her down a side alley, which comes out on the prom beside the hoardings advertising the Palace of Strange Girls. Tiger Woman lifts her fingers to her mouth and whistles. A taxi appears out of the crush of traffic and holidaymakers, and in a moment both Beth and Gunner are ensconced in the back of the car and heading for the hotel.

18

BEACHCOMBING

There's nothing more interesting than walking along the beach after a storm. Things that were hidden are suddenly visible. Score 20 points for a shocking discovery.

Jack looks at his watch as he's buying his third pint at the Albion. It's eight o'clock. Connie will be sat on her bed, dressed up to the nines and waiting for him. But Jack has no intention of turning up. He despises himself for not telling her this afternoon, but it might have led to a scene in front of Sputnik and God knows he can't afford that. It's easier to keep out of Connie's way and hope nothing blows up before he leaves on Saturday. He glances around the bar in case Dougie has turned up, but there's no sign. Jack takes his next pint outside and sits down at one of the wooden tables overlooking the prom. He is well into his fourth pint before Dougie finally appears.

'Evenin', Jack.'

'What kept you?'

'Doug has bloody scored again. The door was locked when I got back to the hotel and there was no way he was going to let me in. In the finish he opened the door a crack, gave me a fiver and told me to bugger off. Considering he'd got another lass in bed, he didn't look that suited. I'd be over the bloody moon if I got my end away half as often as he does. I'd be happy if I managed it once. I haven't been near a woman since his mother upped and left. Anyway, why are you down in the dumps?'

'I'm all right,' Jack says, peering into the bottom of his glass.

'Oh, it's that bad, is it? I'd better get another round in.'

Dougie returns from the bar with two pints and a couple of whisky chasers. He puts the tray down on the table and gives Jack a long look. 'If there's nowt wrong then why were you so keen to meet up tonight? What's up? Have I to guess? It's like that programme on the radio, *Twenty Questions*.'

'The whole bloody thing is unravelling.'

'What is?'

'Everything. It's disaster everywhere I look. I've had enough, Dougie. For two pins I'd bugger off.'

'Give over! You wouldn't leave Ruth and the girls.'

'I wouldn't have to. They'd leave me if they knew.'

It's nine in the evening and the men watch as the wind brawls along the prom, whipping up a rage of dust, chip papers and orange peel. It's fair blustery. You can hear the thwack of waves breaking over the prom across the road.

'Well, if you're determined to get plastered at least slow down a bit and let me catch up.'

The two men sit in a companionable silence, sipping their beer and watching the waves break over the sea wall.

'Come on, spit it out. What have you done that's so bad?' Dougie asks.

'I've got mixed up with a waitress.'

Dougie slaps Jack on the back and cracks out laughing. 'Is that all? For God's sake, I thought it was summat important.'

'It is! She's barely out of school. She's . . . she's not even . . .' The words peter out. Jack's head sinks on to his chest. He can't bring himself to finish the sentence.

Dougie doesn't say anything. He just looks at Jack, waiting for the rest of the story. But Jack is silent for so long that Dougie is finally forced to ask, 'OK, you've been having some fun with a waitress. It was a mistake, but it's not the end of the world. Is it?'

'She's a friend of Helen's.'

'Bloody hell. You've been playing a bit close to home, haven't you? Is it likely to get out?'

'I don't know. She'd fixed up for us to meet up tonight. But I didn't go.'

Dougie starts to laugh again, 'Well, you may be a fair few years older but you've obviously still got what it takes!'

Jack gives him the faintest of smiles.

'It'll sort itself out. If Ruth cottons on then you'll have to tell her that it wouldn't have happened if she'd been a bit more accommodating. Who can blame you if you have to go elsewhere for what, by rights, you should be getting at home? It doesn't mean anything. It's just a bit of pleasure. God knows you could do with it. Life isn't all hard graft and overtime, Jack.'

'I want to go back to Crete.'

Dougie is at a loss to understand. As far as he is concerned they were talking about Jack having a good time with a waitress. Now the subject has changed. 'What's this about Crete?'

'I want to go back.'

'What? Am I hearing you right? Didn't you see enough of it during the war? Have you gone daft? Have you forgotten what happened?'

Jack doesn't answer.

Imbros Gorge, Crete, 30 May 1941

It is early morning. Jack and Nibs have spent an uneasy night in near freezing temperatures. They wake to find muscles stiff from a night without cover, flesh that is numb with the cold, feet and hands that ache with the smallest movement. There is nothing to eat, no dry rations or even foraged berries. They pass a canteen of water between them, shudder at the shock of cold water in their throats. Sitting on the rocks above the track, they watch as a ragged stream of retreating soldiers stumble down into the gorge. This final leg of the journey should be relatively straightforward. It will be a long walk but the high sides of the gorge will provide some protection, and beyond it lie the beach and the prospect of rescue.

They are following a goat track down a shallow gully when they hear the approach of enemy aircraft. The Allied anti-aircraft guns on the plateau above them kick in and the ground shudders with the firing. Jack watches as the bombs topple out of the planes and waits for the sound of the impact. Having discharged its load, one of the Messerschmitts banks steeply to avoid returning fire and begins to strafe the surrounding area. Seeing the approach of the Messerschmitts, Jack and Nibs dive for cover. Seconds later Jack feels the heat of bullets passing his cheek and hears the branches above his head burst into splinters of wood and torn leaves. Bullets ricochet wildly around the rocks. There's a cry from over to his right and Nibs topples forward to lie on the floor of the gully. A mixture of shock and blind terror stops Jack from moving immediately. A bullet has grazed his cheek but he is otherwise unharmed. The sight of Nibs lying in a fast-spreading pool of blood jolts Jack into action. When he reaches the injured man he discovers that Nibs has been hit twice in the leg. These look to be flesh wounds but when Jack turns him over he sees that his friend has been hit in the shoulder as well. The wound is bursting blood across the pale rocks that cover the gully floor. Nibs is still conscious and screaming with the pain. Without a first-aid pack or any way to staunch the blood other than strips ripped from his shirt, Jack is reduced to patching up what he can, all the time assuring Nibs that the wounds aren't serious, that there'll be another aid post further down the gorge, that they'll reach Sfakion in two shakes.

Supporting Nibs with his right arm, Jack starts the long descent. It is pitch black at the bottom of the gorge, the rock walls rising 2,000 feet above their heads, and the floor of the gorge narrows, compressing the disparate groups of soldiers into one long line of retreat. Jack's ears are filled with the constant drone of bombers and the rock-strewn path at his feet switches this way and that like a dog's hind leg. They have not been going for twenty minutes when Nibs's screams change to groans and finally silence as he loses consciousness. Jack stops, panic-stricken. He lowers Nibs to the ground, checks his friend's neck and, feeling a pulse, is reassured. There is no alternative. Jack will have to carry him the rest of the way. He hefts the limp body of Nibs on to his back. It is a crushing weight. Jack can feel his chest straining for breath as he starts forward with the burden.

Halfway down the gorge and the effort of moving one foot in front of the other is overwhelming. Jack is empty of both thought and feeling. He is only aware of the river of sweat that oozes down his back. He wants to stop and rest but the weight and the fear are killing him. His legs, which should have given way long ago, continue to move without any conscious direction from him. He can feel nothing now, not even hunger. Nibs has been quiet for a long time and, despite the troops in front and behind him, Jack has the sensation of being totally alone. He is now barely aware of the weight he is carrying, or where he is heading. He is driven by some automatic response beyond fear and despair. Even the blinding sunlight and the breadth of the open sea that greet him when he reaches the end of the gorge fail to register. Jack is still struggling through the endless darkness, the weight of Nibs across his shoulders, his blood-soaked shirt sticking to his back and chest as he grasps the lifeless hand of his friend.

* * *

Jack is shaken back into the present by the sound of Dougie banging another couple of pints down on the table in front of him. Dougie takes a gulp of his beer and says, 'Look, Jack, lots of the lads were like this after the war. They came home and discovered it wasn't all that they'd hoped it would be. They'd not been back more than a couple of months when they were looking for a way out. Is that it? Is that what's bothering you? You're a daft bugger. You'd be crazy to leave. Especially when you're about to start making a lot more money. There's no reason to go back, is there?'

Jack pulls out the photograph of Eleni and the boy.

Dougie looks hard at the black-and-white picture for a few moments before saying, 'It's a picture of you and a girl. Taken in Crete, was it? I've seen hundreds of photos like it from the war. I've even got a few myself. What's so special?' Dougie hands the photo back. 'Short of wondering what you're doing out of uniform, that is. Who's the woman? She's a stunner.'

'She's called Eleni. The photo was taken last year.'

Doug needs a minute or two to take this in. At last he says, 'Well, if it's not you, who's the lad standing next to her, then?' Jack is silent. Dougie takes the photo a second time and peers at the figures, turning towards the light streaming out of the Albion's double doors in an attempt to see better.

'There's no point,' snaps Jack, snatching back the photo. 'He's mine. He's my son.'

Dougie recovers from the shock of this revelation surprisingly quickly. He takes another sip of his beer and gives Jack a long, cool look. 'What's this Eleni asking for?'

'Nothing.'

Dougie shakes his head. 'They're the worst.'

'What do you mean?'

'I mean why send you the bloody thing if she doesn't want anything? What's the point?'

'She says they'd both like to see me.'

'I'd like to come up on the pools, but that's not going to happen either.'

'It's not that straightforward.'

'How do you mean?'

'I mean I want to see Eleni, and the lad as well.'

'Give it time, Jack. You'll get over it. If you're determined to do something, send her a few quid and then forget about it. She's managed by herself since you left and she'll manage again.'

'No. I can't. I can't carry on the way I've been doing. I'm half mad with thinking it over and over. I've got to see her. A photo isn't enough. I have to see her. I thought she was dead, killed when the village was bombed.'

'But what about Ruth? She'll not stand you buggerin' off to Crete.'

'I'd never have got mixed up with Ruth if I'd known that Eleni was still alive.'

'You've done a bit more than just get mixed up, Jack. You've been married seventeen years and had two daughters.'

'I don't know what I'm going to do about Ruth.'

'Well, God knows, I can understand if you're wanting to get shut.'

Jack stares into his pint while he struggles to make some sort of a reply. At last he says, 'You've got to make allowances for Ruth. She had a rough time when she was younger. She does her best. She's a good mother to the girls and she's a hard worker.'

'Aye, but there has to be more than that. Why did you marry her in the first place?'

'I've told you, I thought Eleni was dead.'

'Aye, but you could have married anybody. Can't you remember why you chose Ruth?'

Jack can remember. He can remember quite clearly. November 1941. He'd got a week's leave and spent it at the Southgate Hotel near Sidi Bishri beach. There'd been a mail drop, the first for a couple of months, just before he'd left. The Southgate was run by an Englishwoman – a sort of home from home. He'd just slept for the first couple of days and so it was the third day before he'd got round to opening his post. There were five letters from Ruth – she'd worked out he was on Crete but still hadn't heard whether he'd got off safely. From the dates on the letters it was apparent that she'd written every few days, hoping for news. Instead of the usual titbits of church news and local gossip, these letters were full of her concern for him, anxiety for his welfare and hopes for his safe return. He supposed that the possibility that he was dead had made her more open about her feelings. Either way, he was touched. He could hear her voice as he read the words. It meant a lot. And the more he studied the letters in the quiet of the hotel the more he felt the strength of her devotion. By the end of the week he had decided. He would buy a ring and marry her when he was next home on leave. The knowledge not only gave him immediate peace but also a reason to carry on after the loss of Eleni.

Back in Blackpool, Jack leans forward and takes up his pint. Dougie is waiting for a reply. Why had he married Ruth? 'She's a good woman,' Jack says. Dougie cracks out laughing when he hears this. 'What's tickling you?' Jack asks.

'I was just remembering, that's all. Remembering meeting you on Oxford Road with a woman on each arm. What was it you used to say? "God help me, I'm not ready for a good woman yet, Dougie."'

'Well, by the time I married Ruth I was. I just wanted to settle down. I lost my appetite for playing the field in Crete. When I lost Eleni I'd had enough. I just didn't want to start again, looking for someone else. I was so tired after Crete. I was never that tired in my life before, or since. I felt like I was hollow, eaten away with exhaustion. And lonely. I just wanted to belong to someone. And Ruth was as good a bet as any. She may not have been as much fun as the girls I used to knock around with, but there again after the war, excitement was the last thing I was after. And Ruth wasn't going to get herself killed like Eleni, or run off with someone else the minute my back was turned like Cora. I thought that Ruth was a safe bet. And I was right. Marrying Ruth was the right thing to do at the time. It only turned sour in the last year since the little girl got ill.'

'And is Beth the reason you don't leave?'

'It's not just that. I've a duty to both girls. Anyway, I'm no use to Beth. I can't bear to see her so ill. When she got a collapsed lung after the operation I caught myself thinking she'd be better off dead than crippled for life with a bad chest.'

'But you said that she's getting better now. She's right enough now, isn't she?'

'Depends what you mean by "better". She has nightmares every night, she's missed the best part of a term and the school says she'll struggle to catch up. Some days she won't talk at all – she just nods or shakes her head. She doesn't trust anybody, I can see it in her face. Not that I see a lot of her what with all the overtime I do.'

'She'll come round. Just wait. Both lasses would be heartbroken if you walked out.'

'You think so? How upset do you think Helen's going to be when she hears I've been in bed with her best friend?'

'Deny it.' Jack shakes his head. 'I mean it. Deny everything,' Dougie insists. 'It'll all settle down. Ruth will think that waitress is nothing more than a teenager with a crush. You're just having a rough time at the moment. Everything will sort itself out in the finish.'

'Well, if nothing else, it has solved one problem.'

'What's that?'

'I may not be able to go out to Crete yet, but I've decided to take the manager's job at Prospect. I'm going to turn down the Union's offer.'

'Well, thank God you're finally seeing sense. You'd be a fool to take less cash with the Union. Principles are all well and good, but they don't buy the bacon. Have you told Ruth?'

'No, I'll tell her tomorrow. We're due to go over to St Anne's for a couple of hours without the girls. It'll be a chance for us to have a quiet chat on the way back. I'll tell her then.'

'Aye, get her told. She'll be over the moon. What are you going to do with all the extra cash? Buy Ruth one of those new semis she's been pining for?'

'I'm not taking out a mortgage to buy a bloody semi.'

'What are you going to do with all the extra, then?'

'I'll send some to Eleni and the rest I'll save. I will go back to Crete. I've a lad there I've never seen.'

It's late before Jack and Dougie leave the pub. Jack is looking the worse for wear. Dougie offers to walk back to the Belvedere with him but Jack refuses. The walk along the prom has a sobering effect on Jack. After a few minutes he's aware of footsteps running up behind him.

'Why, if it isn't the resident fucking gigolo.' Jack carries on walking. 'Are you deaf? I'm talking to you, you bastard.'

Jack finally stops and turns round to face the voice. The man's face is familiar but Jack has trouble remembering where he's seen it before. The speaker is slight but muscular, red hair, pasty white face scattered with freckles. He's already got his fists clenched as he closes in on Jack.

'What's biting you?' Jack asks, raising his hand to ward the man off.

'I'd scarper quick if I was you. After all, you've a talent for scarpering, haven't you?'

'I don't know who you are or what you want. You need to get

home. It's too late to be spoiling for a fight.' Jack turns away. A second later he feels a blow land on the back of his head, forcing his skull sideways, making him stagger forward. Jack grabs on to the railings to steady himself and turns again to look at his assailant. The man is bearing down on him, both fists clenched and guarding his face as if he were a trained boxer. Jack finally recognises the face – it's the chef from the hotel. Jack fumbles for the man's name. 'It's Andy, isn't it? You work at the hotel, don't you? What are you playing at, you daft bugger?'

'It's you doing all the playing around. What about Connie? She's in a right mess because of you. She's less than half your age, you dirty bugger. What sort of twisted bastard gets a young lass into bed and then drops her like a hot cake the next day?'

'Bugger off. It's none of your business.'

'I've made it my business now. You're a miserable bastard. Once you'd got what you wanted from Connie you couldn't even remember her name. You haven't even got the guts to tell her to her face. She's been waiting all night for you to turn up.'

'It's nothing to do with you. Connie was keen enough. I can't remember hearing her complain.'

Andy throws another punch at Jack's face. This time his fist connects with Jack's right temple and there is a thud as the blow lands. Jack raises his hand to the right side of his face, the skin around his eye humming with pain. Finally he is roused to retaliate. Jack may be a good ten years older than the chef and a damn sight less agile, but he's powerfully built. He swings a punch to the man's jaw and follows it with a cut to the stomach as the chef falls. It is all over very quickly. Looking down at the figure of the chef sprawled across the promenade, Jack resists the urge to stick his boot in the man's ribs. He has been seen – there's a small crowd gathered across the other side of the road and the sound of a whistle in the distance. Jack breaks into a run, dodging down the nearest side street and nearly knocking over a couple locked in beery union in the process. He turns sharp left down a cobbled back alleyway punctuated by dustbins and littered with discarded refuse. Jack covers some distance before stopping to catch his breath. The police are streets behind him and it's hardly likely that the chef will press charges – not if he wants to hang on to his job at the hotel. Jack slows to walking pace and considers his options. It's well past midnight. Thank God he's remembered to take the front-door key. He can feel the right side of his face swelling up, now he's stopped to catch his breath. There's nothing for it. He'll have to let himself in quietly and hope no one sees him.

19

THE BIG WHEEL

If you go to a big holiday resort you might see a Big Wheel. They're awfully important, they make a lot of noise and they're known to ordinary people for miles around. But do remember, children, a Big Wheel can be dangerous and there's no such thing as a free ride! Score 50 points for spotting a big mover.

Blackpool, Friday 15 July 1959

'I hope your kids aren't hungry! You're tied on for a fair wait this morning, Ruth.' Following their heart-to-heart yesterday Florrie now regards Ruth as an intimate friend. She has been waiting with growing impatience for the Singleton family to come down for breakfast. Now that they have arrived she is anxious to share the gossip.

'Why's that?'

'It's Andy. You know, the chef. He hasn't come in this morning and the manager has had to step in. We've been waiting ages and

Connie has only just taken our order. You'd think they'd be better staffed mid-season. You've got to get what cereal you want from that table over there. By the left, your Jack looks as if he's been through the mill. Picked up a right shiner there, hasn't he?'

'It's nothing. Just a bump,' Ruth says.

'Been a bit busy with your fists, have you, Jack?' Florrie bellows over Ruth's head.

Jack gives her the nearest he can get to a smile.

'I'd hate to see what state the other bloke is in,' Florrie adds. She winks and nudges Fred, from whom she's already had the whole story.

Fred had been drinking late when Jack had walked past the entrance to the hotel bar. When Fred had seen the state Jack was in he'd pulled him into the bar, sat him down in the corner and ordered a brandy. The bar steward had looked none too pleased, the Belvedere has strict rules. Residents wishing to take advantage of the hotel bar must be properly attired. Fred had ignored the barman's objections and grabbed a bar towel to wipe the worst of the blood off his face. Fred had thought that the steward was going to throw them out, but the wound had looked worse than it was. Jack had said that he'd lost his footing on the prom and he'd given the steward such a look that the lad had pulled down the shutters on the bar and switched off the lights, leaving Fred and Jack to nurse their drinks in the semi-darkness. Fred had recounted the tale to Florrie, who'd pressed for all the lurid details. But Fred had said there weren't any – looking back, it hadn't been funny at all. He'd seen a despair in Jack's face that was even deeper than his own.

This morning he catches Jack's eye and nods his support before turning to Florrie and muttering, 'Drop it, Flo. Let the man eat his breakfast in peace.'

Connie breezes up to the Singleton table and lifts an impertinent eyebrow. She doesn't even bother to write down their order when Ruth gives it. Helen looks up and smiles at Connie, but the waitress looks away. When she brings the full English, Connie virtually throws the hot plate down in front of Jack and, passing behind him, mutters, 'Hope it bloody chokes you.'

Ruth gives no indication that she has heard the comment. Indeed, any bystander would find it difficult to believe that Mrs Singleton is anything less than completely satisfied with the service.

Five minutes later Connie appears again with a tea tray complete with teapot, hot water, sugar and milk. This too is slammed on the table with the words, 'Manager apologises for the delay. Chef was beaten up last night. In case you didn't know. He's off work today with his hand in plaster.'

Jack and Ruth studiedly ignore the information and continue breakfast in silence. Under normal circumstances Ruth would be prompted to complain about the lukewarm tea but she has put two and two together. Whatever Jack was up to last night, it has resulted in the chef needing hospital treatment.

'Now, don't you worry about your girls, Ruth,' Florrie says. 'We'll keep an eye on them. Our Alan reckons they'd enjoy a walk on the pier, depending on the weather, of course. Though it looks to have fined up after all that rain yesterday.'

Ruth has been listening with mounting horror. At last she can stand it no longer and interrupts Florrie's flow. 'I don't let the girls on the pier. It's too rough and there's nothing for them to do there anyway.' Florrie looks scandalised and opens her mouth to protest but Ruth carries on. 'I've told the girls to stay in the hotel. Helen has plenty of postcards to write while Elizabeth is having her nap.'

Jack starts the minute they leave the dining room. 'I can't say I'm keen on St Anne's. It'll mean getting a tram to Squires Gate and then walking. I don't know why you have to see Cora anyway. You can see her any day of the week at home. Why don't we forget about it and just have a couple of hours to ourselves?'

'After last night I don't think you're in any position to complain about anything. From what that silly waitress said, I wouldn't be surprised if it wasn't the chef who gave you a black eye.'

'I told you what happened. It was nothing to do with the chef. Dougie got into a fight. He was outnumbered. I stepped in to help him, that's all.'

'It doesn't make any difference. We're going. It's all settled. Cora invited us.'

'Where is the bloomin' place, anyway?'

'It's at the far end of St Anne's. Right by the golf links.'

'Well, it'd have to be, wouldn't it?'

'I don't think Ronald plays that much.'

'I'll bet he doesn't. Too much like hard work. No, he'll be sat in the clubhouse doing business with all the other bastards with funny handshakes.' Ruth gives Jack a warning look. She doesn't hold with swearing – it's a bad example to set for the girls. But

Jack knows Ronald Lloyd well enough to avoid him if at all possible. 'You should have seen him at infant school. He thought he was the Big Wheel even then.'

Ruth ignores him and continues, 'Cora says the hotel does afternoon tea in the conservatory. Cream cakes baked fresh every day and fancy sandwiches. And there's music. You'll enjoy it.'

'I'm surprised you asked Mrs Clegg to look after the girls. I'd have thought that was the last thing you'd want.'

'I've told Helen to stay in the hotel and ignore whatever Florrie Clegg says. They'll be all right. I don't think I'm being unreasonable taking a couple of hours off from looking after the girls. After all, Helen is sixteen, Jack. She's old enough to keep her eye on Elizabeth. We'll take the girls out this morning. It doesn't look like rain.'

Since it is the last day of the holiday, Jack decides to treat the family to a trip up the Tower. Ruth has no head for heights and spends the morning reading the paper on the prom. Jack glances at Beth as they are queuing for tickets. What has got into her? She is chattering ten to the dozen and skipping from foot to foot. She's a different child. Jack reckons it must be taking Gunner for a walk yesterday that has been the turning point. Victor mentioned it to him and Jack was at pains to keep the news from Ruth. Heaven knows what a fuss there'd be if Ruth found out that Beth had been wandering the streets with a dog. When Jack asked Beth about her walk she said that she'd gone to see Tiger Woman and she'd had a hot dog, and she was going to be a Tiger Woman when she grew up. Jack had retied the ribbon in her hair and told her that she was the best storyteller he'd ever heard.

When they reach the top of the Tower Beth looks down and tries to spot her mother but it's impossible. She could be any one of the thousands of dark specks swarming along the promenade below. From this height the trams crawling along the prom and the horse-drawn landaus look like dolly mixtures. A ragged fringe of bathers hugs the water's edge, advancing and retreating with the waves, and the sea stretches long and wide like a great blue flag rippling in the breeze. Jack urges Beth to take big breaths of the fresh air. He demonstrates, squaring his shoulders and lifting his chest, breathing in through his nose and out through his mouth. Beth looks up at him in admiration. He's like a giant. No matter how cold it gets up the Tower the huge hand that safely holds hers is always warm.

Beth's view is limited to the sight of rusty brown ironwork until Jack lifts her and takes her on a tour of the viewing platform, pointing out all the distant coastlines. 'That's the Westmorland Fells, the start of the Lake District, and that's Scotland,' he says, pointing north.

'How far away is it?' Beth asks.

'The Lake District? About forty miles, as the crow flies.'

'How does a crow fly?'

'Like this,' Helen says, flapping her arms.

Jack and Beth both laugh, ignoring the people who have turned to stare.

'So that must be Ireland,' Helen says, pointing west.

'Yes, and the Isle of Man. And there, behind all the mist, is north Wales.'

Helen follows her dad's pointing finger – all these places she's never been. Helen sighs and turns away.

The fresh air has given everyone an appetite. The Singletons have dinner in a café, and make their way back to the hotel for a wash and change. The whole family is in high spirits, even Ruth and Helen appear to have reached a truce.

It's two o'clock before Jack and Ruth set off for St Anne's. There's a queue for the tram and, although this isn't unusual in Blackpool at the height of the season, there's still a sense of expectation in the crowd. When the bloke at the head of the queue announces, 'It's comin'!' the whole crowd murmurs and leans forward across the tracks to catch its first glimpse of the tram. It's the 'Blackpool Belle', a standard, run-of-the-mill olive and yellow tram transformed into a replica of a Mississippi paddle steamer complete with wheel, or at least the closest any weaver this side of the Atlantic is going to get to one. Seeing the surge of the crowd when the doors open, Jack takes Ruth's arm and they step back and wait.

The next tram goes the long way round. Only half full, it threads its way inland through a long sprawl of red-brick semis, built before the war. To Ruth's eye, familiar only with endless streets of modest terraced houses, these semis look palatial. The patterned brickwork carries with it a sense of solid authority. The entrances are flanked by red-brick pillars topped with huge cream balls carved with the house name. Heavy wrought-iron gates open on to wide gravelled drives. The gardens consist of verdant lawns fringed by ornamental borders filled with roses. These semis, with their coach lights and fancily carved barge boards, exude a private superiority from their high trimmed hedges to their polished and leaded windows that flash like diamonds against the white paintwork. And no two are exactly the same. Not like terraced houses where you could go in any one and find your way blindfold into the scullery or up to the attic. Residents of St Anne's wouldn't know what a donkey stone was if it hit them in the face.

The Links Hotel is heralded by a string of company flags that line the drive leading to the front entrance. It's an impressive sight. Jack and Ruth step through the entrance into a cool reception area that's all Ionic columns. Their ears are assaulted by the sound of violins from loudspeakers hidden behind gigantic flower arrangements. They approach a reception desk that is the size of Ruth's kitchen at home and, having given their names, a supercilious bellboy in green and gold livery escorts them through to a rambling Edwardian conservatory complete with button-back couches and wrought-iron tables.

Cora spots them as soon as they walk in and waves them over. She is heavily made up, powder lies thickly on her cheeks and there is a gash of bright-red lipstick across her mouth. She looks unsteady in her white canvas wedge shoes as she stands up to greet them. Cora is wearing a dramatically tight-waisted dress with a full red polka-dot skirt. The white feathers on her cocktail hat waft in the air as she embraces Ruth. Sunglasses cover her eyes but, as ever, her smile is sufficient to disarm the most critical look. Ronald, every inch the assistant bank manager, lounges back in his chair with a proprietorial air, as if the whole building belongs to him. Ronald has dark-brown hair that is parted thickly on the left and held in place by generous amounts of hair oil. His wide face and blunt nose distract attention away from small blue eyes that constantly shift, taking in everything. His body gives every indication of having escaped the worst deprivations of the post-war economy. He is a man writ large. He exudes from the open pores of his skin an aura of complacent wealth, of gravitas in a world of lesser mortals. His feet alone have resisted the onslaught of middle-aged expansion. They remain small, dainty to the point of absurdity, and encased in diamond-patterned golfing socks and black lace-up shoes.

'Look who's here, Ronnie. It's Ruth and Jack. I told you I'd invited them over.'

Ronald gives Ruth a thick-lipped smile that disappears from his mouth the moment it arrives. He fails to acknowledge Jack other than by pointing to the seats opposite and indicating the visitors should sit. This gesture never fails to intimidate both social inferiors and bank customers called in to explain their overdrafts. Jack, alive to Ronald's calculated superiority, ignores the indicated seating and chooses instead to sit at the other side of Cora.

Cora softens at his approach, pats his knee and says, 'Did you find the hotel OK, Jack? I'm afraid the directions I gave Ruth were a bit vague. I'm not a driver, you see. I don't really pay much attention to the roads.'

'We were fine,' Jack replies, folding his arms. 'We came over by tram.'

'Why, that'll have dropped you some distance away,' Ronald smirks.

'Yes,' Ruth concedes, 'but it was a nice walk. We wouldn't have seen the avenue of limes . . . well, not properly, if we'd come by car. The gardens here are beautiful, aren't they?'

'It took us half the time to get here that it usually does,' Ronald tells Jack, 'what with my new Rover. There's some real power under the bonnet. And the acceleration – nought to sixty in no time. You don't drive, do you, Jack?' Jack opens his mouth to say that he drove during the war, but Ronald breezily continues, 'Still, Cora tells me you're on the waiting list for a second-hand car. A Ford Popular, is it? Small but cheap to run. Thirty brake horse-power. You'll not have to let him get carried away with the speed, Ruth. Anyway, let me order something. What would you want, Ruth? Cora has been drinking pink gin – can I order one for you?'

Ruth shakes her head. 'No, thank you, Ronald. A cup of tea would be nice though.'

Ruth had told Cora about the car (£390 + tax) in the strictest confidence. About how excited Jack was. About it having chrome bumpers and hubcaps. And a spare wheel and even a boot. Jack looks irritated already and they've not been there five minutes.

'And you, Jack?'

'Tea is fine. I make a point of not drinking during the day.'

Ronald raises a lazy paw. A steward hurries up, pad and pencil at the ready, and is dispatched with an order for a pink gin, a whisky sour and a pot of tea for two. Ronald is a heavy tipper. But only in public. Women who weekly provide private services of a personal nature never see this beneficent side of Mr Lloyd.

'Do any gardening, Jack?' Ronald asks.

'No. Not really.'

'Oh, you should. I find it very relaxing. It's the coming thing. You wouldn't recognise The Hallows now. Shrubbery, bedding schemes, herbaceous borders – I've ditched the lot. They're very old hat nowadays. Got a man in to lay the concrete. He made me laugh. Wanted paying in advance, didn't he, Cora?' Cora nods dutifully. 'In case I changed my mind once the concrete was down. No fear of that I told him. I left the beech hedge in though – I don't mind forking out for a new-look garden but I'm blowed if I'll have passers-by gawping. I like my privacy. Not that there's been much of that since the railings went to the war effort. Once I'd got rid of the flowers I got my gardener to lay a lawn along the front. It's immaculate, even though I say it myself. Best lawn I've ever seen. Of course, it takes a lot of care to get it to that standard. My man uses sulphate of ammonia for weeds and iron sulphate for the moss – all mixed with sand, of course. You need a good dose of chemicals to get a lawn looking as good as mine. And plenty of DDT – best pesticide there is. Gardener watched all the concrete being put down at the back and said, "You'll be putting me out of a job, Mr Lloyd; there'll be no flowers to look after at this rate." But he changed his tune when I put in the raised beds and concrete pots. A block of French yellow marigolds just like the ones we saw at the latest Ideal Homes Exhibition, all crammed tight between the concrete walls, and another block of roses, twelve foot by six, at right angles to it. I don't hold with a mishmash of different varieties – you don't get the same uniform colour. All the paths are solid concrete, of course – you can walk round my garden all day and not get a bit of soil on your shoes. Cora's delighted. We're planning a garden party next week to show it all off. I don't suppose you have much of a garden where you are, Jack?'

'No.'

'Still, Cora tells me that you have one of those allotments across the road from where you live. How convenient. I bet you escape out there every Saturday to read your newspaper. You run a couple of dozen hens on the allotment, don't you? They'll be keeping you busy, I expect.'

Jack barely nods. The waiter arrives with afternoon tea and performs a series of deft moves in order to fit the feast on the table.

'Oh, I should let Ruth be mother,' Ronald says when Cora reaches for the teapot. 'I'd say she was altogether better qualified, wouldn't you?'

There is an uneasy silence. Cora pushes her sunglasses further up the bridge of her nose and says in a voice that is brittle enough to break, 'I'll bet the girls are enjoying Blackpool, aren't they? We've been lucky with the weather, haven't we? You're staying at the Belvedere, aren't you?'

'Yes, but it's not like this.'

Jack leans forward and interrupts. 'It's good enough,' he says, shooting Ruth a glance.

'Well, yes,' Ruth agrees, 'but this looks to be a lovely hotel.'

'This place?' Ronald asks, his tone incredulous. 'It isn't a patch on our usual hotel. But there again, this isn't the Costa Brava, is it?

I wish the bank could afford to give me a Wakes Week every year, but we're too busy. It's pure chance that I managed to get these days off.'

Jack leans back in his chair, folds his arms and peers up at the glass roof. There's a four-piece string quartet started up somewhere and the piano accompaniment isn't all it should be. Jack has an ear for music and the occasional flat note from the piano makes him wince. That and the proximity of Ronald bloody Lloyd is enough to make him sick. Jack and Cora had knocked around together a lot before the war. He liked the way her hair curled and fell through his fingers, the perfume she wore that made her smell of wild violets. Never on time, daft as a brush, hopelessly clumsy, Cora had been the perfect complement to Jack. He'd be up on the stage blowing his trombone and she'd be down on the dance floor with all comers. It was only flirting, but Jack had ended up punching one or two of the more persistent bastards. His eye strays across to Cora but she's difficult to decipher – especially behind those sunglasses.

'How's your daughter getting on, Ruth?' Ronald asks.

'Oh, she's getting better from her operation quickly now.'

'No, you misunderstand. I mean the other one. Helen, isn't it? The blonde one. She whose face launched a thousand ships.' The look that passes across Ronald's face prevents both Jack and Ruth from feeling flattered. 'Is she still working at the dress shop?'

'She works Saturdays – that's enough. I won't let her work full time. Next term she'll be starting A-Levels and there'll be plenty of school work to keep on top of.'

'Well, your girl could do a lot worse than work for Blanche,' Ronald says. 'She'd get to know one or two things about the way the world works that she won't learn at school,' he goes on with a smirk.

Cora sees the expression on Ruth's face and hurriedly interrupts: 'I shouldn't be surprised if Helen ends up going to university. The shop may be all right for a Saturday job but the shine would soon wear off if she had to sell dresses for the rest of her life.'

'Well, you don't know. She might catch herself a husband,' Ronald persists.

'Over my dead body. She needs a proper career first. There's plenty of time for boys after she's finished university,' Ruth counters.

'I don't know about you but I've always thought education is a waste of time for women. No man wants a clever-sticks for a wife. You don't need A-Levels to look after a husband. Look at Blanche – now there's a woman who's made the best use of her assets. Anyway, Helen's pretty enough not to need paper qualifications. You never did, Cora, and you've done very well for yourself – you signed on for a life of luxury the moment you married me.' He turns to Jack and says pointedly, 'Cora wasted time with the odd loser before she married me. But she's smart enough to know which side her bread is buttered on. Aren't you, darling? She made the right move when she married me.' Ronald pauses, watches, dares Jack to react.

Jack had been in Italy when he'd heard Cora had got married: a big do, by all accounts. ASSISTANT BANK MANAGER WEDS COTTON QUEEN: the local paper gave it a full page. Jack's sister said it had been the talk of the town – a slice of rich fruitcake for every customer who walked into the bank on the day. The cake was nothing short of a miracle when you considered how ordinary people were struggling with rationing. The effort to remain civil to Ronald has Jack shifting in his seat, crossing his arms and taking deep breaths. He is about to suggest that he and Ruth leave when Cora jumps up and says she's off to powder her nose. Ruth gets up as well and the two of them are off without a backward glance.

'Now that the ladies have left us, let me get you a proper drink, Jack.' Ronald hails a passing waiter and orders a couple of whiskies. The waiter is all over him like a rash: yes, sir, no, sir, thank you very much indeed, Mr Lloyd.

'What happened to your eye, man?' Ronald asks with apparent concern as the steward appears with their whiskies. 'Ruth's not been letting you out at night, has she? Oh, no offence intended! Doubtless you were defending a lady's honour when you got it. I suppose it's only to be expected with our local war hero.'

'Don't be ridiculous.'

'Well, Jack, we couldn't all be swanning around the Mediterranean picking up medals. Some of us had to stay at home and take the responsibility for keeping things going. You can't expect a bank to look after itself.'

'I heard different, Ronald. I heard you'd already got your call-up papers. I heard it was a case of money changing hands, of strings being pulled.'

'You're not above pulling the odd string yourself.'

'What do you mean?'

'I mean the manager's job at Prospect. What did you have to do to get offered that? Oh, you needn't look surprised. John Foster banks with me. I've recommended one or two very good investments to him over the past year. He's cock-a-hoop at the moment. He's pretty sure that there's going to be some left over after the government grant comes through and he's always on the lookout for a decent return. He let it slip that you'd been offered the job of manager.' Jack fails to react so Ronald continues, 'Cora tells me that Ruth has her eye on one of those new semis, but that's the ladies for you, bless them. Always ready to spend the money before it's even been earned. It'll mean a mortgage, of course. Still, you know where to come. I'll be happy to consider your application. Of course, you'll understand, I can't make any promises.'

'I won't be taking out a mortgage with you.'

'No? Got all the money hidden under the Singleton family mattress at home, have you? Or maybe you lack the courage for a financial commitment? Still, you might change your mind when your first salary rolls in. Management will be quite a change for you, won't it? Leaving behind all that worker solidarity nonsense. But don't get me wrong. I admire you, Jack. I really do. Not many men would be capable of the sort of moral and political gymnastics involved in taking the manager's job. Not when you consider the number of lay-offs that John Foster has got planned. It's a bit of a joke really, isn't it? I mean you, of all people, helping management get shut of half the workforce. I have to smile. I wonder what your comrades in the weaving shed will have to say when they find out? John Foster wasn't sure you'd take the job, but I knew you would. I told him. I said you'd swallow your principles fast enough when you caught sight of the money. Meanwhile Ruth must be over the moon. I'll bet she hasn't given you a moment's peace since you told her.'

Ronald watches Jack shift in his chair and starts to laugh. 'Oh, Mr Singleton. Oh, what a tonic you are, with your black eye and your little secrets. Ruth doesn't know, does she? I thought not. I knew the minute Cora said she'd heard nothing about it from Ruth.'

Jack stands up, his fists clenched at his sides. 'You miserable bastard. I ought to give you a bloody pasting. But that would suit you down to the ground, wouldn't it? Getting me thrown out of your fancy hotel.'

Jack grabs Ronald by the throat and lifts him partway out of his chair. Ronald begins to choke, straining his eyes this way and that to look for help. 'I hope for your sake you never run into me again because, I promise you, I'll not let you off so easily next time.' Jack pushes his flabby opponent down into his chair and leans his full weight into the hand grasping Ronald's throat until the banker's eyes look as if they might burst from their sockets. 'Do you hear me?' Jack asks.

Ronald croaks and nods.

'Good.' And with that Jack releases his grip on Ronald, turns and walks away.

20

MERMAID'S PURSE

This purse is really a case filled with eggs from the ray fish. It is a pale cream colour and rectangular in shape with a single tendril trailing from each corner. You will often find a mermaid's purse near the high-tide mark and, if you're very lucky, it may still contain some of its secrets! Score 20 points for a purse full of secrets.

'Come on, Beth. Get a move on! They're waiting for us.' Helen yanks her blonde hair free of her ponytail and empties the contents of her white clutch purse all over the blue blanket. Out come the face powder, the lipstick ('Pink Kisses') and the forbidden mascara, all of which have been purchased secretly over the past week and hidden in the zipped pocket of her bag. Helen opens the blue plastic mascara tray and spits expertly on the block of mascara, rubbing the surface of the black cake vigorously with the tiny brush supplied. She crosses her legs and balances her elbow on her knee in order to steady the loaded brush as she strokes it down the length of her eyelashes. Several layers of mascara are required and she must bat her eyelashes frantically between coats in order to let the previous layer set before applying the next. She squints again into the tiny mirror and applies a covering of face powder, blue eyeshadow and finally a layer of 'Pink Kisses' to her lips. There will be time to rub it all off again before her parents return. Beth watches the whole routine in silent fascination. Beth hasn't seen Helen with make-up on before. When she's finished Helen looks like the picture of the Little Mermaid in Beth's fairy-tale book. The transformation is amazing.

'Don't stand there gawping. Get your coat on and don't forget your scarf,' Helen says.

'Do I have to? It's too hot.'

'It won't be hot on the pier. Mum will kill me if you end up getting a cold. She'll say it's my fault.'

Beth pulls on her coat but she refuses to button it up.

'For goodness' sake, Beth. You're seven. Can you still not dress yourself properly? Come here.' Beth is reluctant. 'Here, you can button up your coat while I tie the scarf round your head. Be quick. They're waiting.'

'It's not fair! You're not wearing a coat.'

'I haven't been poorly. And anyway I'm taking my cardigan.' Helen is wearing her new underskirt and the top she bought from the Co-op yesterday. Her cardigan is draped over her shoulders.

'That's just for fancy. It doesn't count.'

'Do you want to see the rock pools or not?' Beth nods. 'Well, then, button your coat and we'll go.' There's a quiver of excitement in her voice that is infectious. The sisters look at each other and burst into laughter.

Only a matter of hours ago Helen was in the depths of despair. She had spotted Doug on the other side of the prom when she was on her way to the newsagent's this morning. Of course she'd waved at him, and started to cross the road to speak, but he'd made such a point of ignoring her that she'd been stopped in her tracks. There was nothing for it but to turn back before she was halfway across the road that separated them. Helen had laid the blame for this firmly with her parents and their resistance to letting her go out at night. Added to this was Connie's sudden and inexplicable refusal to speak to her at breakfast. Having to spend the afternoon babysitting Beth was the final straw. Nothing would lift her gloom. But the sudden prospect of a trip to the pier with Alan has transformed her mood. Mrs Clegg, who was supposed to be keeping an eye on the girls, didn't bat an eyelid when Alan came up with the idea. She'd nodded, told them to be back by four and shut her eyes for a nap. Helen has never before witnessed such a level of maternal negligence. She is speechless with admiration and gratitude.

Helen is finally going on her first date. It doesn't matter that Beth and Red Hawk are coming too – in fact, it's almost a bonus for Helen – she suddenly feels shy. At last she'll see the Laughing Donkey bar – even if she doesn't actually go in and have a drink. Helen is elated. She ignores the stairs and takes Beth down in the lift. This is strictly against the rules – their mother has a fear of lifts and, as a result, insists that the family use the stairs on every occasion. What, Ruth reasons, if Beth collapses in the lift? She may be trapped and die before rescuers can reach her. Helen has no such reservations, she can think of no more glamorous way to arrive at the ground floor than by lift.

Helen had always imagined that it would be windy at the end of the pier, but it's not. The flags and bunting are stationary in the heat. Still, it's exciting. It's low tide, but if you walk to the end of the pier there's sea on three sides. It's a different world without the connection of land. Helen imagines that it must be like this on board ship, but without the sickening rocking from side to side. All the rush to put her make-up on had been worth it. Alan whistled at her when the lift doors had opened. They had set off with Helen holding on firmly to her sister's hand, but Beth had wriggled and pulled until Helen finally let go. Beth rushed ahead and fell into step with Red Hawk, leaving Helen to walk beside Alan. Anybody seeing them would think he was her boyfriend. It's a dream come true – just wait until she tells the girls at school.

The pier is packed with teenagers lounging against the rails and couples sitting side by side on the wrought-iron benches. The noise is deafening. There's the whirl and clash of the painted dodgems and the blast of organ music, the smell of boiled onions and hot dogs, and the screams of holidaymakers on the swing boats. Helen and Alan make their way along the pier. They have to keep stopping for Beth, who wants to see the sea between the gaps in the planking. When they are halfway along the pier Alan calls his brother over. He reaches in his pocket and pulls out a shilling, which he gives to Red Hawk and says, 'Now bugger off. And take her with you.' Alan tilts his head in Beth's direction.

'Beth has to stay with me. She's not allowed to go anywhere by herself,' Helen protests.

'She isn't by herself. She's with our Rob, isn't she? They'll be all right.'

Helen looks unconvinced. 'Where are you going to go?' she asks her sister.

Beth looks at Red Hawk and shrugs her shoulders.

'You can't go until you tell me where,' Helen insists.

'Rock pools. I want to see the rock pools.'

'OK. Well, don't go out of sight,' Helen says as she reties the scarf under Beth's chin and she adds in a whisper, 'And if that boy does something stupid, don't you. OK?' Helen points back to the clock above the pier entrance. 'Be back here before half past.'

Beth frowns. 'Is that the one when the big hand is at the bottom?'

Helen, conscious of her sister's confusion and keen to avoid embarrassing her, leans down and whispers in Beth's ear, 'See the hands on the clock? When the little one points to three and the big one points to six you have to come back. OK? And don't go anywhere where you can't see me.'

Beth nods briefly and then she is gone, winding her way through the crowd after Red Hawk. Helen is prompted to go after them to make sure Beth keeps her scarf on. She starts forward, but Alan puts his arm round her and says, 'Thank God we're shut of them, now we can have some decent fun. Let's get something to drink for a start.'

It's crowded outside the bar. The drinkers have spilled out on to the walkway. There's music blaring from the open doors. Billy Fury, Elvis, Cliff Richard and Bobby Darin. Helen relaxes and begins to enjoy herself. This date is a sweet revenge for Doug's behaviour this morning. Nevertheless she refuses Alan's invitation to go into the bar. It looks dangerous with all those Teddy boys milling around in their drape jackets fixing their hair with flick combs and drinking beer as fast as they get it. She shakes her head and says, 'I'll stay here.'

'You want a Babycham?'

'I'd love a Babycham,' Helen says and they both laugh because it's exactly what the woman in the advert says. Despite the crush it's only a minute or two before Alan is back with the drinks. Helen is disappointed that the Babycham is handed to her still in its bottle. On TV they always serve it in a special glass. But after a bit of encouragement from Alan she tries to sip it from the bottle neck as nicely as she can and look as if she's used to doing it at the same time. They stand and watch the dodgems slamming back and forth around the ring. Despite the worry about Beth, Helen begins to relax. Somebody puts on a Bobby Darin record and the sound of his voice singing 'Dream Lover' floats through the air. Alan puts his arm round her. This is as near perfect as Helen can imagine. They stand, swaying slightly to the music.

Alan drains the last of his beer and says, 'I'm ready for another, aren't you?' Helen tips the rest of the sugary liquid down her throat and nods happily.

Halfway through the second drink Alan kisses her and it's so romantic. He then steers her to the seats at the very end of the pier. The ornate cast-iron forms are tucked behind the Laughing Donkey bar and, since they face out to sea, they afford a modicum of privacy. Alan swallows the rest of his drink and puts the pint glass down on the planking at their feet. Helen senses that something has changed. The sun is still shining, people are still moving back and forth, music continues to blare out from the bar, but some element she can't quite identify has changed. When Alan leans over to kiss her his body blocks out the sun. He slides his arm round her waist and she can feel his muscles harden and lock as he clasps her. An involuntary shiver runs through her.

'Are you cold?' Alan says.

'A bit,' she lies. Helen grasps the opportunity to stand up and step away, folding her hands across her chest. Another shiver runs through her and she shifts from foot to foot as if she's about to run.

Alan watches her carefully. 'Here,' he says, draping his jacket over Helen's shoulders and picking up his empty glass. 'I think it's time for a refill.'

21

DONKEYS

Everyone loves to have a ride on a donkey when they visit the seaside! How many donkeys are there, and what are they called? Score 20 points for a donkey ride.

It's a dream come true for Beth. She has earned fifteen I-Spy points just by setting foot on the pier. She's seen dozens of lifebuoys fixed to the pier railings at regular intervals – they're five points each, but you can only score for one. If only she can spy a tidal scale then that's another twenty points.

'What do you want to do first?' Red Hawk asks when she catches up with him. He holds up the shilling between grimy fingers.

Beth is torn between a ride on the donkeys or buying a red rock dummy. She takes the money from Red Hawk's grasp. The coin lies heavy in her palm and glints with promise. 'Let's go on the donkeys,' she says.

The donkeys are collected in a little circle a few yards away, but it takes Beth some time to reach them. She labours through the deep sand, the hem of her winter coat brushing the surface and her shoes filling with every step. The decision as to which donkey to choose is difficult. Bronco has a sombre expression and knobbly knees. He stands perfectly still, disinclined to move even when the donkey man tugs his reins. Next to Bronco is Fred. Beth has been watching the donkeys for some days and knows that he is the slowest and always the first to turn back. The next donkey is called Lucy. She has a wary look in her eye and refuses to be stroked, shying away from eager children and jostling the other donkeys if they come too close. Beth is disappointed, she had wanted a donkey with a sunhat, like the ones on the front of the postcards.

'You go on Beryl,' Red Hawk whispers. 'She's the best, but you have to give her a good kick to get her going.'

Beth is shocked. She wouldn't dream of kicking a donkey. Beryl's mane is several shades darker than her creamy white coat and it stands as stiff as the bristles on a yard brush. Her name is in metal lettering across the front of a bridle that tinkles with half a dozen bells every time Beryl moves. She is young and flighty, prone to clearing off at full speed given half a chance. Beth hesitates, suddenly overwhelmed by the magnitude of what she is about to do. She can imagine the look on her mother's face if she ever found out. It is such a vivid sensation that she turns round, believing for a moment that her mother is actually there, her mouth twisted with anger and her tongue sharp with reproach.

The donkey man has already taken the money for the rides and helped Red Hawk into the saddle. He steps forward and catches Beth under her arms to lift her on to the nearest donkey. Beth twitches with pain from her scar and grits her teeth until the sensation passes.

When Beth is settled on Beryl's back she leans forward and buries her nose in the donkey's short fur. The smell is a sour mixture of sweat, manure and sweet hay, and another smell Beth can't quite identify. Beryl is warm to the touch but she's restless. Her legs twitch and her hooves shift in the sand. The saddle is smooth under Beth's thighs but her legs aren't long enough to reach the stirrups. Beryl shakes her head when she senses Beth's weight and a tremor runs all the way down her back. When Beth takes the reins the donkey snatches her head into the wind and snorts. And then they're moving. The donkey man takes hold of Beryl's bridle and the group sets off with all the other donkeys trailing behind. Beth hangs on to the metal handle at the front of the saddle and laughs as Beryl sways from side to side, making her way through sand strewn with litter and droppings. On the way back the man asks if she wants a gallop. Beth nods furiously, too excited to speak, and the donkey man directs a sharp slap to Beryl's rump. A cloud of dust and sand rises as he lets go of the bridle. Beryl completes the rest of the ride at full pelt and is only caught and led back to the ring of waiting donkeys by the prompt action of the donkey man's assistant. Beth's heart thumps and lurches in her chest, and she's covered in sweat but it's the most exciting ride she's ever had.

The two children wander back across the sands. Central Pier rises like a monster, high above their heads. Beth can hear the rattle of stilettos and thump of crêpe-soled Teddy boys on the planking above her. 'Here Comes Summer' is playing at full volume. The song is familiar. She's seen Helen jive across the flagged scullery floor when it comes on the radio. To her right, further into the shadows under the pier, sand-locked lovers wrestle in a muddle of legs and discarded clothes. Beth pulls out her I-Spy book and stares at the picture of a rock pool on the front cover. There are dozens of points to be earned from a decent rock pool. A whelk scores ten, a whelk with a hermit crab inside scores a dizzying thirty-five. But Beth must find a rock pool if she is to stand a chance of earning points.

'I've seen loads of those,' Red Hawk says, pointing to an anemone.

'Where?'

'Over there.' The boy points to a pool of water that has collected round the base of the iron pier supports. 'Come on, I'll show you.'

The rock pools are confined to the cool dark strip under the pier where salt water is marooned in crevices and hollows from the morning tide. Beth looks up and is relieved to spy Helen's pink-and-white skirt billowing out between the pier railings above her head. Helen has her arms crossed behind her back and her hands grasp the sky-blue railings. Beth shouts and waves but Helen is deep in conversation with Alan. Beth can see her sister's blonde hair lift in the breeze when she tilts her head back and laughs.

Beth imagines that all rock pools will be crammed with exciting finds like the one on the cover of her book. It is filled with brightly coloured fish and shells, scarlet anemones, aurelias, sea gooseberries, seaweed, limpets and periwinkles. She only needs to see one rock pool today to spot at least nine different things and so earn more points than she can easily count. It stands to reason – everything else, the birds, the boats, and the seaweed all look the same as in the book – why shouldn't the rock pool? But still she hesitates. The pier is out of bounds. She's already come far too close. But Red Hawk is older than her and knows the beach a lot better. And it would be exciting to see all the different types of fish. Perhaps, if she could find a jam jar, she'd be able to catch one and show her sister. Then it would all be worth it, worth getting into trouble for.

Red Hawk has climbed halfway up the pier's dark geometry of rusted stanchions and he's tired of waiting. He climbs back down and runs over to where Beth is standing. 'Come on,' he says and, when she fails to move, he takes her hand and drags her with him into the darkness.

It's sunny and bright on the beach but dark and dank under the pier with the fierce smell of rotting seaweed and the taste of salt. The iron supports bedded in rough concrete are covered with barnacles sharp enough to rip the delicate skin of a child's foot or hand. Water drips from the planking of the pier overhead and there is the constant rumble of holidaymakers' feet passing back and forth. The rusting iron flakes off in her hand as she threads her way through the bars and supports. The sand is damp and the rocks are covered with seaweed.

Beth is glad of Red Hawk's hand to steady her. 'Watch out here,' he warns, 'it's slippery.' When they come to the place where the iron bars cross the supports he says, 'Mind your head.'

His voice echoes around the maze of rusted iron. The salty darkness under the pier is the retreat of courting couples. The girls' summer dresses are whipped up by the breeze and the men in joke trilbies, with shirtsleeves rolled up, reveal a straining of muscles under sunburnt skin. Beth picks her way unnoticed past the couples wrapped in each other's arms. She pauses, waiting until her eyes become accustomed to the gloom. The first rock pool they come to is a disappointment. It's empty except for a few pebbles and a piece of seaweed. Red Hawk shrugs and leads her on, confident that the next rock pool will contain enough wonders to fill in the whole two pages.

22

PUNCH AND JUDY

If you can spot lots of children sitting cross-legged on the sands in front of a tall striped box it means that there's a Punch and Judy show. Children love to see Mr Punch losing his temper and hitting Judy with his stick until she cries. What a laugh! Score 10 points for some typical family fun.

'What's the panic?' Ruth asks the minute they're out of earshot of their husbands. Cora tips her head towards an arrow pointing to 'Ladies' Powder Room' above a curvy silhouette of a woman with powder puff poised. There are two swing doors to negotiate before they enter the powder room proper. It's an ode to femininity with its cream porcelain, flower arrangements, cotton-wool balls and low-lit mirrors. Cora slumps on a heavily upholstered button-back turquoise velvet chair and puts her head in her hands.

Ruth feels a rush of annoyance. 'Don't you start that, Cora Lloyd. You've no reason. You'd have a good enough reason to put your head in your hands if you were me. Jack has been offered a really good job and he's dithering about taking it! He'd be earning more than enough to cover the cost of a mortgage on that semi I've been looking at. You'd think he'd have the wit to consider what would be best for his family instead of suiting himself. But no. He has to have everything his own way. Now I have to continue struggling to bring up the girls crammed in a miserable terraced house just because he doesn't want a better job. I'm that frustrated with him I could scream. If it wasn't for the girls I'd leave him. See how far his principles would get him then. You're lucky with your Ronald. You wouldn't catch him getting up on his high horse over some silly principle, would you?'

Cora slips the sunglasses from her face.

'Anyway, I've told him straight. An end terrace may be good enough for him but it's not for me or the girls. I . . .' Ruth is cut short by the expression on Cora's face as she raises her head. There's silence while Ruth takes in the sight. Even in this subtle lighting Cora's face is a battlefield. Ruth takes her friend's chin carefully in her hand and tilts Cora's head to the light. 'What happened? Who did this?'

'It's my fault. I got into an argument with Ronnie a couple of days ago.'

'So that's why you rang and asked me to come over. You were frightened he was going to start knocking you around. Dear God. What did you say to him to deserve this?'

'I can't remember now.'

'How can you not remember?'

'I mean it could have been anything. It doesn't take a lot.'

Ruth is incredulous. She struggles to take it all in.

Cora grabs Ruth's hand and says, 'You won't tell anyone, will you? I couldn't stand it if people were pointing to me and saying "her husband knocks her around".'

'It's too late, Cora. They're already saying it. Irene Sykes said as much to Helen the other day.'

Cora puts her head in her hands again and rocks forward in her chair. 'Oh, God. And I suppose it's common knowledge that he spends time down Liverpool Road as well.'

'Does he? But why would he bother with some prostitute from Liverpool Road when he has got you? I can't credit it. How dare he use his fists on you? You should call the police. For two pins I'd give him a taste of his own medicine. I can't believe it. I always thought – you always said – you were happy. I believed you. I mean, you've got everything: a wealthy husband, a big house. For goodness' sake, Cora, you even have a housekeeper. And you've no children. What is there left to argue about?'

'He's out every night with one thing and another. If it's been a bank do he comes home the worse for wear and anything I say aggravates him. It's nothing new, Ruth. He's been doing this since we were married. I haven't told anyone. When people say how lucky I am it's easier to agree. I mean, everyone looks up to him and thinks he's a real gentleman. I must be in the wrong for aggravating him in the first place. He wouldn't shake me about if I didn't deserve it.'

'This is more than a shaking about. He's been using his fists on you.'

'Well, it started with him grabbing hold and shaking me, but then he'd give me the odd kick and I'd lose my balance. He only started using his fists this last week.'

'Why?'

'He thought I was being too friendly with the waiter. You know, smiling too much. Anyway, it doesn't matter. I won't do it again.'

'So he gave you a black eye?'

'Oh, that was yesterday. He'd had a bad day on the golf course. He was annoyed. I'd been stuck in the hotel room and hadn't seen anyone all day and I started chattering at him when he wanted to relax and be quiet. And he always says sorry afterwards.'

Ruth takes hold of Cora's hand. 'Call the police.'

'Don't make me laugh. They're as bad as he is. Ronnie has got friendly with a few policemen since he joined the Freemasons. I'd a split lip last time he invited them over for dinner and not one of them said a word. I can't see them charging him with assault, can you?'

'Then leave him.'

'And go where?'

'Anywhere. You could go back and live with your dad.'

'I can't. Do you think he'd have me back? He'd say, "You've made your bed, madam, now lie on it." I told him Ronald was knocking me about the last time I saw him and he said, "Well, learn to keep your mouth shut then." There's nothing for it, Ruth. I've just got to hang on until things get better. It'd be different if

I could just get pregnant. He wouldn't lay a finger on me if I was pregnant. I can't leave. I have to stay put. That's the way it is.'

'But it's not fair,' Ruth says.

'Oh, Ruth, don't be so naive. Nothing's fair.'

Ruth is offended. After all, she's seven years older than Cora and she's given birth to two daughters. If anyone could be accused of being naive surely it's Cora. 'But why can't you leave? Even if your dad won't have you, you've enough to live by yourself. You could go anywhere you wanted. After all, you're hardly short of money, are you?' Ruth struggles to keep the envy out of her voice.

'I don't have any money,' Cora says and, seeing the look of total disbelief on Ruth's face, she adds, 'I don't! I haven't a penny. Do you think I'd have let you pay for tea and scones on Wednesday if I'd had any money? Why do you think I had the Tupperware party? Everything is in his name. I was better off when I worked six looms at Fosters.'

'Well, then, what was the point in marrying him if it wasn't for the money?'

'Is that all you think of me, Ruth? You think I married for money? That I'm nothing better than a prostitute with a marriage certificate? I married Ronnie for the same reason you married Jack. I was in love with him. I thought he'd look after me.'

'Well, you were wrong there, weren't you.'

'You needn't sound so pleased.'

'I'm not! I'm just saying.'

'Has your marriage turned out exactly as you expected? Has

Jack never disappointed you? You were calling him all the names under the sun not ten minutes ago.'

'Well, at least he doesn't keep me short of money, he doesn't spend time on Liverpool Road and he doesn't knock me around.'

'No. He's not the type, is he? No, that's not Jack's way with women. Jack's way with women is to look after them.'

'It's true, he's a very protective husband,' Ruth says with a self-congratulatory smile. She could almost forgive Cora for calling her naive.

'Well, he was certainly looking after the woman he was walking along the prom with a couple of nights ago. She had his jacket round her shoulders when I saw them.'

'That's a lie.'

'I'm not lying, Ruth. I saw them when Ronnie was driving me back from the restaurant.'

'You've made a mistake. It was someone else. It's easy to mistake people in the dark.'

'He was under the lights. And anyway, I've known Jack all my life. I could spot him a mile off.'

'Well, there must have been something wrong. An accident maybe. Jack's not like that. He went out to see Tom Bell on Wednesday. They had a chat about a Union job that's coming up.'

'A Union job? But Ronnie said . . .'

Ruth interrupts her: 'They had a couple of pints and then he came back to the hotel.'

'So what time did he get in? It was around eleven when I saw him and that girl.'

Ruth pauses, remembers Jack coming in at half past twelve. 'I've forgotten,' she replies. 'I'm not watching him all the time. Why should I? Jack would never go with another woman. Just because your marriage is a disaster there's no need to start throwing mud at mine. Anyway, it's time I got back to the girls.'

'Oh, Ruth. Come back. Don't leave like this. Don't let's fall out, Ruth.'

But Cora's words are drowned out by the sound of the powder room door swinging shut behind Ruth.

23

PIER

The highlight of any holiday at the seaside is the pier. It is an exciting place with lots of things to see and do. It can be decked out with coloured lights – a fantastic place where you can play deck quoits, watch a show, admire the view, have a drink or even dance! Score 10 points for walking on the pier.

Alan is off to the bar again when Helen sneaks a look at her watch. It's twenty to four. Beth should have been back ten minutes ago. Helen reckons she's only got another fifteen minutes or so to find Beth and get them both back to the hotel lounge before their parents return. Helen stands up and looks down the length of the pier. It's difficult to see much with all the crowds. Perhaps Beth has gone down on to the beach? Helen peers over the rail down on to the sands hoping to catch a glimpse of Beth's yellow scarf. At last she catches sight of a girl about the right size standing by herself, but the girl is bareheaded and wearing a pretty cotton dress so it can't be Beth. Helen doesn't know where else to look. She turns round and sees Alan in the middle of a group of porters and kitchen hands from the hotel. She recognises them as the group of lads who are usually hanging on Connie's every word. There's a lot of laughter and one or two of them keep glancing over at Helen and nudging Alan. Anxious now, Helen starts to walk back down the pier to the entrance to see if she can see Beth on her way back. The further she walks, the more desperate she becomes. Suddenly there's a jerk on her wrist and she turns, hoping it's Beth. But it's not. It's Alan.

''Ang on a minute! Where do you think you're off to? I've just got you another drink.'

'Beth. I have to find Beth.'

Alan starts talking, but Helen is in no mood to listen. She twists her wrist out of his grasp and moves forward again, forcing her way through the crowds. Beth isn't at the pier entrance and there's no sign of her under the clock. She seems to have vanished into thin air.

'Don't panic. She'll be all right. She's probably buggerin' about with our Rob somewhere. She'll turn up.'

Helen looks again at her watch. It's quarter to four. She has less than five minutes to find Beth. 'I'll have a look on the beach,' she decides.

'What's the point? If she was down there you'd have spotted her already from up here.'

Alan puts his arm round Helen's waist to stop her walking away, then stands in front of her, blocking her escape.

Helen twists out of his embrace and darts sideways to the pier railings. She looks down again into the seething mass, hoping against hope she'll spot Beth looking up at her.

Alan puts his hand across her shoulders and says, 'Relax. Have another drink. I'll bet the crafty bugger has taken her for a UCP.'

'UCP? What do you mean? United Cow Products? Why would he take her to the tripe shop? She's not allowed in shops on her own. She's too young.'

'Not the shop,' Alan says with a snigger. 'UCP – Under Central Pier for a bit of the other.'

Helen turns and looks at him. He thinks this is a joke. He couldn't care less about his own brother, let alone Beth. His sniggering makes Helen furious, but there are more important things to worry about. He might be right. 'I'm going to look under the pier. She's been nattering to explore rock pools for her I-Spy book.'

Alan looks delighted at the prospect, as if all the hard work has been done for him. He leads her down the wooden steps on to the beach and they step into the shade under the pier. It takes a minute or two for Helen's eyes to get used to the darkness, let alone begin to look for Beth. The pier is supported by a forest of pillars, their tops hidden in the darkness of planking and their bottoms swathed in seaweed and surrounded by pools of salt water and rocks. There's a dank, brown, slow-dripping smell of rust, wood and rot. Alan leads her further into the darkness until she stumbles on a tussock of rotting seaweed and slips. She stretches out her hand towards the nearest iron pillar but misses and starts to fall, grazing her arm against the barnacles that cover the concrete footings. Alan catches hold of her other hand and she doesn't know how it happens, but she ends up flat on her back in the sand with Alan beside her. He immediately rolls on top of her and, before she has a chance even to catch her breath, clamps his lips over hers.

Helen struggles to free herself. His kiss slathers her mouth in saliva. His lips forced on hers, he angles his face harshly against her cheekbone, squashing her nose sideways. Helen is suffocating. When she raises her hands to push him off he grabs both her arms and traps her wrists under her, tearing at the neckline of her top. Her lungs are bursting with the effort of fighting for air. She's afraid she'll faint. She stops struggling and lies still. It's no good. He's too heavy for her to throw off. Her mind races, trying to work out a way to outwit him. She lies quite still and finally his grip on her relaxes in response. Helen manages to work one hand free, her wrist burning with the aftermath of his loosened grip. She pushes her arm between their bodies, the heel of her hand hard against his shoulder and he shifts slightly, allowing her a single breath before his full weight is over her again. His knee is forcing her legs open and his hand scrabbling through the layers of her underskirt, his nails raking her thighs. He lifts his head for a second and she grasps another breath, her scream silenced by the return of his lips. His teeth cut into her lip and there's the metallic taste of blood in her mouth. Her throat retches on the choke of his tongue until he moves again and she turns away, teeth clenched shut against him.

His hand moves over her mouth and presses the side of her

face into the putrid sand now, and she is fighting for air again as the particles of sand cover her lips and block her nose. She is trapped, trussed up in his arms, weak from the effort of trying to throw him off. Helen stops struggling and starts to sob, turning her head away, sickened by the knowledge of what he is doing to her. There in the semi-darkness, six or seven feet away, she can see another couple. The girl is familiar. It's Connie. She's flat on her back with the figure of a man lying on his side facing her. They are murmuring and he bends and kisses her lightly, and there is another burst of laughter. It's Doug. It is a moment before he recognises Helen. When he does his eyes take in the scene. For a second he looks her in the eye, an expression of disbelief followed by anger. Connie turns to see what has attracted his attention and seeing that it is Helen, she slides her arm round Doug's neck and pulls him towards her. They roll loosely together, Connie laughing as if she hasn't a care in the world. Alan too has recognised Connie but now, as she turns away, he renews his assault on Helen. Her panties rip easily under his hungry fingers.

The darkness closes in over Helen, she is weak with trying to resist the onslaught. 'Keep still or I'll do for you,' he hisses in her ear.

Suddenly Helen hears a scream of fury that echoes around them. Above her, out of the darkness, Beth's face suddenly appears. The little girl is screaming, over and over and over again, as if she will never stop. Her lungs heaving with the effort, her face contorted in fury, she hurls herself towards Alan. 'Get off her! Get off! Get off my sister, you big bugger.'

Alan kicks out at the child, sending her sprawling at the foot of one of the pier supports, but Beth gets up again and, heedless of her injuries, renews her attack. It is an unequal struggle. Alan reaches out a lazy arm and pushes her away. 'Bugger off, you bloody cripple.'

Beth renews her onslaught, her fury reaching new heights. She leaps like a tiger, kicking and punching until she is breathless. Her fingers claw at his face and her feet thud into his flesh. This frenzied attack has drawn the attention of other couples who look on bemused. There's a parting of embraces as strangers turn and take in the sight. It is only when Beth begins to shout for help that Alan hesitates. He pauses, releasing his hold on Helen's arms and half turns towards the snarling, screaming child. At last Helen struggles free and crawls towards the light, her face pitted with sand, her cheeks stained with mascara and her mouth bloody.

24

WRECK

There are all sorts of unusual sights you might see at the seaside. A wreck is one of the saddest. Boats that have run aground on sandbanks may be floated again at the next tide. But a ship that has been driven on to the rocks is more serious. When this happens the only question to be asked is 'What can be salvaged?' What unusual sights have you spotted at the seaside? Score 20 points for anything you can salvage.

Ruth makes her way back to the hotel conservatory at a smart pace, leaving Cora hurrying in her wake.

'Ruth! What a welcome return,' Ronald says, getting to his feet. Glancing at Cora, he adds, 'Nothing wrong, I hope.'

'No, not at all. I just wanted to thank you both for your hospitality but it is time we left. Where's Jack?'

'I imagine he decided to wait for you outside. I fear I may

have offended him. I hope we haven't upset you as well?' Ronald asks, his face wreathed in apparent concern. 'Forgive me, I hadn't meant to interfere. I was merely congratulating Jack on his promotion to manager of Prospect Mill. He didn't seem to want to discuss it.' Ronald pauses, waiting for a reaction. Ruth stands open-mouthed, staring in disbelief. 'Oh, didn't you know?' Ronald says. 'Jack been keeping it quiet, has he? Still, I've only known for a week.'

Ruth finds her voice. 'Of course I knew.'

'Of course,' Ronald agrees in a condescending tone. 'Of course.'

Glancing around the room, he snaps his fingers. 'Here, let me get the bellboy to see you out.'

'There's no need,' Ruth assures him. 'Good afternoon.' She turns away and walks quickly to the door.

Ruth doesn't speak until they are well clear of the hotel and walking back down the avenue of limes. A piece of gravel has lodged itself under the canvas at the side of her shoe but she's too angry to stop and shake it free.

'What's got into you?' Jack asks. 'You've a face like thunder, which is rich considering it was you who wanted to come in the first place. Given a choice, I'd have been happier with a poke in the eye from a sharp stick.'

Ruth interrupts: 'What happened with you and Ronald? Why were you standing outside?'

'Oh, nothing. He was just being his usual obnoxious self. Will you slow down, Ruth? If you keep this pace up we'll make it back to the hotel before the tram.'

Ruth stops dead and glares at her husband. 'You've been made up to manager, haven't you?'

'Well . . .'

'Haven't you!'

'Well, yes, in a way. It's been . . .'

'Just this once, Jack, tell me the truth.'

'What do you mean by that? I've not lied to you, Ruth. OK, Fosters have offered me the job. I was going to tell you after we'd finished with the Lloyds. This is the first time we've been alone without the girls for ages.'

'Why didn't you tell me before? Why did I have to hear it from Ronald, a near stranger?'

'I haven't known about it that long.'

'Ronald heard last week.'

'Well, I only got wind of it recently. I didn't tell you immediately because you were so flustered about Beth when I got home. And later we were both busy getting the house straight and the bags packed for the holiday. I felt I needed time to think about it before I started bothering you with it.'

'And what about allowing me to think about it? What about discussing it with me?'

'Well, I was going to.'

'You're lying. You were only going to tell me once you'd made up your mind.'

'I haven't said anything to John Foster yet.'

'You haven't been at work to see him.'

'Bloomin' 'eck, Ruth. We can talk about it till kingdom come, but in the end it's still me who has to do the job.'

'Well, are you going to take it or are you sticking with the Union?'

'That's what I wanted to talk about. There's a couple of things we need some time to discuss. Things that I need to explain.'

'You can explain until you're blue in the face. It isn't going to make any difference. When I think about all the support and care and encouragement I've given you. You don't deserve it. None of it.' She starts walking again and Jack lengthens his stride to catch up.

Out on the sands the retreating tide reveals the rusty ironwork of a wreck, draped in seaweed and studded with limpets, a seagoing vessel reduced by the rush of disaster to a hopeless shell of what it once was. Jack catches hold of Ruth's hand and puts it in the crook of his arm.

Ruth turns to face him, livid with fury. 'How could you?' she shouts. 'How could you make such a fool of me? In front of the Lloyds, of all people?' Ruth pulls her hand away from Jack and they do not speak again.

The three-mile walk has made them late back to the hotel and Ruth is getting anxious about the absence of the girls when they suddenly turn up. Ruth is still angry. When she sees Helen in a torn blouse and muddied skirt she snaps, 'Go upstairs and take that blouse off. It's torn to bits. You look a sight.' Seeing Helen's tear-stained cheeks, she continues, 'It's no good crying over spilt milk. I told you that top wasn't at all suitable for a girl your age. I said it would fall to bits, didn't I? How on earth have you got yourself in this mess?'

'It was my fault,' Beth says. 'I dragged her down the steps to the beach and she fell. That's why she scratched her leg and everything.'

Ruth finally loses her patience. 'What did I tell you, Helen? I told you to stay here, not to go out. You should know, you're the eldest. Does nobody ever give a thought to me? Does what I say matter so little? Go upstairs and get washed and changed. Here are the keys. You'll have to put on your other skirt, it's in the suitcase under the bed.'

Jack has been standing back during this exchange between mother and daughter. He has noted the state of Helen's clothes, watched as the colour in Beth's cheeks rises as she speaks. He is almost convinced that Beth is lying, but he doesn't want to begin thinking about what has happened and how his older daughter got into that state. The sight of her may infuriate Ruth, but it troubles Jack.

The Singletons are first into the dining room at six o'clock. Helen has no appetite, she pushes the fish and chips around her plate and is relieved when the waitress clears the table. Ruth confines herself to two cups of tea and a slice of bread. It is left to Jack and Beth to maintain an air of normality. Sensing the parental rift, Beth fills the silence with an account of her progress with the I-Spy book. It is, she claims, almost full. She pulls the book out of the side pocket of her shorts and, starting with page one, recites all the items she has spied. She hands the book to Jack and asks him to add up the scores. Some of the pages are crumpled, folded back, or have come loose altogether. Her handwriting is a mixture of over- and undersized letters scattered across the page, squashed circles, bent strings and backward-facing 's's.

Nevertheless Jack is moved to paternal pride by the effort his daughter has made. He turns to Beth and says, 'Leave it with me, Sputnik. When we get home I'll straighten out all the pages and tot up your points. All right?'

Beth nods happily.

The family are leaving the dining room just as the Cleggs arrive. Florrie is disappointed and expresses the hope that they'll all meet up later in the Residents' Lounge, but Ruth shakes her head. She has packing to do.

Jack spends the evening closeted with Victor in the office. Together they drink the best part of a bottle of Irish whiskey and, when conversation shifts to the war, Victor talks about how things might have been if his wife had survived. Before they part company at ten, Jack has made up his mind to tell Ruth about the letter from Eleni.

Ruth is busy, as usual, when Jack gets to the room. She has everything they brought away on holiday laid out across the double bed – everything from medicines and cleaning materials to the piles of dirty clothes. She ignores his presence and continues to empty the dressing-table drawers. Eventually she looks up and says, 'You're back early. Dougie finally drunk the pub dry, has he?'

'I haven't been out. I've just been in the office chatting to Victor. I've settled the bill. I haven't made the usual booking for next year. I thought you might like to try somewhere different. You've always said you fancy a week in Llandudno.'

'You think a week in Llandudno makes up for what you've done?'

'I've said I'm sorry time and again. I should have told you about the management job sooner.'

'I'll bet you've discussed it with Dougie.'

Jack picks up a sock from the floor and puts it back in the pile on the bed. 'None of this matters. All that matters is that we get over this and start looking to the future.'

'But why didn't you tell me? Why do you have to keep secrets?'

'I was worried that you'd talk me out of taking the Union job and then I'd regret the decision. But I'm sure now. If you agree I'm going to take the job with Fosters.'

Ruth pauses in the task of stuffing the dirty clothes into a clean white laundry bag and looks Jack in the eye. 'I'm glad. I know it was a difficult decision, but you'll see, it'll turn out to be the best thing. Just think of what we'll be able to do with the extra money.' She turns and sits down on the edge of the bed.

'There's something else I've been meaning to tell you.' Jack slips his hand inside his jacket and feels for the letter. It's not there, it must be in his trousers.

'What?'

'Something that's been bothering me a lot. It's about a girl I got friendly with . . .'

Ruth's heart sinks. She lets the laundry bag slide from her fingers. 'So it's true,' she says, her eyes filling with tears. 'Cora told me and I wouldn't believe her. I told her she was a liar, that just because her husband messed around it didn't mean that mine did. But she saw you with that girl.'

'But she can't have. Cora saw me doing what?'

'She saw you with a girl on Wednesday night. She had your jacket on, Cora said. I couldn't believe it. I couldn't believe you'd be unfaithful. She saw you at eleven and it was well past midnight before you got back here. You had sex with her, didn't you?' Jack refuses to answer. 'Didn't you? You had sex with that girl, didn't you?' Jack drops his head and nods. 'It's true! I can tell from your face. Where did you go?'

'Ruth, please. It doesn't matter. There are more important things we need to talk about.' Jack pulls the letter from his pocket.

But Ruth, blinded by tears, fails to notice. 'What could be more important than you committing adultery? Where did you have sex? On a backstreet somewhere? What's her name, or didn't you bother to find out?' Ruth starts to cry. Jack walks round the bed and tries to sit next to her, but she throws out her arms and shouts, 'Get away. Get away from me. You liar. You cheat. You're nothing better than a dog.'

Jack moves away and sits on the opposite side of the bed, his shoulders slumped in despair. He tries again. 'I'm sorry. I shouldn't have done it. I know that. I'd had a few pints. It meant nothing at all.'

'What if you've made her pregnant? Or is that what you wanted? Then you could have the chance of a son?'

The absurdity of this accusation makes Jack finally lose his temper. 'That's a bloody ridiculous thing to say, Ruth. Rubbish. It's just rubbish. And I'm getting tired of forever making allowances for you. Whatever I do, I'm always in the wrong. It's been obvious for a long time that you don't want me. I've tried to be reasonable. I've tried to be patient. I know you've been upset about Beth, but I have too. Anybody would think you were the only one who cares.' Jack looks down and, seeing Eleni's letter crumpled in his hand, he pushes it back in his pocket.

Ruth looks up at him, her face streaked with tears. 'Well, you needn't worry. You won't have to put up with me for much longer. I shall be leaving when we get back tomorrow. And I'll be taking the girls with me.'

This threat strikes home. 'Don't be daft. Where would you go?'

'Anywhere will do as long as it's away from you.'

'It's a waste of time trying to talk to you when you're in this state.'

'Get out, then. Go on, get out.'

Ruth launches herself at Jack, thumping his shoulder and chest until he pushes her arms away and gets up from the bed. 'I'm going for a walk on the prom.'

Ruth doesn't reply.

There's a south-westerly wind blowing when he gets outside. He buttons his jacket and strides towards the prom. There are still a fair number of people about, spending their final evening in the resort strolling arm in arm and admiring the sunset. Jack finds an empty bench and sits down. Ruth's threat to take the girls has hit him hard. It's ironic that he'd meant to tell her about his relationship with Eleni and ended up having to admit to a meaningless one-night stand with Connie. There's some small comfort to be had from the fact that Cora may have seen him, but she won't have recognised who he was with.

One thing is clear, Ruth is in no state to hear about Eleni now. And he certainly can't tell her he has a son. The prospect of keeping this secret is not as unbearable as he first thought. Jack knows that he needs to make Ruth understand how sorry and ashamed he is about his one-night stand. He needs to ask for her forgiveness and he needs to do it quickly before the argument spirals out of control and he loses everything. Jack gets up from the form and heads back across the promenade to the hotel. Halfway across the road Gunner appears out of the blue and falls into step.

'You shouldn't be out at this time,' Jack tells Gunner. 'At this rate you'll be joining me in the doghouse.'

Gunner looks up at him and wags his tail. It's a heartening sight.

Back in the hotel room Ruth blows her nose on a rag and wipes her eyes when she hears Jack's knock. She opens the door and steps back when he strides in. The sight of him reduces Ruth to tears again. She walks back to the bed and, heedless of the piles of dirty clothes and still empty suitcase, leans forward and puts her head in her hands.

'Don't, Ruth. Don't cry. I've been a fool. I know it's no excuse but I was drunk. Drunk and stupid.'

'Who was she?'

'Just some girl in the bar.'

'You betrayed seventeen years of marriage and two daughters for some stranger in a bar?'

Jack walks over and sits on the bed next to Ruth. Her hair has come loose from its Victory Roll and her cheeks are stained with tears. Jack strokes her hair and puts his arms round her. She resists for a moment, then drops her head as another hopeless rush of tears overwhelms her.

'Forgive me, Ruth. I'll make it up to you. I promise. You know how much I care for you and the girls. How can I make things right again? What can I do to make things better?'

Now it's time to say goodbye, children! Our I-Spy adventure together has finally come to an end. Big Chief I-Spy hopes that you've enjoyed I-Spy at the Seaside and you've discovered lots of things that you never knew before!

EPILOGUE

Sparrow Hawk Hotel, Blackburn, Friday 29 December 1959

It's only when the cloakroom attendant turns round to take her coat that Ruth recognises her. It's Cora – Cora Lloyd in a neat navy-blue uniform with a badge on her chest that reads 'Reception'. Ruth's first reaction is one of shock. Jack had coaxed her into drinking a glass of sherry to settle her nerves before she left home, and for a moment she imagines that she is drunk and hallucinating. 'Is it you, Cora?' she asks, leaning forward slightly. Her high-heeled black patent court shoes creak with the strain.

'Oh, hello, Ruth! I was hoping I'd see you.' This is not quite correct – if truth were told Cora has dreaded this moment ever since she heard she was on Friday night duty and no one was prepared to swap shifts. Ruth appears incapable of immediate reply so Cora continues, 'Gosh, don't you look glamorous! Where did you get the outfit?'

Ruth feels awkward, keenly aware of her last meeting with Cora. This is Ruth's first time at Fosters' Annual Management Buffet and Dance. It's typical that the first year Jack's name has been added to the guest list, Fosters has changed the rules and now even foremen are invited. The card specified formal dress. After some thought Ruth decided upon a long black velvet skirt and a pink pin-tucked blouse with a standing collar and pearl buttons to match her earrings. The whole outfit cost more guineas than Ruth believed she could strictly afford.

'Where did you get it? You never went all the way to Manchester, did you?'

'No. I bought it at that Italian shop on Queen Street in Blackpool.'

'Roberto's?'

'Is that what it's called? I don't really remember.' This is stretching the truth somewhat. Ruth had spent the whole of the train journey back from Blackpool with the foil and cardboard carrier box perched on the double seat opposite. By the time she reached Blackburn the words 'Roberto, Fine Italian Couture' were burnt into her brain.

'Here, let me take your coat,' Cora says. 'Mustn't keep you waiting or I'll be getting the sack.'

Ruth hands over her black fitted coat. 'What are you doing here?' she asks as Cora slips the coat on to a hanger, pins a green numbered ticket on the collar and hands Ruth the stub.

'Cloakroom duty. Usually I'm on reception but we're short-staffed tonight so it's all hands to the pump. I'll be helping on the bar later.'

'Oh!' Ruth says. 'How long have you been working here?'

'Oh, just a few months. I suppose you've heard that I've left Ronnie. I don't doubt that Blanche's shop has been buzzing with the gossip.'

'No, I hadn't heard. Helen's not working there now. She stopped when school started again in September.'

'Oh.'

The conversation is interrupted by Irene Sykes, keen to shed her bouclé wool swing-back jacket. She pushes the jacket across the desk towards Cora with some satisfaction. 'Evening, Cora. You're never on duty again! Put this on a padded hanger, will you? Those wire ones are a waste of time. Doesn't she look a picture in her uniform, Mrs Singleton? Quite the career girl nowadays, isn't she?' Irene swans off before either woman has a chance to reply.

'The nerve of that woman,' Ruth says, but when she looks up she sees that Cora is laughing and, despite her best efforts, Ruth finds herself laughing as well.

'Oh, Ruth. I've missed seeing you. I'm so sorry about those things I said. I must have been mistaken. I never would have said anything if I'd thought.'

'It's all right, Cora.'

'I was wrong.'

'No, really, it's all right. I've missed you too. I could have done with your help when we moved house.'

'Oh! So you finally bought one of the semis! It must have been after I left. His case comes up in February, you know.'

'Jack said there were rumours that Ronald had been arrested. What has he done?'

'Only beaten up one of the ladies he pays for sex. If he'd done it on Liverpool Road one of his Masonic friends would have covered it up for him, but the stupid fool was up in Scotland at one of those fancy golf tournaments. The poor woman was in a right mess when he'd finished with her – she'd got concussion and a broken jaw. And all the usual bruising, of course. Quite a dab hand at bruising, my husband.'

'So when did you leave?'

'The minute I found out. He'd been hoping to keep it all quiet. The case is to be heard in Glasgow. I took the liberty of telling his area manager before I left. Ronnie isn't "on extended leave". He's finished as far as the bank is concerned.'

'So where are you living?'

'Here. This is a live-in job. I have the attic room right at the top. You'll have seen it. It's the one with the circular window. I never thought I'd like it as much as I do. The rest of the staff are friendly and I don't mind the hours. There's nothing better than hard work to keep you from feeling sorry for yourself. Look, can you spare a minute? If you can push your way past the bloomin' Christmas tree we can have a chat in the back out of sight of the manager.'

Ruth slides past the tree and into the dingy cloakroom.

'Here.' Cora grasps her hand. 'You sit on this bench, I won't be a minute.'

Ruth waits in the semi-darkness until Cora reappears with a drink in each hand. 'Go on,' she says, handing Ruth a glass. 'It's only fruit punch.' The two friends sit side by side and sip the ruby-coloured liquid. 'Did you say Helen had finished at Blanche's?'

'Yes. When we got back from holiday she suddenly announced that she wanted to go to university.'

'That's a change round, isn't it? She'll have to do her A-Levels. I thought she was determined to leave.'

'She was. But she met this lad on holiday and now she spends every Saturday in Manchester, campaigning for this CND.'

'CN what?'

'D. It's the Campaign for Nuclear Disarmament. There's a group that's active at Manchester University. She must have made some friends there because there's some lad called Adrian who rings every Friday to let her know what's on at the weekend. I said to Jack it's a good job we've got a phone – otherwise how would our eldest daughter get on with overthrowing the government?'

'It's not that bad, is it?'

'No, I don't think so. Whatever it is she's up to in Manchester it doesn't require fancy dresses and high heels. Jack bought her a beautiful white layered petticoat during the holiday, but I've not seen her in it once since we came back. She's up and down in jeans and a duffel coat.'

'It's only lads who wear duffel coats.'

'I've let her grow her hair – I thought if I made her have it cut short again, no one would believe she was a girl. These friends at the university seem to have some pretty odd ideas. When I started asking her about this lad, Adrian, she got mad. She insists he's just a friend.'

'And is he?'

'Looks like it. Anyway, I'm not complaining. She's too young for a proper boyfriend.'

'She's sixteen, Ruth.'

'She's nearly two years of A-Levels to finish.'

'And how are things with Jack?'

Ruth shrugs and rubs the rim of the glass with her finger. 'He's busy at work since he was made manager. He's a hard worker, you can't fault him on that.'

'No, you're right there. But you don't sound too happy, Ruth.'

'I'm happy enough. I get a lot of pleasure from buying for the house. I've got a set of Venetian blinds on order that'll finish off the dining room. I haven't decided yet what I'm going to do with the lounge. We're not like some couples, arguing all the time. We're doing the best that we can for the girls. You can't expect romance after all these years. It's like everything else – you've got to compromise. That's what living with someone boils down to in the end, isn't it? After all the fireworks, I mean.'

'I don't know, Ruth. I never got past the firework stage with Ronnie, did I?'

Outside there's the sound of someone ringing the reception desk bell with increasing impatience, followed by that of a coin rapping on the counter. Cora lifts her finger to her lips. 'Sh-h-h,' she says. 'It'll be Irene Sykes again.'

The Sparrow Hawk's main function room is heavy with Christmas decorations – the tasteful swags of fir pinned to the picture rails with clusters of holly and mistletoe in the lobby give way to paper chains, lanterns and tissue bells in the ballroom. There's a dance band playing seasonal tunes at the far end of the room. Blackburn's answer to Bing Crosby has just finished 'White Christmas' and has paused to allow the assembled partygoers the opportunity to clap. A ripple of half-hearted applause follows.

Despite the closure of Portsmouth and Waterfoot Mills, the room is crowded with around thirty employees and their wives, all dressed up to the nines. Irene Sykes, decked out in a midnight-blue shift dress with heavy gold embroidery, has caused a stir. It's apparent from across the room that she's opted for one of the 'new fabrics' instead of traditional cotton velvet. The shiny fabric and gaudy gold embroidery constitute open rebellion. But not all the assembled managers are offended by her appearance. Mrs Sykes is wearing a neckline that does more than merely hint at her legendary breasts and the dress itself ends above the knee. As a result there's an unsightly scuffle among the younger men as to who can coax her into one of the alcoves. Meanwhile Harry Sykes is becoming increasingly belligerent as the night wears on. Having failed to secure the manager's job at Prospect mill, he considers he has nothing left to lose. He has spent the last hour 'relaxing' at the bar and now he's in search of a sympathetic audience. Dougie Fairbrother has the misfortune to be passing.

'Well! If it isn't the blushing bridegroom! Little Dougie Fairbrother, as I live and breathe. Not divorced a year and ready to marry again. You're a bugger for punishment. Here,' Harry says, liberating a couple of whiskies from a passing waiter, 'get that down your neck. That'll put lead in your pencil!'

'I've got a drink waitin', thanks, Harry.'

'I mean a proper drink, none of that filthy punch they lay on every year. Of course, you aren't to know that, are you? This'll be your first time. First invitation to the social event of the year – Fosters' Christmas bash. It's a once-a-year opportunity to grovel at the feet of the famous Foster brothers. Say thanks very much for keeping the mill open, sir. Very grateful, I'm sure. And here you are, Dougie, living proof of the Foster dictum – jobs for the boys. Jack Singleton steps out of the foreman's job and you step straight in.'

Dougie has twisted out of Harry's bear-like embrace. 'I only got the job because Tapper turned it down.'

'I believe you. I believe you! But how did Jack land the manager's job, eh? Who suggested that they switch the weaving shed at Alexandria over to shifts? Jack Singleton, that's who.'

'The way I heard it was that it was the only way they could continue running the mill.'

'Tell me another! It was Jack bloody Singleton's suggestion. I was there. I heard him. It was him persuaded them to cut my job in half. They've brought in a night shift manager. He lets his weavers leave the looms in a right state. I spend half my mornings chasing up broken pegs and replacement spindles. Well, I've had enough. I'm finished. Come the New Year I'm off. I was trained on Dobby looms producing top-quality fancy work. If I can't get work here, I'll go abroad. Germany's crying out for textile specialists.'

When Harry turns to grab another pint from a passing bar steward Dougie quickly steps away. He has seen Irene tucked away in the alcove with a couple of supervisors from Bank Mill and reckons there's trouble brewing.

This being Dougie's first time at the mill party he's had to hire a dress suit for the occasion. The jacket is a tad too long and the trousers are a bit tight at the waist, but with his fiancée's help he's managed to struggle into the outfit. The scarlet cummerbund was abandoned early on and is still lying across his bed at home, the black shoes crippled him so he's had to revert to his brown slip-ons, and his bow tie fastens at the back with a bit of elastic, but none of this really matters. Since his recent engagement the world is altogether a brighter place for Dougie. Having escaped the unwanted attentions of Harry Sykes, he makes his way back across the room and finds his fiancée chatting to Jack. 'Hello, love. Jack has got me an orange and there's a pint for you.'

Jack raises his drink and toasts them both. 'Here's to the happy couple. All the best to both of you. Not long now before the wedding, is it?'

'Next Saturday and it can't come soon enough,' Dougie says.

His fiancée is a couple of inches shorter than Dougie and almost as wide. She is dressed in a cream cotton dress with a busy floral pattern, which ties at the neck with a large soft bow. A heavily perfumed crimson tea rose pinned to her shoulder matches her lipstick. She is all fine powder and fragrance.

'Would you like to sit down with that drink?' Dougie asks, his hand resting lightly in the small of her back. 'I'll be over in a minute. I just want a word with Jack.'

Both men watch as she makes her way over to the seating near the finger buffet.

'Another week and she'll be Mrs Fairbrother,' Dougie says. 'I can't believe I've found a woman like her. She's the best thing that's happened to me, Jack. I'd seen her around, of course, but I never thought she'd spend time with me. You should have come to the stag party! We made a weekend of it in Blackpool.'

'I'm sorry. I'm too busy chasing my tail at the moment with all the new machinery.'

'Thank God for Tapper. He's got the measure of the new system with no problem at all. He's done some mumbling about it not being a skilled job any more since the weaving is all automatic, but he's kept things moving all the same. Still, he enjoyed himself at the Belvedere – got in a fight the first night, but after he'd got that out of the way he was downright docile.'

'It was your Doug who arranged it, wasn't it?'

'Aye. He'd heard that they were doing stag nights there.'

'I was surprised when I heard it was the Belvedere you'd booked. I've known Victor since the war.'

'Oh no, he's gone. It's a new manager now. The bloke who's taken over is still in his twenties. They're doing all sorts of coach trips and cut-price weekends. There's been a lot of interest – it's a lot faster to get there on the train with the new diesel engines. Time your trains right and it's close enough for a good night out.'

'Aye, I suppose so. It's changing like everything else.'

'They'd a postcard at hotel reception from that pal of yours.'

'Who? Victor?'

'Aye. It were a picture of a couple of donkeys in sombreros parked outside a large hotel called the New Belvedere. It looked for all the world like Blackpool front, but it were from somewhere in Spain. He'd signed it on the back. I cracked out laughing when I read it – 'All the best from Victor and Connie'. Wasn't Connie that waitress you knew?'

'Aye,' Jack replies uneasily.

'Gets around, don't she? You've got to give her that. And how are things with the other lass? Eleni.'

Jack looks round to see who's listening before he replies. 'I've written back – sent the lad a few quid for Christmas. I don't see anything wrong in that. He's as much mine as the girls are. I've had a word with my dad.'

'How did the old man take the news?'

'He did a fair bit of shouting. Told me he didn't care if the lad was in Timbuktu, I still had a responsibility to him and Eleni. She writes every week or so. I pick the letter up when I see the old man on a Tuesday.'

'And what about Ruth?'

'Ruth's well looked after. She's got what she wanted. I wasn't for selling our old terrace but she got her own way in the finish. I don't think she's really wanted me for a long time. There were a rough few weeks in the summer after she heard I'd been spotted with a lass. I did try to tell her about Eleni a month ago but she turned away, wouldn't listen. Told me whatever it was, this time she didn't want to know.'

Jack shrugs and Dougie shakes his head. Together they raise their glasses.

'Well, I'll be glad to see the back of the fifties. Here's to 1960! All the best, Jack.'

'All the best, Dougie.'

Moorlands, Boundary Drive, Blackburn, 30 December 1959

It is a Saturday like any other. Helen is off campaigning in Manchester and Ruth is out shopping as usual. The house is silent in a way that the old terrace on St Cuthbert's Street never was. Moorlands has been finished with fitted carpets so the rooms no longer echo, but still there's a sensation of emptiness. Jack sits down and polishes the family's shoes under the pitiless glare of a state-of-the-art strip light. This kitchen is bigger but not as cosy as the one in their old terrace. Central heating and clean white radiators have replaced the once familiar open fire and rumbling back boiler.

Jack avoids sitting on the white tubular steel chairs with yellow wipe-clean seats and instead perches on his old wooden shoe-cleaning box. It was cobbled together years ago from old planks liberated from his father's allotment. Ruth urged him to 'lose it' when they moved house, but Jack refused. The shoebox belongs to him, you wouldn't catch Ruth volunteering to clean the family's shoes: it's his job; always has been, since the day they got married. Jack is content to do the shoes, he finds it therapeutic. There's a comfort in setting time aside once a week to make things right, to polish over the evidence of casual scrapes, brush away mud garnered from footpaths and dust from gutters, to restore the shine on scuffed shoes. Whether the damage is collateral or direct, visible or hidden, Jack has learned that some damage defies repair – however skilled the hand that tries. As Nibs would have it, some things can't be saved.

It has been a busy six months since the holiday in Blackpool. Ruth has pinned up a photograph on the new notice board. It was taken on the first day of the holiday by a photographer on Blackpool prom. Jack has his arms round both girls, Beth in her shorts and woollen jumper squints at the camera while Helen fluffs out her skirt. Ruth is clad in her raincoat and scarf despite the sunshine. Looking at it now it seems to Jack like a record of a different life. So much has changed. Beneath him, in the dark recesses of the wooden box, covered by rags and tins of polish, is a brown envelope that holds, with a modest fold of ten-pound notes and Eleni's latest letter, the start of a future for Jack that makes the present more bearable. The icy relationship with Ruth since her discovery of his infidelity has thawed only slightly. They remain polite at all times, but Ruth has made it clear that any intimacy is over for good. If truth were told, Jack has accepted this more easily than she had expected. It doesn't appear to have bothered him at all.

Where once he only had sad memories of Eleni, Jack now has a future with her to think about. He knows he won't lose his daughters. Ruth is happy with her brand-new semi.

Jack sighs and turns his attention back to the shoes. Beth's lace-ups are so small that it's easier to hold the shoe in the palm of his hand as he rubs in the brown polish. He is not a sentimental man, yet the sight of the short blunt toes makes his throat ache. He runs the rag a second time across the leather and looks up when he hears his younger daughter throwing her weight against the back door. The door gives way unexpectedly and she stumbles across the threshold, her lips and cheeks red from the exercise. It occurs to Jack that his younger daughter, despite her mother's constant anxious attentions, is developing into a highly voluble and determined tomboy. Beth turns in the doorway and drags her right heel against the back step to lever off her wellington boot. In doing so she manages to spread a generous layer of mud everywhere but on the mat provided. Undeterred, she performs the same manoeuvre with her left boot, kicking it out on to the path.

'Shouldn't those boots go in the garage?' Jack asks.

'Do it later,' Beth replies as she slides across the newly tiled floor in her stocking feet and cannons into her father's knee.

'Where have you been, Sputnik?'

'Taking next door's dog out.'

'Who? Sandy? Does your mum know?'

'Waited till she went out.'

Jack's smile widens. He catches his daughter round the waist and polishes her nose with his rag.

'Dad!'

'Your mum said you've got homework this weekend.'

'I always have homework. Ever since they moved me back into class A.'

'But aren't you happy to be back?'

'No. I liked it in class B. It was nice.'

'But what about your Eleven Plus?'

'Don't care. They don't have to do homework in class B.'

Beth gets down from his knee by way of protest and slides away across the kitchen, banging into the fitted sink as hard as she can. The stainless steel shudders with the impact. Jack reflects on the uproar Ruth had caused when the school decided that Beth had fallen so far behind that it would be better if she were moved to the lower stream. She was duly moved, but Mr Hartley's professional opinion was no match for Ruth's maternal ambition. She protested to the headmaster, followed by the school governors and finally the Local Education Office, and Beth was moved back to class 4A. Beth might not like it, but family pride was restored. Jack watches as his younger daughter gets herself a glass of milk and a biscuit. She is forced to balance on the bottom drawer of the kitchen unit in order to reach the biscuit barrel which, like the Kenwood Chef, is kept at the back of the wipe-clean counter top. The fridge, with its stiff handle and tight door, requires a good yank to open and a hard slam to shut.

Jack is about to protest when he catches sight of Beth's face and changes his mind. 'Never mind, Sputnik. Cheer up, I've got a surprise for you.'

'What? What have you got?'

Jack slips his hand into his pocket. 'I've got a letter here. It came this morning. It's addressed to . . .' Jack pauses and lifts the envelope out of range of Beth's hands. 'It's addressed to Miss

Elizabeth Singleton, Moorlands, Boundary Drive, Blackburn.' Jack turns the letter over. 'Well, blow me! It's from Big Chief I-Spy. Shall I open it for you?'

Beth's face is transformed with excitement. 'No! Let me, let me. I can do it.' She grabs the letter and tears it open. A single feather floats down and lands on the kitchen floor, followed by a white card covered in copperplate writing. Beth yelps with delight and, poking the feather in her hair, pounces on the certificate: 'I've done it! I'm in the club,' she yells. 'I'm in the club. Big Chief I-Spy says I'm in his club!' She dances towards him, waving the card. Jack catches her in his arms and, heedless of her screams, whirls her round and round until, it seems, the whole world spins with them.

Thanks to the following people for their help:

Susannah Godman for seeing the possibilities in the manuscript which arrived on her desk, for her ideas, enthusiasm and complete professionalism.

Clare Smith for her suggestions and her light editorial touch, both of which served to make the book far better than it would otherwise have been.

Novelist and tutor Suzannah Dunn, who kindly read and commented on the opening chapters – as did Rosemary Howell, Glenis Stafford, Bill Pickup, Dorothy Hurtley and Maureen Ashworth.

And finally Julia Johnson for her patient support.

'The air of ideas is the only air worth breathing.'

EDITH WHARTON

LITERARY CORNER

A NEW VISION

'True originality consists not in a new manner but in a new vision,' claimed Edith Wharton. Few would dispute the truth of this statement, yet the process by which such visions are vouchsafed is a mysterious one. What is it that inspires authors to put pen to paper: curiousity, sympathy, passion, obsession? In her own words, Sallie Day reveals some of the influences that compelled her to write *The Palace of Strange Girls* . . .

The idea for the novel sprang from a visit to the cotton town where I was born and the subsequent discovery that all the mills I remembered from my childhood were gone. Ironically, the only one left standing was the mill where my father worked and which I had visited as a child. Looking at the remains of a once thriving mill I was reminded of the anger, the sense of betrayal and the despair that marked the end of the Lancashire cotton industry. This idea expanded from public to private spheres – the betrayal of a child's trust, a husband's infidelity, a wife's misguided belief in fortune tellers. Blackpool was the perfect place to set the novel since it stood as the ultimate antidote to the grim reality of ordinary life. Meanwhile, the addition of the 'I-Spy' book determined the direction of the individual chapters, and the title allowed me to indulge my fascination with houses, from Ruth's humble terrace to Cora's palatial mansion.

From these bare beginnings the novel very much made itself and expanded into hitherto unexpected areas. Characters came into their own and promptly started misbehaving. Bridging chapters took off at odd angles. And finally, at the eleventh hour, Tiger Woman appeared.

SALLIE DAY

SPREAD THE LIGHT

'There are two ways of spreading light: to be the candle or the mirror that reflects it.'

EDITH WHARTON

From Socrates to the salons of pre-Revolutionary France, the great minds of every age have debated the merits of literary offerings alongside questions of politics, social order and morality. Whether you love a book or loathe it, one of the pleasures of reading is the discussion books regularly inspire. Below are a few suggestions for topics of discussion about *The Palace of Strange Girls* . . .

- **Sallie Day places Beth's story at the heart of *The Palace of Strange Girls*. What do you think the author achieves by doing this? What light does Beth's story shed on those of the other characters?**

- **What does the Tiger Woman represent to Beth? What does she tell us about women in 1950s and 60s Britain?**

- **Ruth has very firm notions of her responsibilities as a wife and mother. What drives her and how do her ideas of 'right' and 'wrong' affect Beth and Helen?**

- **To what extent do you sympathise with Ruth? Do your feelings towards her change as the story progresses? If so, when and why?**

- ***The Palace of Strange Girls* brings to life a specific period in British social history. In what ways has life changed? In what ways has it stayed the same? From the portrait Sallie Day paints, would you say these changes are for the better?**

- What do you make of Jack's character? Do you sympathise with his emotional predicament? What does his dilemma tell us about post-war Britain and the long-term effects of the conflict on those who fought?

- What do you think of Ruth and Jack's relationship? Are they capable of happiness? Could the novel have ended differently? If so, how?

- *The Palace of Strange Girls* is, in many ways, a novel about the death of the Lancashire cotton industry and what this means not only for the mill workers, but for their families and communities at large. How accurate is Sallie Day's portrait of the industry and its demise, do you think? Can any parallels be drawn between the 1950s cotton industry and modern British industries?

IRREPRESSIBLE FRESHNESS

'A classic is classic not because it conforms to certain structural rules, or fits certain definitions (of which its author had quite probably never heard). It is classic because of a certain eternal and irrepressible freshness.'

EDITH WHARTON

If you enjoyed *The Palace of Strange Girls*, you might be interested in these other titles from HarperPress . . .

Broken by DANIEL CLAY

Skunk Cunningham is an 11-year-old girl in a coma. She has a loving dad, an absent mother and a brother who plays more Xbox than is good for him. She also has the neighbours from hell: the five Oswald girls and their dad Bob. And yet terrifying though they are, the Oswald girls are also happy to put it about – so when Saskia asks, shy virginal Rick Buckley for a ride in his new car, he can't believe his luck. When she then broadcasts Rick's sexual deficiencies to anyone who will listen, it puts ideas into her younger sister's head that will see Rick arrested for a crime he never committed. From her hospital bed, Skunk tries to understand the events that follow. And as we inch ever closer to the mystery behind her coma, Skunk's innocence becomes a beacon by which we navigate a world as comic as it is tragic, and as effortlessly engaging as it is ultimately uplifting, in this brilliant and utterly original debut novel. *March 2008*

Bone China by ROMA TEARNE

Grace de Silva, wife of the shiftless but charming Aloysius, has five children and a crumbling marriage. Her eldest son, Jacob, wants desperately to go to England. Thornton, the most beautiful of all the children and his mother's favourite, dreams of becoming a poet. Alicia wants to be a concert pianist, and Frieda just wants to remain close to her family. But civil unrest is stirring in Sri Lanka and Christopher, the youngest, is soon caught up in the tragedy that follows. As the decade unfolds, Grace watches helplessly as her family is torn apart and four of her children make the decision to leave. And yet in London, life is not as they expected. Only Thornton's daughter, Meeka, moves confidently into a world that is full of possibilities. But even she must overcome heartbreak, a terrible mistake and single parenthood before she is finally able to see the extraordinary effects of history on her family's migration. *April 2008*

The Queen's Sorrow by SUZANNAH DUNN

Plain, dutiful, Catholic Mary Tudor is overwhelmed by joy when she becomes England's first ruling queen. When she marries Philip of Spain, her happiness is complete. But Mary's delight quickly sours as she realises Philip cares nothing for his broody, besotted new wife. Desperate for a child and increasingly obsessed with returning England to Catholicism, Mary soon loses the support of a people horrified at the severity of the measures imposed by a queen who is lonely, frightened – and longing for love. Xavier, a member of Philip of Spain's entourage, is a reluctant witness to the unfolding tragedy. As the once-fêted queen tightens her cruel hold on the nation, Xavier's life – and new-found love – will be caught up in the chaos. *July 2008*

The Piano Teacher by JANICE LEE

It's 1952 when 32-year-old Claire arrives in Hong Kong with her new (and dull) husband Martin. Using her marriage to escape a bitter mother and non-existent home life in England, Claire takes a position in Hong Kong as a piano teacher to Locket, the daughter of wealthy socialite Chinese parents. She swiftly becomes intrigued by the family's unconventional English driver, the charismatic and enigmatic Will Truesdale. As their love affair blossoms, the tensions and intrigues of 1950s Hong Kong are interwoven with events a decade earlier, during the island's wartime years – another, very passionate, and tragically doomed love affair, Japanese brutality and secrets betrayed. *January 2009*